A Green-Years Overture

§§

Jon Morrill

Pair of Blue Herons
Colorado Springs, Colorado

Appreciation and thanks to:

Cindy Schrag *for her keen eyes in beta reading* A Green-Years Overture *and her offering of constructive content criticism and encouragement.*

Jim *and* Merry Morrill *for their assistance in propelling* A Green-Years Overture *forward to publication in many ways, including; content correction, expressing their enjoyment of foreshadowing, and motivating me.*

My wife Jenny *for her invaluable patience and support throughout the writing process and for reading and re-reading* A Green-Years Overture, *finding plot flaws, suggesting improvements in my characters' emotional profiles, and offering (sometimes ironic) editorial advice.*

Pair of Blue Herons
P. O. Box 7074
Colorado Springs, Colorado 80933

A Green-Years Overture *is a work of fiction. Characters, businesses, locations, products, are fabrications of the author or are fictitiously applied.*

ISBN: 978-0-9998261-2-6

Prologue

§§

In Italy, there is a phrase *Anni Verde* (Green Years). It alludes to the years of youth and by extension, to one's best years.

My name is Michael Barton; the overture to my *Anni Verde* follows.

§§

CHAPTER 1

Suspension of disbelief makes fiction enjoyable. Automobile suspension helps us enjoy our ride. Suspension bridges are miraculous and beautiful; suspension makes oil and vinegar salad dressing and mayonnaise possible.

Little on earth beats the suspension that rewards one with a moment of weightlessness over water. A whole sub-genre of paintings and photographs dangle kids on knotted ropes over a pond or lake, chased by the ubiquitous mongrel leaping from the embankment.

Let go of the rope. The act itself is frivolous, fun, and formative, and important symbolically, classic, iconic.

§

Verdant maples, oaks, and birches canopied this idyllic natural swimming hole. Leaves were on the fringe, hinting at the coming, famous New England autumn color palette of deep reds, brilliant yellows, and luminous oranges. Crisp early September sunlight shone through.

The Cold River waterfall at the toe of its horseshoe over-hangs and ledges sparkled in the penetrating sunlight. White-noise from the fall's wet conflict with its rock-choked plunge pool dominated all sounds. The water below, cold, shadowy, inviting.

A pair of swallows darted by me to skillfully pluck a mosquito or horsefly from its flight.

Bare-armed, bare-chested, tanned, and buff, if I do complement myself, my light brown hair bleached even lighter, almost blonde, from sun-soaked work this passing summer.

I had labored for a homebuilder hauling dirt, concrete, lumber, drywall, and shingles, fetching tools, occasionally as a gopher, off-site. Any jobs that required a set of opposable thumbs were mine. On the side, I had tutored Jim Weston, the company's foreman, in geometry and algebra, handy tools for construction projects.

More often than not, during the summer, I would have additional evening work helping Dave Harris. He was the farmer who mowed and baled the twenty-odd acres of hayfield that surrounded my family's Acworth, New Hampshire home, he used our barn to store hay, our silo for silage, and he wintered his dry cows there. I would pitch or stack hay bales on his four-wheel wagon until well after sundown. Following a short ride to the barn on the fender of his Allis-Chalmers tractor, I would help stow the bales in the hayloft. On these days, helping into the dusty dark, I wouldn't finish until after ten. It does a body good.

§

Rope in hand, I swung toward that momentary reward of gravity-free suspension. The rope's pivot, lodged in the heights and unfathomable foliage of an ancient and rugged oak, provided a long, free-swinging arc. Clothed appropriately for the neighborhood, in denim shorts, and no longer drawn down and outward, I prepared for the payoff. I let go.

Without my weight as a pendulum bob, finished with its work, the rope returned for its next use.

Its history was lost if ever the rough, tight-knotted swing had a history. The pendulous questions, "Who all were the host of people who had grasped this same rope?" and, "Who was the enlightened person who secured it in the upper branches?" hung unanswered.

Near autumn air filled my nostrils and lungs.

I truly enjoyed that instant when inertia leaves off and gravity struggles to regain its hold. Lofted in a single beam of sunlight that managed to infiltrate the leaves overhead, I bent my knees to right angles, one kneeling the other raised. My arms cooperated, temporarily forming an Egyptian hieroglyphic.

"Woo-hoo!" I yelled, elongating the vowels.

Time stretched out. What made this particular moment languish in apparent isolation from every other activity on the planet, I don't know. One cycle of inhale-exhale crammed minutes of events, reflections, and thoughts. Much more than I could fit into the span allotted. The arrow of time maintained the same trajectory, only in a more dense fluid. Time had decelerated. I was sure that there was a name deep in psychology for feeling this way. Psychology isn't my thing.

My experience, although stretched out, was still transient in the natural world. The reality of the fifteen-foot plummet toward the chilling pool gripped me with the same certainty as the twenty-eight gaining feet per second of gravitational attraction.

Consequence followed choice, and I was in brief and joyous shock at water contact. Arcing water pellets composed my irresistible cannonball splash. If I had chosen to dive, this swimming hole was altogether deep enough. The rocky bottom presented no danger of roughing me up.

§

Deep Hole is a most aesthetically pleasing swimming hole. Natural erosion, powered by glacial meltwater, had scooped and sculpted it. Glaciers estimated at a mile thick covered this area when they receded thousands of years ago. Rocks had swirled, abraded, and dug this natural pool who knows how deep; geologists call it rock drilling. Time and volumes of water belched from beneath the ice sheet, filled the bottom with boulders, rocks, gravel, and sand. Flow from springs and winter runoff had maintained the deep pool over the millennia.

A short distance away, scars remain where rocks, under unbelievable weight, ground into an outcropping of resistant granite as the underside of the glacial ice pushed, pulled, and pressed them.

§

Had I more time, I would have scrambled back for another launch into the pool; this afternoon, I only had time for one quick plunge, that is before I pleasantly spied two girls from our regional high school who had mysteriously preceded me here. My afternoon game plan could tolerate a slight delay.

Not many people knew to take advantage of this out-of-the-way, jewel of a swimming hole, and the girls were from a neighboring town, so my curiosity was piqued.

Both Chelsea and Jill were brown-haired and brown-eyed, much-appreciated beauties, cheerleaders, and my fellow seniors. Perhaps the lack of familiarity accounted for their conservative attire for the water today. I couldn't think of any other reasonable alternatives. I had never seen them here before, and even though I visited here frequently, I was sure they weren't here to see me. Regardless, I stopped for a friendly word.

"Hello!" I said, knee-deep in the shallows of the pool, dripping from head to foot, glad that my unfashionably short hair would dry quickly. Bermuda length shorts drained over my knees.

Hellos returned, accompanied by smiles. A guy could do worse.

The girls leaned back on a rocky beach, half in the water, half out. Their attention, alternately focused toward me and the path coming down to the pool, confirmed that their being here right after school hadn't included any thought of me.

"Jill, Chelsea. Awesome weather. Not always this warm in mid-September," I offered. This was true; it had been great haymaking weather; the local farmers yielded a healthy third cut this year.

"How did you guys get here so soon?" I ventured on.

"Jill and I plan to cut last period study hall every Friday, and Jill has her car. Today was our first," Chelsea taunted in a friendly way. She considered herself older and more mature than her peers. Even though a high school senior, she was already a socially active college girl in her own mind.

"Hey Cal, there's a party tonight at my brother's house in Keene. Want to come join us?" Jill was sincere.

Chelsea's smile waned ever so slightly.

Jill did use my self-adopted nickname, the tail end of my surname, rather than the unimaginative and prevalent Mike. Mike was a highly popular name in my age group, six in my grade alone, seven in the school I had attended before my family moved here two years ago.

Jill knew me better than Chelsea and thought me to be shy, possibly true, although I thought differently, that I was respectful, with the right mix of naiveté.

That is the definition of shy. My unspoken thought fluttered by.

"I can't, although I'd like to. I'm headed to the Keene airport to pick up my parents' car. They flew to North Carolina for a computer seminar this morning, and after that, I'm driving down to Boston to take some things to my brother. I'll be staying the night. Phil invited me to a coffeehouse concert with his friends." A perfect blend of truth and avoidance; besides, I could be a fifth-wheel as the only high school guy at a college party.

A splash behind me announced the arrival of the genuine reasons for the girls' presence. Jill's six-foot-six brother Steve had just hit the water, assisted by the same rope I had, minutes before, taken advantage of. Chelsea beamed; she had been dating Steve since I'd known them.

Another body flailed in the air and looked to have a painfully inelegant entry into the water. It was Steve's college roommate, Jack, Jill's interest.

"You guys going to the football game tomorrow? Monadnock, isn't it?"

Duh! We're cheerleaders! Was their unspoken, nicely softened, demeanor. Their actual response came back, "Yeah. We'll whoop their butts this year."

Pretending not to notice their eyes refocusing on the center of the pool behind me, I bent down to pick up a quartz rock that showed thick dark veins.

Steve and Jack approached, sloshing gingerly over the rocks. *Tenderfoots.*

§

Steve, I had helped to pass his physics final the previous year. I busted the normal distribution in math and science grades but never realized that I had a reputation. Steve had made the thirty-minute drive from the south of Walpole to look me up last spring before the end of school.

"Hey, Cal, can you help me?" He'd humbly asked. "I need a good grade on my physics final to graduate and get into Keene State."

"Well, come on in, Steve. Let's review your year in Physics." I put my planned twenty-five-mile bike ride on hold.

Even though we were in the same physics class, we hadn't had many interactions, different circles and all. Steve was an exceedingly gifted athlete but never arrogant, a rare, disarming combination. He never had the time, motivation, or support to realize his ability to approach any subject, including physics, intelligently.

We leaned over my kitchen table, where I outlined the major themes of the physics we had studied that year with a diagram that ended up resembling the Connecticut Charter Oak.

"You need to remember that Heinrich Hertz quote Mr. Chase started the class with, 'We can not study the theory(s) without feeling that mathematical formulas have a life of their own, and that they appear sometimes more intelligent than we ourselves, and even than the master who established them, giving out more than he looked for in them.' With that and paying close attention to units of measure, you'll get a good grade, a C or better."

Steve was skeptical of my grade prediction.

"Hey Steve," I'd said as he settled into his jade Camaro to leave. "I love your ride, but I'm more impressed with how brilliant you are. I'm glad that you came to me for help.

"At Keene State, you should study anatomy and physics, and then apply what you observe to sports: ball inflation and elasticity, coefficient of friction, aerodynamic drag, angles of deflection, conservation of kinetic energy, joint movement, musculature, all that."

We had done three hours of cram for a school year of physics. The potential for a disaster turned out to be an exceptional final test score and a grade well down the surfing side of the bell curve.

Jill had been stunned when she found out how Steve had gotten his high grade. On the first day of school, she found me in the hallway and thanked me for helping him.

§

"Are you coming tonight? We're having a party. It's at my place on Green Street," it was Steve's invitation this time, fast and choppy with what he wanted to say; it helped in football, basketball, and baseball, but not always in social conversation. He was sincere.

He glanced down at Jill, "Jill invited you, right?"

She nodded.

"We were just talking about that," I smiled at Steve's reissued invitation. A ray of sunlight made it through the canopy of leaves and made a pretense of a disco ball, forcing me to squint.

"Thanks for the invite, but I'm headed to Boston tonight."

I tossed the rock I'd picked up from one hand to the other, then rolled it around in one hand.

"Too bad. You know our parties."

"Yeah," I didn't know though; I'd never been to one, "I was just hitting the dusty trail. I'm riding my bike to Keene."

The mention of a distance ride produced the usual jaw-dropping disbelief from both girls and Jack.

"Hey, Steve," I wanted him to show off his physics knowledge, "you just swung into the pool as the bob of a pendulum. How do you measure the amplitude?"

"Angular. Somewhere between twenty to twenty-five degrees," he grinned.

"When did you let go?"

"When velocity and acceleration were zero."

"Sweet, Champ," I affirmed.

"You guys should have been there when this guy tutored me at the end of last year." Steve, in a burst of praise, pointed at me. "Mr. Chase was a good teacher, but when Cal went over the concepts from class, it was like I always knew what they were. I didn't have to memorize anything. I knew it and understood it. This guy is smart."

Steve, Chelsea, and Jack all started toward deeper water. Jill hung back with me.

"I've seen you do that before," Jill watched me toss and catch the quartz, "you know, pick up a rock, look at it, and toss it back and forth. I know you're not nervous. Why do you do it?"

Jill tended to be smarter, more curious, and more observant than most girls I knew.

"Do you know much about the geology around here?"

"Not really."

The other three, in the water, noticed our conversation. I gathered that Jill wanted it that way.

"On the other side of the pool from where you parked your car is Beryl Mountain Road," I gestured in that direction. "So let me ask you, does 'beryl' ring any bells for you?"

17

CHAPTER 2

Lance recalled his reflection from earlier that morning, in the polished midnight blue finish of his new Fleetwood Edition Cadillac DeVille. His mirrored image was perfect, of course, dark brown hair, fashionably over the collar, styled and exquisitely captured with the Paul Mitchell men's spray gel recommended by his salon stylist.

Most lawyers scurrying about Boston area courthouses, Lance noticed, were no match for his smart attire, more dashing than the corporate bigs that employed those lawyers and far outclassing his Revere Street, Brownstone neighbors.

He smelled fantastic, too, with an overly ample dose of Lacoste Elegance. Women dig that. A regular swill and swish of Lavoris and a freshly popped peppermint Breath Saver didn't hurt, either.

He was always his own best company.

Lance wasn't here to meet and greet today; no introductions, not yet, only observe and protect his interests.

"Amy Farina, did you ride your bicycle today? I drove 150 miles just to see you, my young fiancée," he was bordering on impatience, breaking the silence of his vigil, speaking to himself. "Don't disappoint your Lance. I am your destiny."

Lance knew better than most that Amy Farina was only a sixteen-year-old high school junior. He humored himself with an old Beatle's tune, *She's Only Sixteen*. This year, for the first time in the last three, he didn't have to modify the lyrics.

He had gotten up early, especially for this trip to Lenox, Massachusetts, a review of one aspect of his five-year plan. From this vantage point just off East Street across from Lenox High School, he could observe the Friday afternoon exodus. He didn't mind the wait, short-term, for the students to exit, or long-term to marry Ms. Farina. It was an arranged marriage. There was no requirement for anyone other than Lance to know, was there?

He felt the roll of Breath Savers on the seat beside him and helped himself to another.

According to his perfect plans, he would tell Ms. Farina of his unilateral marriage arrangement in four years. He would find her after a university class and knew exactly how the meeting would occur.

"Amy. Amy Farina. I'm Lance Grimaldi. I've watched you mature and develop for many years, and I want you to marry me. Let's go to any nearby five-star restaurant tonight for dinner and discuss your future with me as my wife."

"Lance, you appear to be a rich, important, and successful man," she would say, "I would like the opportunity to know you better before we marry. Over dinner?"

Later in the evening, he would say, "Amy Farina, marry me."

She would offer her ring finger to his three-carat diamond white gold engagement ring. And, he would allow her to bask in the thoughts of marital bliss with him while she completed her senior year in college.

She might have a minor objection, he admitted to himself. He couldn't imagine what, but he would overcome it. He was Lance, wealthy, suave, and handsome. Neither would he let his low estimation of higher education interfere with her attending a university of her choice; it wasn't his money spent on tuition. College was a status thing; in fact, his marriage to Ms. Farina was a social and business rung up for himself. This aspect of his future was inevitable.

§

Lance Grimaldi defined his world. His definition of morning was for the rest of the world, early afternoon, which never occurred to him, why should it? Sunshine meant it wasn't necessary to turn on his headlights. Clouds presenting fantastic imagery meant he didn't need to shield his eyes with the nuclear protection of Oakleys. Rainbows meant rain, which in turn meant he would need to have his car detailed the next day. Flowers were not beautiful but a burden. You were obliged to give bouquets at weddings and funerals, so you had a *soldato* call a florist. Brilliant autumn colored leaves

21

were only sticky note reminders to have the furnace serviced and the window screens replaced with storm windows.

Beauty and joy were superfluous, meaningless; money was the measure of success, with money, he purchased power and happiness.

Who had money and power? That's right, Lance Grimaldi.

§

At three-thirty, Lance checked his Rolex against the electronic dash clock. He stroked the leather seat beside him, admiring his Cadillac's golden laurel hood ornament, tracing affectionately, the very same laurel, an embossed replication, in the cream-colored leather seatbacks.

"Happy birthday, Lance."

Lance's twenty-second birthday had been two weeks earlier. He'd purchased his new Cadillac as a present to himself, with cash, and planned to do the same next year as well.

The DeVille's exhaust manifold clicked as it cooled. He rapped the steering wheel with his index finger a split second after each click, a recently acquired skill; instinctive and instantaneous was the aim. It was another opportunity to further practice for his critical performance tonight.

How far he had come from his humble beginnings, how far from his Gloucester home. So lucrative was his business that he had dropped out of high school his sophomore year to pursue it full-time, with vigor.

The genesis of his business involved his high school principal's son. Lance, socially inept, struggled and suffered while he jealously observed the son frequently make off after school to a shed in the pinewoods behind the school. Lance knew that drinking alcohol, getting high, and exploiting female classmates was not the desired image for someone who was also involved with high school sports. Coaches had high standards, too.

One afternoon, armed with a camera, he became at once a voyeur and an entrepreneur.

Lance confronted the honored son, "Your dad would be disappointed by the photos I have of you from yesterday afternoon. He doesn't need to know about them or the coach either. Tell me what you want to do. You pay me fifty bucks to start and twenty bucks every month, or I mail the photos. Or, option three, you can get me proof of three of your friends doing bad or worse. Then I'll let them pay me, and you won't have to."

"You little twerp," he had answered as he weighed the consequences of punching Lance in the face, then, thinking better of it, he reached for his wallet. "Here, take your freak'n fifty."

"Good. But know this, if you snitch, I'll tell on you, too, and any of the dirty friends you supply me with."

That was the power of multiplication.

Lance had followed through on his word and had grown an immense client network. Often he would have repeat clients due to subsequent misconducts. If clients paid with lucrative information, he would let them off his hook until they hooked themselves again.

Surprised and pleased with the frequency of relapse, he applied the same methodology consistently. Not only was he an entrepreneur but a multilevel marketer. With a surprisingly small amount of legwork, he had been able to leave home and move into his own furnished apartment.

Humor abounded in his work. His first adult client was the high school principal, whose son had started Lance in business. Lance's tipster of the principal's financial impropriety was none other than his son. This had supplied Lance with many hours of amusement and a milestone increase in income.

Some things, though, he couldn't rush, but the last six years had been very good to him. He'd managed his increased client and employee base well. A superior planner, he was already a year ahead of schedule in his five-year plan. With his income base and his vast network of contacts in influential places, he had already insinuated himself into the position of made man and then underboss for a man whom Lance considered a weaker friend of ours. Lance was a big earner. In time, he would be Boss of the Office.

Extortion, properly executed, was a wonderful way to wealth.

§

Lance's suit was not his newest, nor was his overcoat his best. Both had been custom-tailored by a Boston client with a Devonshire Street shop off Post Office Square. Lance considered his current attire expensive but adequate and expendable.

Careful selection, tailoring, attention to his clothing, and his concern for his meticulous appearance would allow any component of his wardrobe to pass for new off-the-rack. His double-breasted suit coat, vest, slacks, and light wool overcoat were genuinely charcoal in color and exhibited zero wear. He had decided on a plain white tailored shirt and a bright green silk tie for this evening's activities.

Everything that he wore since he left his house this morning would be ashes by dawn. On this occasion, like several others, Lance would donate his clothes to the recently deceased. Even his patent-leather Prada lace-ups, so lovingly cleansed with distilled water and chamois, and his Charles Tyrwhitt black silk evening socks would have to go. Lance had no particular concern for the departed unless they had been one of his clients, in which case it would have meant a loss of revenue for him. He didn't give a rip whether his clothes would attire a worthy corpse or end up wadded in the corner of a closed casket. His concern was their destruction by cremation. When he didn't need this niche service, the funeral director owed Lance's full monthly silence fee.

§

Near the Boston theater district and Chinatown, there is a vivid and colorful area known affectionately, or with malcontent, as the Combat Zone. Lance's long-term wait for the proper marriage required of him frequent sojourns there. These visits were efficient and less expensive than spousal maintenance. If variety was the spice of life, then a chef of high regard located the Combat Zone so conveniently to his home.

"Lance," he chuckled slightly, "you comedian."

The other variables in his equation for a successful lifestyle were restaurant dining, a maid service to maintain his Central Boston home, a scheduled laundry service, and his Cadillac regularly detailed.

Not to diminish the savings he realized with his Combat Zone patronage, his visits often turned out to be lucrative. From time to time, he would catch sight of a well-heeled socialite or a politician, and better yet, magistrates when they were there for entertainment. A call from his car phone to one of his detectives could increase his monthly income by thousands of dollars.

If events dictated, he would bait his marks to return then document their frailties with photos. He was close to perps, pimps, and doormen, with whom he had piecework arrangements, contracts, or simple extortions for information.

He felt compelled to nurture weaknesses and failings in others. Easy to accomplish, he created situations guaranteeing his clients' eventual moral failures. It was a gift and an essential component of his productivity. Lance's business, after all, was a direct leap from those failures. He determined the amount of money the avoidance of emotional or physical pain was worth to his clients, then demanded they pay it to him. He proposed reasonable down payments and monthly installments. To opt-out, they could add three more individuals to his client list. He never varied from his initial formula for success.

In what was a useful personal disconnect, Lance had no capacity for compassion, sympathy, or empathy. The resultant pain of others' failings was merely an avenue to his enrichment; that was pain's function.

His pain, he rarely experienced it, was fuel for vengeance.

The use of physical pain for enforcement was also a requirement. He had subcontractors for retribution and coercion, and for the past several years, he had augmented his subcontractors with *soldati* of the organization he had joined and would soon inherit.

§

"Okay, Amy, show yourself. Pedal by my pretty princess. I have crucial business to attend to in Boston tonight."

His thoughts wandered off again while he maintained a watchful eye on the school.

A new Breath Saver rattled on his teeth.

His political ambitions would take time, possibly within ten years, if things went better than planned. The US Senate would challenge him adequately with a place to practice and perfect his particular skill set.

"The distinguished Senator Grimaldi" sounded powerful. He mouthed the words, venerating them, infusing them with the power to achieve.

Domineering, and with his wife of youth, beauty, and education as a protective mask, he would mesh with the DC in-crowd, applying all the delicate exploitation he had had so long cultivated. No dirt could adhere to him; nothing and no one could touch him. He would have more Teflon than John Gotti or DuPont.

In the same way he had recalled his reflection in his Cadillac's shine, he also recalled his plan this evening. The details were impeccable, as was his appearance.

He consulted his Rolex once more; in precisely five hours, his guys would collect Tom Kean Boyle from Ian McCrory's Place, Boyle's favorite haunt.

Tonight would be another milestone, completing an extraordinary piece of work, eliminating two ethical birds with one stone.

"Amy? Did you stay late after school? I don't think so. Are you being chummy with some guy? Don't be too nice 'cause I'll fillet him and feed him to the dogs." He thought for a moment that he'd laid eyes on Amy's distinctive blue bicycle at the north end of the school building, and that boy who he'd seen before with Amy, but there was no Amy, no boy, and no bike.

"Amy, it's not nice to pull a vanishing act when your Lance has made a special trip. I'll see you next time. I've got to get back."

With that, Lance fired up his DeVille and idled forward. He'd had no reward for his efforts today, having not seen his future wife anywhere. His evening had better be an improvement. It had to be; he was all in. His whole stack of achievement rode on his roll of the dice. Then he smiled to himself, *Loaded dice. Ha, ha.*

He shifted into neutral and raced the engine in an un-Cadillac like manner. At high rpm, he snarled as he dropped the transmission into drive.

The result was shrapnel; pebbles and gravel, rooster tailed into the shrubs, maples, and oaks that lined the street. Debris flung onto the School Zone Ends sign, which shot back the distinctive ring of sheet aluminum. The short grass just off the shoulder suffered a brutal mowing. Flying chunks struck a Ford Taurus on the windshield as it approached. The Cadillac's tires squealed, leaving a pair of curled licorice stripes on the asphalt.

Parental heads turned in the parking lot.

"Oh, yeah! And there's a lot more where that came from!" Lance screamed, windows closed, secured comfortably in the confines of his passenger compartment. He fed on the lavish admiration of his audience for his superior skill with a clearly superior automobile.

Lance liked gravel. Lance loved dirt.

His tires continued to mark up the pavement. The drift completed his U-turn, heading him toward the Mass Pike and Boston.

§§

CHAPTER 3

Her L. L. Bean backpack, pale blue, black-trimmed, flipped up on her right shoulder. The familiar toss caught twists of the girl's wavy dark brown hair in the process. Amy Farina rocked her head from shoulder to shoulder, then forward to free her captive locks. She burst out from the high school's double front doors in concert with the colorful hoard of Lenox High students who all wanted to be the first to get away from the confines of brick, mortar, and glass for the weekend. Amy, like most girls, dressed in knee-length shorts and bold, wide-striped polo shirts. The guys wore, predominantly, khakis and solid polos, with a handful of blue jean wearers.

Outdoors in the sunshine, the air was fresh, crisp, and clean, unlike the stale, shared school air. Invigorating, refreshing, it encouraged chatter of weekend plans. Students happily shared noisy greetings and partings.

Amy quietly reviewed her agenda for the next two days while she jostled with her schoolmates. She would juggle her work duties and assist with the tenth anniversary of The Josh Billings Runaground, aka The Josh, or The Runaground, a run, bike, kayak triathlon.

"*Finire è vincere.*" Amy voiced, in Italian, the triathlon's "To finish is to win." slogan. It helped. She found it difficult, at times, to maintain her spirits and press on as the respectable daughter of a single, self-employed mom. She always kept herself active enough to avoid the appearance of being emotionally down. Italian, spoken in her bilingual home, afforded her a lift, as did her increased appreciation for Josh Billings' humor.

"*La piú rara delle cose che un uomo fà è il meglio che può.*" She stated another Josh Billings quote from the promotional literature that appealed to her.

A new senior classman overheard Amy's muttering and gave her a peculiar look. Too aloof, too shy, or too uninterested, he didn't say anything, not, "that's not English," "that sounds Italian," "what does that mean?" Nothing. Thrown a perfect icebreaker, he failed.

"The rarest thing a man does is the best he can." She translated loudly for his benefit and within the hearing of several other students. She met his eyes straight on with a smile, challenging him to converse, but she had no taker.

Her point proven; she didn't speak her thought, *codardo (coward)*. Her nimble chiding fortified her.

The boy looked away, cowed, and moved on.

Too bad, he's not too hard to look at.

Amy took note of his appearance. Six feet tall, hunkier than any of his classmates, he sported a mop of brown hair and an unremarkable, wide face. A Ralph Lauren striped, sage and white polo shirt, brown belted grey Dockers, white and teal Nike running shoes marked him as not yet comfortable with the high school's dress culture. He appeared more college-junior than high school senior.

§

The Josh was a Lenox mainstay, honoring a nineteenth-century contemporary of Mark Twain, Josh Billings, a humorist, more popular than Mr. Twain in their era. The Runaground was competitive, but it was also inclusive. Engaged contestants were there to compete, the less involved were there for the T-shirt, and all were good with that. Revering its namesake, the Josh Billings Runaground had a mission, to allow the cycling, kayaking, and running contestants to choose where on the scale from silly to serious they wanted to fit.

This weekend was a time of excitement and enthusiasm in the Lenox, Stockbridge area. It was the unofficial conclusion of summer, a celebratory rite. The craziness of day and night parties, that last hike up Mount Greylock, swim parties at the quarries or a private dip in the Roaring Brook, competitive or fun cycling, kayaking or sailing on the lake, those final runs on the asphalt or softer wooded trails, The Josh provided the excuses and the time to savor them.

Automobiles, bicycles, and people filled the streets. Restaurants and stores, especially the sporting goods haunts, walk. She saw none and cranked up her cadence. Dexterously as a tour racer, she shifted her derailleur, propelling her way toward Kennedy Park.

§§

CHAPTER 4

Wet denim shorts were the monkey wrench in my machinery. I toweled off and donned my dry tee shirt. I had cycling togs to change into but no place to do it. I hadn't considered what number or gender of folks might have been at Deep Hole.

I couldn't afford to take fifteen minutes extra to head home. Sunset would be at five, giving me an hour and a quarter to face the nerve-racking Keene traffic in daylight.

Fifty feet in from the other side of the roadway, the native flora afforded me the seclusion to change. It was a worthwhile side trip. Checkerberries and low bush blueberries were delicious. The mayflowers, trailing arbutus, beautiful and aromatic.

§

My Trek, I'd purchased just after my family arrived in Acworth. It was a dark blue 12-speed, with Sun Tour derailleur, downtube shifters, and skinny tires with Presta valve stems, accessorized with trap pedals, a Zephal pump, an under-seat utility bag, and a water bottle holder. The titanium frame made it light and fast.

My rural New Hampshire neighbors thought a twenty-mile automobile ride from Acworth to Keene, a notable outing. They considered me off my rocker. Any day of the week, I would ride my bicycle to Keene and back if I had a few hours to spare. On the other hand, I would ride to Newport, Sunapee, or Dublin, in New Hampshire, or anywhere from Windsor to Chester to Brattleboro in Vermont.

With no cyclist friends, I only enjoyed the company of other riders when I met them on the road. These were the times I learned to draft, engage a paceline, double echelon, and all the associated etiquettes.

CHAPTER 5

Amy, the speeding cyclist, quickly approached the stop sign at the intersection with Route 7. Traffic accompanying her there was composed of parental school pickups, mostly moms. She had passed them all on the short, Housatonic Street stretch.

Inside the gold Volvo station wagon rolling to a stop in front of her, she could see Janie Biafore and her mother. Janie would probably assist backstage for the school play; a sophomore this year, she might even try out for a part. The nearly opaque back window spoke clearly of the noses of their family's two friendly spaniels.

The Jaguar Executive lined up behind the Biafores was an early summer addition to the Arnold Thomas family. The Thomas family had been a fixture in the Lenox area since Edith Wharton had settled there. Janis Thomas was a classmate and friend of Amy's. Her dad was away much of the time on business, placing his family's financial provision in higher priority than role modeling. He spent considerable time around the Pacific Rim in trade development for his employer, Digital Equipment Corp., and promoting Massachusetts trade in general.

Amy's most recent get together with Janis had been a visit to the Boston Museum of Fine Art in early June.

§

Amy had taken the center spot in the back seat of the Jag in order to visit over the console.

"Hi, Mrs. T., Janis. Thanks for thinking of me today. Is there something special or just a fun thing to do?"

"I love Boston," Janis was the first to respond to Amy's question as they eased back out of Amy's driveway, "tall buildings, restaurants, the culture. Lenox is fashionable, but Boston has much more variety. Don't you love it too, Amy?"

Janis wore her enthusiasm for city life on her sleeve. Her effusion gave Amy the impression that there might be another reason for today's invitation.

"Amy, sarebbe troppo chiederti se noi parlassimo in Italiano oggi? Io e Janis incontreremo Mister Thomas in Italia. Fa parte del regalo per la promozione di Janis. Potremmo usare la pratica." (Would it be too much to ask if we spoke in Italian today? Janis and I are to meet Mister Thomas in Italy. It's part of Janis' graduation present. We could use the practice.) Mrs. T's Italian was passable with the inevitable pronunciation, word choice, and grammar errors.

"Certo. Non ci sono problemi." (Sure. No problem.) That cat was out of the sack early. Were there any others?

They talked in Italian about school, Mr. T's work, Lenox, its history, and Amy's mom.

"So, gossip has it that you and your mom have mob connections. That's why it was incredibly easy for you to get a house in Lenox." The topical shift by Mrs. T. was acutely abrupt, insulting, and accentuated by the jolt back to English that Amy flushed with anger.

"Mom!" Janis pleaded.

It wasn't a new conjecture. It had been rude for Mrs. T. to bring it up, but then, Amy knew her prepared and detailed answer.

"I can squelch that gossip." Amy steeled herself. She was pleased enough to correct the misinformation. "I've heard that claptrap before, so I tracked down where it came from, and this is what I found out.

"The whole thing started in the mid-1800s when Castille Canfalierre came to visit Harriet.., her last name escapes me. I'll remember it. European authorities had imprisoned this Canfalierre in Monrovia's Spilkberg Castle for membership in the Carbonari.

"Romantic and mysterious already, isn't it?

"The Carbonari's crime was seeking the political unification of Italy. Called the Risorgimento, the government considered the Carbonari to be revolutionaries. The Carbonari organized and borrowed ceremonial fare and coded communication from the Free Masons. They acquired a lot of Free Masons, too. The outlawed Carbonari was Canfalierri's

41

criminal affiliation. From what I could tell, a Sicilian branch of the Carbonari had eyes on liberalizing the Catholic Church, whatever that means.

"Arthur Conan Doyle's *The Adventure of the Red Circle* was a Sherlock Holmes story about them.

"Canfalierri didn't stay very long in Lenox. He did sign coffeehouse registers where he promoted his political philosophy. His personal card showed up at this house or that.

"He had no money to speak of. He ended up using his persuasive powers to raise financial support in Lenox and Stockbridge to start a charcoal manufacturing company north of town. That was the primary legitimate business of the Carbonari in Italy. His company failed, but it confirmed his connection with the Carbonari.

"To avoid his creditors, he changed his name to Farina, which is why people think he's related to us. He presumably moved to Boston but went straight back to Europe. There wasn't time for him to propagate a family in Massachusetts. He had no wife while he was in the States.

"Besides, mom and I moved here from Newburyport; we're not Lenox natives.

"So it's true, there was an Italian guy in Lenox who was a member of a secret society with Sicilian affiliations, illegal in Europe. Mom and I share the same last name with him, but we aren't even in-laws, and his secret society connection was political, not criminal. Our mob connection is only rumor-mill stuff with a life of its own, like that party game."

"I'm sorry, Amy. That was a question that I've had on my mind. I just wanted to be sure. Janis told me that you want to attend Wellesley College when you graduate. She wants to go there, too. It would be convenient if you two could be roommates. But we'd be too uncomfortable if you had, you know, mob ties."

Tutoring Italian and defending the Farina family name were two of three impressive memories of that trip.

The third memory was of a John Turner painting in the Fine Art Museum's American Art section. For Amy, it was indelible.

The center of Turner's seascape was bright with a gray ocean, rough with swells. In the foreground, the wide eyes of a black man were white with terror as he struggled to remain afloat in the waves; slave ships sailed away in the distance. Turner captured perfectly and horrifically the futility on the man's face. It spoke of a time when slave ship crews would throw slaves with smallpox, measles, scurvy, or amebic dysentery into the ocean chains and all.

The painting's legend said this was a common practice in the slave trade era. It enabled the captain or "cargo" owner to collect insurance money for his loss. No insurance claim would be honored if the slaves came into port and left the ship alive. It was estimated that from five to twenty percent of the slaves purchased in Africa did not make it to their West Indies destinations.

John Turner's artwork was of a genre that purposed to abolish England's slave trade by revealing its brutalities. Amy had remained transfixed by the painting, absorbed by the horror, even nauseated by it. She felt that those castoffs were less sick than those who had cast them, but futility and fatality fell to the slaves.

Fascinated by its composition, she admired the use of light and dark. Several patrons strolled by without Amy noticing.

"Do you think she's on dope?" one older couple commented brusquely, and loudly enough to be heard when they lingered nearby.

A concerned Janis tugged Amy away ten minutes after the painting had drawn her in.

In one last bit of fun, they dined at an Italian restaurant in Wellesley on the way home. Amy had ordered the Carbonara to the raised eyebrows of both Thomas's

§

Amy shifted from memories to reality. She slipped into her clips and rode out behind the Volvo through the intersection.

§§

43

CHAPTER 7

Once through the Lenox village, Amy blazed past the picturesque Old Church on the Hill.

Adjacent to the old church was it's delightful and exceptionally photogenic cemetery surrounded by a granite post and iron-pipe fence with openings topping the periodic granite stairs in the short rise from the street. Soon the grand maples would brandish their golds and reds, and tourists would snap hundreds of photos of the church and its broad field of grave markers. They would miss the wonder of the bed and breakfast across the street with its well-maintained grounds, gardens, and elegant interior. Unless, of course, they were to stay the night. The Whistler's Inn was an overshadowed treasure. It touted a library containing hundreds of literary masterpieces some authored by those who had lived and composed works nearby or within its walls. One rare item known to Amy was the calling card of Castille Canfalierri.

Amy and her mom occasioned the inn for special talk times and was the place that her mom, Cecelia, years earlier, had said she would tell Amy about her dad when she was old enough. Amy thought sixteen was old enough, but she would rely on her mother's judgment.

Amy downshifted to boost her cadence for the slight pitch beyond the church.

§

Standing on one pedal, Amy coasted to the registration tent set up at the back of the Kennedy Park parking lot. While she expected the usual traditional army hospital tent, featuring off-white canvas, straight sides, and a roof ridge down the middle, she was surprised and excited by what she saw.

The tent had three spires and not one straight line anywhere, curved on every surface; circular was the most compelling nod to traditional. Even the spires, slightly offset, didn't form a straight line, creating, instead, a shallow triangle. She would find that the tent's lower edges kept their shape with graphite rods inserted into the hems. It lit up the lot, the canvas, shimmering white, under a semigloss coating.

A committee had spontaneously formed to bicker about the Josh Billings Runaground registration banner's placement, a three-by-fifteen-foot, red canvas with white letters. The banner had hung on one of the straight tent walls in years past, an impossible situation for a tent with no straight lines.

"We'd be better off if they'd never set it up!" The chairperson flamed against the red-faced volunteer who had ordered this tent. "Why didn't you verify the kind of tent we were getting? Did you even give them a decent description?"

Mrs. Annette Smith was upset over the disruption this gleaming monstrosity had caused to her thoughtful plans. This diversion was a continuation of a day, for her, that hadn't started at all well.

Mrs. Smith, Amy didn't know her well, had been a trophy wife, replaced by her former husband with another trophy wife. Compensating, she involved herself with volunteer efforts at athletic events, wanting to counter the effects of her minimal exercise. Next year she vowed to herself to be a casual contestant in The Josh. The Josh T-shirt wouldn't conform with her wardrobe, but she would wear it, a testament to her physical improvement.

Today Mrs. Smith presented herself in a red and white checked cotton blouse, high-water peg pants, white footies, and brown, "golfie" loafers. Chained, horn-rimmed glasses lent her all the authority of a schoolteacher.

Amy locked her bike's back wheel to the 10 mph speed limit sign.

"This is the coolest tent ever!" She enthused in unmistakable support. Ambling closer, she knew that there was a controversy looming.

"So *you* think," shouted back, the middle-aged woman in charge, who then squeaked, rhetorically, "Where will we hang the banner?"

"*That's* the problem?" Amy questioned loudly, envisioning *Status Quo* tattooed on Mrs. Smith's forehead.

47

The small group obsessed on the difficulty the tent's serpentine lines posed, not seeing the beauty that Amy saw in it. It was visionary. *Mr. Billings would be proud,* Amy thought, *after all, the rarest thing a man does...*

Ted North, rather than vilified, should be praised. Ted was a personal computer salesman at A-Tech Computer, a small shop in town, and was a runner and cyclist, sidelined today, with a fractured left heel bone. His lightweight cast was hardly noticeable. Tent procurement had been Ted's responsibility. His request to the rental company was for a tent to hold fifty to seventy-five people.

"Set up a line of posts over there." Amy pointed to the left of the tent. "Hang the banner on them."

"Well, I don't know how..." The lead protagonist of the banner conflict was embarrassed that there was such an obvious and straightforward solution.

Amy wasn't well acquainted with these volunteers; however, in less than a minute, she had acquired one's animosity, another's friendship, and had relieved the stress level of those in the balance.

"I'll set up the posts and hang the banner after the 'org' meeting. We should have posts and guy-lines over at Berkshire Sports. I'm sure they'll let me borrow what we need."

"I'll drive you there and back," offered the still red-faced Mr. North. "I'm Ted."

"I'm Amy. It'll only take a few minutes."

"I can help, too."

"Count me in."

"Can you say, fresh look?" Amy was zealous.

Politics were suddenly not in favor of Mrs. Smith.

"Let's get started. Otherwise, it'll be dark before we finish," Mrs. Smith launched the words over her shoulder.

"Ooh, there's an unhappy alpha today," Amy whispered loudly to her limited audience.

Mutters of agreement followed as they trailed their leader into the avant-garde tent.

§

Folding chairs had already been set up expressly for their meeting, along with a sturdy music stand to posture behind and an easel-mounted dry erase board.

"When we remove the chairs, we'll set up a queue with stands and ropes to control access of the contestants. I'll need volunteers for several tables. We'll have two people to take names on the appropriate clipboards and two to assign and pull numbers at each table." The committee chair regained the high ground and control.

"Excuse me." Amy's first request for recognition, ignored.

"Excuse me!" Amy stood.

"What, dear girl, is it?" The social friction machine discharged a bolt of acknowledgment toward Amy. All felt the disparagement intended by Mrs. Smith's emphasis on *girl*. The volunteers' hair rose a bit with the static.

"The Josh is supposed to be fun. That's the reason we're all here, Mrs. Smith, you too. We all want to contribute, and thank you for coordinating this year. You've done a lot more work than most people recognize." Amy led a scatter of appreciative applause.

"With our outlandishly stylish tent this year, we ought to complement it with a way to speed up the sign-ups. If we had two people at the entrance, they could classify the contestants when they come in; they would point out the tables that specialized in one of the three races. We wouldn't need stands, ropes, waits, and long lines." All eyes were on Amy. They supplied a friendly reception.

"The tables for individual races could be spread out just to the back of these three spires. Three races, three spires. If a contestant wants only to kayak and run the 10K, the triage pair will send them to the kayak table, and the kayak table will send them on to the 10K table. There will be more open space in the tent for people to mingle, they could even form spontaneous teams without the Match Maker, and there will be less wait time."

Murmurs of "Yes, yes." and "Great idea." signaled approval before Mrs. Smith could object.

"We've never done it that way before."

"Exactly my point. It'll be fun and dissimilar, like this extraordinary tent. Thank you again, Mrs. Smith; it's a credit to your resourcefulness and flexibility."

Teenage Girl Arrested for Blatant Flattery and Assertive Manipulation. Amy could foresee the *Berkshire Eagle* headline above the fold, front page.

"How do you propose to accomplish this?" Mrs. Smith yielded, holding out the black marker and subtly directing Amy to the dry erase board.

Instead, Amy tugged on her neighbor Ted's sleeve.

"Grab a table with me." She nodded in the direction of the cart of folding tables.

Ted jumped at the request, with an undeniable limp favoring his damaged foot.

"Can we get three people to register for the bike race over here with their chairs? While we get the tables for the other two races set up, would two of you stand by the entrance to greet contestants? Thank you," all the while, Amy moved tables, qualified volunteers, and spoke out her proposed organization.

"And, by this table, who covers for the Kayak race? Thank you. For the 10K? Who can man this one? Bring your chairs. Thank you. Thank you very much."

Amy three, chaos nothing.

As Amy's order engulfed the interior of the tent through a flurry of activity, a newly inspired and observant Annette Smith took notes on the dry erase board and wrote down their assignments. The benefits of Amy's concept flowered in Mrs. Smith's mind. Even the tent became attractive; it was a beautiful thing.

"Miss Farina?"

"Yes, Mrs. Smith?"

"Will you join the three at the bicycle race table?"

"Yes, ma'am."

She finished the diagram and wrote Amy's name.

"That leaves only me without a job."

"Oh no, ma'am. You have this entire area of circulation in the middle." Amy gestured widely. "You're the concierge, and you'll socialize with everyone, ensuring that everyone gets through quickly. It'll be a party atmosphere. You'll also see to it that we all have our jobs done correctly. That's your job."

"Are we done already, then?" Annette Smith happily inquired of everyone; again, it was a rhetorical question.

Rather than diagram and argue, the tent was cooperatively set up and ready for registration. "We'll see everyone here tomorrow at 7:58 AM. I'll have pastries, coffee, tea, and juice. Thank you so much, everyone."

"Annette Smith, everybody!" Amy led another round of applause.

Undeniably, Annette's day, and maybe much more, had turned around. She gave Amy a thankful nod as the group dispersed.

§§

CHAPTER 8

The talented group in concert at the Ellery Street Coffeehouse was not a well-kept secret. Heck, if I was from backwoods New Hampshire and had been lucky enough to get in, who all else was here?

Phil paid our cover charge immediately inside the door minutes before nine. The glass windows behind the stage revealed the line, waiting patiently, still formed outside. If the Fire Marshal's occupancy limit prevailed and no one exited, they remained in vain.

I surveyed the small stage.

"The drummer isn't out of Berklee yet. I probably know him. I'm glad you came with us, Cal." Phil scoped out the uncomplicated stage set up; drums were a simple trap set; a Korg keyboard and Yamaha electric bass graced the side furthest away, a Les Paul and another Yamaha bass were on the side closest. Mics and stands stood left and right, none for the drummer.

I found an iced coffee doctored with cream and sugar in my hand as the lights dimmed; Phil's roommate Andy, our drink courier, had returned to the remarkably smoke-free room. The crowd quieted as the musicians approached the stage.

These are not the musicians we were looking for, was the thought of everyone in the room. These guys had slicked-back hair, light blue button-down Oxford short-sleeved shirts, skinny dark blue ties, blue or black pants, I couldn't tell, with white Converse deck shoes. The band member opposite the keyboardist carried an acoustic double bass and skillfully set its endpin in a stand I hadn't noticed.

The audience was strikingly quiet and attentive, their expectations challenged. The keyboard player spoke into the mic; at the same time, he drew a small black comb through his hair, single-handedly.

"We'll start tonight with a tribute to the late, great, Johnny Maestros with a song by The Crests, *Angles Listened In.*"

Amused bewilderment circulated throughout the audience. As the band played through the ballad, several couples rose and left.

Fifties songs all beautifully played, followed for the next forty minutes.

§§

CHAPTER 9

Amy's ride from the sports store to her home was a hilly and curve-filled two miles without streetlights. Amy and her mom lived west of the ridge that made up most of Kennedy Park. The paved roadway past their house was limited to use by their neighborhood. A No Outlet sign kept out most wayfarers.

Amy stopped at the foot of her driveway before she came under the influence of her home's exterior lights, gazing at the stars to make the most of the temperate night. Sagittarius backdropped the moon, Mars made ready to set in the southwest, and Jupiter rose over the southern end of Kennedy Park ridge. She weighed her insignificance in the vast luminous band of the Milky Way.

Conceptually, she knew that even the cosmic distances of space were measurable; at least Einstein theorized that. The infinite, by definition, wasn't measurable; she asked herself, *was there a true infinite, beyond the seeable, beyond the tangible?*

Amy pressed the button on her garage door remote. The clatter of the garage door opener would alert her mom to her arrival. It was nine twenty, ten minutes before her unofficial curfew.

With her Bianchi safely dangled from its designated ceiling hook next to her sporty minded mother's brand new BMW M6, she shed her Adidas in the mudroom and stepped into the kitchen. Nabbed by the aroma of fresh-baked chocolate chip cookies, she helped herself to two from the Fiesta Ware plate, without remorse. She snagged a glass from the new oak cupboards and poured it half full of milk.

Cecilia was at work in the living room just beyond. A few months ago, contractors had completed the new fixtures, installed new kitchen appliances, and reconfigured the space between the kitchen and living room, allowing a cook the opportunity to socialize. The formal home's remodel also included transforming the front drawing-room into a home office and library for Cecilia.

"Hi, Sweetie. You're home early."

"There wasn't much left to do at closing; work was slow. Just before The Josh, that's surprising." Fully occupied with her snack, Amy joined her mom, took the leather recliner, and used the side table to place her plate.

"That means you would have liked it busier."

"I can see that your day was busy. You made cookies. Thank you." Amy held up her second cookie in acknowledgment. "You're not in your new office."

"No, I'm working at home tonight so that I can connect with my busy daughter."

"Congratulations on closing the Williams house, and you've listed another two."

"Deduction time, is it? Yes, I made cookies, and you can see the comp Polaroids from two different neighborhoods, so there are my two new listings. But what about closing the Williams house?"

"Too easy, you're drinking the '78 Barolo, not the '85 Valpochella." It was a game between daughter and mother. Amy excelled at matching her mother's wine consumption with her moods.

"Young lady, your wine knowledge is too scary. Have you tried either of those..., or anything alcoholic?"

"The answer is still no, Mom. Except for communion. Thanks for asking."

"No problem. While we're at it, how about any drugs?"

"No, Mom."

"How was your day?"

"School was okay. As I was leaving, Paul asked me to try out for the *Imaginary Invalid* this year, then he tried to set me up with a blind tennis date this afternoon. I told him that it would be better if he, Ann, and this other guy would meet me at the Josh awards ceremony at Tanglewood.

"I kind of took over The Josh meeting. The tent was anything but a MASH tent; this thing has style with a capital *S*. Mrs. Smith was outrageously stressed and let everyone know it. I helped her make the most of it. The situation that is."

"Amy, you should go easy on Annette. She's gotten short shrift from her divorce."

"I know, and I think I left her in good spirits and positive self-esteem." Amy made her way back to the kitchen, rinsed her milk glass, and set it in the dishwasher's top rack.

"Before I talked to Paul, I brushed off a senior guy who seemed like he wanted to talk. Then, once I was outside, I don't think that it was that same guy, but I felt that evil presence again. Why is it, Mom, that I can't pinpoint what causes that stalked feeling? It's been almost three years. Is it just hormones? Or, should I take myself less seriously?"

"I think about it, too. All I've come up with is that you're right. It may be that you're so observant you see danger, but you don't have all the pieces to put it together. When your mind struggles, it magnifies your feelings. I wouldn't put it aside, dear. Sorry. That's why I worry about you riding willy-nilly after dark."

"That's what I come up with, too, except for the riding willy-nilly after dark." She chuckled because the conversation was a familiar one. She and her mom were in the process of resolving that conversation by developing mutual trust.

"Mom, am I ever going to find a guy who appreciates who I am? Most guys that talk to me don't look me in the eyes: they focus lower. I want to find someone who cares about compatibility, about relationship, first. I get positively frustrated because there isn't any guy I can talk to about trigonometric identities or the historical origins of folkways. Isn't there someone that will just ask if I want to go for a bike ride?" A tear trickled from Amy's eye as she turned her head to hide it and wiped it away.

"Sweetie, one man's trash is another man's treasure. A lot of guys are jerks, only after one thing, and that type attracts some girls. You are an exceptional young lady, and there is an exceptional young man out there for you." Cecelia thought of her husband and quelled the rise of loving emotion. Part of Amy's struggle, she knew, was not having him as part of their family. "You'll know when you meet your guy, and you'll confirm it as you get to know him. He won't be flawless, and that will make two of you. You'll have to work through those flaws if a true, solid relationship is what you both want."

Amy stepped toward the front hallway and leaned against the hall corner.

"I'm headed upstairs for bed. I've got an early morning tomorrow. We need to go to Whistler's Inn soon for tea and scones."

"Next Saturday before work?"

"Sounds great, Mom. Good night."

"Good night, Amy. Love you."

"Love you, too, Mom."

§§

CHAPTER 10

"Thank you. You're such a thoughtful audience," the keyboardist spoke. He couldn't have helped noticing that a quarter or more of the audience had left, even though the music was excellent, and he didn't seem to care. Others immediately replaced those who had departed, but the crowd outside had thinned considerably.

"Hey, Phil, what is this?" I quizzed, puzzled and entertained.

"Just wait for it..." Phil held up his right index finger.

The coffeehouse reduced to low-level white-noise.

"We wanted to ensure we had the right crowd." It was the keyboardist again.

Following a wave of recognition of who this duo was, the patrons slowly opened up with applause and whistles. They were still unknown to me, and Phil was too busy to elaborate. The performers removed their ties and shook out their longish hair to another round of applause.

"We picked up Ted Reigns for drums tonight." There was another enthusiastic applause. Ted acknowledged his introduction with a nod, then pulled another floor tom out from under a black cloth at the back of the stage and expertly adjusted a vocal mic.

The double bass yield to the electric Yamaha.

A few paradiddles from Ted confirmed the new tom's tuning.

Odd selections from the late sixties finished their first set, ending with *Going Out of My Head* by the Zombies.

Perceptive couples in the room were delighted.

The group imitated the original performers in the best cover style. Rowdy appreciation met their departure from set one, and expectation in the room was high for their return.

Phil was bursting with enjoyment. An enchanting girl smiled beside him, having shoulder-length blond hair, a heart-shaped face, and totally, totally beautiful.

"The Zombies were avant-garde, atypical. They weren't big on commercial appeal, but they were more creative than most. Most of them, at least to start, were actual choir boys," he explained at length the Zombies' musical appeal and techniques, "their *Hung Up on a Dream* is even more illustrative," he spurted excitedly, "key changes, in and out of minors."

How, I wondered, *could "even more illustrative," work into a conversation with an attractive female stranger.* I eavesdropped. He surely had ruined his chance of romance.

"Is that why they sounded different from those other sixties groups?" the girl asked. She hung on his every word, fascinated with his musical expertise.

Inexplicably, in the midst of his music rant, he managed to have his drink refilled and had an additional one to place in the girl's hand. Coinciding perfectly with the musicians' return, Phil finished.

My Sharona's distinctive two-note bass hook clicked in as a girl with straight, pageboy cut, light brown hair, and admirable curvature stepped in front of me. Conveniently, she was a full head shorter. Inconveniently, she was close enough that I had to raise my newly refreshed iced coffee to keep from spilling it on her. She wiggled an impulsive dance move. In sync with the song's lyric, her hand was on my thigh.

I was startled and thrilled. I knew I should step back, a task more easily contemplated than accomplished. Both because of the restrictive closeness of people around me and because knowing better was not always a compelling motivation.

She tilted her head back and slurred what I interpreted as, "You go to school in Cambridge?"

"I should be starting at MIT next year."

Immediately her hand separated from my leg, and thankfully, didn't return as the musicians struck up *Down Under.* Another fellow not well-groomed, slightly taller than me, strolled up next to this overtly playful girl. "Step out for a Vegemite sandwich, doll?"

She responded to his tempting lure.

My concept of amusement was not that of a constant crush of bodies; well, not all crush was terrible. My ideal for a meaningful encounter would be to establish a social and intellectual relationship first. *Fairy tales, would I ever part from them?*

A woman, markedly assured, approached the stage and raised a flute to the bassist's microphone. With Vocoder accompaniment, she drew an extra positive audience response.

Finally, at midnight I interrupted Phil from his musical critique in which he somehow continued to engage the same girl.

"How would I walk to your apartment from here?"

"You're going to leave us? Okay. Outside go right on Broadway to Prospect, Prospect to Mass Ave," his directions were hastily delivered, "Mass Ave. to Boylston, Boylston to Hemingway. You'll be going through the MIT campus."

As an afterthought, he added, "Stay away from the Fens."

"Listen to him on that," offered his girl, surprising me. It was the lengthiest attention I had from her all night. Her voice was amusive, buoyant.

Perhaps Phil wasn't hopeless after all.

§

An impenetrable fog had crept into the high-walled streets, chilling the air and any desire I had to see any sights on my walk back. Headlights and taillights faded in and out, and wisps of vapor swirled in the wake of automobile outlines, intermittently clearing for a moment then closing in just as rapidly. I heard fellow pedestrians before I saw them, the scrape of sand under shoes gave away shrouded approaches. It was a fog New Englanders called pea soup, known for its ability to strain eyeballs out of their sockets.

The streetlights held their halos tightly. Diffusion lit the night softly, evasively.

There were a surprising number of wandering couples.

I sensed the Rogers Building, central to the MIT campus. If I could have seen it, I would have recognized the six Ionic columns at the entrance, the stairs, five in the first rise, twelve after the short landing, and the brass railings. I would schedule my classes here next autumn, though I could have skipped my high school senior year and been enrolled here now.

Gut-felt, I apprehended the power of the Charles River's deep currents beneath as I crossed the Harvard Bridge. Once across, I decided to detour on Beacon Street and walk by a row of MIT frat houses to gauge the students' activities in the early Saturday hours.

I picked up on a few quiet conversations until I heard one bitter, drunken, self-directed monologue, presumably from high on a fire escape landing I knew to be unfashionably bolted to the buildings' fronts. The young man harangued, denouncing his lost love and a traitorous former friend.

"What's he got that I don't got?" the liquored up, unlucky in love, soul slurred, well sauced in self-pity.

"Approach your relationships with less self-centeredness." Moderation escaped me as I hollered up my advice for this lovelorn drunk, my second calling. I received several hoots of approval from adjacent fire escapes that developed into applause from an illusory, surrounding, apparitional audience.

"Bite me!" was his erudite response. The lonely heart then retched and showered the shrubbery below.

§

Fenway Park, the famed Red Sox home, was less than a mile distant. Derived from the same root as Fenway, the Fens, which my brother and his friend warned me to avoid, were considered the clasp of the Emerald Necklace Park System. A beautiful image, the creative upshot of landscape architect Frederick Olmsted whose broad vision had graced public places in Boston and New York City, among others.

The Boston Common and Public Gardens began the Emerald Necklace. It connected thinly, along Commonwealth Avenue, then more broadly in the Back Bay Fens of Muddy River with its sundry ponds, lagoons, and pools. Proceeding from there were the Arnold Arboretum grounds, which offered room to explore. The Emerald Necklace concluded with Franklin Park and the Franklin Park Zoo.

"Of this park system,..." its creator penned, "a ground to which people may easily go when the day's work is done, and where they may stroll for an hour, seeing, hearing, and feeling nothing of the bustle and jar of the streets, where they shall, in effect, find the city put far away…" Olmsted was hugely successful; walkways and bike trails abounded, trees, shrubs, and flowers flourished for the park's guests' enjoyment. Indeed, it was the way he had penned it, during the daytime.

Late on a foggy night, the Fen's character was dark, moody, sinister, and grasping. From the undergrowth off the trails, toward the river, came sounds recognizable only as human.

"A little help here," kited at me through the swirls in the gloomy mist by a tormented phantom protected by impenetrable fog and the dim illumination that the city called night. Bondage and despair came to the forefront.

Warnings to heed. Requests to ignore.

I approached the Agassiz Street Bridge and recalled it having several stone arches, narrow concourses for the Muddy River's sluggish flow. Its top was broad enough for a two-lane street with bordering sidewalks. Leaves would collect in low-walled alcoves, poetically called *tourelles*. Beyond the further bank, I would find Phil's apartment where a sofa, a pillow, and a blanket awaited my tired body.

Off to my left, a loud, harsh, one-sided conversation intruded into the caliginous night. Phrases I could make out, but not the context.

"Tom Boyle… not business… family…" laced the fog.

Attracted, drawn toward the indiscernible speaker, I swiveled instinctively and stopped. The man's speech was crisp Boston Brahman.

A chilled draft formed between the river and the bridge's cold stones. It wafted by, creating a lens of clarity between the quarrel and myself, a fleeting vortex, the same as I'd seen in the wake of fogbound automobiles earlier. It provided a furtive but clear line of sight to the unfolding drama. Corner streetlights were no longer halos in the mist but became stage lights for the open-air live theater.

A dozen yards away, a man was kneeling, hands behind his back. Two men stood behind him; one, a distinguished older man with gray temples below his dark fedora, bushy eyebrows, doleful, crow's footed eyes, a wrinkled forehead, and a large nose, a profile to remember. Alongside the older man, another man, with a younger stance, memorable for his sharp tailored lines, very stylish, although his longish dark hair didn't go well with his fedora. Both men who stood wore long black dress coats, and glints from the nearby streetlight divulged shiny black lace-up shoes.

A trace of cologne flitted across the fragile stillness.

I looked away. Not my fight. My averted gaze took in the presence of two limousines with similarly clad men who stood beside each one.

"Tom Boyle, make your peace."

My attention shifted back to the three men on the grass. The older man extended his hand, exposing a stubby pistol. I looked away again, protectively closing my eyes. I feared, I knew what was to follow. Two consecutive flashes of light registered red behind my eyelids; two loud echoes of the reports, in equal volume, ricocheted off the apartment buildings across the empty, fog-filled street.

"What..." I bellowed involuntarily.

The kneeling man slumped forward, a tumbled lifeless mass that might have been a pile of clothes turned out from a laundry basket.

The older man looked directly at me. His right hand faltered, fell to his side, and the pistol dropped to the ground. The man's stunned and contrite expression etched itself in my mind. He had an oval face, thinner than I expected, and a mouth slightly wrinkled at the sides, a once contented face, horrifically altered.

The younger of the two men went down to one knee and picked up vague items from the ground. He also retrieved the dropped gun.

"Get that kid!" the embodiment of the voice was lost. The fog resumed its grasp on the Fens, frustrating the vision of all. "Mr. Belluno, get into the limo."

It took me paralyzed seconds to realize that I was that kid to be gotten. I had just witnessed a cold-blooded murder.

Running for my life, I had pursuers in my ears. I heard two distinctive styles of running from the stiff leather soles and another softer set. The two leather-shod runners wouldn't last, not proper shoes for a race; the third chaser was sneaker-shod.

Among the beachfront shops, I spied a wooden, sandblasted bakery sign. The bakery lit up inside as I passed; with plentiful places to park at this hour, I had all the invitation I needed.

With my legs, back, and arms stretched, I knocked on the glass oval in the door. It rattled loosely in its frame, adding an impatience I hadn't intended.

A friendly looking, middle-aged man, accompanied by a woman equally friendly-looking and middle-aged, came to the door. They stopped short of opening it. The man was fit and the woman much less round than I would have expected of bakers. Both wore white aprons.

The woman remained behind and to the man's right.

"Do you have any coffee?" I asked through the glass.

"Open it, John," I heard the woman say. "I'll start the urn. It'll take a few minutes."

"Thank you. It's been a long day."

The man locked the door behind us.

"We're just starting ours. What brings you here this early?" The woman sniffed casually. Breathalyzer.

The bakery had an inviting vibe. The front section had chairs inverted on the tables, all scooted to one side. A fresh, red-checkered tablecloth was folded, ready to spread, on each one. Clean display cases were unlit and bare, and behind them, the appealing kitchen was open to view. The register drawer was open and empty. Black and white floor tile, white acoustic ceiling tile, and walls neatly adorned with common-place seascapes created a comfortable, familiar feel. Entic-ing scents abounded, ghosts of delectable baked goods past. Ovens pinged in preheat mode, heralding the freshly baked pastry and bread aromas to follow. Their coffee mill started at a touch, churning out lusciously aromatic grounds. John, meanwhile, hauled bins of flour and other ingredients.

On the wall by the register was a framed dollar bill, a testament to the bakery's humble beginnings. A cross-stitched Bible verse hung next to it. "'As for me and my house, we will serve the Lord.' Joshua 24:15," a testament to the owners' faith.

"I visited my brother in Boston last night. I'm from Acworth, across the state from here. A couple of hours ago, I saw something that made me want to head home."

"And that was... what?" the woman invited particulars. John listened in.

Hesitantly, I evaluated how much or what to say. I knew whatever I spilled, it wouldn't be any of their tantalizing coffee.

"I was walking in really dense fog, back to my brother's apartment from a coffeehouse in Cambridge. I was on the Fenway side of the Back Bay Fens when the fog cleared for a few seconds. I saw a man shoot another man kneeling in front of him. Twice in the back of the head." A stress cough punctuated my story. "The shooter saw me."

The bouquet of brewed coffee diffused through the little shop. Measuring devices, bowls, and more ingredients arrived noisily on the preparation surfaces, filling a void in my description.

"Have you reported this to the police?" The woman poured three ceramic mugs of coffee.

"Not yet. Three men chased me after it happened, but I outran them."

"John? What do you think?"

"It sounds gangland and providential that our young man, here, got away." John interrupted his baking set up, retrieved a pad of paper and a pen from a cabinet above their prep area. He also brought a chair from the front of the shop, cleared off a low counter, and made a place for me to sit.

"Write all that you can remember, of time, location, what happened, what you were doing there, and a description of the men; take it with you when you go, and fill in other details when they come to you."

It was advice, not a command, from an efficient Yankee.

"Have some coffee," offered the woman. Steam rose off the top of the warm, white ceramic mug, which said welcome much more so than a foam cup.

I sipped, initially cautious of the hot beverage.

"Thank you so much. This is delicious. My name's Cal. What are your names?"

"This is my husband, John. I'm Martha."

"You're both very kind. I didn't expect to invade your time."

"Not at all. What else would we do at four o'clock in the morning? Usually, all we have is each other and our daily routine. Today we start with tales of high adventure."

I narrated my encounter while I wrote and finished my coffee.

"When you get home, I'd call the Boston Police. They'll want the information that you have. You might be a witness for the prosecution. A lot of times, they don't have a lot to go on." John was earnest.

"Thank you for the advice, the coffee, and opening up your store for me before business hours."

"Stop anytime that you're in the neighborhood and recommend us to your friends."

"I'll do that."

Martha poured extra coffee into a Styrofoam cup for me. A fiver whispered its way into the empty tip jar.

John came to unlock the front door.

"Thank you both again."

What a welcome respite, regardless of the situation. All the more, I appreciated the couple's hospitality. I would remember them, and John and Martha's Bakery.

As I backed out of the parking lot, I glanced in the bakery window. I saw the two, backlit, facing each other, each holding both hands of the other.

§

Milford, New Hampshire, provided me with a 7-Eleven pit stop and a Pepsi before the final stretch into Keene.

Caffeine barely sustained me. I read aloud the drive-in movie features and the familiar signs on Marlborough Street: Miniature Precision Bearing, Markum, and Kingsbury Machine Tool. I took a short detour, heading down Green Street, where Steve and Jack had their apartment. There were no lights on, no Camaro, and no sign of activity.

Once home, I left the car in the driveway with my bike and all my gear. The sky blushed, anticipating the sunrise. Dave Harris would be in his milking parlor cleaning his milking machines.

I sloughed my jacket over the back of a living room chair, ran up the stairs to my room, and tumbled onto the bed. On the comfortingly cool sheets, I closed my eyes, sacked.

§

Not in a long time had I slept past eight in the morning, but at ten, I was distressingly aware that the phone was ringing downstairs. I was at the top of the stairs when it stopped, and before I had time to slog back to bed, it began again. It could only be Phil.

"Hello?" was my dull greeting.

"Cal, where are you? I mean, why aren't you here?"

"Good morning, Phil." A scrap of sensibility returned. "Sorry I left without leaving a note. I was chased out of town."

"What does that mean?"

"It means you Bostonians aren't all that friendly. I saw a guy get shot last night while I was walking to your place, then, because I crashed their party, they wanted to take me out for a nightcap."

"Over by the Agassiz Bridge?"

"Yeah, how'd you know that?"

"*Boston Herald*, front page, headline. 'Kean "Tom" Boyle Found Dead.' I've got the story right here in front of me. Irish Mafia. Petros Aristide Belluno, an Italian Mafia guy, turned himself in. Says here in the sidebar, a turf war is likely. Anyone with any information should call the Federal Bureau of Investigation."

"Shoot, I've got two pages of legal pad filled with info, and it's still growing. Did they give a number?"

"Are you going to call them?"

"Yeah, I kind of have to, don't I?"

"This is deep stuff, Cal. Most people wouldn't."

"Just give me the number. How did you make out with that girl last night?"

"Her name is Jill. If you want to talk to her, I'll wake her up. We came back here last night and stayed up talking 'til dawn. You'd like her. She's at MIT, engineering. A sophomore."

"Cool, dude, bring her out the next weekend you're free." Great, another Jill. At least Phil wasn't a Jack. Otherwise, I'd have to do that Jill, Jack thing, all over again. "What's the FBI number, please?"

"800-555-2121."

"Thanks, Phil, ttfn."

Not wanting to rationalize my way out of making the call, I ran out to the car in my flannel shirt and lounge pants. The legal pad was where I'd left it. I grabbed it along with the John and Martha's Bakery pen. Back in the house, I dragged the phone over to the recliner and dialed.

"Federal Bureau of Investigation. How may I direct your call?" The voice was delightfully feminine and airy.

"I have information about the murder of Kean Boyle last night in Boston."

"May I have your telephone number, in case we get disconnected?"

"Sure, it's 603-555-2828."

"Hold one moment, please, while I get a detective."

Faster than a speeding bullet, a voice, more math teacher than cop show cop, was on the line.

"I'm Detective Asbury; before we start, may I have your name and telephone number?"

§

Sleep tingled in my arms, my hands, clubs at the ends of my wrists. I rotated my body to swing my arms into motion. It was a painful transition from sleep to wakefulness. I fought to sit up against the cradling of the recliner.

A dream? Would that it was, but it wasn't. My scribbled notes were still on my lap.

Saying goodbye to Detective Asbury was the last thing that I could recall. We had exchanged numbers and set up an appointment for me to see a sketch artist in Bedford on Monday morning. My parents wouldn't be back from their conference, but Detective Asbury said he would discretely acquire an excused absence from my high school.

My wake up was utterly wrenching; I decided that a bike ride would clear the dogged cobwebs. Marlow's millpond had a secluded sandy beach, if one knew where to find it, for a swim and a relaxing nap in the sun.

"Snap." Mentally, I slapped myself on the forehead. Tool sharpening beckoned to me from the wood frame shop.

§§

Chapter 12

A red and black striped picnic blanket lay under the prodigious twisted oak, spread over the evenly manicured lawn of the Tanglewood grounds. The curved portico of the impressive Tanglewood Music Shed yielded to the temporary, makeshift Josh Billings Runaground award stage.

The nearly cloudless sky appeared unusually blue with vapor trails of passenger jets flying out of Albany and Bradley Field. A dulcet breeze played with the blades of grass and caused the slightest rustling of oak leaves, a refined composition. If ever there was a day for Amy to make a new friend, she was sure that day was today.

Paul and Ann waved. Hand motioning, Ann outlined the large wicker picnic basket that presumably contained a picnic lunch. Fittingly, Ann had over-the-shoulder blonde hair, parted down the middle, a brilliant smile, shapely, and tall even without heels. She clapped her hands in conclusion.

Shade from the oak was welcome protection from the unclouded, late summer sun. The Josh contestants and volunteers staked out positions closer to the stage with folding chairs or blankets, better poised to jump up for five to ten seconds of recognition for their earned awards.

Amy's approach was characteristically deliberate. She wriggled her nose in disgust at a rude smoker who couldn't refrain from his detrimental habit. She returned Paul and Ann's waves then continued the motion, fanning in front of her face to rid herself of the cigarette's noxious fume. She received affirming nods.

The public address system on the distant stage didn't attain the same high standard as the jazzy, spired tent she'd worked in yesterday. It cackled to life announcing the first award.

"Third in the over fifty, competitive cycling event, Russ Sherman." Met with sparse applause.

"Where's your friend?" Amy inquired.

Paul's grimace forewarned Amy that nothing was the way he had wanted. He pointed with his eyes, past the trunk of the oak.

As if waiting for that cue, the same obtuse schoolmate Amy had spurned Friday afternoon, stepped from behind the great oak tree. He cast a smoldering Winston close to the crooked trunk and crushed it under his white and teal Nikes. Wearing a pastel blue Alligator polo and denim shorts, all six feet of him still fell short of tasteful fashion.

Amy stopped short, standing feet apart, arms folded, and silent.

"Hello, we meet again. I'm Sam Wilson."

"We haven't met at all. You walked beside me when you left school on Friday. I was speaking Italian, and you looked at me. I translated, and you walked away. You never said a word." Amy could muster no more warmth than that of a marble rolling pin. "My name is Amy, and now we're introduced."

Amy continued to stand, resolute.

"I stand corrected," Sam said while he sat on the blanket.

"No, I'm standing. You're sitting."

Paul's eyes appealed to Amy's for peace.

"That's funny. Like the stage business you do, Paul." Ann attempted a conversational rescue.

"First in the over fifty, cycling event..." intruded the PA.

"You're new." Amy lobbed.

"Yes, I am. I'm from Gloucester, moved here this summer. It's nicer there, being closer to Boston and all, with so much more to do. There are beaches. It's great fun in the summertime, just to go to the beach and tan. Take in the scenery. I like the mountains, too. I want to go hike one sometime."

Don't say it, please, Paul's eyes again pleaded with Amy, knowing the obvious reply. Sam was out of his league. If he couldn't rise to Amy's taunts, she would shred him and reduce him to hamster cage lining.

"Maybe you should take a hike right now."

"Hey, sorry. Ah, maybe we could sit and have lunch and start over. I brought turkey club sub sandwiches from Benny's. I heard it was the best place for takeout."

Amy, still disturbed at a level even she didn't entirely comprehend, sat only on the slightest fringe of the blanket.

"I got a pie from Village Inn and a bottle of Mateus to wash it all down with," Sam rambled affably, blissfully unaware of the new wave of anger that swept from Amy's disturbed face throughout her entire body. "I love the shape of the bottle. Don't you? Pretty stylish, all squat and curvy, not the tall boring regular wine bottle. I went all the way to Chatham, New York, to get it. You guys are so lucky to have a state so close where the drinking age is eighteen. We should have a lush club. Tell you what..."

"Don't you presume to tell me anything, *Sam*," Amy paused, using Sam's name to highlight her scorn. She rose purposefully to her feet. "Right now, I can't think of a single decent word to describe you, and I'm not wasting a minute trying to find one. I can't begin to catalog all the indecent ones.

"Paul, a minute with you," Amy demanded.

Paul unfolded his legs and followed Amy a short distance to another scraggly oak that would obscure their conversation from Sam, Ann, and the close neighbors distracted by Amy's rise in volume and passion.

"Paul?"

"I'm truly sorry, Amy. I had no hint of where this guy was coming from. My fault."

"I believe you. But, he's disrespectful, cowardly, uncouth, stupid, demeaning,... if he had any notion of a future that exists beyond the next fifteen minutes, I would drop my jaw in amazement."

"So," Paul was cautious in his inquiry, "how do you mean?"

"Cowardly? He had you ask me to set him up for a round of tennis. Why not ask me himself? He could have right after school. Disrespectful? Wine? Really? I'm sixteen. You and Ann are eighteen. Can you imagine how angry our parents would be if these people," agitated, Amy wildly waved her arms inclusively toward the crowd, "told them we were drink-

73

ing alcohol? Do you think you'd be involved with the Thespian Club or be acting at all if someone saw us? That's what he's disrespecting, my reputation and my future, and yours and Ann's. What's his point with the wine anyway?"

"That's fair."

"I can't tell you in all of the ten minutes that I have been exposed to that creep, how deeply I loathe him."

"I'm kind of stuck; he's working at the music store with me."

"Watch him like a hawk. I'm positive there is something rotten about him. Let him know that if he gets within ten feet of me, I'll fix him."

Paul returned to the failed picnic and noticed that two wine glasses were out. Ann and Sam were still on the blanket.

Sam pulled out a third glass.

"She's one spitfire Italian, isn't she?" Sam smiled, relishing the idea of continuing conflict.

"You had better keep clear of her. She doesn't like you," Paul delivered evenly.

"I'll take that as a challenge."

"Don't. She's serious. Ann, we should go."

"Okay," Ann agreed, with a trace of indecision.

Paul weighed the implication.

"Sam, I'll see you tomorrow."

"If you guys aren't just spoilsports and I thought you were cool," was Sam's parting remark. "What do I do with the wine and sandwiches?"

§

As Amy walked away from the ill-fated picnic, she caught sight of the Stockbridge Bowl over the high hedges that segmented the Tanglewood grounds. Blue undulating hills beyond called on her to cool down. Still angry, she decided to ride a lap around The Josh's 10K run course to quell her dog-eared nerves before going home. If that didn't work, she would do a second. After her ride, she would talk with her mom.

She removed her Bianchi from the Tanglewood Café's bike rack and walked it along the path toward the Nathaniel Hawthorne Cottage, a small footprint, two-story home in a relaxed setting. She leaned against the wood rail fence surrounding its adjacent lawns. The easygoing yard and homey yesteryear charm made her yearn for a simpler time. She noticed relaxation seeping in and recalled Hawthorne's underestimation of himself and his bouts of loneliness. She could identify.

In a flash of fantasy, she imagined she was in the Julian Alps with rugged mountains and green alluvial valleys. To fill the bill, the cottage would be her home. High mountains with remnants of snow would replace the low, hilly Berkshire horizon, but such was not the case.

She rolled away, her mind beginning to function in sync with her pedal strokes. *There had better be a day, someday, to make a new friend. At least,* she thought, *there will be school tomorrow. Mr. Adams will be assigning his required reading for English class, Shelley and Keats. The rigors of advanced math and physics will be there to take my mind off this dismal day.*

Her legs kicked out a comfortable cadence. The sparse traffic on Hawthorne Road consisted of kayakers headed to the parking lot to retrieve their boats.

Analytical gears meshed in her mind, trying to make sense of the day.

§

Cecelia heard the garage door open. It was late afternoon, later than she expected for Amy's return, given her plans for the day. Real estate papers spread, in typical fashion, across the coffee table with a glass of wine at the far end.

Amy grazed in the kitchen before she settled down in an oversized armchair. She crunched into a Macintosh apple, chewed, and washed it down with water.

"Last of the good stuff?" Amy asked lightly.

"Sadly, yes," Cecelia smiled, paused, then continued, "I drove down to Tanglewood to see if I could say 'Hi.' to you, Ann, and Paul."

"Not a stellar afternoon, Mom, the only thing stellar was Paul's acquaintance, who is a stellar jerk. He's the same guy I put down after school on Friday. I lit into Paul for being a horrible judge of character and left without joining the picnic. I'll have to track Paul down tomorrow and apologize."

"That's why I didn't see you. But, you left early, and you're just now getting home?"

"I went for a cool-down ride to sort out my thoughts."

"And how did that work out?"

"This guy's definitely a misfit. I told Paul that I'd beat him up if he even tried to walk near me. He smokes, and he brought wine, cheap wine to boot. He hadn't opened it before I left, though. He told us he went to New York State to get it, but I saw a Great Barrington Liquor bag at the bottom of his picnic basket.

"He couldn't even bring himself to invite me to tennis Friday afternoon. He had the opportunity while we were leaving school. All of his connections here are through his attachment with Paul, to me, and for work. If I read him correctly, he may make a move on Ann. Yeah, he's a jerk."

Cecelia always cultivated Amy's honest expression and appreciated her judgment.

"But here's the weird thing," Amy continued, "he didn't strike me as having any designs on me, but he does have an agenda. I don't quite have it. He's gotten close to Paul and presented himself as everything I'm not. Any advice?"

"Are you challenged, fearful, or none of the above?"

"Mostly, I'm concerned about Paul. Me? Challenged or fearful? Nope," Amy popped the p to emphasize her no.

"I'd go ahead and apologize to Paul tomorrow. I'd let him know that you're concerned for him because of this guy."

"Jerk, Mom, he's not a guy. He's a schmuck. His name's Sam. Calling him a schmuck is even too generous. Honestly, Mom, I have an obscenity in mind for him."

"I'd tell Paul that you're concerned about Sam and that you believe he may have an agenda that's suspect. It's good judgment for you to avoid him."

"I've got some puzzling to do."

"Let me know if I can help."

§§

CHAPTER 13

Finals week at Lenox High followed Memorial Day. It seemed incredible that the school year had already flashed by, already five full months into 1987.

Reminiscent of when Amy first encountered The Misfit, her school was letting out, but on a Tuesday, not a Friday. She knew that Sam would try to humiliate her during this last week. He had kept his distance ever since Paul relayed her ultimatum the previous fall.

She noticed times when he chatted with his acquaintances; he would cast his eyes in her direction, mutter indistinguishably, then laugh or snicker. He might field a comment, with a knowing nod of the head. She hated it.

She hated it, too, that he hadn't stood up for Paul when Tangled Music's owner had Paul arrested for the theft of four guitars. Paul was the one who had gotten Sam his music store job.

She knew that Paul hadn't stolen the missing Les Pauls. The irony in the name alone would speak against it. Not enough of a guitarist to desire one, he didn't need the money and had no means of fencing them. His clean three years of prior history at the store contradicted it. Paul maintained his innocence, but no one aside from Amy believed him, not his parents, not even Ann stuck with him.

The theft conviction removed him from his school acting gigs, and over spring break, Paul's family moved back to Dayton, Ohio. Ostensibly, they relocated for a better job for his dad. Regardless, Paul had written to Amy that the move was because of his conviction. He'd only sent the one letter and had not responded to her reply. He was very depressed.

Rabbit trail, Amy thought and quickly attended to her surroundings.

Behind her, she sensed sounds dampened. A body was immediately behind her. Mirrored in the glass double door exit, she saw Sam's reflection.

"Guess who," he said maliciously, simultaneously covering Amy's eyes from behind.

Amy stopped short.

Sam collided with her, his full body against her back.

She jammed her left heel on the top of Sam's customarily sneaker-shod left foot with all her hundred and fifteen pounds, a self-defense move that she had learned and practiced.

Sam dropped his hands instantly, shrieking with surprise and pain. Students in the hallway gave way to the central aisle conflict.

Improvising, Amy pivoted on her left heel counter-clockwise, her right foot kicked hard against the side of Sam's left knee.

Sam screamed. His knee bent unnaturally and buckled.

Amy's eyes met his, unashamedly blazing the messages:
Trust me when I say, 'Stay away from me.'
I don't pull punches.
I can beat you more now or again later.
You just got thrashed by a girl in three seconds.
Try that again...

Principal Alford, hurriedly responding to wounded animal sounds, surveyed the shocked students. He quickly inquired, "What happened here?"

Shrugs from all but Amy and Sam were his answers.

"I didn't do anything," Sam forced, sucking for air, between clenched teeth. He stifled his expressive style and tried to save face.

"No, sir. He assaulted me from behind. So I kicked his...," she *so* wanted to use an expletive, but her filter of better judgment replaced it with "knee."

Sam writhed on the floor, looking from face to face; each one nodded in assent to Amy's report. His eyes narrowed vengefully.

Amy would have another long talk with her mom; she envisioned support and criticism. She would receive both.

§

"Mom? Would you sign me out from school today?" It was the first time Amy had seen her mom since Tuesday morning. They were having breakfast together. Cecelia had been out very late the previous night with business in eastern Massachusetts. Amy had been at home just under curfew despite the year-end school parties, which she studiously shunned, preferring, instead, to work at the sporting goods store. "I don't have any finals today, and I wouldn't want to relieve my boredom by crippling Sam more. He's already on crutches."

"What did you have in mind?"

"A bike ride."

"I know that tone, young lady. What were you thinking of, specifically?"

"I want to drive to Williamstown and bike the half-century circuit from the Cozy Corner, around through North Adams, Searsburg, Bennington, and back to Williamstown. That will keep me out of mischief." Amy sensed maternal doubt and added, "I'll call along the way, and it shouldn't be much longer than a four-hour ride. You could call it an early day, and meet me for dinner at The Williamstown Inn, my treat."

"If you bribe me, and if it would save on attorney fees, how can I refuse? Besides, I had a warning when I saw the half bottle of Gatorade in the freezer this morning."

"Thanks, Mom. I'll change into my bike gear while you write the note."

"What shall I write, 'out sick'?"

"I'd prefer 'mental reorientation break.' Apt?"

"Very."

§§

CHAPTER 14

Detective Asbury worked his angles, persuading my school through channels, not I, my parents, nor even my teachers, had any inkling. The result was, no one at school figured out how I had managed to reschedule my calculus final from Friday to a week earlier. Chelsea and Jill admired my cunning in arranging no after Memorial Day finals. They only knew this much; I wouldn't be there. I'd see them at commencement and graduation.

Sunrise was at five forty-five this Friday morning, coinciding with the black Chrysler 300 abruptly crunching to a stop in my driveway. I sat, perched atop our white rail paddock fence, where I had been for the last fifteen minutes.

"Agent Palmer," he introduced himself tersely. Agent Palmer's close-cropped dark hair topped a solid six-two frame. "My apologies for being late."

I wondered if all FBI agents dressed from the same closet. His white shirt, solid blue tie, shiny black shoes, charcoal suit told me he was concealing a firearm and sunglasses.

"That backpack won't pass courtroom security. You know that." Matter of fact. Detective Asbury had said that security would be very tight considering the trial's high profile.

"I wanted to bring a book for reading, water, and snacks."

"Uncle will take care of our refreshments and lunch. What's the book?"

"*Hunt for Red October.* Tom Clancy."

"Pretty thick. They'll check it for concealed weapons if you try to take it into the courtroom." Not to be mistaken as short-tempered, he added, "Where are you in it?"

"It's the ping standoff."

"Nice. Take the book, leave the backpack," Agent Palmer said, with a curious, familiar inflection. *Intentional humor or staid FBI talk?*

"I'm your chauffeur today. I can't talk to you about the trial or your testimony. It would be best if you took the back seat and enjoyed the ride."

My analysis of Agent Palmer, this chauffeur duty was beneath him, but business was business, and this was business.

Mom and Dad were inside watching from the living room window. I lifted my pack for their attention and rested it on the grass just inside the fence. After I waved good-bye, Agent Palmer held open the land yacht's back door.

I would have preferred that my parents take me. They agreed with Detective Asbury, though, that it would be best if they went to work as usual. I would be the only atypical Barton.

"What's the best route that you know of to get to Boston that includes a good cup of coffee to go?"

"We could stop at Lindy's Diner. That would do it."

"Really? How far, timewise?"

"Only farmers on the road right now, no cops. No offense, sir. Twenty minutes."

§

Boston was outside; Agent Palmer once again opened the door for me to disembark.

Art Deco to the core, the John W. McCormack US Post Office and Courthouse covered a full city block, inspired by a stuffed chair built of Legos. Vertical window insets in the white limestone gave the building relief and guided the eyes upward. The decorative metal grillwork darkening those insets obscured the lighter, deco style, aluminum frames. Thankfully and artfully conceived, the ground floor grill-work was bronze.

"This does it for me," Agent Palmer interrupted my book reading.

He had been earnest about not discussing the trial or my testimony. At Lindy's Diner, he had chatted with a couple of early shift Keene police officers about his witness transport duties. They exchanged business cards.

From my first appreciative sip of coffee, I was on my own to read.

"Thanks for the ride, sir."

"You're welcome, Cal. Agents Moretti and Fisher will escort you to the courtroom. I'll be here to pick you up for the return trip when you're done. Hopefully, the prosecution and the defense will finish up with you before afternoon recess."

Gleaming high-rise buildings clashed with a dirty little park across the street more suited to vagrants than lawyers and businessmen. I wouldn't want to eat my lunch there.

Agents Moretti and Fisher were no more sociable than Agent Palmer. With efficiency and lack of appreciation of the spectacular building, they guided me through the middle of three double glass entry doors. They didn't notice the wheat stalks that interrupted the upper flutes in the columns that bookended and separated the main doors. They missed the art deco eagle motifs in relief higher up on the exterior. Neither did they glance at the inset bronze placard that announced the building's name with its construction and funding credits.

A round brass rail up the center of the stairway led to the ground level hallway. Post Office features abounded, again lost on my personal agents. Straight through the lobby, through the post office service area, and clear across the length of the building was a bank of elevators. Suspended from the high, embossed tin ceiling, a massive two-foot cube of a clock in patinaed bronze intruded on the lobby. It showed that Agent Palmer had made excellent time from Acworth, five past nine.

An inlaid graphic of an art deco eagle with a laurel of wheat graced the marble floor, light gray on black. I stamped my foot on the marble floor to draw attention to it.

"Leg asleep?" It was Agent Fisher.

"Yeah." My effort was pointless. Either they were not at all discerning or lost on the details through repetition.

"Tell me," just to let them know that I was paying attention, "were the guys outside reading the *Herald,* casually drinking coffee, they're on our side, right?"

"Good eye, kid."

§

From elegance to elegance, five stories up the elevator opened to polished blond marble walls, mirroring busy lawyers, plaintiffs, witnesses, and reporters, echoing their conversations. Attractive dark stained cherry wood benches lined the business end of the courtroom hall.

"Restroom?" I asked expectantly when the agents motioned for me to sit.

"Sure, we'll all go."

We left the well-furnished restroom with satisfactory relief. With no pause, I heard my name called in the hallway. I looked inquiringly at my black-suited friends.

§§

Chapter 15

"Good timing on the potty break, kid; testimony is taking less time than we thought."

"I just want you to know; I'm really nervous."

"Listen carefully to the questions; answer the questions completely and truthfully. Don't offer any more or less information than what the question calls for. With your observational skills, you'll be a jewel of a witness." And here I had thought that Agent Moretti was the silent partner.

Two men were leaving the courtroom when we entered. The first was tailored better than a movie spy before the fight scene. The other, atypically dressed in a wide striped polo, was a big guy favoring his left leg. Arrogant, even at a glance, he jarred me, walking straight into my left side. I doubted that he was clumsy, more attempting to knock me off my balance. Regardless, instead of a fluffy snowdrift, he discovered that I was the fire hydrant hidden beneath. Agent Moretti, who had politely stepped behind me to allow the pair to exit, hip-checked the offender as well.

"That's okay," I whispered, "I'm a lot more substantial than what he was planning on."

"You're good, kid. Want to be an Agent?" Moretti whispered back.

The judge, whose nameplate identified him as Judge Taylor, interrupted our brief conversation. Silvering hair topped his round, clean-shaven face. More eyebrow than anyone should have without first obtaining a license crowned his brown eyes, and crow's feet framed them. Wrinkles fashioned his sober lipped mouth into a parenthetical expression. Faces tell of various histories, of laughter, of pain, of puzzlement, of contentment..., his spoke of concentration.

"The witness will approach the bench. The bailiff will administer the oath. Bailiff?" The judge was precise, solely intent on business.

"State your name for the record." The bailiff recited.

"Michael Barton."

"Do you, Michael Barton, affirm that the testimony you're about to give in the case now before this court will be the truth, the whole truth, and nothing but the truth, this you do affirm under the pains and penalties of perjury?"

"I do."

"Take the stand."

"Mr. Royce, you may question your witness."

"Very well, Your Honor."

Mr. Royce was a fit individual and evidently had an excellent tailor. Longish blonde hair, blue eyes, and anachronistically small gold-rimmed glasses gave him a distinguished air.

From the knee wall separating the gallery from the proceedings section, he stood and stepped quickly to the right of the prosecution's table and glanced briefly at the judge.

"Michael, may I call you Michael?"

"You just did." This rejoinder gained a stare from the judge that spoke volumes and caused stifled laughs and a smile from the not yet identified defense attorney. They reminded me of the grave nature of the trial. My lesson was quickly appreciated. "My apologies, everyone. I joke when I'm nervous. You may call me Michael."

"Thank you. Michael, would you relate to the court your activities on the evening of September 12, 1986, a Friday, and following Saturday morning, the thirteenth. Please give all the detail that you feel is significant."

"Let's see; That Friday, I had driven to Boston to visit my brother who attends the Berklee School of Music. He had told me of a musical event at the Ellery Street Coffeehouse in Cambridge. At about midnight, I left the coffeehouse alone. He and his friends stayed. It was an extremely foggy night, the kind of fog that keeps you from seeing your hand in front of your face. Phil, my brother, gave me directions on how to get back to his apartment, walking."

"Let me interrupt for a moment, Michael. Are you not familiar enough with Boston to know the way?"

"Not really, sir. I've been to Boston several times either to go to the Museum of Science or, more recently, to move my brother's stuff down here. One time I visited the MIT campus. I had intended to go to school there when I graduated from high school."

"And what were the directions that your brother gave you?"

"From the coffeehouse, Broadway to Prospect, Prospect to Mass. Ave., Mass. Ave. to Boylston, and Boylston to Hemmingway, then Symphony. After I crossed the Harvard Bridge, instead of Boylston, I took Beacon Street past some MIT Frat houses; I couldn't see anything, though, because of the fog. I got on the west side of the Fens. I do know enough of the area that if I walked further, I could cross the Agassiz Bridge not too far from where I had parked."

"Okay," Mr. Royce interrupted again, this time for emphasis, "when you reached the Agassiz Bridge, what happened?"

"It was early morning, about one thirty-five. I heard bits of a conversation from off the sidewalk. I looked that way out of reflex. Then, as an upshot of what I can only describe as a hole in the fog, I saw three men at first."

"Your Honor, objection," it was the defense attorney, "this is highly far-fetched; a hole in the fog?"

"Your Honor, Mr. Van Gelder, I have a meteorologist present, ready to testify to the high probability of just such a phenomena occurring in that location and under the weather conditions at the time," Mr. Royce snapped back before the judge could comment.

"Very well, defense concedes that such an event could occur. I withdraw the objection."

"Michael," Mr. Royce prompted, "proceed with your account."

I was amazed at how everyone in the courtroom was concentrating on my summary.

"When I had this open line of sight," underscoring my opportunity, "I saw one man kneeling, hands behind his back with two men who stood behind him. One of those standing men held his arm out toward the back of the kneeling man's head. I closed my eyes, anticipating a gunpowder flash; I couldn't imagine any other scenario. I heard two gunshots and their echoes from the apartments across the street. I felt slapped. The kneeling man slumped forward. One of the standing men squatted, plucking up two small brass looking objects from the grass. I never saw that man's face. The man who had extended his arm toward the kneeling man let his arm drop. I saw a revolver with a bluish barrel, which he let fall to the ground."

"Do you know what type of revolver?"

"I didn't then, but I researched on my own, and I believe that what I saw was a snub nose revolver, perhaps a .38 caliber."

"What happened to the gun?"

"The second man picked it up."

"Could you describe the second man?"

"I never saw his face. I do recall that he was wearing shiny shoes, cuffed dress pants, a dark full-length overcoat, a nice one, a fedora, and he had longish dark hair over his collar."

"Is he in the courtroom?"

"I'm certain that I wouldn't know it if he was."

"What about the man that dropped the gun? Would you be able to point him out in the courtroom?"

"Yes, sir. He's seated next to the defense lawyer, Mr. Van Gelder."

"Your Honor, again," Mr. Van Gelder jumped to his feet, "this is too farfetched. It was foggy that night."

"Your Honor, I can clear up Mr. Van Gelder's doubt and any that the court or the jury might have concerning Michael's ability to identify the defendant. I promise to give the defense, wide latitude in questioning Mr. Barton on cross-examination."

"Very well, but to be very clear," Judge Taylor weighed in, "Mr. Barton, you understand the seriousness and the penalty for committing perjury before this court?"

"Your Honor, I do. I assure you that this is what happened."

"You may continue."

"How can you be certain that the defendant is the man that you saw?" Mr. Royce nodded at me.

"When I reacted to what I had seen, the setting and the gunshots, I made a sound. I gasped. The man who had the gun turned and looked at me. I have a vivid recollection of the look on his face. He impressed me as being in disbelief and having real sadness.

"The fog started to collect again, and the man who had picked stuff up shouted, 'Get that kid.' All of a sudden, I heard several kinds of footsteps start running toward me. I took off, too. I'm fast and outran whoever was after me."

"Did you stay with your brother in Boston Saturday morning?"

"Leading the witness."

"Sustained."

"What did you do after you outran your pursuers?"

"I got into my car, the family car, and drove to my home in Acworth.

"I slept until my brother woke me with a telephone call wondering where I was. I told him why I left. Then he read me an account from the *Boston Herald* with background information but less detail on what happened than what I've been describing. The article included a phone number for persons with information to call. My brother said not many people would call even if they knew what happened. But I did. The number was for the FBI, and I talked to a Detective Asbury. I told him the whole story, even more than what I've spoken of here because he kept asking questions, cross-checking my answers to see how accurate I was."

"Is Detective Asbury in the courtroom today?"

"I wouldn't know that either. I've not met the man face to face. The only time that we have spoken has been on the phone."

"Very good. Detective Asbury arranged for you to do what on the Monday following?"

"He arranged for me to meet with an FBI sketch artist in Bedford, New Hampshire."

"I introduce, for people's exhibit number five, this artist rendering, drawn under the direction of Michael Barton," Mr. Royce hammed it up. When he unrolled the paper he had withdrawn from a mailing tube, there was a corporate gasp. Whispers mounted from the courtroom attendees. The resemblance to the defendant was evident to all, almost photographic in quality. More than a similarity, it captured Petros Belluno's striking expression of *what have I done?*

"Michael, can you identify this sketch?"

"Yes, sir. The FBI artist drew it following my instructions. That's where I signed it, in the bottom right corner."

"Your Honor, I have no more questions of this witness."

"Mr. Van Gelder, you may cross-examine."

"Your Honor, due to the lateness of the hour, I ask that the lunch recess commence at this time."

"Very well. Mr. Barton, you may step down. I remind you that when you return to the stand, you will still be under oath."

"Yes, sir." I hadn't ever said, "Yes, sir." this many times in one day. It was a personal best.

"The court will recess for lunch and reconvene at one-thirty."

With a gavel rap startling those in the outer hallway, all the gallery rushed to the doorway, reporters especially, clutching their notepads and stampeding anyone in their way.

§§

CHAPTER 18

I hadn't taken the time before the lunch break to study the courtroom. A large United States map backdropped the judge's chair. Hanging from the white, stamped tin ceiling were light fixtures, large cylindrical frosted glass pendants finished with octagonal leaded glass frames. Twelve foot high windows presented an unrecognizable skyline. Sconces hung on both sides of the judge's chambers door at the right of the bench and the court workers' passages to the left. An American flag stood in the far right corner, beyond the jurors' box.

Jurors filed into their seats.

"All rise," the bailiff intoned tediously, "The Honorable Judge Taylor, presiding."

"The witness will retake the stand. The court reminds you, Mr. Barton, that you are still under oath. Mr. Van Gelder, you may proceed." The judge at once established his control.

"Mr. Barton, or shall I call you Michael?" Mr. Van Gelder asked with a sly smile. He was an older man with graying hair. His voice, friendly but tired, projected well from the defense table.

"Michael will do fine."

A few small chuckles arose from the gallery.

"Thank you, Michael," Mr. Van Gelder looked over at his client, "do you think the defendant is a bad man?"

"Objection. Calls for an opinion from the witness." Mr. Royce was on his feet in a flash.

"Your Honor, Mr. Royce, before lunch, promised wide latitude in questioning this witness."

"I'll withdraw the objection, Your Honor, Van Gelder. Force of habit."

"Understood."

"The witness will answer the question."

"I have no opinion, favorable or unfavorable. I've never met Petros Belluno. I can only testify to the events that I saw on the morning of September thirteenth."

"Fair enough." With a green, legal-length notepad thoroughly covered with notes, Mr. Van Gelder stepped to the side of the defendants' table and looked at the jury establishing eye contact with each of the twelve. He addressed me again. "You are an observant young man."

"I try to know my surroundings."

"You managed to instruct the FBI artist in creating a superb likeness of Mr. Belluno. How long of a look did you get of the person you saw that Saturday morning?"

"About twenty seconds."

"And you want the jury to believe in this artist's rendering created from your *recollection* of a man you saw, in the fog, for only twenty seconds?"

"It's not up to me to persuade them, sir, only to tell to the best of my ability, what I saw. The illustration was made entirely from my instruction."

"When you first entered those doors this morning," he pointed to the back of the courtroom, "you were clumsy enough to bump into another witness who was exiting. Describe him, please."

Mr. Royce stood and began to speak again. Judge Taylor lobbed a quizzical squint in his direction. A slight shake of the judge's head returned Mr. Royce to his seat and refocused a certain amount of heat to me.

"He had a slight limp, left leg, and was wearing Nike sneakers with blue, aqua accents, cuffed olive Dockers, pleated front, two pleats, recently ironed, but he forgets to hike the legs when he sits down; his knees were baggy. His polo shirt was wide-striped blue on white and tucked into his pants. Six feet one or two inches tall and a hundred seventy pounds, give or take. He had light brown longish hair, oval face, eyes..."

"That will do, Michael."

"It won't, sir. I swore to tell the *whole* truth. You said I was clumsy. Not true. He very purposefully knocked into me."

"That's enough."

"I haven't finished with his ears, mouth, chin, nose..."

"Michael, you were coached on the answers you would give today, weren't you?"

"Only to answer truthfully and completely. The agents and detectives all thought that the attention I paid to detail would be all that I would need."

"Give an example of your attention to detail that the agents noticed."

"I spotted law enforcement personnel, trying to be incognito, watching the entrance to this building. The agents that escorted me up here were impressed."

"How are you able to establish the time so accurately of your observations from the morning of the thirteenth?"

"I only ran for about two minutes from the west side of the Fens, and when I got into my folks' car, I noticed the clock said one forty. I changed the radio station to Worcester, and *A Dream of Your Smile* was playing. I called the station later, on Sunday, to ask for the broadcast time of that song from their log, they confirmed it did play at one forty."

"You seem to have a certain enhanced memory. Is that true?" Mr. Van Gelder's questions were coming more rapidly.

"In a sense, I stopped for coffee on my drive home from Boston. When I explained what I had seen, the bakery owner suggested that I write down all the details I could remember, those things that I saw and heard, of time, and place, and people. He said that I should fill in blanks as I recalled more. He gave me a pad of paper and a pen."

"No further questions," Mr. Van Gelder shrugged toward his client, then paused thoughtfully. "In fact, I do have a few more questions.

"You said, Michael, you intended to attend MIT after you graduate from high school, correct?"

Mr. Royce again twitched but didn't object. Mr. Van Gelder looked pleased with himself.

"Yes, though I've enlisted with the Navy instead," right away, I regretted offering the additional information.

"You're good with numbers?"

"Yes."

"You enjoy watching lightning storms?"

"Of course."

"Because you're interested, you calculate the distance from where you are to where a strike of lightning occurs?"

"Doesn't everyone?" another chuckle floated from the gallery.

"The apartment complex that is across from the Agassiz Bridge, how far is it from where you saw the gunshots?"

I considered Van Gelder's insightful implication.

"You testified that you saw and heard the gunshots and the echo of them. What was the delay? How far away was the reflecting surface?"

"I hadn't thought of it. That's clever. If I could have a moment of quiet, Your Honor?"

"Silence in the court," ordered Judge Taylor, intrigued. Someone coughed and rustled noisily in his seat.

"*I said silence!*" Judge Taylor shouted and rapped his gavel, this time realizing his order.

"About two hundred seventy-five feet," I spoke to the silence of the court seconds later, the gallery surprised at my confidence. "I had to approximate the angle of deflection and recall the delay, but I should be close."

"No further questions, Your Honor." Mr. Van Gelder resignedly dropped his legal pad to the defense's table.

Petros Belluno's body language expressed sadness throughout my whole testimony. I looked straight at him when I stepped down from the witness stand expecting a challenge. There was none. He granted me a slight nod that conveyed; *you did well, young man. It was the right thing to do.*

§§

CHAPTER 19

The blue suits left the Court Street sandwich shop and walked toward the Bartons' insurance office. The Barton Insurance Agency sign hung from a black metal bracket over the sidewalk.

"Mr. and Mrs. Barton?" One blue-suited man asked the couple as Mrs. Barton unlocked the office, returning from lunch.

"Yes, may we help you?" Cal's mother asked in her lilting voice.

"We'd like to see you inside if we could." One nodded to the other and followed the Bartons through the door.

"Certainly, have a seat. I'll be ready in my office in a minute or two." Cal's dad responded.

Two chrome frame chairs, on each side of the centered entry door, decorated the small reception area. Full front picture windows opaqued gray, on the inside, from the bottom up for two feet, added privacy for their clients. Above the painted section of glass, gold leaf restated the agency's sign in a horizontal oval. Potted palm plants, an area rug, and two side tables with *Time, Newsweek,* and *Sunset* magazines completed the setting. A hallway led to the offices.

The four of them stood in the waiting area.

"Business insurance, right?"

"You could say that," answered the first blue suit.

"You won't need to prepare. What we have to say we can say right here," chimed the second. "Please, both of you, kneel facing your reception desk."

"We don't keep any cash here," Cal's dad choked, suddenly frightened for Cal's mom and himself.

"Do what I say and be quiet. This won't take a minute."

Both men pulled revolvers, .38 caliber snub nose, from their shoulder holsters. The sight of the guns instilled immediate cooperation from the Bartons.

One man leaned toward the street and looked for anyone approaching; a head nod indicated all clear. Each man stepped behind one of the Bartons, raised his gun, and shot two rounds each into the back of their heads.

The men made no attempt to silence their shots. They holstered their weapons and walked casually out the front door toward Court Street.

The Keene city police station and fire department were not five hundred feet from the Bartons' office. Sirens of quickly converging police cruisers cleared the street.

As the pair of assassins walked, nearing their parked car, police officers were running to the insurance agency. One cruiser raced past them with lights flashing, driver and passenger prepared mentally for weapons fire. Tires complained loudly at their powered turn.

After giving the chaotic activity the curiosity that it was due, the blue suits took seats in their late-model gray Impala. Their cautious departure avoided attention, disappearing, assimilated by ordinary, everyday Keene traffic.

They shopped at the State Liquor Store a few miles distant and took advantage of the opportunity to yellow-ribbon with other Friday, Massachusetts patrons who came to buy New Hampshire's less expensive liquor. Before they strolled out with Johnny Walker Blue and Macallan Sherry Oak 30 Year single malt, they used the payphone inside the store to call the Boston office with their report.

§

Cello in hand, Phil worked his way through bowing techniques, through fingering techniques and speed, through arpeggios and scales: diatonic, Mixolydian, Phrygian, and even blues scales. Jill had brought her integral calculus book and one on fluid dynamics.

Slow tempo, chromatic scales were the most boring for Phil. His task was to begin the bow motion at the precise tick of the metronome or at a variety of note subdivisions, a challenge requiring more concentration than it would seem.

Phil's music practice had made it easy for Jill to study. Her presence made Phil more exacting in his exercises. Synergistic.

At two, he would pull out Sammartini's Sonata in G Major and Eccles' Sonata in G Minor. At two forty-five, fifteen minutes before they left, he would bring out his compositions. In those last fifteen minutes, Jill would close her books and enjoy. Phil would locker his instrument; then, they would walk to his apartment, prepare dinner, and talk. She, delighting in the music, knowing the physics of harmonics and resonance, and he, learning the physics, added to his musical knowledge. That was their routine for Mondays, Wednesdays, and Fridays. Later, on Fridays, they would head to Acworth or to Jill's home in Schenectady, New York. Or, they might go to the Cape with friends, or north to Freeport, Maine. This week they planned on Schenectady.

Except for classes, they spent most of their time together and agreed to live together in Boston next summer.

The Berklee Performance Center practice rooms had acoustic treatment on the walls. Designed for only one or two instruments, it had a minimum of reflected noise.

A knock on the door disrupted their reciprocal vibe.

"We're reserved until three." Phil raised his voice, annoyed at the interruption.

"There's an emergency. We're evacuating the building. Didn't you hear the alarm? Everyone needs to leave the building now."

Phil, closest to the door, set his bow on his music stand's shelf and reached to twist the door lock. Two men hurled the door open. Phil's premonition was a split second too late.

Jill startled from her seat.

Phil stood, his cello falling to the floor. With feline quickness and canine protection, he stepped in front of Jill and snarled.

"That won't be necessary," observed the man who had given them the emergency warning. His right hand slipped under his jacket's left lapel.

Phil's assessment was correct, but these unfamiliar thought processes were slow. He struggled for more options

98

than there were available. There was only one exit from the tiny room.

Phil lunged at the original warning giver. He saw that action as his only way to save Jill's and his own life. Before he was able to grapple his target, the other less talkative man cracked him on the side of his head with the butt of his revolver.

Phil dropped without grace to the floor.

Jill screamed and adopted Phil's protectiveness, kneeling and cradling his head.

The men nodded at their respective targets and fired two bullets into each of their heads.

A sheet from the Eccles piece drifted lazily to the floor stirred by the brief commotion, catching a few droplets of blood on its way.

The men used no silencers on their now reholstered weapons. They left the room and walked to the rear emergency exit expressing no haste.

§§

CHAPTER 20

Agent Moretti entered the courtroom hurriedly. He and Agent Fisher were to meet me in the hallway for an escort out of the building when I was ready for my ride home.

Without comment, Agent Moretti steered me into one of the bench seats. With a compassionate stare, he commanded me to sit. He continued toward Mr. Royce, under the curious and cowering glare of Judge Taylor. Moretti whispered into Royce's ear, who then stood angrily and looked at Petros Belluno. Agent Moretti spoke in hushed tones to Mr. Royce once more.

"Your Honor." Anger of the deepest, unfeigned, sort infused the request of Mr. Royce. His emotional pronouncement stunned the gallery. "May it please the court to clear the jury and courtroom? And may opposing counsel and I discuss a matter of *extreme importance* and *urgency* before you in chambers?"

"Chambers! Mr. Royce. Mr. Van Gelder, you will join us."

§

Three ashen faces returned to the courtroom from Judge Taylor's chambers. Reporters were at the ready to take notes. I hadn't moved from the seat where Agent Moretti had guided me.

"All rise."

"Agent Moretti, Michael Barton, Mr. Royce, Mr. Van Gelder, the court recorder, and Petros Belluno will remain. I, hereby, order the bailiff to remove the jury and clear the courtroom." Judge Taylor, intensely on edge, vehemently pounded his gavel.

Court officers swiftly and expertly removed all spectators and journalists. Any resistance encountered greater and opposite force.

Mr. Van Gelder leaned over to the standing Mr. Belluno and whispered. Mr. Belluno turned toward me, shook his head, and slumped resignedly. When he resumed a forward-facing position, his knees buckled. Quickly recovering, he supported himself. He raised his hands to his face, rubbed his eyes, and shook his head from side to side again.

Quiet and seriousness underscored my isolation.

"Michael Barton." The judge's voice was an aggregate of multiple emotions. Incongruous with one who is very rarely emotional, rage penetrated what he intended as compassion.

Man, was I in trouble. I thought, standing in response to my name, unaware of what else I might do.

"Michael, sit down. Please." Judge Taylor's tone was much kinder. "The court has been made aware, and I don't know of any simpler or more compassionate way to tell you; this afternoon at two o'clock, your parents were found shot to death in their place of business. Keene City Police, New Hampshire State Patrol, and FBI are cooperating in..."

The judge paused, sensing that I had tuned out what he was saying. When I tearfully regained composure, I recalled Phil's words on my willingness to testify.

Not many would; I could hear his voice warning me.

"I'm sorry, Michael, to be the one to tell you, there is more," the judge, anguished, "also at two o'clock, your brother Phillip and a female companion were found shot to death at the Berklee Performance Center.

"That is the sum of the news. Please take all the time you need and let me know when you are ready for me to continue. For the record, this court is adjourned for the remainder of the day."

No one moved.

Agent Moretti, the silent one, sat next to me. I leaned forward, elbows on my knees, hands clenched, eyes to the floor. The judge, attorneys, the defendant, and the bailiff were silent.

I was aware of each breath; each one was searing emotion and soul with recall and unfathomable loss. If I had been observing instead of the one who was experiencing my inner heartbreak, I would have been uncomfortable long before I broke the silence.

A quarter of an hour later, I cleared my throat.

"Yes, Your Honor, you had more to say?"

"Michael, I fear, the court, the attorneys, both defense and prosecution, and all the law enforcement involved, we all fear that your life is also in danger."

I nodded, but fear was not on my mind.

"You will exit by way of my chambers; Agent Moretti will accompany you."

I tried not to look at Petros Belluno, but the urge was irresistible. He continued gaping with his hands folded in front of him, palpably baffled, tired, red-eyed. However, resolution grew too, a mental reorientation.

He returned my fleeting glance as though he felt my gaze.

Wrenching as was this turn of events, bewildered, pained, and shocked as I was, the emotion composing Petros Belluno's expression was even more stunning. His face was that of a father who wanted to comfort a son, a look of reassurance that I would be okay. He appeared as one who had satisfied his inquiring mind, completing all but a few pieces of his bedeviling speculation. The result was a face set with tenacious determination.

§§

CHAPTER 21

Lance reclined in his leather La-Z-Boy while waiting for his new RCA television to warm up. It was only nine, and he wanted the ten o'clock news. He reached for his Breath Savers, then opted instead for a two-yard jaunt to his wet bar. Picking two cashews from the nut bowl, he slid a rocks glass from under the bar, loaded it with ice, and poured himself a generous Glenlivet.

It had been a glorious day. He thought it curious, the speed that the news of Michael Barton's family had arrived in the courtroom. A better coup for Lance would have been to cleanly eliminate the entire Barton family.

Once the Barton boy went into the judge's chambers, there had been no trace of him. For all anyone knew, Michael Barton was still in the McCormack building. Lance Grimaldi knew better than that.

His last bottle of Glenlivet would have to do for his celebration. He had, for a backup, in his estimation, a lame schlock brand, Loch Indaal, that a client had used to appease Lance's collection efforts. *Whoever heard of that? What do people take him for?* Besides, tomorrow, his liquor supplier would deliver a case of his favorite.

Lance surveyed his big-ticket surroundings. His cleaning crew had neatened, tidied, swept, vacuumed, and dusted well. Two months extortion he'd deducted from his contractor's account for the refined, remodeled living and dining rooms. The interior remodel met his much-needed requirement for additional storage. The decorator had used all wood furniture, the upholstered items were custom, donated by their talented manufacturer, similarly acquired elegant Arabian carpets covered his refinished hardwood floors.

He strolled across the room to the narrow, six-foot-high windows in the alcove facing Revere Street, then drew the heavy draperies closed to keep out the darkness. He loosened his tie, pleased with the silk.

The television splashed light intermittently.

Lance wished he could better appreciate the beauty of his possessions; he had original and expensive artwork on the walls, and impeccable craftsmanship surrounded him. He thought about the statement his possessions made about him, rich and powerful to the extent that he arranged the outcome of legal proceedings, and tomorrow, he would be boss, pro tem, of an entire criminal organization. Few pieces remained for him to have his full ordination.

He reclined and sipped his Glenlivet before setting his beverage on a coaster.

"We will return to Frank Herbert's *Dune*, after these messages." At first, Lance had thought that his television's color needed adjustment, then he realized that he had experienced a moment of artistic understanding. He was impressed with the dark nature of the images he had just seen. It felt good.

On the other side of the messages, he would watch more of *Dune*, but he would have to be aware of the time. The ten o'clock news was a gold mine, offering much to his line of business. He might see coverage of Michael Barton's family.

Piano music from the television came through the stereo system for enhanced sound. An announcer listed, with eloquence, several holdings of classical paintings at the Museum of Fine Arts.

Spare me, thought Lance. Another sip of Glenlivet.

"Hundreds of masterpieces are on view now at the Museum of Fine Arts. Let your imagination take flight with the *Pyramidal Seal with Birds Preying on a Goat*. Feast your eyes on the inscrutable *Still Life with Bread, Ham, Cheese, and Vegetables*."

Lance rose to retrieve a few edibles from his kitchen.

"Enjoy Edgar Degas' *Visit to a Museum*, only by coming to the Museum of Fine Arts for your pleasure and betterment." The announcer continued, oblivious to Lance's departure.

High class. Big money. Lance thought. *It might be profitable, no telling who I might find in a compromising situation.*

104

He returned to his recliner, in his hand, a plate of French bread, deli ham, wheel cheese, and vegetables, which he set down next to his Glenlivet.

He maintained the thought that *Dune* must be a classic film until a skinny waif had his heart plug pulled.

I should watch television more often.

§§

CHAPTER 22

Set in a substantial sixteen story, modern structure, four massive, five-story arches, forming a square and supporting a circular rotunda, composed a stunning vertical architectural feature. If I were inclined to be impressed, I would have been. The boxy marquee sat off-centered over the entrance. For such a sensational building, obviously a five-star hotel, it had no establishment name emblazoned on it.

Peculiar too, there were no people visible, aside from my entourage; no valet, no porters, no guests, and the concierge was absent from his station in the lobby. The registration desk, ornate in its wood paneling décor and dark green marble countertop, was unmanned; there was no wait staff, no doormen, and no phones rang.

Four men and two women whom I didn't know, and whose duty it was to protect my well-being, accompanied me. The lead, a woman, had gestured not spoken, to each of two men to inspect and clear side rooms.

Anger had slipped in alongside my grief, and I was critical of everything. The architect of this building had given the feel of marble but used a more durable stone for the flooring and archway frames, Vermont Verde granite. I'd seen it used in the high-end post and beam homes I'd helped to build. I'd also detected wood grain variations where a workman skilled with stain had artfully covered a costly carpentry error, masking sassafras as oak.

One room, an elegant dining area, had stacks of boxes and a floor cleared of any furniture. At the far end, a high glass wall opened out to a broad deck, exposing a magnificent panorama of Boston Harbor. White sails billowed on yachts in motion. A counterpart adjacent to the main lobby was a similarly appointed room, complete with more furniture boxes.

Both teams simultaneously issued the all-clear sign from the forward investigative duos.

I wished I were on the harbor yachts escaping with the wind.

My escort, a human cocoon since leaving the judge's chambers, was a cadre of US Marshals. Their badges, well displayed, complemented their tactical vests and unconcealed Glock 2340's. They stayed close enough to defend me against any assault and appeared very ready and very willing to do just that.

"Patrick, take the security room, radio confirmation that the cameras are working," directed the lead Marshal.

The whole building smelled of new, a swanky hotel right on the harbor. Today at a little past seven in the evening, it was ours alone. Odors of carpet adhesive were noticeable and gave way to fresh paint, in other places, drywall compound, familiar and comfortable construction smells. In the wood-lined elevator, a classy, polished brass floor selection panel had a whiff of mineral oil.

"I have you on surveillance; I see you in the elevator with the subject, yourself, and four other Marshals." The lead Marshal's radio had come to life with surprising clarity.

"Thank you, Patrick."

The building was not yet complete. A few weeks at best, maybe months would elapse before this grand hotel had a certificate of occupancy. The lack of activity made the Marshal's surveillance jobs easier. Rightfully, there should be concern about compromise with a traditional safe house. Hadn't the FBI assured my family, assured me that our identity and pretrial whereabouts were secure?

We would be occupying before the granting of an occupancy permit. The resourceful Marshals wield a lot of pull.

When we reached the tenth floor, again, the lead had signaled rather than spoken for two Marshals to assay the side rooms. They proceeded with pistols drawn, safeties off, to inspect all surfaces and enclosures; within minutes, they had satisfied themselves that there were no threats.

Katherine, as she had introduced herself, briefly reminded me that I had to stay in my room unless I was with a bodyguard, and I should radio for any needs I might have.

A change of clothes would be forthcoming, and due to changes in the legal proceedings in Petros Belluno's trial, there was no need for any further testimony from me. Two Marshals would be outside the door of my suite until my morning departure.

§

Left alone in my hotel room, I drained myself of tears.

I should let my parents know where I am, or Phil drifted with futility through my mind until no surge of emotion could produce tears any longer.

A knock on the door announced the delivery of new clothes. I took them in, confirmed sizes, then showered and changed into the hotel's complimentary cotton pajamas.

I lay on the extremely comfortable bed. I didn't want it to be comfortable.

Hunt for Red October was a distraction, but I found that I couldn't remember any words moments after having read them.

The room overlooked the harbor. The water below came right up to the hotel's very own dock, where several moored yachts and watercraft bobbed on the tide, freeloading since the hotel was not yet open. My Marshals surely had inspected each one.

With the window cracked, I could hear the occasional bell buoy tossing in the wake of freighters navigating the harbor. Not a morose toll or happy little tinkle, it was a brazen midrange call for all boats to stay in the channel.

In hopes of scoring a cheap meal, gulls squawked in flight and dove randomly to the harbor's surface. A flock of the same feather would harass the successful bird, crying loudly, ready to take advantage of any possession error the first bird might commit.

I looked down on a reddish copper-roofed gazebo that bobbed almost imperceptibly, built on flotation devices. This building and all that surrounded me was empty except for the eyes that were looking out for me.

"Looks like they plan on taking in guests from the moorings." No one heard my observation.

Further out, across the harbor, Logan International was conducting business as usual. My room was in line with one of the runways, parallel rows of lights guided strings of jetliners from over the Atlantic. Beyond that, far out to sea, a light flashed twice every ten seconds.

No fog tonight.

I wondered what a Bible might have to say about my plight. I checked the bedside table, but the Gideons had not yet made their distribution.

My room was a chrysalis. A different person would emerge in the morning with a different name, different home, and different past. Whoever I became would be up to me. That was the gist of the US Marshals' *Memorandum of Understanding* I had signed. I was in WITSEC, the Witness Security Program.

The question was, would I fly away as a moth or butterfly?

A pillow tag prodded my neck. I pulled at it to read Fretta Classic Linens, 100% Egyptian Cotton Percale.

I flipped the pillow and slept not at all well.

§§

CHAPTER 23

Lance thought that one of his living room windows had shattered, struck with a brick or a rock, only to realize that it was his telephone after the third jarring ring.

"Glenlivet bites," speaking to no one before he pulled the receiver roughly from the phone.

"What?" he said equally roughly.

"Boss, you've got to see the *Globe* this morning, section B, page two, on the bottom. Michael Barton surfaced in San Diego. He was taken out even before he had a chance to start basic training."

Lance knew it was his unconventional, contract assassin, Breathless. He'd been itching to finish the one Barton family loose end.

"To bad for you."

"The story says that the Naval Criminal Investigative Service opened an inquiry."

"Fine. Take the afternoon off," Lance hung up the phone, then went to retrieve his copy of the *Globe* from his front steps. Bending down to pick the paper up, Lance nearly had his head split open.

He slung the B section of the paper to his kitchen table.

"Good use of tax money. Feds sweep him out of the courtroom and then kill him," Michael Barton dead, wouldn't cost him a cent.

Lance picked up the phone and dialed seven digits.

"Get up to Keene. Check out the funeral, and make sure they all get in the ground."

§

Associated News, June 3, 1987

San Diego, California. In a tragic accident at the Naval Training Facility in San Diego, California, Michael

James Barton was killed during an orientation of the RTC facility yesterday at 9:45 AM. The accident occurred in proximity to a live-fire drill, and details are under review by the Naval Criminal Investigative Service. Burial arrangements are pending the investigation's conclusion.

Mr. Barton's death attracted national attention due to an investigation involving the apparent gangland slayings Monday of Mr. Barton's father and mother in Keene, New Hampshire. In a synchronized event, Mr. Barton's brother was killed in Boston, Massachusetts, along with Jill Taylor, a female companion. Graveside services for the Phillip L. Barton Sr., Stephanie K. Barton, and Phillip L. Barton Jr., are scheduled at 2:00 PM Friday, June 5th, at the Monadnock View Cemetery in Keene, New Hampshire. Michael J. Barton's service is yet to be determined.

Michael Barton had testified as an eyewitness for the prosecution in the trial of Petros Aristide Belluno. Belluno was convicted for murder in the gangland slaying of Thomas Kean Boyle, both, allegedly, notable Boston crime figures. Michael Barton's testimony at the trial coincided with his parents' and brother's murders.

§§

Chapter 24

The person who named Monadnock View Cemetery must have done so from a different vantage point than from the three recently excavated graves. Next to them, marked out with lime green spray paint, was a fourth grave for Michael James Barton.

The hearses and the limo had arrived, the honor guard was assembling, Barton family friends were gathering, cars lined both sides of the cemetery roads. The clergyman from Saint James Episcopal Church, where the Bartons occasionally attended, reviewed his notes once again.

"Dearly beloved, we are brought together here to celebrate the life (lives) of (name/names)..."

He stood from his folding chair and walked a few paces from the wall-less canvas canopy into the warmth of sunshine. In understatement, this would be one of his most difficult funeral services. How to make sense of unspeakable ruination stemming from the best of intentioned, heroic deed of a young man, and how to put the tragedy to rest.

Among the attendees, rapidly becoming a crowd, were a few barely noticeable FBI agents and a few even less identifiable US Marshals. Reporters, mostly local, with several from Boston, blended not well with their cameras, microphones, and notebooks. WBZ-TV from Boston had a camera crew assigned for a sidebar if it was a slow news night.

The wind fluttered in the few maple trees that lined the roadways. On the otherwise flat terrain, blades of grass shimmered. The canopy ruffle flapped lightly.

A Case backhoe approached slowly and quietly, stopping on the grass within earshot of the service. Those milling in small groups first glared in its direction then looked away, annoyed. No one wanted the crude reminder that it would soon be filling these empty graves.

§

Seven guns fired three times. A distant Barton relative received a folded flag for the elder Barton's Vietnam service.

Words said. Bible read. Flowers tossed. Tears shed.

The attendees formed small groups then cleared, except for Dave and Betty Harris. Betty tried to lead Dave away; instead, he waved her toward a pair of folding chairs under the canopy. Dave's Erinmore Flake came out along with his best briar pipe. He smoked in silence, broken only by a word or two to Betty; not until most cars had departed did he stand to leave.

Betty headed straight for their dark blue '85 Marquis, then corrected her path to match Dave's roundabout course.

A short distance across the well cared for lawn, Dave began a lengthy arc toward their car until he and Betty were walking directly away from the backhoe. The operator was waiting patiently to restart his engine and get about his business. Dave maneuvered to put his arm around Betty's shoulder, without looking he waved directly behind him toward the tractor.

The backhoe operator started his engine, returned Dave's wave unseen, and headed slowly to the maintenance shed. The excavator, whose job it was, would complete the dirt work.

§§

Chapter 25

Lucas Construction, my recently acquired employer, would be working west of Durango, Colorado, my recently acquired hometown. Our job was to prepare the underpinnings, footers for a house foundation. The commute was courtesy of the company's Ford F-350 crew cab, with Jamie the foreman driving.

Any conversation was laborious between my three coworkers and me. They sat on the front bench seat together. The new guy, me, settled alone on the crew seat. They expected me to be a burden; I got that. I was, in their eyes, still wet behind the ears. It was common in the trades, but this bunch seemed extra chilly.

About a half-hour distant from the shop, Sandy, short for Sandoval, decided to break the ice that had been building up between the front and back seats.

"White guys your age should be in school. Why aren't you?"

Sandy twisted from his shotgun position, wanting to see my response.

"Long story, Sandy, maybe another day."

"Anti-social," Sandy announced and then returned his attention and conversation to the front seat. That was that.

I didn't like Sandy's attitude. His brief question did expose my unpreparedness, though; I should be ready with quick answers.

Jamie, Robert, and Sandy, animated and humor-filled, conversed amongst themselves in Spanish, mixed with English. They left me to my daydreaming though I sensed many jokes were about me.

One WITSEC perk was that the Marshals would find and place their ward in some employment. I was a teen and had been unconventionally set in the program; this job was my perk.

Perk indeed.

I gazed out the passenger side window. As we rushed past the Silver Restaurant, I looked up the La Plata Highway. Its few miles of paved road into the La Plata Mountains would give way to gravel, then deteriorate, in arterial fashion, to less and less passable tracks. I'd explored them and found mountain bikers and hikers were the only ones to defy the No Outlet sign.

The Silver was a large, modern log building with an attached motel of the same motif. Inside, log furniture and blue checked tablecloths welcomed the traveling diner, with little play to faux Old West miner decor. It was all one might expect from a restaurant in downtown Durango. It also had a small stage, which graced local talent some evenings. Those old enough could enjoy a host of beers from near or far.

I discovered this comfortable out-of-the-way establishment during my summer biking and hiking adventures in the La Platas. For breakfast, The Silver served up French toast with bread sliced an inch thick, drenched in egg, milk, and cinnamon; they had genuine maple syrup, too.

"Where does your maple syrup come from?" I dared ask once.

The waitress, impressed or working for tips, came back with the answer, "your syrup comes from Vermont," which was close enough for her. Not nearly so, for me. I wanted to know down to the specific tree. Most Vermont maple syrup is distributed out of St. Johnsbury. *Could it be, from Brattleboro, closer to home?*

How to ask for more information without asking? After all, I was a recently relocated kid from a vaguely defined area close to Phoenix, Gilbert, in which I'd spent all of half an hour. I would have had little interest in, or discriminating knowledge of, maple syrup; never have climbed the trees or run a car head-on into a sugar maple. I would never have known the methods of collection or production, or taps and buckets, or plastic tubing, or about using the skimmed froth for composting. I would never have savored sugar on snow, never inhaled the steam from the sugarhouse boilers, never seen the skill of grading, never rejected the imitations, never have stolen a kiss from a daughter when her dad went out to get more wood to stoke the boiler.

On another stop at The Silver, the waitress, remembering my, more than customary, gratuity, disclosed that their maple syrup came from Bennington, Vermont.

Bennington. Bennington College. I loved touring the Vermont Covered Bridge Museum in Bennington. I admired the wood joinery the bridge builders used and the fascinating covered bridge process.

I once climbed the steps of the three hundred-foot Bennington Battle Monument commemorating General John Stark and the New Hampshire militia. They had battled the Hessians and British in Walloomsac, New York, ten miles distant. In effect, he turned the British away from the American Revolutionary Army's military stores cached in Bennington. Pivotal in the war, Stark's success weakened Burgoyne's attack on Saratoga. History.

There was also that long, winding, picturesque, Green Mountain Molly Stark Highway, Route 9, that descends into, or ascends out of, Bennington. I bicycled up that five-mile exhausting climb from Bennington into the Green Mountains when I'd ditched school during senior finals on an idle day. Hard to believe; less than a year had passed since then. Starting early in Townshend, Vermont, I embarked on a solo century bike ride through Manchester, Bennington, and Wilmington. Verdant mountain beauty combined with challenging hills.

Nearly at the top of the Molly Stark climb, I remember glimpsing a pretty, solitary cyclist decked out in proper cycling attire starting her descent. A kindred spirit, she had shouted, "Great form!" followed with a thumbs up.

"Thanks! Be careful! Have fun!" I shouted back across the highway. I waved and picked up my rpm a few strokes, appreciating her great form.

So hazardous was the Molly Stark into Bennington, many commercial truckers stopped to check their brakes before they attempted it. The convenience store in Woodford had a suitably broad, gravel pull off for just such an inspection. Drivers would get a full-on view of the Woodford Cemetery when they returned to driving and would be glad of their ounce of prevention.

In an instant, I could get lost in my thoughts even about the very fringes of my old stomping grounds, caroming from one recollection to another.

Just seeing The Silver Restaurant had prompted these wayward thoughts. I already knew that I had a mental battle brewing, so I would have to resist the impulse to travel these Michael Barton rabbit trails. Study, new challenges, and work were to be necessary distractions.

I am Calvin James.

Maple syrup would have to become no more than a tasty topping for pancakes, but not for apple pie a la mode. I had to dislodge all the anchors drilled deep into my memory.

My mind, left alone, was a mess.

Less than a minute after the Lucas crew and I passed an abandoned, small-scale ski area, we slowed and turned onto a newly developed access road. I expected a rough ride, but bumps and loose rocks were equally as sparse as the camaraderie between my new workmates and me. It was a smooth, but faster than necessary, trip up the gravel road considering the loaded materials trailer we were hauling.

We doglegged under high-tension wires, and within five minutes, we parked in the worksite driveway. Before the dust had settled, Jamie, with a string of cursing, railed about the absence of batter boards.

"We can't start without the batter boards. How can we set forms without knowing where they go? I just knew it!" then he cursed the excavator, abusively and darkly. A speech impediment, I called it. Jamie seemed to think expletive use was a talent to cultivate.

Then, as if the sun had suddenly emerged from behind a black cloud, Jamie laughed out loud. Sandy, who had been, a moment before, contributing epithets of his own, also broke into laughter.

No explanation was forthcoming.

Jamie barked orders with a Jack Russell bark, not the Rottweiler bark that he should have for the command he wanted to project.

Note to self, be wary. Small dogs are freakish and unpredictable.

117

"Chock those trailer wheels," Jamie instructed me. "Unhitch the trailer. Unplug the electrical. Disconnect the safety chains."

Sandy and Robert watched as I complied.

Jamie pulled the pickup forward and then backed up to a stepped platform, equal in height to the pickup bed.

"Drop the tailgate. Get the gang box off."

I pulled the heavy, tool-laden, Knack crew box toward the back of the pickup bed and wrestled it onto the platform. Sandy and Robert continue to watch.

Tasks accomplished, Jamie leaped from the cab, a roll of blueprints in hand, and made his way back to the platform. He rolled out the prints on the plan table, opening to the site plan page. He shook his flaxen hair, and with a single nod, tossed it back to its very proper place. The message was loud though unspoken. He planned on looking and feeling good all day, no mirror necessary.

"Cal, it's your first day on the job; I'll make the line out for you and the crew real simple," Jamie was all business, distinctly different from the ride up. Sandy and Robert were his attentive audience. "We're forming footers today. They're the *footings* for the foundation walls. We'll form and pour the foundation and basement floor later."

"Cal, you'll finish your tasks and clean up. Sandy, Robert, and me are . . ." he paused to stifle a laugh, "Sandy, Robert, and me are going to The Silver for coffee. It's your first day. You didn't get the memo. It's a beauteous day; we've got our fly boxes and rods, so we're going to liberate trout from the stream up La Plata Canyon and lunch there. We should be back around four-thirty or five. You'll cover for us if Ben Lucas comes around."

I laughed heartily along with the three of them. Re-up the new guy gag. Tradition allowed leg-pulling, demanded it even, on a new guy's first day. If I suffered this prank, I shouldn't have to deal with board stretchers, left-handed pipe wrenches, or be on the watch for jack-a-lopes.

I was still laughing when Jamie handed me the key to the crew box.

"Get your Knack box off the truck. Grab your lunch cooler, too."

Sandy and Robert made their way to the pickup's front seat.

§

Dust blasted up from the Goodyears then dispersed in a low cloud across the meadow. Jamie spun them hard with the crew-cab fishtailing down the driveway. In a moment, all was quiet, and I was by myself.

Barton to James, observe, neither safety, nor teamwork, nor sociability is close to Job One around here.

Would my new James follow my old Barton? True to self, had for me an element of choice. Calvin James still had a self to develop.

Let's set up the transit to see what we've got.

The crew box had to contain a transit or builder's level to do layout work; there hadn't been one in the cab. I rocked my head and twisted side to side in an effort to shake off the day's unusual timbre and assure myself that Jamie, Sandy, and Robert would return shortly with coffee for everyone.

The jobsite was an alpine meadow in the southern foothills of the La Platas. A peninsula of tall yellow pines rose toward the mountains, intruding into the dry grasses and fading flowering weeds. Past the pines were the slopes of the La Platas in clear view. In an otherwise clear blue sky, the peaks were ridding themselves of morning fog. At least I was in good company.

Scrub oak and aspen patches, leafy green islands, dotted an expanse of dry grasses. The wind velocity was zero. Rocky Mountain jays, quail, and nuthatches scratched away noisily in search of breakfast. Squirrels scuffed up fallen crisp leaves scouting for acorns.

This was a beautiful setting, and from my glimpse of the blueprint drawings, the house promised to be beautiful, too.

I could see a portion of the major highway from Durango to Cortez. Further on, I saw a ridge-top lift tower at the ski area we had passed; below that, I could see high-tension towers. I caught sight of the Lucas truck rounding the bend, barreling back toward The Silver Restaurant.

"Large!" I yelled in their direction. "With half a pack of raw sugar! No cream!"

§

In the last two months, since settling in Durango, I had kept busy hiking, bicycling, rafting, studying, four-wheeling, exploring, reading, planning, and camping, a respite to sublimate grief and anger and to mourn.

Awe-inspiring, brilliant, varied, and fantastic are apt descriptors when used to describe Southwest Colorado. It is a beautifully wild country. I was already becoming partial to the sparsely vegetated, alien countryside compared to lush, flourishing New England.

The western yellow pine's double needles were course compared to the tight, smooth five needle clusters of the eastern white pines. New England oaks were stately, under which the village smithy could stand; here, oaks were glorified shrubs. White Mountain's sugar maples provided vibrant reds to the autumn palate. Rocky Mountain aspens would turn predominantly yellow. Alpine streams, I'd found out the hard way, were too cold to drop into for a dip after a hot day of strenuous play, unlike Deep Hole in Acworth.

The air was dry and rarefied.

I reveled in the area's geology, with its mix of sedimentary, glaciated, metamorphic, and igneous. The local college, Fort Lewis, had in its library a great map selection, which included satellite images. These, when accurately overlaid, pointed to startlingly neglected areas for precious metal exploration, worthy of future pursuit.

After our turn in from the highway, I'd seen a National Forest Service sign that announced a trailhead further up. I wondered then, how is it that I had not yet wandered here? It would be a great place to hike.

§

I could check several things while I awaited the crew's return. For one, I found the property's corner survey marker next to the access road and an orange-ribboned stake that marked a jog in the northern property line. Blue lumber crayon marked the elevation.

If I had help . . .

Cal, let's not be a victim here.

In the crew box, I found a David White transit with its tripod, a twenty-four-ounce bob, and a collapsible survey rod.

Good, I was familiar with this model. I scavenged materials for a makeshift survey rod holder.

I'll call my rod holder Jamie. Heh, heh. I judged that the jury-rigged rodman was smarter and much more reliable than my coffee imbibing help. Now I could at least verify the excavation depth.

"You're doing fine, Jamie," I sneered. Working solo was new ground for me.

I retrieved my programmable calculator, which had trig functions. Manufactured in Italy, it didn't help that the instructions that came with it were in Italian. I'd written to Texas Instruments to get an English version two weeks ago. A spiral notebook and a mechanical pencil joined me. I flipped the prints over to the foundation page; I found there was only one level for the footer.

I jotted a calculation in my notebook. My monopod rodman, Jamie, jumped into the excavation with me, along with the transit, which I set up and leveled again. I had to jog back and forth between moving Jamie, reading and recording the rod markings. Every place I checked, in what appeared to be where the concrete forms should go, the elevation was within a half-inch but consistently low, the excavation was perfect.

Why would anyone pull the batter boards and waste the original layout work? If they had remained, I could have started locating the footer forms.

And where's my coffee? I pondered. Probability said it went into the mountains, fishing.

"So, what can I do?" To reset the batter boards would require an extra pair of hands and someone technical enough to hold the dumb end of a 100-foot tape.

I climbed back out of the excavation and looked hopefully toward the visible piece of highway. Nothing positive. 8:05 AM.

"It's okay, guys; I can take cream in my coffee if that's going to be a problem."

I decided to build the corner forms as a unit. Setting the corners first, in picture puzzle fashion, then fill the rest in between, made sense. Better to use the company saw than dull my blade on the two by ten form boards. The previous users had neglected to scrape them of caked-on concrete.

As I poked around in the depths of the crew box for a worm-drive saw, I found a vintage tripod. Even with its lower deck treatment, it was in excellent shape. Deeper yet, under a torn section of tarp, was a large mahogany box. I drew it out by its stitched leather handle. Kneeling close, I opened it.

It held an engineer's transit, and with it, there was a current record of certified calibrations, a dust brush, a lens cloth, and another twenty-four-ounce bob. I slid the instrument out with its mounting bracket. It was irreconcilable with the mental capacity of my coworkers. Out of place in precision and time, it was a World War II Army Corp of Engineers transit. With black matte metal, brass screws, silver circles and verniers, and an internal focusing mechanism, it was a David White, too.

No one heard my low whistle.

The horizontal circle vernier, with thumbscrews for pinpoint settings, was accurate to twenty seconds. Rugged and precise, it held an accurate internal magnetic compass.

My thoughts raced, now I hoped the guys didn't come back with coffee. I wanted to be alone with this machine. My fingers flew, punching numbers into my calculator; I found that at seventy-five feet, I could sight in a point within a quarter inch.

I know this! I had, in my hands, an instrument that would help me accomplish an impossible task.

§§

Chapter 26

Sixteen months ago, Melanie Howe, a bright, inquisitive girl and I, spent a day together at the end of our school year. Pretty and shy, she devoted more attention to her writing compositions than to conversations.

Our precalculus teacher rewarded the juniors in our class with an unconventional post-finals field trip. There were six of us left after the seniors, as expected, ditched.

We knew days ahead to plan for hiking. The permission slips we took home for our parents elaborated on how to prepare for the day and about the specific educational objectives for our activity. "Orienteering is an exercise in hiking, compass usage, map reading, and distance estimation. The subject matter of your field trip is to practically apply trigonometry and vectors."

Mr. Wells had set out two orienteering courses, one east of the school, the other west of the school. Each course's combined destinations were six miles in total length. At each of the fifteen stations was a token to collect, a large, brightly painted washer, clearly noticeable on a distinctive landmark. A stash of apples and soda, water, or other snacks might be there too. Mr. Wells designed zigzags and crossovers from destination to destination, and each course had multiple legs. How Mr. Wells had time to create two such courses was a mystery.

"Your school day ends tomorrow when your team returns with all fifteen washers from your course objectives, or at 3:00 PM, whichever comes first," Mr. Wells said as he returned our final exams and gave us our assignments. "I've established two teams, team A: Melanie, Cal, and Paul, team B: Spencer, Susan, and John.

"We'll meet at the football field at 8:20 AM. The team winning a coin toss will start first with their initial compass heading; the remaining team will follow after a delay of ten minutes."

At our fifty-yard line starting point, Mr. Wells armed each team with a compass, a topographical map, a straight-edge, and the list with compass bearings and distances. Team B won the coin toss that morning.

Team A had the excused absence of Paul as an additional handicap. While Melanie and I waited out our ten-minute delay, I pulled out my Texas Instruments calculator, and out of my backpack came a pad of paper and a pencil.

"Melanie, would you read me the bearings and distances of all the legs to our first destination, one at a time?"

With trigonometric functions, I reduced the multiple legs of the first destination to the end-point.

"Cal, you are such a clever nerd," Melanie laughed out loud when she saw what I was doing. "I'm going to have to write a story about you."

"We're supposed to use what we learned, right?"

I remember the joy that radiated from that smile and marveled that I'd never seen it before. She had the type of good looks that didn't need makeup. She gathered her shoulder-length blond hair into a ponytail and donned her white baseball cap, all the while gauging my reaction.

We took the topo map, plotted our first destination. We found it was opposite a pull-off on a paved road.

Before Mr. Wells had returned to launch Team A, we had approximated the second objective's location on the map. When he did appear, he only stepped out of the gym door and waved us on. We waved back in acknowledgment but didn't leave.

Our second objective was close to a pasture easement, also just off a paved road. The third had a similar placement. The fourth was on the side of a dirt road. If we had taken the analog orienteering approach, we wouldn't have noticed all the objectives were easily accessible by automobile. We'd solved Mr. Wells's time-saving preparation mystery.

"Melanie, do you remember anything in Mr. Wells' rules that says that we have to hike? I drove my dad's Saab to school this morning."

"No?" Her answer was more of a question. Then she smiled, laughed, and asked, "Can I drive?"

Before we started, we'd plotted all fifteen objectives. We were back at the school in fifty minutes. Not finding Mr. Wells anywhere, we left a note at the school secretary's office.

> *Mr. Wells,*
> *Thank you so much for your being our teacher this year and for the excellent field trip today! Enjoy your summer.*
> *Team A. The winners,*
> *Melanie and Cal.*

We had the school secretary write the time with her initials on our note and left our bag of washers with a copy of our calculations.

After I'd suggested swimming holes in Newfane, Vermont, or Deep Hole, in my neighborhood, we settled on the beach at Sunapee State Park to spend the rest of the day. Melanie drove us to her Charlestown home to get a swimsuit and towel and leave a note for her parents.

Having her company was delightful. We lunched at a Victorian inn in Sunapee proper, where she and I talked more than all our previous conversations combined. The state park beach had public restrooms with changing areas. We swam, splashed, sunned at the beach, and talked more. She was stunning in her one-piece bathing suit.

I never had the opportunity to speak to her again after I dropped her off that evening. Melanie said she was moving to Maryland in a few days. Relocation for her father's machine-tool software design job precluded her family from staying.

Mayflower Van Lines was at her home the next day, and movers were packing their belongings. Both family automobiles were gone. I'd checked.

Our few letters exchanged made me consider our possibilities had she stayed. Her's, she crafted skillfully, the product of her writer's talent. They softened her unwillingness to engage in a long-distance relationship.

§

Thanks for the memories, Barton.

When the time came that I referred to myself as Cal again, that would be welcome progress.

There's a broken up hundred-foot steel tape in the crew box with eighth-inch increments.

There are a lot of calculations,...

Animated and excited, I conversed with myself back and forth, Barton and James. Calculations escaped from my pencil, captured by my notebook pages, details for each corner location.

Melanie, where are you? I had seen her and her boyfriend at my family's funeral.

From the readings I'd sighted on the judiciously distributed steel tape pieces, I pressed a duplex nail at each corner point then spray painted it.

All forgotten was the coffee, the co-workers, everything except plotting the foundation corners and conversing with Barton and Melanie.

Done, I climbed out of the hole and opted for a long cold drink. In anticipation of hot weather, I had poured out and refrigerated a half-liter of Gatorade in an empty pitcher the night before. The other half liter, I'd frozen in the original bottle. This morning I restored the liquid portion to the frozen bottle to keep a cold, undiluted drink.

The crew box platform offered scant shade.

On the sliver of highway where I had last seen the company truck barrel off toward the rising sun, I now saw a blue Sierra pickup parked on the shoulder. I refocused the engineering transit on it. The driver was leaning over the hood, scoping the hills with powerful binoculars for deer or elk, in preparation for hunting season.

I waved in the hunter's direction.

The hunter waved back.

Was that funny or disturbing?

§

I set the carefully reboxed transit beside the crew box.

The lucent blue sky and the unfiltered, bright sun made the slight, cool breeze welcome.

I decided to work the reinforcing steel next, starting with the corner bends. Later in the afternoon, the iron would be too hot to handle. In my notebook, I jotted seven additional tasks to prepare for a concrete pour.

Whoever had dug this hole had been spot on with dimensions, elevations, and orientation, validating my calculations.

§§

CHAPTER 27

Charging up the jobsite driveway, sending dust flying was the blue Chevy pickup I'd seen a few minutes before. I was sitting on the crew box with my mostly eaten sandwich and Gatorade nearly half-consumed with just a chunk still frozen.

The middle-aged driver was clean-shaven with perceptibly graying dark brown hair sprouting from below a well-worn John Deere baseball cap. I touched my head, wishing I still had my old John Deere hat.

The man catapulted from behind the steering wheel, sporting a fierce semi-smile and furious gray-blue eyes that hid nothing. He wore a construction worker's uniform: Carhartt jeans, Red Wing boots, and an open Levi denim jacket, revealing his blue work shirt.

The dust had not yet settled when he strode the distance between his truck and me.

I stayed sitting.

"I see you found my David White."

I followed his stare to the box on the platform, then looked at him.

"It was at the bottom of the Lucas crew box. What makes you think that it's yours?"

"My name's on it."

"You can tell that from there?"

"The name's Dave Cravath, take a look." There was a statement of respect in his stance and set off distance, and an edge to his tone.

I slipped the last bite of my sandwich, not wanting to risk interruption, and looked at the box. Under the leather handle was a brass plate that identified its manufacturer to be David White. When I twisted the handle for a more thorough look, it revealed the engraved name, Dave Cravath.

"That's one darn fine instrument, sir. My name's Mi...,
Calvin James."

"Calvin. I knew it was my transit when I saw you with it
from the highway. The boys anywhere around here?"

"They went for coffee about seven-thirty. I thought they
were razzing when they said they were going fishing after
that," I said, miffed. "You work for Lucas, too?"

"I wouldn't consider working for Lucas a wise choice.
I recommended against them doing any work at all on this
project."

"Why wouldn't you want them working on this?" A sincere inquiry. I was glad that he realized that.

"Jamie and his sidekick Sandy stole that transit a week
ago, from this jobsite. That's the Lucas way. They took it to
slow me up. I imagined that they'd pawn it in Farmington."

"I didn't know. I did take good care of it."

"Hey, the fact that you focused it and saw me on the
highway puts you in a class way beyond those boys. First day
on the job?"

"Yes, sir. Let's get this thing into the cab of your truck
before it wanders off again. Are you interested in seeing how I
used it?" Admittedly, I was proud of what I had done.

We walked over to the excavation.

"I see paint spots." Dave was unimpressed.

"Yes, sir. I painted the nails locating every outside footer
corner. Accurate to a quarter inch." I waited for the information to digest, which didn't take long.

"You, what?"

I reveled in Mr. Cravath's incredulity.

"I take it that you did the excavation?" I asked.

"Yes, I did."

"And when you finished, you pulled the batter boards
so that whoever worked here next would have to do the layout
work again and be in agreement with your start."

"I did that, too. But it didn't make up for the stolen transit." Dave was still dumbfounded at what I had done. "I wanted
to show how stupid the Lucas boys were when the excavation
didn't line up with the prints."

"Sixteen degrees declination, true north to magnetic,"
I volunteered. "That would have stumped them. It would have

stumped me too, but I entertained myself on a rainy after-noon this past summer with some maps up at the Fort Lewis library. That's where I discovered this area's magnetic weird-ness. I created an east-west shadow line for confirmation."

"I need to check this out." Dave pulled a twenty-five-foot tape measure from his jacket pocket and started down the backhoe access. "I'll take the smart end. You hold on your marker down there. I remember the backside dimension from the corner to the inset is twenty feet. With clearances, that makes twenty-one feet four inches. If you're right, I'll help you this afternoon, but you'll have to explain how you did this by yourself."

Dave walked carefully and deliberately toward the paint spot and stopped when he had gone a step beyond. We stooped down together; I held my end to the nail as he low-ered his tape measure. He shook his head.

"*Il ragazzo è un genio!*" (The kid's a genius!)

I heard him mutter something that sounded Italian.

"What did you say?"

"I said, what's next, boss? We've got three hours before the boys get back; I'm gone before that happens."

"Let's prefab the corner forms as a unit...," I read off the seven tasks I'd written in my notebook before lunch.

"Your first day on the job, eh?"

Evaluation on my part, *how should I respond?*

"I've worked as a laborer. I faked the rest as I went along."

We trudged our way out of the excavation side by side. The fury in Dave's eyes had transformed into hedged admiration.

"You faked the rest as you went along?"

"I had a little help from Melanie." Too late, I thought better of mentioning her name. "She and I experimented with orienteering a year and a half ago. If she'd stuck around, I'd be in a different situation today, but she moved."

We sat on the crew box. To fulfill my part of our bar-gain, I referred to my notebook again. I went through the calculations while pointing at my references. Dave nodded. When I mentioned the broken steel tape pieces, he whistled.

"That was my hundred-foot tape that got run over. Okay, kid, let's get busy."

§

In two and a half hours, rough forming was done, and the rebar placed.

"Do you want a ride back to Durango, Cal?"

"Thanks, Dave, I'll wait for Moe, Curly, and Larry. I'm pretty sure they'll want to check any progress and won't leave me here."

"Be careful; they'll try to take credit for your work. I've heard they'll threaten you with your job, maybe even physically, if you don't let them paint you as hardly worth having around. Don't give them any details. They wouldn't understand anyway; don't tell them I was here, either."

Dave wrote his home number on his DC Excavation business card and handed it to me.

"Call me later. Let me know how the day finishes up. I have to check in on another job. I would have been there all day, but I thought I'd better come after my David White when I saw the chance. You've given me a lot to regard, of you and this job, Calvin James."

"I'll call. Thanks for all the help, and thank David White for me, too."

Dave's blue Sierra rolled peacefully down the drive. He idled to a stop before easing forward in a sweeping turn.

I packed up the power cords and worm drive saws that belonged in the crew box, along with the prints, and locked it up.

I found a comfortable spot for a nap against a yellow pine. The wind rustled the dried grass and the pine boughs above; birds chirped the same way they had at the day's start. Specks of sun flitted over closed eyelids. Slow breathing lasted for a half-hour while James and Barton made peace with each other. Cal was a nearly cohesive unit after three months of identity turmoil.

§

Spanish from the two laborers was recognizable, mixed with English. Did I have a nice relaxing day while they did all the work? Was I pouting in the back seat?

"Your daddy must have been a wuss to raise you, a lazy, soft kid," Sandy, even less careful with his accent, derided brazenly. "You spend a lot of time in the kitchen with your mama? And hold onto her long apron strings? Bet she's pretty, though, good-looking boy like you."

My hackles bristled.

Jamie quelled the chatter that had been constant since our departure from the job.

"Calvin, listen to me," Jamie laid out his revision of the day, "if you want this job with Lucas, this is what happened. Sandy, Robert, and me had to carry you all day today. You didn't know the work. You didn't know the routine. It would be great if we'd give you another chance to show that you can keep up."

"That's not gonna happen." Dave and I had all but finished the forming. They had found me sitting on the locked crew box. Jamie had checked two dimensions after seeing what I'd accomplished and tried not to look mystified.

"We'll see." A simple, bald-faced threat.

§

Close to the old Durango Drive-In, the club cab rode rough down the gravel driveway to the steel building that held the offices of Ben Lucas Construction. It was doubly rough in the back seat. No seat belt, combined with the slick plastic seat cover, gave the front seat riders opportunity to laugh at my discomfort, already sore from the labor of the day. Jamie intended to make the last 500 yards most uncomfortable. Shovels clanged together, and steel form stakes threatened to fly out of the pickup bed. Other tools, digging bars, rebar bender, spare pieces, and bends of rebar, all loose in the back, merged into a pile, which would require sorting. A fifty-pound box of nails burst and scattered.

We pulled up to the shed to unload.

Jamie gave his orders.

"Sandy, you're with me. We'll go in to report on lazy bones. Robert, help Worthless here unload the truck." There was an added head nod toward Robert, an unspoken instruction.

In the shed, I laid the rebar bender flat where I had found it that morning. In the meantime, Robert gathered a dozen of the spilled nails, threw them into the box, and managed to get a Camel filter lit.

"So it's this, right through the end of the day."

"End of the line is more like it." Robert grimaced and flicked his cigarette ash. "I'll get a shovel."

"One? Mister Big Help."

I'd grabbed a shovel myself, which is when Robert grazed his shovel against the back of my right calf. Not a nick, it sliced through my jeans, parting skin and muscle in one stroke. I turned with my shovel, stunned, in pain, and bleeding; I prepared to defend myself.

"Jamie gave you a chance. He must like you. He wants me to persuade you to take his offer. Or make sure that you don't work at all." Robert fainted a few jabs with the shovel. "Construction accident, call it. How's that feel?"

He pointed with the blade of his shovel at my calf.

I could feel blood trickling into my new Red Wings, soaking my socks. I parried Robert's jabs. He was accustomed to the obviously sharpened tool. His assurance in speech, posture, and handling told me that these few jabs were only intimidation. I back peddled.

"Well?" he said, "do you want the work?"

More ash fell from his cigarette, hands busy with the management end of the shovel; his lips made an adjustment. He gave his spade a lacrosse stick spin and swung the shovel's curved back at my grip.

"Time's up," he said flatly and jabbed the shovel point toward the back of my knee.

Not well, I deflected the thrust. Robert bore down. His spade twisted and advanced. Our shovels interlocked, and I found myself having to pull toward myself to maintain my grip. This ensnaring put Robert's shovel point closer to me than my own. Given my lack of fighting experience, I didn't like the situation.

I thrust in return and rolled to my right, not the best foot for me to pivot on, but I made it work. This move surprised Robert and inspired him to be more aggressive.

I knew that this would turn out horribly for me if I didn't change something.

"You and your buds can stuff it." With that, I threw my shovel at his head. He turned to avoid my sudden harpoon toss. He helped it along its trajectory with a well-connected tap and watched it fly by.

I moved in toward him too fast and too close for his shovel to have any meaningful advantage. Just under my right shoulder, I formed a fist, with a sudden scrape backward on my right foot, I punched. The footwork hurt, but it enabled me to deliver the blow with power.

Furiously, I struck Robert's nose, which sweetly approached my curled fingers. No telegraphing; it was a straight jab. My body recoiled from an added twist of my torso.

Robert staggered back; his cigarette disappeared on the ground. He sluggishly tried to bring his shovel to bear again. I repeated my previous skip forward, staying close with the same movement, same contact, same effect. I followed with an undefended left hook.

Pumped with rage, I'd had it with their talk about my parents. Someone had brutally murdered them. I vented pent-up brutality spinning again, a left foot pivot; I reached for and caught the shoulder of Robert's shovel on the front side of my right foot. Wresting it from his loosened grip; It flew away. When I faced him again, I saw his blood-drenched hand covering his nose.

Robert let out a painful gasp and spluttered. His eyes, fearful.

"It's broken," Robert shrieked of his nose.

"Construction accident, call it." I heard my own loud, cold voice deliver fiercely.

Violence controlled by anger was dark and sweet.

Jamie and Sandy stepped out of the Lucas office fifty yards distant. Robert looked at them and pointed at me as unintelligible noise bubbled thickly from his face.

With both hands, I grasped Robert's accusing finger, quickly snapping it back sharply. The finger's proximal phalanx, the bone nearest to his palm, fractured. Robert screamed, fell to his knees, and pulled his hand protectively toward his chest.

His coworkers froze momentarily, then rushed toward us. I grabbed Robert's other index finger and bent it toward the wrist, then held up my left hand, palm out, in the universal halt signal to the running pair.

"Stop right there!"

"*Por favor! No! Por el amor de Dios, ten piedad de mí,*" (Please! No! For the love of God, have mercy on me,) Robert cried, swallowed up in pain. He heaved, "*¡Basta! ¡Basta!.*" (Stop it.)

Team Lucas stopped in its tracks at my insistence. There was a moment of silence except for Robert's sobs. I hadn't so much heard the sounds of our conflict or felt pain as I had observed both; it all now collapsed inward. Timepieces regained their natural speed. I scowled; my calf was throbbing.

I stepped away and dropped Robert's left hand, uninjured, to his side.

Jamie was the first to speak, voice raised, not minding the awkward distance between us. "Hey, dude, I like the way you handle yourself. I can use you. Can you come back tomorrow? I'm short on help."

"Talk to the hand," I shouted, keeping my traffic directing hand up, and twisted away from Robert. I limped toward my 4Runner, accompanied by a noticeable squish in my boot.

§

"Dave Cravath? Calvin James here."

"Hey Cal, thanks for calling. How are you?"

"Oh man, the day ended nowhere nearly as enjoyable as it started. You were right about the Lucas boys." It was good to talk with a person who at least knew some of my day.

I dumped the whole story on my new friend, from my nap under the pines, to Jamie's alternate version of the day's activities, to Robert's bloody face and his broken finger, to the twenty-four stitches in my leg and megadose Ibuprofen.

"Well, here are a couple of things you don't know yet. Lucas is off the job. I talked with the owner today. He's in Italy doing a basketball thing, and now he's peeved that the Lucas crew was negligent by getting such a late start. He was already considering terminating the Lucas contract for nonperformance."

"That Warthington? The Suns' coach? You know the guy?"

"I'll introduce you over the phone tomorrow if you'll come over to my office."

"Yes, sir! Sure, I'd love to." I was eager to find out what Dave had in mind.

"I want you to look over the full plans for the project before we talk with him.

"Also, if you can find it within you, check out Bobby, that is, Robert. He's smart, skilled, and a hard worker from all that I've heard about him. The company that he had been working for, Best Way Management, folded. Not the company's fault; they didn't have enough financial resources to fight a bogus lawsuit. He took the job with Lucas as a *very* last resort. Bobby has a wife and three kids, from what I understand, Sandy and Jamie threatened to harm him and his family, too."

"He knew his business with a shovel." I started to unload on Bobby's expertise with his improvised weapon, then cut myself short. "Truthfully, Dave, I was out of control. I should have stopped after I bloodied his nose. I'm better than that. I'm sure he's more hurt than I am. I'll see if I can talk to him, or if he really does hate me. I don't think he intended to carve me up that badly with his first slice."

"Many folks would have retaliated in far worse ways."

"Thanks, Dave, for your ear. I needed to talk to more than my biking buddies this evening."

"No problem. You still have my business card?"

"I have it right here." I verified, with Dave, his address in Bodo Industrial Park.

"Eight-thirty. My office?"

"Absolutely. See you there."

§§

CHAPTER 28

Promptly at nine-fifteen, Friday night, the second week of September, Amy pressed the button on her remote garage door opener. The door's whir and grind was a comfort to Cecelia. Amy had kept her bike-riding curfew as usual. This winter, when she would give up her bicycle in favor of her CJ5 and would have a later return home time. Even now, if she cared to, which she rarely did, she could go out again, driving, until the time Amy and Cecelia agreed upon. It was the bicycling after dark that most concerned Cecelia.

Amy hung her bike, ditched her Adidas in the mudroom, and sock-footed her way to the kitchen. She served herself a slice of leftover coffee cake, delicious with milk, crumbly enough to require a large plate; then, she joined Cecelia in the living room.

Their evening banter usually started while Amy foraged in the kitchen; tonight, she was already sitting in her favorite recliner. A fork full of cake and a sip of milk had already disappeared in the thoughtful silence.

"Rough day?" Cecelia ventured.

"Most of it was just fine. Great job on the coffee cake. Are those apple chunks?" Another fork full, and another sip, interrupted her from completing either divergent thought. "Mr. Adams posted a tryout list for *Guess Who's Coming to Dinner*. It was disheartening not to see Paul's name at the top. I couldn't do it."

"What about Paul? We haven't talked about him for a while. You still don't think that he stole anything from the music store?"

"No, Mom. The more I mull it over, the less likely it seems; he had the same means and opportunity all his three years working there. Nothing changed. He had no money consuming bad habits, no dissatisfaction with work. He wasn't reading *Crime and Punishment* and wouldn't want the intrigue. No, I'd say that my old nemesis, Sam, framed Paul; the jerk's motive is the only question I have. There was no change of lifestyle for Sam either that five grand could offer a high school bully. I haven't heard that they've even found the loot. If I could prove Paul didn't do it, I'd put all I had into it. "

"I know you would, honey, tooth and nail." Cecelia put down *I libri, la città, il mondo* that she had been reading and picked up her wine glass. "Let's go to Whistler's Inn tomorrow for tea; I have an idea of something you and I might enjoy doing together afterward. It's the second Saturday of the month; you're not working. Right?"

"Right. Diversion required. Tea would be great. When did we last take tea there?"

"Too long. Beginning of June, wasn't it? I was the one in the dumps then." Not a memory Cecelia wanted to revisit. "So we can tea early, then do a little focused clothes shopping for me; I'll need your expertise, then a drive followed with a surprise."

"I'm in." Already diverted, Amy transitioned into detective mode and swept aside her longish hair to fall over her right shoulder. "You opened that Lambrusco Tuesday night. If you need my expertise to shop, it's for sporting goods. Bicycle gear? No, why would we drive afterward? Why would that be much of a surprise? How do I gauge your thought processes with Lambrusco at night and tea the next morning?"

"I'm not giving you anything else to go on. You figure things out too quickly."

"I'll have it out of you before our tea steeps."

"Not so fast there, young lady, no matter how wise you are for your few years."

"Thanks, Mom. I feel better already. Did I say how much I enjoyed your coffee cake?" Amy padded to the kitchen, rinsed her plate and glass, and placed them in the dishwasher.

"Yes, you did, thanks. I hope Mrs. Fisher felt the same way."

"Me too. If you don't mind, Mom, I'm headed off to the Land of Nod."

"I don't mind; you have a lot to think about." Cecelia winked knowingly. "I think I'll slip between the sheets soon, too."

"Good night, Mom."

"Good night, Amy."

Cecelia was right; Amy did have a lot to think about. There was the school play that she had been a part of for the last three years, Paul's wrongful theft conviction six months ago, the school year was starting up, she also had her mom's surprise outing tomorrow, and a significantly omitted conversation this evening. Hardly ever did Amy bring an observation about the wine Cecelia was drinking that didn't lead her mom to go through their accountability questions, have you had any wine, except for communion? Any other alcoholic beverages? How about drugs? What are your dating prospects?

Was it a sign of respect for Amy's depressed mood? Or, was it her mom's concession to Amy's growing maturity and responsibility?

All of these were good things; all probably weighed in. Amy smiled to herself; perhaps this was a harbinger of another neglected topic to be discussed.

§

Earl Grey was Amy's favorite tea. Cecelia's was Darjeeling. They sipped their teas in silence and sipped between their talking, and they nibbled the venerable Whistler's Inn breakfast quiche. Seated among the bookshelves, fireplace, and Victorian furniture, Amy's topics and Cecelia's, weighty for each of them, made it into the open, save two, one being the surprise of the day.

§

Berkshire Sports employees' discount was substantial enough that Amy and Cecelia purchased all of their sporting goods there. Her mom had advised Amy to wear her cool-weather cycling gear. The same garb was on Cecelia's shopping list.

"Mom, you could borrow any of my gear that you wanted. You don't have to buy your own." The offer was bona fide, Amy had plenty for her to choose from, and they wore the same sizes. Amy was still subtlety digging, unable to determine yet, their final destination for the day.

"I know that, Amy, and thank you, but we might need this type of clothing regularly, though, so I should have my own."

Regularly? Amy's mind took the word, torturing it for every ounce of meaning that it might have. There was no mention of a bicycle yet. The term was empty. It yielded nothing. *Rats.*

Cecelia purchased according to Amy's recommendations, Pearl Izumi for Cecelia's base layer and gloves. Amy found a stretchy headband and thin wool socks that would fit well with Cecelia's Adidas runners. A Woolrich flannel, mostly green, caught their collective approving eye on the sale rack. Patagonia finished off their outfitting with a fleece vest, a shell, and slick athletic pants.

After paying, Cecelia returned to the dressing rooms to remove tags and change from her street clothes. They left the store fashion twins, cut from the same cloth.

§

Their drive took them through Pittsfield, then at Brodie Mountain Road, Cecelia maneuvered her M6 deftly through the almost hairpin intersection and headed toward Hancock.

"Still cluefree?" Cecelia asked good-humouredly.

"I've got quite a few clues. It's just that they don't connect very well."

"We'll catch lunch at that little sandwich place in Hancock. It'll give you a chance to deduce more."

"Mom!" Amy pleaded.

"I'm enjoying this. It happens ever so rarely that I can keep one over on you."

"It's not the Alpine Slide. You're not doing that regularly or dressing especially for that." Amy leaned forward to look up at a hang glider that had launched from the Jiminy Peak Ski Area. The pilot had spied a soaring bird and was attempting to catch the same thermal.

"You watch the road, Mom." Amy cautioned light-heartedly when Cecelia tried to see the same thing. "I'll report. There's a red and white hang glider trying to chase a red tail hawk."

"Any hot air balloons?"

"No, Mom, just red herrings."

§

Both Amy and Cecelia enjoyed BLTs with fries. Amy had a root beer, Cecelia, an iced tea. Their wandering discussion had moved on to Hancock's Shaker community with their remarkable skills in construction, furniture building, weaving, quilts, and their peculiar religious practices.

In the Beamer, they chatted briefly about Wellesley. Was it the school Amy wanted to attend? Yes, it was.

Cecelia enjoyed the thoughtful, delving look on her daughter's face. Her magical mystery tour afforded all the therapeutic distraction she had hoped it would. Retracing their route, Cecelia slacked off the accelerator and steered into the Jiminy Peak Ski Area, basking in Amy's perfect bafflement.

After parking, they walked toward the small base lodge. It was then that Amy caught sight of six resting hang gliders hidden behind a modest rise at the end of the parking lot.

"Mom?"

"Yes, dear?"

"You are brilliant, Mom! Absolutely the best! "

"These are beginning lessons. We won't fly today."

"That's okay, but how soon?"

"We'll have to find out."

"And, you Mom, you're doing this, I mean actually fly one of these?"

"I believe so. What are moms for?"

§

The first part of their lesson was a walk around the wing. The instructor, fortunately, was not ruggedly handsome, more a pocket protector kind of guy. It helped them attend to the topics of his instruction. He spoke about the wing construction, the aluminum frame components, the redundant safety systems, and how to harness up.

Following the basics, covered to the instructor's and the instructed's satisfaction, the four in this class took to the hill and ran enough to have the glider lift off their shoulders. The lesson finished with a short, low glide for everyone in the class.

Mother and daughter rested their adopted gliders, nose down after their last run of the day. Delight showed on both their faces.

"Well?" Cecelia quizzed.

"Out of the park, Mom! Glorious, fantastic, absolutely what I needed! Thanks, Mom." Amy leaned over and gave Cecelia a peck on her cheek. "When do we come back?"

"Two weeks?" Cecelia sighed happily. "Weather permitting?"

"If we're doing this *regularly*," Amy overemphasized, laughing, "I'll be off work again. Berkshire can get us gliders. I'll call the lessons, sales development; maybe I'll get paid."

"I'm sure you will, dear."

§§

CHAPTER 29

Comfortably settled in his living room, Lance decided to make a few afternoon "social" calls to delinquent accounts. He was irritated with the sluggish rate of money flowing into his coffers.

Lance's first call was not satisfying. His client, a state senator who needed to maintain secrecy about his campaign fund usage, said that he had the cash. Should he bring it to Lance's Post Office Square office? Would Lance prefer to send a courier? He'd even offered to up his payment for being a slow-pay and intimated that he had three juicy tips for Lance, the silver linings Lance loved and lived for.

Lance declined the increased payment offer but was appreciative. Better to keep things simple, stick to basics. Why create an unnecessary obligation, no matter how slight? Even if the senator had the three tips, he would contribute to Lance's coffers again soon enough. The senator's pretty and diminutive staffer had just moved into an apartment on Revere Street not too far from Lance and had no means to support that lifestyle.

Shooting fish in a barrel.

Still, he was restless, spoiling for a fight. He knew the next call might do the trick.

Richard Drummond, CFO of Auric Enterprises, had been cooking the books of his small gold plating firm in Woburn. The company gold plated copper-etched circuit boards and pin connectors for Digital Equipment Corp.'s prototyping unit. Auric was too modest a company to touch the production side of DEC. Tyler Simmons, Drummond's business partner, had dreams of growing into that production potential; however, the capital necessary to make a move never materialized.

Drummond had embezzled gargantuan sums. Gold market fluctuation, metal stocks, and currency manipulation had made it easy to hide his financial discrepancies. Lance owned a thirty grand a month cut of Drummond's skim thanks to his highly valued, well-placed tipster. The days for the company were lean. Drummond was currently having difficulty shaving funds while under the scrutiny of an SEC audit. Not Lance's problem, only that the additional attention denied Lance his rightful share. Payments were past due.

"Hello, Richard."

"Yes, Lance, I've been expecting your call, although not at my home. Can I call you back tomorrow?"

"Your office says that you are a busy man." Lance ignored the attempted brush off. "Too busy for your other business partner. Me, Lance."

"Oh, that, I'll have the receptionist expedite your calls."

"That would be nice. How's the audit going?" Point and advantage for Lance, he could tip the auditors.

"Lance, you want your money. I know I'm behind, and you've been patient. I owe you what? Ninety thousand? It's impossible right now. If you spook the auditors, I'll never be able to get anything to you."

"Richard, I'm a reasonable man; I won't whisper a word."

"Huh? You won't?"

"No, but I have lost, I mean, *absolutely* lost my faith in your interest in paying me what I'm due. To be out this much cash is new territory for me, so I'm putting out a contract on Tyler Simmons."

"What? No, please. He hasn't done anything. You can't."

"Actually, I can. I have suitable, highly qualified resources. Tell me, should I arrange it so that you're close when it happens?" Lance felt a comfortable warmth fill his body. "You can be a witness. Business partners, especially dirty ones, make great suspects when a financial audit becomes a murder investigation. You don't know it, but you took out a key employee life insurance policy for $2 million on Simmons."

Richard Drummond stifled a remorseful groan.

"Lance, listen..."

"No, Richard, let me explain. One of my contractors is a specialist." Lance already had Breathless in mind, the most terrifying killer in his stable. "You may have read about his successful projects in the papers. His expertise is depriving his subjects of oxygen in quite creative, even ingenious means; what's more, he's very psychological. In the instance of Tyler, he would restrain him in a chair, perhaps, with self-tightening knots to make him work for his breath. He'd then take his time with a detailed exposé of your embezzlement, dates, times, and amounts. Tyler would struggle, causing the ropes to tighten further. My man would tell of how *you* had robbed Tyler of his dream of an expanded Auric operation, how *you* had abandoned him to his last long journey toward death. He would destroy every vestige of trust Tyler had in you. Then he would completely divest Tyler's life-sustaining breath from him.

"Tyler's son and your son play hockey together, don't they? When's the next game? Who do they play?"

"Okay. Okay, I'll get the money."

"How about tomorrow, two o'clock?"

"I need to liquidate assets. That can take time."

"You, Richard, have all the time in the world. Tyler Simmons, not so much. I'll watch my bank deposits. You can wire the money before two.

"You and your *beautiful* wife, Stacy, enjoy your evening."

Now that was more satisfying. If Drummond came through, Lance would have to come up with some different work for Breathless, who was looking forward to just such an undertaking, it would come soon enough. Maybe he would send him on a drive up-country to cruise by the old Barton home. He could take a gander at the Bartons' former business office, too.

Lance had hard evidence of the death of three out of four Bartons. The closed coffin burial and curious circumstances of Michael Barton's death left Lance with a trace of uncertainty.

On to more collection calls...,

"Oh, my amphetamine dealer in Plymouth is behind. Only three grand, still, I have to pay the help."

§§

Chapter 30

Durango is a small town of fourteen thousand if you don't include the college students. It wasn't surprising to find that my recent combatant lived only five blocks from my rented apartment. I parked at home then walked those five blocks while settling on my conversational approach.

Dave had called Robert, Bobby; I would call him that if he decided to talk to me. There is power in the name you call someone.

Not wanting to stress my stitches, I chose to cross at the light on the abundantly trafficked North Main.

Bobby's home sported a low white picket fence, a shot-gun-style house some would call a bungalow, with shake siding stained brown, white trim, and an extremely well-manicured yard. Raised flower beds and flower boxes contained marigolds, bluebells, roses, clematis, and cinquefoils. All the plants were beginning their autumn decline but showed signs of extensive care.

Only a block away was Mercy Hospital.

I paced the sidewalk in front of Bobby's home and midway beyond, in both directions. Ten minutes passed before I saw the curtain in Bobby's front window move to the side as someone peaked out. I paused by the low gate and waited.

Bobby stepped out onto his covered porch.

"What do you want?" It was more contempt than an invitation. Visibly beaten up, he had purplish bruising below his eyes, a swollen cheek and nose, and a not well-fitting aluminum splint to immobilize his fractured finger. I had no idea that I had done such damage. I was appalled at myself, yet this man dignified my presence with a civil question.

Yesterday, I battled with the identities of Michael Barton and Calvin James. Today, right now, I was battling with my inhumanity.

"An apology on my part is in order; I wanted to offer it. May I come into your yard so we can talk?"

"We don't get many polite white guys coming around here."

I took that as a yes. Carefully, I opened the gate and closed it with the same care.

"Do you mind if we sit on your steps?" I looked down at my leg as I asked. "I walked over here from my apartment and might have been overly ambitious."

"Help yourself." Bobby was leery, not convinced of any sincerity from my quarter.

I sat on the middle of five thick oaken steps. He took a seat at the porch level.

"You know," I chose my words carefully, "defending myself yesterday, you probably get that. I went way overboard. I am truly sorry, especially about your finger; that was nasty, cruel of me. I don't know what came over me. Your nose, just bloodied, I hope, not broken?"

I looked at the sidewalk. All I received from Bobby was a nod of the head. I went on, finding no trust there.

"But how are you? I mean, did they give you pain meds. What did they say about the finger? It'll heal okay?"

"You're not from around here, are you?" Bobby was angry, in part, a reaction to his medical treatment. "This face, this brown skin, these brown eyes, they don't get the same care as your face, your white skin, and blue eyes when it comes to Worker's Comp or anything medical. Since you asked, it hurts like hell. I'm trying to space my pain relievers. Will it heal? The doctor wasn't concerned. 'You get what you get.' he said."

"Bobby, you're right. I might just as well be from another planet." I allowed myself time to think of all that meant as I said it. I felt alien. "I don't understand how you could be treated differently or didn't before now. Seeing how the doctor fixed you up, yeah, I get it."

"Did you know that when Jamie dropped me off at the emergency room, he fired me? I hadn't been working for Lucas even a whole week. Worker's Comp is only going to get me two-thirds of my pay while I'm laid up. I've got a family, a wife and three kids. We were already pressed hard before all this."

"First, let me say, don't worry, but let me tell you why. It'll take a few minutes."

Another nod from Bobby, dismissive, but a nod; good, I was getting agreement.

"I've been doing some checking around today. I didn't know about Lucas firing you, but it doesn't surprise me after all the trash I've learned about them. I'm sorry that you had to work for them in the first place. I don't have any family, a wife, or kids to support and protect. I don't know the weight of that responsibility. I won't until I do have a family of my own.

"Let me tell you about some other checking that I've done. Aside from that sore finger there, you are a superior carpenter. I went over to the racketball club and looked at the impressive inlay stuff you did for the flooring and cabinetry. I went to the Lost Pelican, too. You did the cabinetry and wood-work on the bar there. Am I right? That is fine work.

"That's thing one. As a result, you and I are going to go over to the orthopedic surgeon tomorrow. I'll put *my* face, *my* white skin, and *my* eye color on the bill for that finger. We'll get you a Hexcel cast. Have you ever seen them? Super light-weight and strong, they don't wear away, and the best part is, they're porous, so they breathe. Before we leave there, we'll have you on a restoration plan, even if it requires surgery, to get your finger as good as it was before yesterday. I want to make sure that you can point at me with that finger, with style, and say, 'That's the guy who broke my finger.' Interested?"

"Nobody's going to pay for all that, especially Worker's Comp."

"Let me say it this way, *my* finger, *my* wallet."

"No way..."

"The second thing," I interrupted him before he had a chance even to think about turning down my offer; after all, I had been getting agreement from him, "I have a job for you starting today. It pays better than Lucas or BWM. What do you think?"

"You don't know what I was making."

"Doesn't make any difference. It pays better. Period."

"I can't swing a hammer."

"That doesn't matter either, because you think, observe, and learn. See, some folks I talked to today, the former owner of BWM was one of them, say that you not only did carpentry, you understood carpentry, the concepts, the math, the layouts, and the precision. All were very high on your work ethic. What I'll have you doing for work, along with finishing Warthington, is to study with me. We're going to test for our general contractor licenses together."

"So, why...? How can you afford...? Wait. Warthington? I'm not working for Lucas anymore, and you're definitely not."

"Yeah, about that. Dave Cravath took over that project; Warthington is terminating the Lucas contract for cause. I was in Dave's office this morning, and Dave had Don Warthington, the owner, on the phone from Italy. Very cool guy, basketball player and coach, and good friends with Dave. They talked yesterday about Lucas's nonperformance. The paperwork reassigning the job will be finished up tomorrow with zero chance of a lawsuit.

"Dave enjoys his excavation business, but he has a GC license too. He's given that project to you and me if you're with me, minimal supervision.

"Why, you ask? Because I have plans. I need good people to carry them out, and even considering our rough introduction, I think you're good people.

"You were about to ask how I can afford to get your finger fixed. You're just going to have to trust me." I was on a tear, desperate to knock down all barriers.

"Okay," Bobby was skeptical, "if all this is true and you're going to do all this stuff, tell me how you pulled off the impossible forming job. You've created a lot of buzz in the field today with that stunt. I've even heard about it at home."

"I cheated."

"No fooling."

"Really. You're in, aren't you?" With Bobby's nod, I was off again. "It started with finding Dave Cravath's army engineering transit in the Lucas crew box."

I told him everything, including "Jamie," the monopod rodman. Bobby tracked with all the details even when I explained the trigonometry. Sometime along, as we talked,

Bobby's perceptive wife, Rosa, had brought a tray with two iced teas, for which we were both thankful. Bobby laughed when I relayed the part about the exchange for Dave's help. The laugh was good for both of us.

I stood to leave.

"I'd shake your hand, but you might have some residual, reflexive recoil."

"I'd shake yours, but some jerk broke my finger yesterday."

"Virtual shake?"

"Deal."

"Bobby, take your meds the way the doctor prescribed them; we'll get you a new regimen tomorrow. Ten o'clock, I'll meet you here. We'll walk over to Mercy together."

"Shouldn't I make an appointment?"

"I've already made one, ten-thirty, with a darn fine orthopedist. Between you and me, I hear through the grape-vine; he's color blind."

§

Bobby was proudly sporting his new cast, sea-foam in color.

"It complements my eyes." An upbeat joke in light of my "My finger, my face." comment two days ago. The doctor wanted to re-evaluate in just a few days and was very optimistic about the outcome.

I favored my right leg, lifting my heel slightly. We didn't have long to wait in Dave Cravath's outer office. Dave returned from an early morning check on his site-pad projects within minutes of our arrival. He had acquired a new client with gas-patch work close to Navajo Reservoir and was expressly concerned with his crew's performance.

His smiling face told us that he was pleased with his findings. The door closer delayed the swing of the door behind him; its slight thud on closing coincided with Dave's left hand-clapping my right shoulder as he grasped me with a hearty handshake.

"Dave, this is Bobby. I don't think you've met."

Dave extended his right hand, then, in a savvy motion, raised it to slap Bobby's left shoulder in camaraderie.

"Pleasure to meet you." Dave grinned unapologetically. "Come this way."

He motioned us aside through an open door helpfully labeled Plan Room.

"I'll be right back. Drinks?"

Bobby hesitated.

"Do you have Pepsi in the fridge?" I knew he did. He had made the same offer the day before. I also knew that there was Molson Ale and Saint Pauley Girl, but that was two years down the road and later in the day for me.

"Absolutely. Bobby? There's Snapple, Sprite, bottled water?"

"Sure. I'd take a Pepsi, too."

"Make yourselves at home; I'll be right back."

Dave's plan room had a central reviewing table, an eight by eight-foot custom oak table surrounded by several elevated swivel task chairs. For current job plans, Dave hung the blueprints' binding side on split bamboo rods, perfect for the job. I couldn't tell if Dave purchased or custom made them. These rod-bound plans hung vertically on one of three stepped racks.

His office help rolled the completed project plans with elastic bands or tucked them in mail tubes. These found their place, cataloged on shelves that resembled extended library stacks covering the plan room walls.

Track lights abruptly beamed down on the table as Dave flipped the switch, returning to the room. He distributed our pint Pepsi's, opening Bobby's before opening his own and leaving me to my own devices. He promptly retrieved the Warthington blueprints from their place in the racks and flattened them quickly.

"Cal, you're the note taker by default." He slid a pad of graph paper toward me along with a sharpened number three Ticonderoga.

"Don Warthington wants to celebrate Christmas in his new house. Cal, you heard him the other day," Dave said, conveying urgency. "How are we..., you guys going to do that?"

"Easy," popped out of my mouth with a little laugh.

"Come on, Cal. All you have are the footers my guys poured for you yesterday. I don't know you all that well, only that you're smart. You need to be serious here."

"Do you think, Dave, we can sell Don on a detached building for an indoor basketball court if we do it at no extra cost?"

Dave, catching a sly smile from Bobby, suppressed his second get-real comment.

"Okay, what's up?"

"Bobby and I were thinking that we had to compress the timeline to make a pre-Christmas, Permit to Occupy, a realistic goal. Don's offering a hefty early completion bonus, right? We thought about overlapping tasks and trades, not relying on just pushing hard to hurry things along."

Dave glanced back and forth between Bobby and me, probing and gaining confidence from our positive smiles.

"We're going to pour a waste slab," Bobby picked up the detailing, "to prefab on. I know some concrete guys that need work right now. I know some fast, accurate framers, too, thanks to BWM. Good guys, good workers, we can contract them at a good price. Cal and I talked about that. Usually, a waste slab would be broken up and hauled away after we've finished with it, but then Cal spins up this metal building idea."

"Here's the run-down," I broke in, "the future metal building floor is our prefabrication site. Class A finished, not your average waste slab. If we push, we can be ready to use it after this weekend.

"Can we get a permit? I mean, if we get it engineered to the right specifications? The slab will accommodate all the framing, all pre-drilled for plumbing and electrical. With a boom truck, we lift the pieces into place."

While I paused for breath, Dave interjected, "how are you going to deal with measurement errors? One mistake will kill your efficiency."

"Cal and I will do the initial layouts," Bobby threw in, onboard and excited. "the lead framers and concrete guys will confirm our layouts with their own, then Cal and I will do quality control on the finished product."

"Can we use your army transit, Dave?" I asked. "We can check control points with it quickly. I want to show Bobby the calculation and follow up process anyway."

"Sir?" Bobby began, addressing Dave.

"Bobby, you need to call me Dave. Otherwise, I'll be looking to see who you're talking to. You were saying?"

"This is a good plan. If we're careful not to rush and get the subs on board, our timelines are stacked, not sequential. That's the concept that Cal and I came up with. The guys I know are great. With a good schedule, they can work for less. I'd suggest that we give them a lowball target price, with a bonus for early completion. That would bring them in under the cost of hourly work, and it would give them ample reason to perform fast and accurately."

"That's how we pay for the metal building," I added.

"You guys make me dizzy. It sounds like a lot of head work." Dave exhaled deeply. "I don't have the time for it."

"You can check on us anytime you like. We'll show you all the supporting detail you want. *We are* up for it."

If it were Dave Harris from Acworth, not Dave Cravath, he would have had his pipe and Erinmore Flake out and be puffing. As it was, Dave exhaled deeply again, thoughtfully wondering what he had gotten himself into.

"You guys start looking at the plans. I'll see if I can arrange a miracle and get a concrete floor with plumbing engineered overnight and approved by the La Plata County Building Department just as fast."

"The out building's going to be seventy-two by one-twenty."

This comment netted me a roll of the eyes from Dave. He stood, looking around the plan room. From this rapid survey, he recalled his beginnings. After a moment of introspection, he nodded, agreeing with himself that he had complete assurance in our abilities.

"I have two sets of plans. You can take one set home with you tonight. I'll have a couple of coffee table sets made and overnighted from Denver.

Collect your thoughts and meet me in my office in a few minutes. You two are selling your ideas to Don Warthington."

§

Dave had begun the phone conversation in what sounded like Italian. When he hit the button for the speakerphone, Don Warthington sounded as American as anyone.

We left Dave's office with the approval we needed to proceed. Outside the office, the corridor had been the same temperature as the office when we entered. Exiting, it felt ten degrees cooler.

"Bobby, Cal, you've got some layout work in the morning, be on-site at eight. I'll help."

"Dave, thanks, but if you can bring us a backhoe with a front-end loader and a compactor, Bobby and I laid out the slab yesterday. I'll get you the orientation specs for your miracle engineer. We reset the batter boards for the foundation form setters and reverified the layout, too."

Dave looked at Bobby, who nodded sheepishly, then at me. He paused and then laughed.

"This is going to be fun, but don't you two get cocky. You're going to need a lot of cooperation to make this work. You'll need to lead, not just manage, and you'll need to listen to your people whether you like them or not." Dave grinned. "I'm off my soapbox. Have at it. Line up your contractors and materials. The lumber package has been in at Red Barn Lumber for two weeks, which you had better double-check for accuracy. Use my phones in the plan room."

§§

CHAPTER 31

The Barton Conservatory Trust now owned what was formerly the Bartons' property with Dave Harris as the paid conservator. His charge allowed him $30,000 per year to "maintain as if occupied." He didn't ask for the position, he didn't ask how the funding came about, but he was grateful for the additional income and continued use of the property. He and Betty took their appointment seriously.

Dave emerged from the Bartons' barn to assess the dark blue Chevy Impala bearing Massachusetts plates, positioned such that he wouldn't be able to close the driveway gate. This was annoying.

The dark-haired, olive complected man with a perpetual five o'clock shadow wore a three quarter dress coat and slacks thin enough and full enough to flutter in a light breeze. He also was an annoyance. Walking along the inside of the property's front fence of sturdy posts and board rails, painted white, the antagonist inspected everything with the attitude that he had purchased the property.

It was the ruler of all he surveyed demeanor that inspired Dave to retrieve his shotgun, a Remington twelve gauge side by side, from his pickup's gun rack, it was accompanied there by an ancient Winchester 3855 and .22 caliber Kimber. He took four narrow-pattern, double-aught buckshot cartridges from a box under the seat. They would make sufficient noise or do considerable personal damage if necessary. Barrel opened, bent over his right arm, he loaded two shells without looking, sliding them down the groove between his index and middle finger.

"You own this place?" The other man began the conversation from too far away and was too loud. He would just as soon be snuffing Tyler Simmons.

"No."

"What are you doing here?"

"That's no business of yours."

"How do you know that?"

This elevated Dave's usually stable blood pressure, but he felt no need to respond.

After what, in normal give and take, would be an uncomfortably long pause, the other man continued.

"This place for sale?"

"No."

The men stopped with about twenty feet distance between them. Again, Dave offered nothing more.

"You are just a bundle of talk, aren't ya?"

"When I choose."

"You need to talk to me."

"You're mistaken."

"Don't be too sure."

"You know," Dave, always the tactful Yankee, "you're dumber than that tree behind you."

"What do you mean by that, farmer?"

"What I mean by that, intruder, is that tree knows when it's time to leave."

The other man flipped his coat back to intimidate this agrarian ignoramus with his .38.

Dave was quicker. His shotgun's break-action barrel latched with a flip; simultaneously, the stock came to rest on his shoulder. If the other man hadn't been sluggish and had completed his draw, his gun hand would have intersected the ripping blast of eight 8.38 mm pellets.

Astonishment interrupted the other man's intent. Dave's demonstration was that of a competition shooter.

"This trigger is *surprisingly* responsive," Dave understated.

"Do ya think?" the other man yelled, appalled and temporarily hearing impaired by the near-miss.

"Maple tree." Dave made an indication toward the large maple with the shotgun, then pointed it just away from the man, "Smarter than you. *Capisci.* My other barrel's chambered. Never can tell what might happen with these sensitive triggers."

Dave didn't vary his relaxed stance, continuing evenly, "Go. Now. Leave."

Without another word, the man holstered his pistol, jumped into his Impala, and hurriedly departed.

For Dave Harris, this confrontation deserved a thoughtful smoke. He drew out his corncob and hinged-nail pipe tool with his free hand, not abandoning the stance he first adopted while engaging the other man. He kept the shotgun in the crook of his elbow and scraped out the remnants of his last smoke.

Before Dave had his tobacco tin out of his denim jacket pocket, the Impala raced by in the opposite direction putting him unnecessarily on alert. It was the flatlander, lost in the countryside.

Funny, he didn't ask for directions. Dumber than a maple.

A chuckle emerged from behind the pipe stem clutched between his teeth. Deftly pulling a wafer of tobacco from his tin, he crumbled it into the bowl, packed his pipe, and nimbly lit it. Dave turned and walked reflectively to his truck. A flicker of a smile plied his mouth and eyes. Someone else had his same suspicions.

§§

Chapter 32

It was Sunday evening, and a dozen or more expensive cars lined the Warthingtons' driveway, Mercedes, Beamers, Audis, most with Arizona plates.

Christmas cheer abounded in Don Warthington's new home. Dave Cravath, with his wife Meredith, had corralled Bobby's family and me when we arrived. New dad proud, he ushered us through the entryway and aside into the drawing-room.

During construction, Bobby had appropriated, for his own particular project, the impressive open foyer, its finish carpentry, the stairs, the railing, and the two landings, encircling the entrance hall with refined, beautiful results. Inlays on the stair treads and risers, and ornate geometric inlays on the landings, were all Bobby's creations from design to finish. The marble tile floor echoed the same geometric designs and was engineered to absorb and store solar heat, shaded in the summer, and exposed to the winter sun. The stonework on the two-story foyer walls was also a solar feature. Three months ago, only a hole in the ground existed, rightly oriented and well dug. Today it was an immaculate living space accomplished by Bobby's and my sweat, hands, and heads.

Dave collected a pile of winter coats from Bobby's family and me, which he parked and then rounded up Don Warthington. Don had made a special request of Dave for Don to greet us personally before we joined the celebrations.

Party noise murmured from deeper within the two-story Colonial Revival home. The county had awarded its certificate of occupancy the week before.

Formerly, my poster child for tall was Steve Chauklin. Don Warthington was six foot nine, instantly becoming my new tall, though his height was not a surprise. Bobby and I had needed to modify the door openings and clearances on the back and upper stairwells. He didn't need to stoop to enter the drawing-room behind Dave.

"*Rosa, Bobby, Cal, vi presento Don.*" (This is Don.) Dave wanted to show off how quickly we had assimilated Italian.

"*Piacere di incontrarvi. Voi avete condotto il migliore dei lavori, e piú veloce di ciò che potevo sperare. Grazie.*" (I'm pleased to meet you. You men have done the best job, faster than I could have hoped for. Thank you,) Don complemented, shaking hands all around. "*Dave non può chiudere bocca di voi due.*" (Dave hasn't stopped bragging about you.)

"*Grazie di averci dato l'opportunità di costruire questa casa,*" (Thank you for the opportunity to build your house,) Bobby gratefully and humbly offered. "*E' stata una gran fatica, un grande insegnamento e un gran divertimento.*" (It was a lot of work, a lot of learning, and a lot of fun.)

"*Grazie dell'invito alla festa di Natale. È piú di quanto ci potessimo aspettare. Noi non resteremo a lungo come i tuoi invitati,*" (Thank you for inviting us to your Christmas Party. It's more than we could expect. We're bound to be shorter than the rest of your guests,) I added.

Bobby and I spouted our prepared greetings.

"*Vi ho in alta considerazione.*" (You guys are highly regarded in my book.)

"*Questi due...*" Dave ventured, "*Questi due ragazzi sanno come portare a termine.*" (These two know how to get it done.)

Don and Dave couldn't have demonstrated any higher estimation of Bobby and me. Rosa's smile expressed the pride she had in her husband.

"You folks learned all that language from watching my Italian dubbed movies? Come on in; I'll introduce you to my family and my players."

§

The kitchen, family room, and living room held the majority of the festivities. Rosa surprised Don's guests with detailed directions to various facilities. We had employed her to head up our post-construction cleaning crew.

Don's guests were effusive in their praise and had questions about the house's features. Others had questions about our construction techniques. They had heard generalities from our progress reports to Don. Still others, inquired if Bobby and I had our own company. Or, could we come to Sedona, Scottsdale, or Flagstaff to build houses for them?

Bobby's and Rosa's kids wandered well among the tall trees, but they needed to observe established bedtimes and left much earlier than the party would break up. The kids did acquire huge name dropping ammunition for school.

Later, Don and I wandered to the outbuilding that was to be his gratis basketball court. Natural cedar clapboards sheathed the lower outside walls, above, was mostly glass. The intense overhead lighting inside illuminated the surrounding area. I told Don equally strong portable lighting enabled Bobby and me to quality check our prefab at night and not interfere with daytime construction. The plan had been to construct the outbuilding with a metal frame, but with the superabundance of savings, it had morphed into a timber frame structure with clear spans.

Bobby made the call to my old timber frame workplace in New Hampshire. At my instruction, Bobby asked for Ron and ordered the frame from pieces I knew they would have readily available. I even specified particular joinery methods to produce the long spans from shorter beams.

Our carpentry crews, already enthusiastic over their bonus checks, jumped at the chance to work in a new, timber frame, medium. It was only a matter of days to assemble the frame once it arrived, tarp-covered on eighteen-wheel flatbeds. They had finished out the building completely; the flooring was all that remained unfinished.

"By New Year's Eve, we'll have the court finished and striped," I explained to Don. "We kept a half-court open toward the end of construction for more than a few late-night pickup games."

"Beautifully done, Cal. Tell me," Don's confidential tone put me at ease, "how old are you?"

"I'm just over twenty," I lied. I was eighteen, but twenty fit Calvin James' license, passport, and birth certificate.

"Dave tells me you're brilliant. Can I ask you why you're not in engineering school?"

"I thought that practical building experience would be helpful before I went on with school."

"That sounds wise. It's not a money issue, is it?"

"No, I'm fixed okay." True. "Thanks for asking."

Five grand a month was my WITSEC allowance. That put me up with the local trust funders. US Marshals were also in the process of funneling my parents' life insurance proceeds to me. Their money laundering would result in making me a multimillionaire. Until they worked it through, they were allowing me to borrow against it.

Money for parents or brother? Not worth the exchange.

We stepped into the warmly lit interior. I still marveled at the open expanse of it. The temperature was cool. Our coatless attire was comfortable.

"I was just thinking if there was anything I could do for you." Don leaned over to the basketball cart, selecting one of the dozen balls. He picked up a fast dribble and made a twenty-five-foot jumper, all net. "You've got the placement right."

"Here's a thought, Don, you've already done plenty, though." I picked off a basketball and dribbled. Don stepped between the basket and me and grinned.

"This place has been one risk after another, hasn't it?" I continued, "I mean, I risked being right on laying out the foundation. Dave trusted me. That was a risk. Then you and he risked that Bobby and I would get it all done correctly. The people we contracted with risked being set up for failure by a couple of young hotshot know-it-alls. You risked your friendship with Dave to allow us the chance. These long span beams, they're a unique risk to me. The joinery connecting those long spans up there is called a wedged stop splayed scarf; it's a very distinctive technique, not many carpenters can even say what it means these days. A few people know that I love to see it used. It's a risk to me that they do and that we used it."

A shoulder drop fake that Steve Chauklin once showed me enabled me to sidestep Don to get a shot off. Both of us watched the ball glance off the backboard and drop.

"You play?" Don asked.

"No, except for a pickup game now and then, if it's basketball, I'm a one-trick pony.

"Don, I'm out on a limb here. You can't let anyone, *anyone*, know what I'm about to ask you, agreed?" A vision of a livid US Marshal, my handler, crossed the back of my eyes.

"Of course, what is it?" Don looked at me curiously.

"The next time you're in New England, catch a Keene State basketball game."

"Recruiting? Who am I looking for?"

"It'll be obvious. He's the guy you'll see bring up the level of play of everyone around him." In this, I knew that I was acting both recklessly and selfishly; recklessly, because if discovered I risked exposure and dying; selfishly, because I wanted my friends close, yes, but I also wanted to give my father's, mother's and brother's, even Jill's, deaths meaning and impact. I had a plan of what I was going to do if Don was favorably impressed.

"Sounds like you, Cal. How do you know this guy?"

I glanced at my wrist where a watch would have been had I worn one.

"Oh, look at the time."

§

Dave, Bobby, and I sat around Dave's plan table and relaxed in the tall task chairs. Each of us, with a steaming Carver's coffee mug, enjoyed the silence for a few minutes along with the coffee and the sociability.

"We haven't had much opportunity to talk about it, but what's up next for you two?" Dave was the first to break the reverie.

"We'll take a study break; the GC test is up in January. Then watch out, we'll be Brand X." Bobby was proud, rightly so, of his preparedness for the test.

"I have ideas on how to stay profitably busy this winter, along with the crews that we've worked with." I breathed in steam from my coffee. "I've gotten to be a zealot."

"Tell me, will I be in trouble for this?"

"No. I don't have it all straightened out yet. I'll need legal help mostly."

"Now, I'm worried," Dave laughed.

"Well, hear me out, Dave. I'd want your counsel on this, too."

Bobby smiled broadly. Dave was now accustomed to the Bobby smile, which had become a great confidence builder. In Bobby, I had a friend who realized that I had a shrouded past. He didn't pry.

"It's midyear at Fort Lewis. Many students aren't coming back. When downtown landlords are placing vacancy ads in the *Weird Old Herald*, they read, 'Rent with option to buy.' It gives them the chance to demand higher rent, and nobody ever exercises the option. Usually, the option language is vague anyway.

"What I have in mind will make the owners angry. I'll formalize the option language with an exercise price and unrestricted right to improve. We'll flip property without having to invest in ownership upfront. Cool, huh? The profit comes when we exercise the option and sell the property."

"Bobby, are you ready for this?" cautioned Dave.

We all laughed. I would expect, if there were any conflicts from our contracts, a judge would decide the outcome.

"I approve. Do you have enough capital to fund subcontractors and materials?"

"With the proceeds and bonus from Don, yeah, we do, and if not, I have reserves."

"How many of these are you taking on?"

"We've spotted five good candidates so far," Bobby pitched in.

"Bobby," Dave, not at all privately, confided to him, "you and I are looking at a man who is destined to be a self-made millionaire before he's twenty-one."

"Dave, you should see him distance himself from the girls who want to spend his money for him. When he walks down Main Street, he has a target on his back with a dollar sign in the bull's eye. My Rosa is impressed that he's smart enough to look for more in a relationship.

"I know he's definitely an inspired salesman. I don't even know why I let him sit on my porch steps four months ago. Now he stuffs money into my wallet and bank account, then he says, 'Let's do this other thing.' Thing is, it's my money, money I earned. But it wouldn't be there if I hadn't listened to him."

"I'm right here where I can hear you guys. If you want to fix me up with a date, make it a girl I can have a conversation with. And, no way can I call what *we're* doing as *me* being self-made. I have too much good help to credit," I objected, inhaling another waft of vapor followed by another swallow. "But I'll also have you know that I have my eye on that acreage west of town, Dave. It looks good for a classy development. You'll need to save me some excavation time next spring for a few spec houses."

How do I explain to Dave and Bobby that money and possessions are okay, but they don't drive me? I can't tell them I'm escaping from one life into another.

§§

CHAPTER 33

The Spaulding Gymnasium athletic offices were central to the Keene State College campus. It was the first day of classes after Christmas break; snow had fallen the night before.

"You wanted to see me, Coach?" An elbow to Steve Chauklin's face during Friday night's game had left a lambent bruise high on his cheek, earned from hard play, not animosity. Steve wasn't clear on why his coach had requested a pre-practice meeting with him. His grades were excellent; he helped his teammates keep theirs up, too. He supposed that it was in preparation for Tuesday night's game.

"How's the eye, Steve?"

"It's fine, Coach. No problem. I'll be fine to play Tuesday."

"Very good to hear. That isn't why I wanted to see you. I wanted to be the first to say so long and best of luck."

"To say, *what?*" Steve's voice edged up with stress.

"Not to worry. I'll have you until summer."

"Come on, Coach. Not funny. What's happened?"

"Steve, did you see, in the stands at the Plymouth State game last week, a guy about six-nine, well dressed, and black?"

"Not really. I had my mind in the game."

"Yes, you did, Steve. You were your usual, impressive self. That guy must have told someone he wanted to keep an eye on you. Starting fall of '87, you've got a full ride at the University of Arizona, Phoenix."

"No way. That's impossible, Coach. No way. Too cool." With Steve's sudden excitement, there followed an equally sudden realization, "With all due respect, sir, I have two amazing friends and a sister that I couldn't stand to leave here."

"I'm sure you all could adjust to the circumstances if you were in Phoenix, and they stayed here. They would be happy for you, Steve. Wouldn't they? You're the one who picks up everyone else. You deserve this kind of break. Who knows why the Sun's coach came to our lowly game, or if he would ever call on us again?

"The grantor may have anticipated your concern for Chelsea, Jill, and Jack. There is an offer for you to distribute three additional full rides. I've never heard of anything like this, Steve. It couldn't happen to anyone more deserving. Hope you thrive in hot weather."

"Coach, who is it? Who did this?"

"Can't help you there, Steve."

"Incredible, Coach. If there's nothing else..., Is that it? Nothing about Tuesday's game? I've got to go tell the guys. Amazing. See you at practice."

"Don't be late, son."

§§

CHAPTER 34

A beautiful, blue-skied, crisp early June morning promised comfortably warm temperatures later in the day. Today marked four years since I arrived in Durango, an auspicious day to reflect. Even so, the first one to arrive at the office made the coffee, which I did.

The Smart Start Builders' answering machine flashed, announcing a call that had come in earlier that Friday morning.

I had scheduled inspections on three building projects. When I was not in Boulder, I would do half, Bobby the other half. We rotated one at a time, the jobs on which we would do our site visits. I had two spec houses and one custom contract home to review, all three west of town.

Our methods had not changed since our first project three and a half years ago with the Warthington home. We each stepped up to supervise multiple projects. Mornings involved monitoring the project managers' reports from the previous day. We made sure that plans and schedules were on track. When necessary, we would do multiple site checks during the week. More often than not, a weekly visit sufficed. On those visits, we reviewed blueprints, checked dimensions, listened to any concerns from the foremen, subcontractors, owners, architects, engineers, and any other interested parties.

Bobby finagled artful carpentry projects when he could.

We still carried with us our fearsome truth detectors, David White engineering transits. All of our jobsites had at least six Do Not Disturb pads with established reference points.

New subcontractors groaned or mocked when they first saw us set up our transits over our indicators. Those duplex nails embedded in small concrete pads spray-painted with fluorescent paint had become part of the Smart Start mythology. It only took, at most, pointing out a dimension or placement error in their work to convince them that our control logs were to be trusted. Contractors had argued and lost the argument; others had argued and lost their contracts. By our third visit, those that remained had coffee and donuts waiting for their crews and us.

Our employees and our contractors savored our second week in June shut down. It was, for us, a pre-summer celebration. We then scheduled start dates in the third week for projects that we would complete in the fall. Bobby and I included in our list of employment benefits, that second week off, paid. In doing this, we avoided the logistics of crewmembers randomly scheduling vacation dates throughout the summer. Our competitors believed that we were nuts to give up the best work weather. Instead, we should make hay while the sun shines. They couldn't deny, though, that we made payroll, paid our bills, and made a lot of money for Smart Start and our contracting partners.

I was looking forward to *my* upcoming week's vacation on Makapuu Beach, Oahu, Hawaii, a real but rare treat for myself.

I'd just finished my junior year at the University of Colorado in Boulder. My studies in Engineering, Construction Management, and a minor in Construction Law kept Smart Start on the cutting edge of legal and operational advances.

I assisted Bobby with blueprint reviews and planning via FedEx while school was in session. Material takeoffs, Bobby's domain, was tending toward computerization. Ahead of the curve in all facets, we produced our control logs with Lotus 123 and employed Microsoft Project to establish, evaluate, and maintain our schedules.

§

With a fragrant cup of freshly brewed coffee in hand from just ground Carver's beans, I released the blinking answering machine from its tedious duty. The Friday morning phone message was specific and brief.

"This message is for Calvin James. My name is Jeff Teller, an architect with the firm of Bell and Teller of Boston."

He had a genuine, but thin, Bostonian accent. "Mr. James, I would value, in terms that you would appreciate, your design assistance for a large home project here in Durango. I have several references for your tenacity for excellence. I want to meet you this morning, Friday, on-site. The location is south, off Junction Creek Road, about a mile and a half west of Main Street. I have a mobile phone in my automobile. Please call me at 1-800-555-1717."

Note to self, get phones in all the company vehicles, and portable ones for the foremen, as an addition to the jobsite office phones.

§

"Jeff Teller? This is Calvin James; you called my office."

"Yes, Mr. James, you heard my proposal. Are you interested?"

"Please, call me Cal, Jeff. I am curious: 'Interested' is a term I usually associate with a dollar figure. I'll come out and have a look. I do have project inspections scheduled later this morning; I can give you an hour or so."

"Very good. Do you know the location?"

"I believe I do, an unpaved road secured by a green bar gate a hundred yards in, through the notch in the ridge on the south side of Junction Creek Road. Is that right?"

"Then you know of the older abandoned house? That's the proposed new home site."

"I can be there in twenty minutes. Will that work?"

"Yes. Excellent. Thank you for making yourself available. The owner's representative will be here, too." I could hear through his slight Brahman that Jeff was less than impressed with this owner's representative.

§

My Chevy Sierra pickup made a dusty approach to the waiting group of vehicles and workmen. Although we upgraded the rest of our Smart Start fleet to new, three-quarter-ton F-250's, I was too accustomed to my truck. Bobby called it stubborn; still, it bore the same Smart Start logo on its doors.

Standing next to a Land Rover with New Mexico plates were two men with backs toward me. The backsides, I thought unintentional, until the outfitter's hat and fringed leather jacket announced, ridiculously, the presence of Jamie Thayer of Lucas Construction.

I had to chuckle despite my persistent dislike of the man; today, the man next to Jamie outdid him in audacity. An oversized, beige Stetson hat, complete with a braided brown leather band and tall feather, crowned a self-proclaimed stranger to the west. A cream-colored, gray, yellow, and red, banded Pendleton three-quarter length jacket broadcast the wearer's avoidance of physical labor. His awkward stance announced his brand new, glossy, Tony Lama boots. The kicker, his jeans were Ralph Lauren.

I can see by your cowboy that you are an outfit. All hat, no cattle, I evaluated critically.

The Land Rover was slightly off the drive to the left, close to the old house. Tall, dry grass brushed against its four-wheel-drive hubs.

The proud old structure was tired and no longer stood straight. Maybe it welcomed the prospect of replacement. Green asphalt shingles sided the house while a dented, loose, rusted, formerly galvanized roof ill-protected the interior.

On the far side of the Land Rover, also with New Mexico registration, was a white Econoline van. Several men, with one attractive female who could have been Diné (Navajo), all wore lightweight maroon windbreakers. Making their way past Jamie and his companion, they carried their surveying equipment, a state-of-the-art Zeiss. I would have to ask them about this equipment and maybe get a demonstration to assist my investigation of a suitable technology upgrade for Smart Start.

I recognized the Higgins name and logo, a respected engineering company from Albuquerque. This second group moved toward a Jeep Cherokee, with Colorado tags this time, parked in the most advantageous working location.

It was there that I would find Jeff Teller.

Sociably, I intercepted the engineers.

"Did you see the gold chains on the fancy cowboy?" the girl in the middle of the bunch commented to her companions.

"Yeah," one of the younger surveyors ventured, adding derisively, "and he *smells* like a *flower.*"

"If I had my guess, the swell is the owner's representative. I don't think much of his companion, either," I added.

"And you are?" asked the smiling Diné girl.

"I'm Calvin James," smiling back. "Jeff Teller called me this morning to help with this project. I know next to nothing about it. I know of you guys, though. A friend of mine, Dave Cravath, uses your company to survey for him down in the gas patch. And your name?"

Before chitchat could evolve from our brief comments, a man jaunted toward us, more respectfully and sensibly dressed, but doubtless, not from the southwest. His right hand prepared for handshaking extended from the sleeves of a new Levi jacket. He found my hand first.

"Jeff Teller," he announced with confidence.

"Cal James."

"Thanks again, Cal, for coming on such short notice." He was happily comfortable with his foreign accent.

"Thanks for the invitation," I said, equally comfortable with my adopted, but slight, western drawl. "These folks are your admirable survey crew; they'll have to introduce themselves. I only know them by their great reputation. Do you want to line them out before we chat?"

"If you wouldn't mind waiting a few minutes."

"Not at all."

"This way then." Jeff beckoned them to the Cherokee.

I followed them to the large-format aerial plot maps rolled out on the hood of the Jeep. One by one, each of the survey group craned their necks to see the logo on my truck. The same young man who made the "smells like a flower" observation registered a look of recognition, gave a nod and a discrete thumbs up to his fellows.

While Jeff and his surveyors talked, I studied the property. This house, graced with abundant character, was exceptionally isolated considering its proximity to Durango. It occupied a corner of a vast former pasture, which showed signs of needing a brush hog and irrigation to bring it back. The land sloped away from the house, offering a tranquil view down the Las Animas River Valley.

North of the house was a high rock-strewn ridge, steeply sloped on this side and nearly vertical on the Junction Creek side, broken only by the deep notch I had just driven through.

The San Juan National Forest, treed with evergreen, rose steeply into the La Plata Mountains. If followed, the

Forest Service road, on the other side of the forest boundary, degenerated to a miserable trail in less than a mile. Beyond, it was a challenge to mountain bike and horse alike.

Skunk Creek bordered the pasture on the south, seventy feet below or better. At best, an extremely steep and narrow section where game trails converged limited the access to it; otherwise, the drop into the creek was a vertical rock face, or in places, overhangs worthy of technical rock climbing expertise.

Between the high ridge and Skunk Creek was this hundred acre, gently sloping, once upon a time, pasture. The grassy clearing tapered to the meeting point of the ridge's precipitous slope and the creek's cliff, making the whole plot in the shape of an arrowhead, the narrow tip pointing toward town. A neglected apple and cherry orchard survived in the narrow strip of vegetation between the ridge and the access road.

The location was singular in its limited approachability.

"I'm sorry to keep you waiting." Jeff had sent off his help and the survey crew.

"Not at all; I love this place. It's good to have time to catch my breath and appreciate the space. If I'd known it was for sale, I would have bought it for myself. Look past that thicket of trees toward town; you can see a buck, and I count five deer." I inhaled and exhaled slowly, "You said that you wanted design help?"

"True; here's the situation. The owner, who will remain nameless, initiated this project with my firm six years ago. This location just became available within the last month. The real estate agent has been relentless in finding land that fitted the owner's objective of being easily defensible if you catch my drift. He wants a home, expansive, luxurious, in tune with the natural habitat. He was prepared to purchase land anywhere between El Paso, Texas, and Spokane, Washington, that fit his criteria.

"Money is not a concern. He wanted to entertain guests for long stays, but in-house, not in a carriage house or cabin. He also wants the master bedroom suite on an upper level in a separate wing from the rest of the residence."

"Nice. That mostly satisfies my curiosity and gives me a few hooks."

"Got it." Jeff Teller was a quick study and matter of fact. "I'll pay ten grand for a workable concept and perspective sketches with elevations."

"And to build it?"

"Has to be an open bid." Jeff gave a nod that said, *you know better.*

"Worth a shot," I chuckled. "I assume that my late invitation was due to... complications."

"Perceptive. I want results within a week."

"Preliminary? You write up an intent agreement, then we'll compare notes. I have a newsprint pad in the front of my truck. Let's get together here in forty-five minutes."

"You do justice to your reputation."

For the last comment, Jeff earned, from me, a smile.

§

Jeff, for his part, had boilerplate design agreement forms that weren't too lawyerly. While I skimmed through the legalese, Jeff flipped through my sketches. I lined through a provision requiring dispute resolution to be done through arbitration. Satisfied that I wasn't signing away any other rights that I shouldn't, I attached my signature and handed it back to Jeff for his. Ten grand was not an insignificant take before a third cup of coffee.

"I'll walk you through what I have." I closed the newsprint pad and reopened it to the first-page sketch.

"Let's start with the sitemap. Here's the compass rose. The north face will be nearly parallel to the forest access road, and I've offset the house from a strict north-south orientation for efficient solar gain.

"I've accounted for a separate, fenced, trash disposal area just west, with a short approach to the road. I thought of an outdoor room over here, south of the house, close to the forest. It would be a place to entertain, not connected to the house, and not designed as a living space. Conversations or meetings needing privacy could occur there. Those are the only two detached structures.

"The house concept is expansive with exposed oak post and beam, high cathedral ceilings, and open throughout.

There's lots of ballistic glass, with an eye to passive solar. Metal roofing is over three by four double tongue and groove decking. All the second-floor flooring will be oak over a sprung floor for sound isolation." The sprung floor, a feature of barns in New England, or turn of the century ballrooms, caught Jeff by surprise. "Oversized river-rock accents a native feel."

I flipped the page for the front perspective. The concept, without question, engaged Mr. Teller.

"So, here's the front. Two stories constitute most of the house. The entryway is a grand vaulted ceiling, double glazed glass top to bottom, but only to reveal the foyer with its floor to ceiling, river-rock fireplace and chimney. There are stairs right and left, and a second-floor balcony that looks continuous, but from the south wing, a person will have to go to the foyer on the first floor to get to the north wing. Ground floor, right, will have a library, the second-floor above it, a sitting room. From the balcony, there is secure access to the master suite. To the left of the entryway is the great room that essentially faces south." I turned the newsprint to the next page.

"This is the uninteresting north side; a four-car garage caps the west end toward the forest. This north wing contains the second-floor master suite. From a closet, a walkway through the trusses leads to a concealed spiral staircase accessing the garage. A rabbit hole if you will."

Jeff Teller pensively bit his lower lip as he thought about what kind of character I was attributing to the owner.

"The first floor under the master suite has a game room with billiards, darts, and a wet bar. The south face is mostly double glazed glass; we can discuss the passive solar application. There'll be a full width covered deck, exterior. Inside the great room are exposed post and beam trusses free-spanning the room. The back has a capacious river-rock fireplace flanked by another full-service wet bar. Next to the great room is a formal, closed dining area. Also separated is the kitchen with eating capacity. Over the kitchen and dining area are two second-floor bedroom suites.

"I didn't do the west view. It's well defined by the other three."

Jeff reclaimed control of my drawings and flipped from one page to another. He looked up occasionally to visualize the contents.

"Cal, your drawings capture the owner's requests. You've also included some well-fitting items that the owner didn't specifically ask for."

The jean jacket over the blue pinstripe shirt and blue tie, along with his accent, caused me to chuckle. The fact that Jeff Teller pulled off the look impressed me.

Jeff looked over my shoulder. Distantly, I heard grass giving way to booted feet.

"Cal, quickly, before we have another set of ears. The owner's rep was out on the town last night when he met up with an unsavory fellow who drew up a house plan on the back of a bar napkin. You saw the fashion plate cowboy on your way in, "he smells like a flower." He wants my firm to consider that fellow's scribbles."

"Hey, James," Jamie blustered, swaggering over, "go back to Denver, or wherever it is you go to school at. This thing is all wrapped up."

"On the contrary, Jamie, I've just freed you up to spend more time with the family."

Jamie increased the pace of his last few strides and pushed me back at the shoulders with both hands.

"You and me, James, you and me. We need to settle our differences, right now."

"That's your need. I'm settled." Quick to gain my balance and composure, it would have been easy and gratifying for me to sweep his feet and land him on the ground.

"I see that you two are acquainted." Among Jeff's other appreciable qualities was dry wit. Then addressing Jamie, "Where did your friend get to?"

"I sent him to the woods on a bear's errand."

"Tell him this. I'm using Smart Start Builders' concept and drawings as a basis for design and construction. I will also consult with Smart Start on all design issues."

Jamie lunged at Jeff. I never expected him to make good choices, but he did catch himself midstride, changed trajectory, and flung his sinewy frame at me. I sidestepped. He missed with flailing limbs and flopped past me. I gave him an extra shove to assure he wound up with a face-plant to the ground.

When Jamie sat up, he tossed his perfect hair and began a blue streak of colorful metaphors that would have shriveled a concrete truck. He strode loudly and unhappily back to the Land Rover.

"Your Jamie and the owner's rep are equally heinous. I'm sorry I didn't relate the challenge I was having beforehand. I'm surprised that he didn't go for you again."

"No problem. Jamie and I have a history. I have a reputation for being an obsessed, maybe dirty, fighter that grew out of his and my very first meeting. That's why I asked you about complications. I wish I could say that he was all bark and no bite."

"It's *decidedly* not true about his friend." Jeff displayed an uncommon self-assurance.

"Take care of yourself then, my friend. I have to attend to my schedule. If Smart Start gets the bid award, my business partner, Bobby, an excellent craftsman, would supervise the project. If you need post and beam assistance, call our office and talk to Bobby. He'll put you in touch with the outfit we use out of New Hampshire, close to your neighborhood." Jeff and I shook hands. "Here's my business card; mail me a check for the ideas you use. I've got to run. Thanks for the call, and it's been a pleasure meeting you."

"Likewise. I'll be calling. It'll be a week before I have formal drawings developed. That's a week better than I was planning. I'll send you a copy to see if we have it right. You take care."

"Hey, Jeff, if you're in town this evening, I'll be back at my office at five. We could chat over dinner at the Ore House?"

"I'd love to, Cal, but my flight's out at two." Jeff shrugged. "Next time."

§§

CHAPTER 35

As my first act as an official University of Colorado Senior, with all courses scheduled, I stooped to pick up a stray Almond Joy wrapper that campus maintenance had missed. For my second act, I judged my ability to strike up a fruitful, relationship-building conversation with a pretty girl.

This pretty girl had longer than shoulder length wavy brown hair, parted right, smiling eyes, and high cheekbones accentuated by a sun-blessed complexion. Beautiful without makeup, shapely and fit, she lent style to her pale-green-and-white-striped sleeveless top, khaki shorts, and low cut Merrell hiking shoes. She sat on a landscape rock situated on the most direct route from me to my car.

I wasn't usually a socially calculating guy. My calculations were mostly engineering in nature.

Not a snowball's chance in the nether regions, Cal. She's beautiful. At the very least, she's in a committed relationship, more likely engaged, or married, was my underbreath assumption. *Forget it before you embarrass yourself.*

Chance, imputed to a snowball or not, was insistent, unrelenting. The notion had sprouted a life of its own, flourishing undeterred by my estimation of likely failure. I was fated to make the attempt.

The grounds crew had, hours ago, mowed the CU Boulder quad leaving the scent of fresh-cut grass, just the lift I needed to spur me on.

Unlike some girl in a photograph or movie, this live version could, at any moment, see me looking at her. A split second's worth of no thanks on her part, and it would be over before it began.

My first line?

"Hey." ingenious in simplicity, popped out of my mouth before I could reel it back.

"Hey." was her surprisingly simple response.

Her delivery, so even-keeled, so without a hint of do I know you, caused me to do a double-take, perhaps I'd known or seen her for years and artlessly not recognized her, maybe a hairstyle was different or a style of clothing?

"*Lavori con questi ragazzi?*" (You work with these guys?) She asked, indicating the grounds crew with a look. Her voice was ariose, good-humored, and flirty.

She initiated, engaged in, and directed our conversation all in one fell, social swoop; her eye contact was unwavering. There was no condescension, associating me with the maintenance folks. Her question was honest and put me on the defensive. Practiced. A good-looking girl would quickly, and very ably, discard unwanted advances.

"*No..., non lavoro con loro.*" (No..., no, I don't.) Except for their coveralls, it would have been easy to mistake me for one of the workers.

Reminiscence smote me.

"*Sto andando al negozio di biciclette. Ti interessa venire con me?*" Finally, I recognized that we were conversing in Italian.

"I'm headed over to the bicycle shop. Would you like to join me?" I repeated, apparently translating for myself.

"Sure," she acceded, adding with a sincere smile, "You're fluent in Italian. I like that."

She leaped up with surprising agility, fairly dismounting from the rock as a balance beam gymnast might have done.

"But, you'll have to explain your hat to a nice Catholic girl, like me, on the way." Emphasized with the slightest touch to my shoulder, she pointed openhanded toward my head.

I had to take my hat off, literally, to see what I had to explain to this nice Catholic girl. I'd left in the dark this morning and had grabbed anything convenient; of course, it was my Ski Purgatory hat, complete with lipstick script.

Defensive still, but now I had humor and Italian on my side, exactly where this girl had relegated them. I donned my hat and adjusted the visor to the right spot.

"Let me drop this stuff off in my car," pointing with my hat's brim, past the rock, "and I'll explain the hat."

The loose-leaf notebook and yellow legal pad had already served their purposes for the day. An impossible spot to get during the school year, I'd parked close to Old Main, a central campus location convenient for the errands I had set out to run.

Optimism lapsed briefly as I wondered how short a time it would be before I had added her to the long and growing list of people I have lied to. I'd never wanted to lie to them. *Would nanoseconds be the measuring unit?* For me, it was the bane of witness protection. Always a dreaded, and 99.44 percent chance of disappointment.

We didn't walk quickly. She listened to the pitiful trickle of a stream that ran through this part of the campus. Elm leaves mottled sunlight and shade. *Sole e ombra.* The grass was well-trimmed but dry. Obscured through the trees was a small stone arch bridge, unused in the undergrowth. I'd never investigated how to get to it, but her glance toward it made me wonder why.

"Purgatory," I continued our conversation, "is a ski area just north of Durango, in southwest Colorado. It's about 350 miles and about five hours away. Durango's my summer home. Dressing in the dark this morning should explain my appearance. I came up early because I needed to change one of my classes before the start of the semester."

"Purgatory can't be the name of a ski area; you're pulling my leg." She gave me an, *I'll be terminally annoyed with you if you think that I'm that dumb,* expression.

"Yeah, oxymoron-ish, but I'm not kidding. I love skiing there; you would, too. You ski, don't you? It's a beautiful area, unpretentious, with lots of lifts and lots of vertical drop. Its name comes from Purgatory Creek that runs through it.

"Purgatory Creek starts at the top of the ski area and drops two thousand feet in elevation. Beginning to end, it's only three miles, with half a mile of it being a section called Purgatory Flats.

"Conventional lore on how the creek was named has to do with a trail that follows it from the Flats to Cascade Creek a half-mile and nine hundred feet lower in elevation.

179

The saying goes, 'Easy to get in, a lot of hard work to get out, just like Purgatory.' And that, as they say, is a long way to go for a nickel candy bar."

"So when you say 'Ski Purgatory,' what you're saying is that a snowball does have a chance in the nether regions." She laughed, a good omen.

I was thinking of the same euphemism just a few minutes before and similarly toned down. It was a straight out sign.

"Okay, ask any question about me that you want to."

"Let me tell you what I know about you first, tell me where I'm wrong, then I'll take you up on your question."

"What is it you imagine that you know about me?"

I conjured an imaginary audience and gestured to them.

"Ladies and gentlemen, this beautiful and charming lady and I have never been introduced. You affirm that we have never been introduced prior to five minutes ago."

"That is true. We're not even introduced yet," she followed in step, addressing our cooperatively imagined audience.

I closed my eyes, feigned a swami pose for dramatic effect, one hand outstretched into the air, fingers spread apart, wrist cocked, palm pressed forward.

"You... are a short notice senior transfer... you like CU because it makes you feel more at home than another campus might. The last time you saw a symphony orchestra, the men wore white tuxedos. Hmm..., and..., you drove..., a '91 green Ford Explorer before you came here."

"My, aren't you Sir Arthur Conan Doyle. You are very close. A little short on the reason for coming to the University; otherwise, you are spot on. My name is Amy, Amy Farina. Tell me how you did that."

"I'm Calvin James. I'll tell you how, but first, here's a question to test your powers of observation. Which one of these vehicles is mine? It's a trick question, and it's in addition to your promise that I can ask any question of you because this one is about me."

We were stopped in front of an '86 light blue 4Runner, not recently washed, next to it my clean metallic green Volkswagen Corrado, and next to that, a blue '87 GMC Sierra pickup.

"It's the VW." No pause, no confusion, only a *this is so absurdly simple,* grin on her face. Her expressions were thoroughly diverting.

"I deserved that," I said with a good-natured shrug, "I do have a 4Runner for the mountains here in Boulder, and I have an '86 Sierra at my other home in Durango for work. Tell me how you knew, then I'll tell you how I came to my conclusions about you."

"You said just a minute ago that you wanted to put your stuff in your... car. For confirmation, if I needed it, you said that Durango was 350 miles and only five or so hours away. You could do that in a 4Runner or a Chevy pickup, but better done in a Corrado. Sweet car." Already her smile was becoming infectious.

Across the street from Old Main was Varsity Lake, a pretentiously named small pond, home to ducks and geese. It reflected another well-used, street-width stone arch bridge with multiple arches. Two couples and an individual of indeterminate gender strolled across it. In a week, both clued in, and clue-free students would crowd that bridge. What good fortune I had to have encountered this intelligent, delightful, engaging, attractive, bilingual lady today. It wouldn't have happened a week from now, misplaced in crowds of students.

A hint of a breeze rustled dried leaves on the pavement in front of us. I stole an admiring glance at Amy Farina when I opened the driver's side door. I placed my books on the back seat.

"I did say car, didn't I? Okay, I will now reveal my Sherlockian prowess.

"Let's come back to my first guess since you say I was only close on that. My second was, 'The last time you saw a symphony orchestra, the musicians wore white tuxedos.'

"Speech wise, you have a slight but distinctly New England accent with an Italian influence. It's not Brahman Bostonian, not down east Maine, not New Hampshirite, not Vermont, at least not upper Vermont, potentially Rhode Island, but not Connecticut. Western Massachusetts accents borrow more from northern neighbors. There's upstate New York in there, too. Therefore, I say you're from the Berkshires.

"Your last symphony would have been the Boston Pops at Tanglewood this summer. The Boston Symphony Orchestra wears white tuxedos when they play the Pops."

"That was wonderfully Sherlockian, with a dash of Mister 'Iggins. Please continue."

We resumed our walk toward the bike shop along Pleasant Street.

"My third guess was, 'You drove a green '91 Ford Explorer before you came out here.' Don't take me wrong, but evidence points to your being financially sufficient. You're doing a last-minute transfer, so you can cover the cost of out of state tuition. There's a Yale lock key hanging out of your back pocket. The University only outfits its buildings with Schlage locks, so you're staying off-campus, confirming upperclassman status. Your hands say that you are industrious. That's part one.

"Eddie Bauer is part two. I get their catalogs, too, great stuff. The top you're wearing, I liked, when I saw it buried about page ten or twelve in the summer edition, although you're better looking than the girl who modeled it. Your shorts are Eddie Bauer, and the Merrells that you're wearing could have easily come from Eddie Bauer."

"It's a good thing I changed into comfortable clothes," Amy interrupted, "I usually dress up when I fly. This morning I was wearing a skirt, a nice blouse, heels, the whole shot. But, you're right. I do adore my Eddie Bauer."

"If I thought that highly of Eddie Bauer, and were able to, I'd get myself one of those new Eddie Bauer Explorer packages Ford offered this year. They're green."

"I did test drive the EB package before I came here, but I didn't like the driver's under knee support. Yes, I drove a green '91 Ford Explorer." Amy flashed a smile. "I can be rough on vehicles. I need durability. I ended up with a Land Rover instead. It's green. And, I will call you Sherlock unless you have a nickname that you would prefer."

She appreciated the unpressed attention, smiling playfully and casually swinging her arms. We walked on.

"Call me 'Cal.'"

182

It was nice here under the umbrella of shade trees. The trees and shrubs on both sides of the street made it seem secluded as we approached Broadway. However, I began to hear automobiles and motorcycles. Broadway is a heavily trafficked street, and when the semester starts, university students mob across it recklessly from the campus to the University Hill shops and restaurants.

"Conclusion one was a stretch anyway," I allowed a little show of deflation, "but I wildly guessed you to have attended Wellesley. Resources, Massachusetts, Catholic, female. Charles Klauder set up design specifications for the University of Colorado buildings. He also designed some buildings at Wellesley.

"Hold on, wait a second. I didn't say that the reason you transferred was that CU made you feel at home. I said you liked CU because it made you feel at home."

This day was going so enormously better than I could have expected. We were almost to the Broadway traffic light and crosswalk. Overhanging shrubs from a landscaped "shrub island" retained by a raised, fitted stonewall, prevented an open view to the left. The shade had given way to bright sunshine; wavy heat rose from the highway north, distorting the distant automobiles.

"Very nicely done. I am... I was a Wellesley student. I'm very impressed. A different carrot and stick got me here, though. The stick, I had a stalker. This pervert introduced himself to me less than a week ago, walked up to me on campus after a summer evening class, told me his name was Lance Grimaldi and expected me to go to dinner with him so he could propose marriage. He said that! Creep! And he said that he had been watching me for the last eight years. Sick, I mean when I was thirteen-years-old. Really? The whole thing was demented and revolting. Not much gets to me, but I was petrified; I knew right then that I would transfer to some other college, far away, for my senior year.

"The carrot is a course in mathematical anthropology. A friend, Amalia Montoya-Aragon, she's a professor at Wellesley, referred me to CU, just minutes after I ran away from my stalker. Mathematical anthropology is going to be the topic of my thesis. A former student of hers is teaching a class here."

The face that I had been enjoying for the last ten minutes, with its perpetual smile, suspended over a perfectly narrow chin, and happy hazel eyes that had taken on a fiery green, for the briefest moment, when she stood next to my Corrado, was abruptly flooded with panic.

I snapped my neck to see what she was looking at.

From behind the obscuring shrubs came a fast walking man, clean-shaven, with longish dark hair, lawyerly in appearance without the suit coat. He wore a gray pinstripe shirt with a bold red tie, pleats in his creased, cuffed slacks, and black patent leather shoes with white vamps. Distinctly, not from Boulder.

I was paying attention to the object he clenched in his right hand, extended toward me.

"*Ohimè*, Calvin," Amy squeaked, recoiling in loathing. She took both my elbows from behind, turning me toward the stranger. "This is the sleazeball who's been stalking me."

"You know why they call me Lance, mister smart college kid?" addressing me. "It's because of my stiletto."

Lance sprung his blade with a melodramatic wave.

It was a high-quality knife, probably new. Lance didn't appear to be the knife-sharpening or knife-wielding kind of guy. His stiletto did have all the appearances, unlike its owner, of being razor-sharp. It wasn't that he looked particularly unintelligent, but automobiles were whizzing by us, and in seconds, the traffic light would change, providing a whole line of cars containing potential witnesses to whatever fool-thing he might do. Not only that, two of us knew his name.

He crouched several feet from me and lunged, arresting in its cliché and covering only a third of the gap between us.

I stepped toward him onto the sidewalk and motioned with my opened hand for Amy to move to a spot well behind me from which she could run.

It was a multiple *déjà vu* experience. My friend, Kirkland, had me help him with a very similar scene in his play. He had written, produced, and performed *Jet Girls* last spring. We had gone over and over the blocking for a *mano a mano*, Weaponless Guy versus Stiletto Guy for weeks. Fortunately, in Kirkland's play, Stiletto Guy loses Weaponless Guy wins.

Lance was making an invocation to fear.

Amy gathered herself up, uncertain of my ability to shield her.

"This little friend of mine is going in my trophy room right after I gut you with it right here. You're messing with the destiny of the wrong guy. She's mine. Amy's mine. She's my destiny." Lance emphasized "my," "mine," and "destiny" in his unmistakable accent, stereotypically JFK.

He lunged once more and came up short again.

Stepping back, I sensed the curb's edge. I gabbed to annoy and ridicule this Bostonian rube.

"Did you know the stiletto gets its name from the Latin word stylus? A stylus is a writing instrument scribes used to make linguistic impressions in clay tablets. That stiletto that you're holding is OTF, isn't it?" Seeing a hint of puzzlement at 'OTF,' I clarified, "OTF is short for out the front. Who's the maker?"

Lance only glared, confounded at my homily.

"You know Lance, a stiletto's strategic advantage is that the blade is concealed within the handle then spring launched, without a thrust, into the intended victim. Like, pressed up against the ribs, or neck, or abdomen." I illustrated the placements with my hand on my body, then opened both hands toward him, palms up. "What you have now is just a sharp knife. So what's all this? Bad strategy and bad form are what this is."

The fear Lance had invited didn't attend our dance.

Amy glared, openmouthed, incredulous at the theater playing out in front of her.

If Lance held true to form, his third thrust would be intended to draw blood.

§

The construction trades had offered me multiple opportunities to be a recipient of confrontational behavior, which included defending against actual or improvised weapons.

Items that frequently became weapons on the jobsite were cutting tools, knives, rock saws, framing axes, but the less obvious could be the most insidious. Concrete finishers inadvertently sharpened and honed their trowel blades when they hand-finished floors. Concrete with its abrasive sand and aggregates hone the steel trowels as finishers work to seal the surface, much as one would steel a butcher's knife.

I recalled my first hostile encounter on the job with Robert... Bobby, I was seventeen, nineteen, if you looked at my license. It was experience gained at the cost of twenty-four stitches and self-confrontation with an ugly, volatile, violent side of myself that I hadn't known existed. Knowledge of that brutality was a dark place that still haunted me, but nice to know I could summon that brutality, not so nice if it summoned me.

After that fight, I had educated myself in the use of a shovel, keeping the one I used sharp enough to cut sod easily and practiced its versatility, as a stave, to swat, to thrust, and as a means of vaulting. Lacrosse like, I could be infernally accurate, hurling rocks with precision and ample force to command attention.

It was advantageous to have firsthand experience, even if I didn't have a shovel.

§

Third lunge.

I stepped backward off the unbusy, Pleasant Street curb and leaned back. Lance matched his slashing trajectory to my step down. Twisting, I grabbed the wrist of his knife hand with my left hand reaching across my body. Lance managed a slice to my palm in the process and produced a moderate amount of blood; regardless, I pulled him forward while turning toward him to displace his knife thrust. Lance lurched clumsily off the curb.

My rotation continued so that our right sides were adjacent. Lance fell, face first, into the pavement while I landed on my back with Lance's arm trapped under me. My grip remained solid on his wrist, which still clutched the positionally harmless stiletto. My right elbow, positioned at the base of his skull, drove his forehead scraping into the asphalt. Not only did I hear the thud of his forehead recoil; I also heard the satisfying sound of joint cavitation in his shoulder... loud, deep in tone. The unusual coiling of his arm and the added weight of my torso had dislocated his right shoulder.

Lance screeched an incoherent howl of rage and pain as the knife sprung from his hand and clattered away.

I regained my feet and retrieved his weapon, which had traveled a foot or two. I checked my wound. It was still bleeding, but not severely.

Amy was horrified at the brief, injurious altercation.

Lance attempted to get up.

A police car rounded the corner onto Pleasant Street with lights flashing to prevent any automotive addition to any injuries. The officer disembarked, weapon at the ready.

"Hello, Peter," I greeted casually, "what took you so long?"

"Hello, Cal, everything okay here?" Peter looked his fittest in his uniform. He was muscular, confident, and on top of any situation. Humor and seriousness reflected in his Japanese American face.

"Timing is everything. Sure, we're fine." I helped Lance up, right hand grasping right hand. I twisted his arm. Brutal, I know. His facial contortion confirmed his painful dislocation. My hand came around his back and under his left armpit leaving a bloody smear on his shirt, no harm in seeing if he was carrying concealed.

I shook my head, *no*, to Peter, who was observing my surreptitious pat-down.

"Lance, let me pop that shoulder back in." Without waiting for approval, I slipped my forearm under his armpit, pressed his elbow into his side, and released it quickly.

Lance shrieked again as his shoulder reset.

"Peter, this is Lance. He's from Boston. He caught Kirkland's play last week. He knew that I had worked to develop the stiletto theatrics and wanted to see if I would show him what we had done. Theatrical." I pressed the knife's release button, moved the blade in and out, and handed it back to Lance, protracted.

His rage, so scarcely contained, was glorious.

"This is Amy who, coincidentally, is from Massachusetts too, and my great pleasure to have met not fifteen minutes ago. Amy, this is Officer Peter Nori."

"Amy, I'm pleased to meet you. Lance." Peter was all curiosity.

"I saw you at the play with Rachel." I was still sociable. "She had quite a lot to say to Kirkland afterward. I hope it was all positive."

"Sure was. She loved it." He looked at Amy, then at Lance. "These guys coming to your party this evening?"

"Lance needs to go back to Boston. I hadn't asked Amy yet. Amy, I am having a party at my house later, do you want to come?"

Lance evaluated whether he could walk away; his egalitarian facade was shredded. Although he stood, his honor and bravado remained in the gutter. Scuffed shoes, knees rent out of his slacks, shirt with dirt ground in, a spectacularly abraded forehead, completed a total alteration of his appearance. He tried to restore his perfect hair to no avail.

"Peter," I asked, "would you take care of Lance's damages for me? I didn't know that I would get him all messed up, and I need to get Amy somewhere else. Sorry, Lance."

Peter would be okay with the separation I had requested. I'd relayed what I knew.

The walk light had come up. I waved my bloody hand at Peter. My uninjured hand took Amy's while we ran across the street, letting go once we were across. I didn't want to release her hand, but now, I reasoned, was not the time to hold on.

"Party! How can you ask me to a party after, during that?" Amy exploded. Her nerves were a pincushion. Her facial expression changed from relief to anger, to confusion, to frustration. Her hands were on her hips unless they were flailing in the direction of the Lance altercation. She didn't know one emotion to hold onto.

"Easy," although I was short of breath. "You promised I could ask you any question I wanted to. I never got to ask it."

Amy almost choked on a burst of laughter.

Good. I thought. *Endorphins.*

"Let me sell you on coming." We walked again. "This year will be the fourth that I've hosted a back to school party at my house. It's tradition, and you can't argue with tradition. By my estimation, over the years, it's been a beneficial and entertaining get together.

"The party is by invitation only. The invitation is good to one degree of separation. Each of my invitees can invite one person. I'll have forty to fifty people this year," I rambled purposefully, "so I either know my guests or who invited them."

"We start at five, although you can show up anytime. I do the steaks, potatoes, salad, and beverages. Bring a side dish if you want." I tried to gauge Amy's reaction. "I don't allow underage alcohol consumption. Not to worry, right? Peter and his wife will be there."

Amy was speechless, not that I had given her much opportunity to respond. I could tell that unless not talking was a conscious decision on her part, she wasn't accustomed to it.

"Let's go to the café," I placed my hand on the small of her back to direct her, "and get you settled down. The bike shop is right next door."

§§

CHAPTER 36

Officer Nori was glad for the diversion from his routine patrolling of Boulder. Without the CU student population in full attendance, there was little challenge to ferreting out the community's misdeeds.

Peter always appreciated Cal's intriguing and varied topics of conversation, finding, inevitably, that he could learn something. Today's clash, though, was not Cal's standard operating procedure.

Directing his newly acquired ward to the back seat of his cruiser's passenger side, Officer Nori rechecked his sidearm to assure that it remained secure. He then disengaged a first aid kit from its mount in the front seat, pulling out latex gloves, disinfectant wipes, and bandages.

Lance still suffered from overall body trauma. His shoulder pained him, and he was unable to keep quiet about it.

Peter spoke first.

"Drivers license, please."

"Are you arresting me? I'll have a lawyer on you so fast your head will spin. You cops are all the same." Lance surprised himself with the glaring conclusion to his last opinion and chided himself for being so off his game. He could grease this cop.

"Calm down, sir; you're injured and not yourself."

Peter addressed all minors as a young man or young lady; nonminors always received sir or ma'am. He had received flack on occasion for doing it, but he maintained that it gave him an additional margin of control over a situation.

"My driver's license is in here." Lance held out his wallet.

"Remove your license from the wallet and hand it to me."

"Yes, sir, Officer Nori."

Lance ignored Peter's first refusal, folded a hundred dollar bill behind his license, and handed it to Peter.

Peter took the license by its edges, another self-imposed custom. Circumstance might warrant a lift of prints, and he wouldn't inadvertently accept anything in addition to the ID. The C-note floated to the ground at Lance's feet. Peter didn't avert his attention from the license and made no mention of the fallen bill.

In exchange for the ID, Lance received antiseptic wipes, a small mirror, Tylenol, and an unopened bottle of Arrowhead Springs.

"In my experience, you'll avoid a lot of discomfort if you're the one to clean up your forehead. The inside of your arm could use attention, too. Here's gauze, and if you need help taping on bandages, let me know." Peter apprised his vexing passenger. "I'll need to radio this in."

"You know, I really don't need this. I'll have a lawyer here in a heartbeat. You can't hold me."

Peter chuckled to himself from the driver's seat.

"The door's open, you're not in cuffs, you've had no Miranda reading, and the one person who can file a complaint against you has left. Consider yourself lucky, also pick up the trash that you dropped, or I will arrest you for littering.

"Protocol," Peter continued, "is that I radio in an incident. The ID check is routine to see if you have any outstanding warrants. If you have any in Colorado, then I'll hold you, and then you can have your lawyer."

Lance picked up his hundred, reinserted it in his wallet, and scrubbed. Each groan, ouch, and flinch received a corresponding quiet snicker or muffled chuckle from the cruiser's front seat.

After lifting clean prints from the license, Peter cleaned it up without Lance observing and then conversed briefly with dispatch.

"How long have you been in Colorado?"

"Since this morning." was Lance's dull reply.

"Been in Boulder before?"

"No."

"We won't be able to use those answers in a court of law." Peter gauged Lance's almost nonexistent response. "To make up for your introduction to Boulder, sir, let me take you to a men's clothing store I know of. They can't match your shirt's tailoring or your slack's for price or prep time, but this shop does pretty well on quality. I wouldn't want to put you on a plane looking abused, and it's my treat.

"Should I FedEx your stiletto to the address on your license?"

Lance began to boil again. He wasn't exactly sure how Peter had maneuvered him into it, but he felt that he was being run out of town. In truth, Peter was personally running him out of town, and he'd call ahead to have the Massachusetts State Police confiscate the knife when FedEx delivered it.

Peter was acquiescing to Cal's wishes. He replayed the incident in his mind.

Cal had reason to suspect that this well-dressed adult punk might be carrying. He had cleverly concealed his pat-down and the smearing of his blood on Lance's shirt. Peter knew that Lance had not seen Kirkland's play performance last spring. Lance's admission to being a first time visitor to Boulder clinched that. Therefore the quarrel was real, not improv theater.

Cal had shown Peter the stiletto but had indicated his desire for Lance to keep the knife. He handed it back to Lance. Don't complicate his immediate departure with a complaint?

The altercation had been spontaneous and spurred by conflicting designs on the girl, Amy, who needed protection. Maybe the relationship between Lance and Amy stemmed from some connection in Massachusetts. Speculative, highly probable.

"Lance needs to go back home." Cal had said. How clear was that? Lance needed to go.

"Amy, I'm having a party at my house later, do you want to come?" True, Cal had met her fifteen minutes ago. He knew her well enough to aggressively defend her, though. This was a bit of a puzzle that he could straighten out later.

"Take care of Lance's damages," fix up his wounds, yes. "Damages" rather than "injuries." Replace his damaged clothes. Keep the ruined ones for evidence. Pay for Lance's flight to Logan? He thought so. Otherwise, why would Cal have slipped him his credit card?

"I need to get Amy across the street." Amy and Lance require separation to avoid further unpleasantness. "Somewhere else." Cal

doesn't even know where this girl lives... yet. Peter chuckled to himself, seeing a bond forming between the two already.

"Sorry, Lance." That was no apology. It was a challenge.

"Sorry, Lance, you lose." This was not how Calvin James operated. The confrontation probably jacked Cal up. He had the girl. At least she was willing to take his hand when they crossed the street.

Peter would have probing questions of his close friend, Mr. James, this evening.

§§

CHAPTER 37

The café's wide pine plank steps were three inches thick, ten feet long, and about halfway to another dark brown paint job, the treads with exposed, light wood grain noticeably smoothed. The railings were rustic and painted with the same dark brown paint. A well-worn deck, with umbrella-garnished tables, was ready for replacement too.

"The outside is rocky. The inside is a lot nicer." I said by way of apology.

"Like you?" Amy's intent was unfathomable. She had maintained a measured distance between us from the traffic light on Broadway to here, shivering occasionally. Any attempt to reassure her with an arm around her shoulder would have been designedly awkward, unlike our casual stroll before seeing Grimaldi.

The door, I held open for her. It was part of the café's recent interior remodel with thick beveled glass, frosted border design, framed in light oak, incongruous with the exterior.

Inside, the display cases were new, with chromed steel and bent glass. The owners had the old, worn oak floor entirely replaced and newly finished. The walls had shed their cluttered appearance, repaired and repainted above the chair rail and wainscoting. In good taste, the remodeling contractor left the ancient fans hanging six feet from the ceiling, replacing the old blades with transparent Plexiglas. Stylish track lighting provided brilliant illumination. The renovation's best, untouched part was the sixteen-foot high, stamped tin ceiling. True charm.

I would have been proud of the results if my crews had done the work. There was much to appreciate in what the new owners had done.

We slipped into opposite sides of the only vacant booth toward the back, where I had a line of sight to the door. I had great faith in Peter's abilities, especially to take care of that despicable jackass. Still, I was on edge myself.

Immediately our waitress greeted us. The wait staff was mostly intact from the time before the new owners and their remodel, so was the menu. I considered both to be our good fortune.

"Do you have a city medium roast coffee? An exotic bean that we could get iced?"

"Is Jamaican Blue Mountain exotic enough? We fresh roasted it early this morning from coffee berries that came in yesterday. It's a full city roast, but I guarantee it's tasty." This waitress I recognized from times last year when I had become frequent in my visits. She had beautiful brown mid-tone skin. Indigo Levis, with a light blue button-down short sleeve Oxford shirt bearing the café logo, was the approved apparel. Her nametag said, 'Camilla.'

"That sounds perfect, Camilla. Two talls. For Amy here, let's have a bocconotto. For me, biscotti, anise if you have it."

Camilla sped off.

Conversations throughout the café amplified into a cacophony aided by the reflective ceiling and fan blades. The patrons, housewives, lawyers, hippies, trust fund kids with their unkempt appearance, and respectably dressed, less well-off, resident students, all had disparate interests and dialogs.

"Thank you, Cal. I'm sorry I blew up at you back there on the street corner." Amy's breathing was more regular as she regained her composure. "I do feel better now, sitting down. I hardly know you, and you hardly know me, but you definitely could have been hurt by that maniac. I'm confused. Why didn't you let that police officer know what happened? We left without you saying anything."

"Apology accepted, but unnecessary. Peter, Officer Nori, is an intelligent guy, on track for the FBI, smarter than most of the grad students at the university, and a great friend, and I told him a lot more than what you heard.

"Lance will be on a plane to Boston this afternoon, my treat. Peter will have Lance's shirt with my blood on it, as evidence, without your stalker even knowing what happened. He knows that you and Lance have a history based in Boston." I watched the comely cogs of reason mesh behind Amy's eyes.

Two glasses of ice water had materialized at our table, along with a couple of cloth napkins wrapped around forks and spoons.

"I have more questions." Amy stared across the table at me, her hazel eyes once again delving into my character. "That was a proficient takedown. You didn't seem at all phased by the whole thing; I mean, you were carrying on a stinkin' intelligent conversation with him, albeit one-sided. What's up with that?"

"*Ho preso la miglior decisione in una brutta situazione.*" (I made the best decision in a bad situation.)

"*Che è* Kirkland?"

"Kirkland, you can meet this evening if you decide to come along to my party. He's a playwright and grad student. Loves to act, and he does improv at a LoDo comedy club in Denver. He has a dinner gig there tonight. Very immersed in the thespian culture. He wrote a play based on two minor characters in *West Side Story*, and he's had hints of off-Broadway interest in it. He asked me to help him choreograph a knife fight. Did you know that there is a whole theatric or cinematic profession called fight choreography? Anyway, he couldn't afford a professional. What you saw was almost an exact replay.

"Was I affected? Yeah. Differently. It has to do with experience, that's what Kirkland wanted to tap, and it has to do with my personal philosophy. Not to brag on myself, I do construction management and consulting, but I started my career at the working end of a shovel. Since then, I've been the hostile focus of more than my fair share of unhappy co-workers and rivals."

My fair companion's face flickered with controlled alternation between curiosity and study, discerning how sincere and truthful I was. As her eyes searched my own, her jaw relaxed. I could see trust prevailing in the slightest turn of her head, and the tension that had concentrated in her shoulders melted away.

"Philosophically, I prefer endorphins over adrenalin. It's a conscious choice between the two most of the time. Mr.

Lance intended to instill fear, so I mocked him. Having fun keeps my thought processes clearer. I experience less fight or flight and realize more options and more control over my actions." I enjoyed Amy's presence while she considered and dissected my answer.

Coffee and pastries arrived, artfully, unobtrusively.

"*Questo bocconotto è meraviglioso.* (This bocconotto is wonderful.)

"Fight choreography, you say?" Amy pondered the thought. A raised eyebrow revealed that her inner conflict was passing, and she was nearing playfulness once more. "Are all your friends like Peter and Kirkland?"

"You can find out for yourself. Are you coming to my party? I hope you will."

"Yes. Okay. I'll be there. Where is your place, and how do I get there?" Her feigned exasperation attested to growing confidence.

"I'll show you on a bike trail map when we go next door. My new Trek is ready, and I'll want to ride it home. I still have party prep work to do, too."

"Maybe I'd better have a look at your hand." Amy flagged Camilla. "Do you have a first aid kit I could use?"

With great care, she attended to my cut palm. Her touch, light as if she held a kitten, was anesthetic. My mouth went so dry that I couldn't speak, and the back of my neck tingled. This was magic. I didn't even notice the Betadine sting.

"This cut is worthy of stitches. The butterflies will hold if you're not too strenuous over the next couple of weeks. If you don't promise, I'll suture it up right now." Amy stroked my palm, a tactile check of my calluses. Her mused smile spread.

No way could she mistake how her hand's caress was silk to my soul.

The same way our water and setups had arrived, our finished pastry plates and now empty iced coffees disappeared. I made sure that the tab disappeared, and a good tip remained.

§

Thomas stepped up from the back of the bike shop when he heard the bell on the door, pivoted without a word when he saw me and headed to the storeroom.

"I'll get your bike," he hollered over his shoulder.

Amy turned aside to the bicycle display racks, targeting the *celeste* (*che-el-estè*, light blue) Bianchis.

Judy, the shop's longtime salesperson, wound her way through racks of apparel to where Amy was standing.

"My name's Judy. Can I help you with a bicycle?"

"Sure. I don't see the bike I want on the rack. What I want is a Bianchi Mondiale, but I need a 54 cm frame."

"Let me see if we have a bare frame in the back. If we do, we'll have to build your bike. I don't know if we have all the stock parts, though."

"That's fine with me. I have ideas on the components anyway. Do you have a Dura-Ace HyperGlide 8 speed cassette, 12/23, and their 39/52 chainring? I'd like a Shimano 600 STI shifter to go with that, and how about Campagnolo Croce d'Aune pedals?"

"Nice, sure. That's a great set up! I'll ask Tom how soon we could get that done. You must ride a wee bit."

"Avid, yeah, distance rides, centuries. My name's Amy, by the way."

"You've hooked up with the right guy, Amy. Cal gets out and puts on the miles. He rides like something's trying to get out of him, or he's chasing something he'll never catch."

"Thanks, Judy. I only met him an hour ago. He's different, affable, and he's already been my guardian angel. He bought me coffee next door and invited me to a party that he's having this evening.

"The first thing he said when we met was, 'I'm going over to the bike shop. Would you like to join me?' Who was I that I could resist?"

"You'll like him a lot. He's good to a whole bunch of folks. He's decent and hangs with a fun, smart crowd. Good people."

"But? I can hear a 'but.'"

"Yeah. Only because you asked; I think it's a dark, sad thing. Nobody but Cal knows for sure. Don't get too deep into his past, especially about his parents, because he gets weird. I've heard that he has a violent reputation in Durango. Someone from there described him as composed as a claymore. You surely didn't hear that from me. He's very particular about who and how he relates to people. You'll like him, and I have never seen anything in him even close to what I've heard. I've only known him to be kind and wise beyond his age. If I were you, I'd take him up on the party invitation. Tom and I will be there."

"Thanks, Judy."

"I'll be right back with an estimate of time and outlay."

Amy pondered Judy's description of Cal while she continued to look over the hanging frames. The image of Cal taking down the stiletto-wielding Lance with self-assurance and ease was not one that she would *ever* forget.

§

"Hi, Judy." I walked up to the pair with my new Trek.

"Hi, Cal. Your friend, Amy, has your tastes in bike gear, Dura-Ace, STI, and Campagnolo." Judy headed toward the back.

"True? Check this out." I was excited, waving my well cared for and bandaged, open hand up and down my new Trek. "Here's a thing, too. Shimano has a license to manufacture the Look pedals and cleats now. Tom talked me out of Campagnolo a couple of weeks ago and recommended these."

"Except for the Trek frame, yeah, and the pedals, what you have is what I spec'd out to Judy."

As Judy crunched numbers in the back, I found a Boulder bike trail map on the cluttered counter. I traced the best route from the bike shop to my house with a highlighter as Amy looked on.

Judy arrived with the numbers. The Bianchi wouldn't be ready until Saturday morning. Amy settled with Judy for the deposit and made the change to Look pedals.

"I'll walk you back to my car."

"But my house is back this way, past the cemetery. I've only toted in my luggage and changed from my travel get up to comfortable clothes."

"Right. I forgot. Not I forgot where you live, because I don't know where that is. It's I forgot I wanted to ask a favor of you. Would you take my car and bring it when you come to the party? You can use it if you need to run any errands."

"*Sei pazzo.*" (You're crazy.) "Take your car?"

"*Chiavi.*" (Keys.) I fished in my pocket. "Here."

§

On the walk back to the Old Main parking, Amy questioned me about store locations, to purchase hardware, kitchenware, natural foods, groceries, furniture, and where to get gas. She confided to me all her secretive college transfer arrangements and her undercover bolt to the Albany, New York airport. She wanted to know about the Colorado climate and if I knew everyone in town.

"*Com'è che tu parli italiano così bene?*" (How do you speak Italian so well?) It was a venture on Amy's part.

"*Io guardo video in lingua italiana. Un amico, per il quale ho costruito una casa a Durango, me li manda dall'Italia.*" (I watch Italian language videotapes from Italy. A friend, who I built a house for in Durango, sends them.)

I was thankful that we were discussing Calvin James' past.

Our casual stroll tranquilly contrasted with the banter and altercation earlier. My Trek's hub ratchet provided its minimal click for accompaniment. The felt need to keep the fires of conversation stoked was absent; there was present, an ability to relax in each other's company. So soon, so pleasant.

We welcomed the early afternoon heat. Pleasant Street, I'd never apprehended the relevance.

Amy's beaming smile was doing invasive work on me, filling a long-standing void and plastering a smile on my face. I would need a fast bike ride home.

"I should have brought cycling togs with me for the ride," I pondered aloud.

"*Ti depili le gambe?*" (Do you shave your legs?)

"Here in Boulder, it wouldn't be out of the question for me to ask if you shaved yours. *È quasi come in Francia.*" (It's almost like France.)

"Not a rhetorical question, Cal," was Amy's faux demand.

"You'll have to wait and see. Won't you?"

Too soon, we arrived back at my car. I stood by the driver's side front fender and indicated that Amy should open the door, wondering if she could do anything but glide comfortably into the bucket seat. Yes, decisively. She adjusted the driver's seat up two notches, adopted it confidently, made a perceptive instrument survey, and gave a whimsical frown combined with a practiced eye roll at the automatic seatbelt pivot.

"You have a phone in your car?"

"Doesn't everyone? If you get lost, you can call me. Here's my Boulder number on the back of my business card. Do you have a local number yet?" It would be my one shred of accountability.

"Not yet. But *you*, Cal, will be the first to know it when I do."

"I was going to orient you with the controls...," I nodded, acknowledging that she didn't need my help. "If you're driving aggressively, keep the tach between forty-four and sixty-five hundred. See you later this afternoon or evening."

Less than one hundred minutes had elapsed from my picking up an Almond Joy wrapper to watching Amy Farina drive away with my Corrado. What hope and promise of relationship this girl was to me. I could not wait until I saw her again.

§§

Chapter 38

Airplane cabin air was an irritant for Lance, stale and recycled; the atmosphere was harsh. His neck and arms tightened involuntarily. Stretching didn't help; it only reminded him of his intolerable soreness. He knew his muscles would be unbearable at the end of the flight. Worse, he was in coach, with ordinary people all around him, ill-dressed and ill-behaved. He should be with the wealthy, important people in first class. If he didn't think that the lowlife police officer was waiting in the boarding area until the 747 pulled away from the concourse, Lance would have disembarked and made changes. Yes, he would.

He gingerly touched his forehead, his scarlet badge of shame. It briefly shifted his awareness from the lightning jabs between his temples; thinking was agony. Would that he had his Oakleys; shutting his eyes was worthless.

How could this have happened unless it was to turn the situation around to benefit his power, position, and wealth?

A flight attendant began the boarding check.

Lance opened his eyes as he sensed the young woman approaching.

"That's a nasty scrape," she said in feminine empathy.

"You must be a brain surgeon," was the gist of Lance's expletive-laced response.

"I was going to ask, is there anything that I can get you to help you feel better?"

Her offer released from him another string of expletives, demeaning the flight attendant, denouncing the airline, and questioning every passenger's parentage.

All eyes were fixated on the woman to see if her confidence withered.

"Sir," she spoke with command.

Her referencing him as 'sir' reminded Lance of Officer Nori, beginning a brief and quickly interrupted tirade against law enforcement.

"Sir, if you continue to be loud and obnoxious, disturbing the other passengers, I will have you escorted from the plane. The officer who brought you said he would be happy to comp you secure sleeping accommodations for the night." Her gaze upon the foul-mouthed passenger was unflinching.

Lance stared back hatefully.

"Is there anything that I can do to help you feel better?"

"Four aspirin, Glenlivet, and for you to shut up."

"I can get you two aspirin. If you can show that you are mature enough to handle an alcoholic beverage between now and the in-flight service, you may have your Glenlivet then. As for me to shut up, no. It is my job as a flight attendant to speak to and for the passengers on this flight. For you to interfere with my job is a federal offense." There was no backing down this young lady. "I repeat my offer to have you removed from the plane."

Spiked cogs of thought attempted to mesh behind Lance's forehead. Sparks arced and ached; rage tensed his already testy facial expression. Lance did not interact with his world this way.

Think this through. Think. You control yourself, not these peons. Get a grip. Get even with them. Make them all pay. Pay dearly, with pain, misery, and money.

Finally, the thought bore the fruit of speech.

"I'll take two aspirin."

A smattering of applause cascaded to universal endorsement. Lance was the only one who thought the approval was of him.

§

Lance put to good use the interval between takeoff and the in-flight beverage service by listing his offenders of the day.

His hired idiots were only barely able to inform him of his fiancée's evasion. He paid them to know what Amy Farina was doing. How could a huge event, moving out of state, have eluded them? Fortunately, he coaxed a departure out of Logan that landed only hours after Amy's flight out of Albany.

That college punk, he was the worst; first, he'd seduced his fiancée and then walked away with her. Then there was his mocking, disrespect of Lance's weapon. He had lectured him with supposed superior knowledge. To not be threatened, unthinkable. How lucky he had been to get the better of Lance, armed and dangerous. His apology was no apology.

His fiancée and that interloper had left him with the insufferable Officer Nori, then the two of them ran across the street hand in hand. He would skin that vile kid and boil him in his own blood.

Officer Nori was such a stooge. He could have been a hundred bucks richer or more if he had any brains. He'd called Lance's C-note trash, insulting him and his money.

This stupid plucky flight attendant, she would be the easiest to deal with, loss of job along with a degrading lifestyle change.

Farina, she was the grand offender, spurning his offer of proposing marriage, running away, then taking up with a complete stranger. But was he a stranger to her, to come so quickly to her defense and to gain her confidence more than he ever could? He would have to regain control over her.

An idea percolated through his brain, bubbling up from the effluent of his being, a poetic dip from a familiar lagoon. *I'll have the best of this deal yet.*

The flight attendant, unseen, brought Lance his disdained pain relief medication. He swilled his aspirin with water.

§§

CHAPTER 39

"So, Peter, what's the scoop on our ugly Bostonian?"

"Not a good guy, Cal. I put him on the plane myself. I pulled a print from his driver's license, and when I got back to the station, I called a friend on the Massachusetts State Patrol.

"Let's wander. How's the paint on the north side of your house looking?"

"Are you painting your house before winter?"

Peter's inquiry was tangible, tactile. We slipped between the house and my property fence to a narrow, secluded strip of lawn.

"Lance Grimaldi, the guy you beat up a few hours ago, is acting head of an Italian crime family in Boston." Peter served up a non-verbal, *bet you didn't know that.* "He's been underboss for a don convicted for the murder of an Irish rival. That don's been in prison for five years. Grimaldi is a dangerous, stinkin' guy, well connected and so far, untouchable."

Covering defensively, I looked down and brushed fresh-cut grass from the top of my Sketchers.

"The don's name is Petros Belluno. The guy he offed was Tom Kean Boyle. Double-tap, back of the head."

Had Peter seen my astonishment before I had a chance to recover? With Peter, I knew that even a poker face was a tell.

Peter relayed, from his friend, two theories of what happened. One was that Petros Belluno was trying to go straight with legitimate business interests, and likewise, the victim. A State Police detective had testified that such was the case. Two was the prosecution's argument for motive, in that Belluno never intended to go straight but that he had promoted this idea specifically to lure Boyle into a meet that ended in his execution.

"Belluno insisted that a subordinate within his organization set up Boyle to take the fall for arranging a near-fatal accident involving Belluno's wife. He and Boyle had common goals and mutual trust. They were both ready to turn state's evidence in return for witness protection. Belluno said that he and Boyle had agreed to stage a mock execution. He had loaded his gun with blanks. Boyle was to lay low until Belluno discovered and dealt with his internal problem.

"The prosecution dealt away with Belluno's scenarios with circumstantial evidence.

"My trooper friend said that they never found the murder weapon. The testimony of two eyewitnesses clinched Belluno's conviction." Peter was tenacious. "Without the weapon, the prosecution couldn't go for murder in the first.

"The first witness wasn't credible. The other witness, a young man, was extremely precise and unshakable in his testimony's details. But, this was tragic. At the very time he was testifying, some mafioso executed his family gangland style. Thugs shot and killed his parents in their New Hampshire insurance office, and, at the same time, thugs also killed his only brother at Berklee College. The young man's name was Michael James Barton. He died in a naval basic training exercise just days after the trial."

"Mi..., *Cal James*..., Barton?" Peter stared at me. He was slow and deliberate in his delivery. "Michael James Barton?"

"Peter, you and Marcia have a Shel Silverstein book that I've read for your kids. *The Bagpipe Who Didn't Say No.*" I tried to deliver it straight, but a waver caught my voice.

"Sorry, Cal. I know that this doesn't go anywhere except between you and me. I'm not into cracking WITSEC, and I'm very sorry about your folks, your family,.... Are you okay? How could you possibly be okay? Yet, look at you. I don't know anyone who's more okay." Peter paused in admiration and because he cared.

"Do you suppose that there is any reason, other than Amy Farina, for Lance Grimaldi to be in Boulder? Do you

think that he recognized you? The underboss for Petros Belluno would certainly have been at the trial."

"I don't think so, Peter, on either count. Amy was very
clear; she'd only met that guy once. He admitted that he
stalked her for the last eight years and wanted to propose
marriage over dinner, wingnut *du jour.*

"No fooling, Peter, that loon's a crime boss? His being
here had to be a last-minute reaction. Amy's transfer to CU
was a secretive, spur of the moment thing. Talk about an
obsessed stalker.

"All he would remember of Michael Barton would be
that of a punk kid who should have gone to MIT or Cal Tech,
a three-quarter nerd. Me? I'm a construction guy. Michael
Barton, the kid, is dead. He died while observing a live-fire
exercise. You didn't say live-fire, did you? Anyway, I'm an adult
messing with this goon's perceived destiny. I think that if he'd
made the other connection, you and I would have known."

"This explains a lot of mystery about you."

"Mystery?"

"You don't know the street on you? It's about how you
have a past, of which you are particularly protective. Word is,
your past is dark, melancholy, and violent, with all kinds of
speculation. Nothing that approaches WITSEC or what happened to your family."

"I hadn't heard. Mysterious, you say?" I managed a
good-natured squint. "If I'd known that, I might have come
up with my second best pickup line ever."

We had turned into the backyard, where a few friends
were already gathering.

"So, what's your best line?"

"It's 'Hey.'"

"You don't say." Peter reassuringly laid his hand on my
shoulder for a moment, enlisting a droll smile.

"I did say, just this morning, about fifteen minutes
before we all had our little get together. Right now, I have to
churn the charcoal."

"That's Marcia I hear laughing in the kitchen. I should
find out how her day went; it was supposed to have been a
tough one."

§

A few minutes after five o'clock, my Corrado's distinctive down gear shifting proclaimed Amy's arrival. I temporarily abandoned the charcoal in favor of greeting Amy and ushering her to the backyard. She was bending into the back seat when I rounded the corner; to my surprise, she had brought a companion.

"Hi, Camilla, glad you could join us."

"I'm thrilled to be invited." Camilla was buoyant and cheerful. "I was surprised when Amy asked me."

"I hope that's okay." Amy straightened up, holding a stack of pizza boxes. "It seemed, Cal, that between the time I saw you from my perch on that landscape rock and the time you let me borrow your Corrado, everyone we met except Camilla was already coming to your party. Well, there were two, actually, but the jerk one doesn't count."

"Perfectly okay. That's the way it's supposed to work."

"I left your books in the back seat, and I made A-1 pizzas to go with your steaks. Where should I put them?"

I looked toward the backyard. Immediately, she was on her way and brushed past me. Before I knew what had happened, she'd pecked a kiss on my left cheek.

I stood flat-footed.

Camilla laughed.

"She told you that she would do that, didn't she?" I asked with a grin.

"Yes. Yes, she did."

"Let's go find her, Camilla." I gestured for her to go ahead. "She's gone."

Amy had found the serving table, parked the pizza boxes, and opened one. Inside I saw that A-1 pizza was literal, possibly hand-tossed pizza crust brushed with olive oil, lightly brushed again with A-1 steak sauce where you'd expect the tomato sauce to be, topped with roasted diced garlic, and crumbled goat cheese, then pie-cut into sixteen slices.

"It makes a great appetizer." Amy affected.

Camilla saw Judy and Tom from the bike shop on the back deck. She grabbed an RC Cola and joined them, welcoming the chance to hang out with these regular café customers.

"So, where did you get the pizza crusts."

"I baked them, a family recipe. I've been busy, Cal. McGukin Hardware had the utensils, appliances, and pizza boxes. Alfalfa's Market had all the baking ingredients for the crust except for the beer. They sent me over to Boulder Beer Company for that. Fortunately, the oven at my house works fine, and the dough rise left me enough time to stop at the café to invite Camilla. And I took your car for a test drive; that was fun!"

"These are good, Amy," I said, sampling a slice. "I'll take another over to the grill. I need to bank the charcoal."

My grill was a steel pipe, two feet in diameter, split lengthwise down the middle, and hinged. I'd welded it up myself, not ten feet from its current station.

"Would you tell me where your bathroom is?"

"It's through the kitchen, take a right, and keep going. There's one at the far end. If that's busy, there are two upstairs, one jack and jill, and one, off my bedroom.

"Take time to socialize, too."

§

Amy followed my instructions, including, "take time to socialize."

A half-hour later, she returned.

"Hi, Cal. Nice house, not your typical college student housing. I talked to a few people inside. Peter Nori introduced me to his wife, Marcia, but you called his wife Rachel, earlier today."

"Ah. That was Peter and me having a sub-rosa conversation. His dog's name is Rachel. Beautiful and smart. But the Rachel comment was intended to clue him in that all was not right with the situation."

"Devious." She nodded and added mischievously, "there's a situation here, too, that's not right. You don't have anything to drink. Can I bring you a beer?"

"Fat Tire, if there are any left. I'm in no hurry, so go ahead and mingle. There are people here you'll find a lot more interesting than me."

"I very much doubt that."

§

The ribeyes were ready, and a line had formed for serving. I started to fill orders for rare, medium, and well done. Amy bypassed the line, wine and beer in hand, and made her way to my side.

"I'm sorry I took longer than expected; here's your beer."

"Find any interesting people?"

"You have incredible friends."

"Yes, I do, to their credit, not mine. Rare, medium, or well? If you prefer well done, get a medium. This beef is from a farm outside Lyons, far better than the drug-laden stuff you get in the supermarket. I'll join you in a few minutes."

"Your few minutes are up," Peter said authoritatively, pulling up on my blind side. He adroitly disarmed me of tongs and spatula.

"I can join you right now," I observed, happily relieved.

"Here's your plate and flatware. Be careful, Amy, the steak knives are sharp as a stiletto," Peter joked.

"Cal's the one you need to warn about sharp knives. Two of those, medium, please. Make mine a smaller one," Amy spoke to Peter for both of us as we held our plates out. "It's a perfect evening, isn't it?"

"Yes, Amy, it is," Peter served up.

"Let's claim the blue Adirondacks." I nodded toward them.

We set our drinks on the side table between the two slate-blue chairs and headed over to the side dish table.

"Split a potato?" I sidestepped to create space.

"Sour cream?" Amy dolloped her own.

"Not too much." As she half-dolloped mine.

"Grated cheese?"

I shook my head.

We danced while filling our plates.

"Salad?" I waved my hand over the tongs.

"Croutons?" She invited, only grasping the serving spoon on her second attempt as she looked for my answer.

"Oil and balsamic?" I gazed at her.

"I'll take some ranch on the side."

"A-1 pizza?"

We filled our plates cooperatively in moments, oblivious to our observers.

We relaxed in our chairs, and after several bites and chews, I ventured forth.

"So you met Marcia Nori, I haven't seen her yet this evening. She still wearing scrubs?"

"She apologized but said that she had come straight from work. She's a doctor."

"True and a good one at that. Pete says that if she comes home in scrubs, the day's been rough."

"Did you know that Camilla is trying to save money to do premed at the university?" Amy punctuated her question with a raised eyebrow.

"That is a tough row to hoe. I didn't know. Let's get Marcia and Camilla to talk before the evening is through."

"You would do that, wouldn't you?" thoughtfully nodding.

More sips, slugs, slices, and chews.

"When I was in your house, I overheard some fascinating snippets. I listened to a couple of guys while they talked about Boolean Algebra. That digressed to Gödel's theory of incompleteness. I introduced myself and told them of my mathematical pursuit of anthropology. They attempted to respect that and then asked what Gödel had to do with anthropology. Pretty cool for party talk. I told them that every time a culture develops a system of logic, inherent contradictions arise. Therefore, Gödel is proper anthropological fodder. That hopped them up."

"Sure, the math nerds. Those two are into cycling, too. They're great guys. We get into math discussions occasionally. I get abstract algebra, groups, rings, fields, logical foundations of math, and all that. I gather you do, too, but I love to push their buttons. I argue that math has beautiful, practical applications, not an end in itself as they maintain. The discussion usually ends with a chess challenge."

"How does that usually end?"

I guffawed with affected overconfidence.

"Okay, you and I'll have to play soon. Now tell me, Cal, who's the Romeo in your house, the smooth dog with the lines?"

"That would be Nick, an English lit major. He's encyclo-pedic. What line did he use on you?" I was accustomed to his hitting on anyone who might wear a skirt.

"He came up beside me in the kitchen. If he'd gaped a second longer without saying anything, I would have slapped him. Most likely, he'd forgotten the line that he'd memorized. Then he said, 'I'd like to be stranded on an *uninhibited* island with you.'"

"So I said, 'Nice wordplay. Get yourself a plastic palm and a sandbox.' He bruises easily, doesn't he?"

"Yeah, but he keeps on working at it. If it's any consola-tion, that script sounds new."

"It wasn't Italian. He cuts no ice." A flicker of recogni-tion and a glimmer of disgust crossed her face.

"The thing is, Amy, he'd follow up with lit stories; Shel-ley, Byron, Keats, then bore you with Trollope. I've watched it before. You did the right thing. Anyone else?"

"Oh yeah. I heard two other guys and a gal who com-mented about you helping them with a difficult theoret-ical physics problem, chaos stuff, and how you, Cal, wasted your time with engineering and law." She halted. "A friend once suggested that I should give up studying math and be a detective."

From the sudden change in her expression, I knew how somber nostalgia looked on her. There was personal pain behind the look.

"Did this friend not think that you could hold onto both pleasures? You lace up your observations with great deduc-tions. I've seen that. In math, I think you're on my side when it comes to practical application."

"I'm sure Paul, he's an old friend from high school who I haven't seen or heard from in years; he knew that the two were inextricably tangled."

"You'll have to tell me about him."

Just then, the neck of an acoustic guitar shell preceded by seconds, a less than averagely dressed, short-bearded, short-haired, unacquainted rover. He ventured into the yard, eyes not resting on anyone in particular.

"So, Amy, what do you make of him? Should I ask him to leave?"

"You should talk to him. You're Sherlock Holmes in the twentieth century. He might be the evening's entertainment or more."

I set my plate aside. After I swirled and finished the last swallow of Fat Tire, I rose to follow her positive advice.

§

"Do you know anyone here?" My new arrival looked tired and hungry, so I dispensed with my stern approach. His jeans and gray pinstripe Oxford were clean but worn.

"Not really. Looks like a discriminating bunch of folks."

"Do you know what a first-degree party is?"

"We talking John Guare?"

"Stanley Milgram. You're close enough, that's good. What's your name?"

"Ted, and yours?" Ted was quick and curious. He faced me attentively to remember my name when I spoke it, a good quality.

"I'm Cal. My house. My party. My guests. Not proud, just sayin'."

"Cal, I'd be happy to play my guitar for them."

"Show me your hands." I looked over my shoulder toward our Adirondacks. Amy was watching closely.

His extended hands were slender but calloused on the fingertips and strong. I choked. I knew these hands; they belonged to my brother, Phil. They spoke of natural ability and diligent practice at their craft.

I offered my hand for a shake. Ted accepted quickly.

"Play for us; when you're ready for a break, help yourself to the food, or if you'd prefer, eat first. Drinks are inside. Two sets max, forty-five on, fifteen between. Meet me in my office later; I'll pay you. No open case for tips."

"Cool, thank you. All I need is a stool or an armless chair."

§

Ted arranged a tall wooden kitchen stool in the middle of the flagstone patio. No doubt, he planned on being the center of attention. Confident.

I found my way back to the Adirondack next to Amy.

"You had quite a satisfactory greeting, but you were startled when you looked at his hands. What was that?"

"I have some ghosts to deal with." A dangerous admission. "I hope to tell you about them someday."

"What did you two say?" Amy deferred again, the opening to quiz me on my past, keeping an unbroken accent on the present. What a welcome trait.

"I told him this was a first-degree party. That didn't deter him. He knew what I meant by it, though. I could see he's devoted to practicing, so I let him play."

§

"Hi. I'm Ted. I'm here to play for you all." Ted announced, all entertainer, ready to perform.

He began by tapping his Reeboks in rhythm until he was comfortable with it, all the while tuning his Tama guitar. Then he literally hammered out, with fingers and thumb joint, Scott Joplin's *The Entertainer*. Ordinarily a rag, I knew it was a piano piece, with left and right-hand parts. It was standard ragtime fare at the Diamond Belle Saloon in Durango. It wasn't suitable for guitar, not until Ted wrenched it away from the honky-tonk piano man.

He kept metronomic time with his foot. Thumb in conjunction with plucking fingers, he fingered the neck with pull-offs, hammer-ons, and strums, delivering fantastic musical interpretations. His renditions emptied the house and had all of my guests in the backyard. They gathered where they could watch and hear the marvels of his dexterity and applauded his presentation profusely.

Never Been to Spain, miraculously carried bass, lead, and rhythm. *Summertime* took a jazz twist. The Beatles *Blackbird* had us all mesmerized; *Classical Gas* followed.

"I'm going to play Vivaldi, for those who might not recognize it, *Trio Sonata for Two Violins and Continuo in A Major*," was Ted's only commentary.

§

"Ted, my guests may kill me for this, but could you stop for a while?" His musical presentation had minimized social interaction for more than an hour, "Mingle a bit; grab yourself a plate. Have a steak and potato, salad, and beer or wine. There's soda, too.

"We'll talk later on. A friend of mine has a booking agent if you're interested. I'm sure he could get you some well-paying gigs. You've already developed a loyal following among this crowd."

"Thank you so much. I think I will pause for a bite. This spread looks better than anything I've had to eat in months."

§

When I found Amy, she was chatting with Marcia. Both were drinking Valpolicella, recently refilled.

"Peter's driving me home," said Marcia of her designated driver. She twirled her wineglass with an impish grin.

"Amy and I were talking about Camilla. Camilla is wildly, uncannily smart. You wouldn't know it until you start to ask her specific questions, which I did. She has a better than an undergraduate-level understanding of biology, anatomy, and chemistry. She's a self-study, never been in a classroom, ever. That could be a problem for her getting admitted to the University."

Amy stepped away, answering the beckoning of Peter and Camilla.

"This girl Amy, you invited, Cal, where did you find her?" Marcia leaned into my side and added confidentially. "Don't answer, I've already heard. If you don't already know it, Cal, listen to me. She's a keeper. Did you know that she's an EMT?"

"The way my day has gone, Marcia... Amy has raised the bar on what can amaze me. I'm still reeling. I have lived a whole extra lifetime today. You know, that nice life I'm supposed to live."

§

I loved the office that graced the front of my home. It was a lockable stand-alone. Bookshelves bracketed the room behind the desk where a Murphy bed hid. What might pass for an oversized wine rack held blueprint mailing tubes, a couple of comfortable guest chairs, two four-drawer metal filing cabinets, and a side table finished the furnishings.

"Ted, come on in." Ted brought his guitar with him. I sat next to the desk. He took a guest chair.

"You met up with Kirkland tonight," I began. "He saw your second set. Did he say that he could hook you up with his agent for bookings?"

"Thank you, yes. He was stoked."

215

"We all are."

My eyes caught Amy's as she peered in.

"Join us? You should meet Ted."

"Camilla and I are cleaning up in the kitchen. I think it's just Kirkland and us in the kitchen, and you two, now." Amy stepped into the room. "I'm Amy Farina."

"Any relation to Geoff?" A question that went nowhere. "I'm Ted, Ted Commons. Pleased to meet you."

"Likewise, Ted." Amy winked at me. "I'll get back to cleaning up."

"We'll catch up with you in five minutes; Kirkland is assisting you, right?"

"He will." She swung away from the doorway, lithe and sublime.

I wanted to get used to that sight, coming and going.

"Anyway, Ted, I have three hundred in cash for playing tonight." I handed him a plain white envelope.

"For that, I'll go play three more sets even if everyone's already left. Thank you again." Ted started to get up to leave.

"You're welcome, but don't get up; there's more. So here's the thing, you have extreme talent. I see other exceptional qualities in you, too: persistence, diligence, creativity, and passion. I propose that you gig around Colorado with the help of Kirkland's agent, and maybe you should consider a music school next fall.

"Are you set up with a place to stay for the night?"

"Kirkland said that I could crash at his place," Ted said with relief, "but you know, even with a season of good gigs, school tuition would be a killer. There's a music school in Boston called Berklee, where I've only dreamed of going. I'm destined to be a hack."

"We'll talk tomorrow about getting you a semi-permanent place to stay." I stood.

"Sounds good to me."

Ted's talent had stirred me; the Berklee comment had me slightly shaken.

We walked to the kitchen. Kirkland sat at the table, watching the girls put away the last of the dishes and utensils.

"I want you to know that I applied my directorial expertise regarding the proper storage places, I am a director, and I helped them immensely by staying out of their way." Kirkland's beret gave credence to his smooth, put on, French accent.

"Kirkland, Ted, let's do a group meet tomorrow at the café. Nine-ish. I have other things I need to attend to tonight."

"Very well, good night. Thank you for another fine party, exceptionally enjoyable."

§

"Camilla, Amy, thanks for making my place presentable again."

"I'm afraid that we've kept at the Valpolicella," Amy confessed, "it is so good."

"I have another wine I'd like to uncork," I offered. "Let's have new glasses; it's not Valpolicella."

I removed the cork, set the bottle down, gave the cork a sniff check, and poured a slight amount in Amy's glass. She rolled the glass, inhaled, then sipped. Her eyes grew wide with recognition. I poured, with her nod of approval, for both Amy and Camilla, and filled my own.

"Camilla, you spoke with Marcia for a while this evening."

"I did. When she discovered that I wanted to pursue medicine, we talked about anatomy, nervous and circulatory systems, and chemistry. It was fun to talk about the subjects I've studied." Camilla looked relaxed, happy, and enthused about her social exchange with a bona fide doctor.

"Oh, that is good." Amy sipped her Barolo. "Camilla, you're from Jamaica. What part?"

"The windward side, the opposite from Montego Bay, geographically, socially, and economically. In Portland Parish, a small village called Moore Town."

"Maroons have a place in your lineage?" Amy surprised both Camilla and me. "Maybe Asante?"

"Very good; you know more about me than you thought."

"You're here. You're brilliant, unique, on an ambitious quest, and you have the determination to see it through. I might attribute those traits to the Maroons." Amy shifted her focus. "So the Jamaican Blue Mountain coffee that we had this morning so, so long ago, holds particular significance."

"I've been on the plantations."

"How is it going, Camilla, your preparations to get into premed?" I expressed my concern.

Amy looked on. I knew she shared my thoughts.

"It's hard to save and live at the same time, but I must do this. There are places in Jamaica with a real medical need, places where only one who knows the people could go. Hurricane Gilbert wiped out a lot of medical facilities, too." Her Jamaican origins surfaced with a more pronounced lilt in her speech. "There is a limited window of opportunity that I have before..."

Camilla took a sip of wine to cover up the emotion she felt at the real potential of missing the whole purpose of her journey.

"Are you naturalized?" I knew I was intruding.

"This past spring. Why do you ask?"

"Camilla, here's the thing. Marcia, Peter's wife, says that you are smarter than any premed graduate that she has ever met. The whole physician thing, what is the estimated start to finish, ten years? Does that include residency?"

I could see Camilla's resolve dwindle.

"You can't get it done working for tips at the café. It's as simple as that."

"What can we do to help out?" Amy intervened, catching on.

"You don't have any time to waste," I continued, complimenting Amy's offer, "if I'm right, long-term monetary support is your largest concern. We're all sipping on nice wine. I've had a terrific day start to finish. You don't leave here without letting me..., us," I received a nod from Amy, "join you in your quest."

"Camilla, would it help if you spent less on living arrangements?" Amy didn't skip a beat, as if we had rehearsed for this.

"How long have you known each other? I thought at the café it had been a half-hour tops. I saw you guys samba around, filling your dinner plates; everybody did. Suddenly you two are an us and completing each other's thoughts. I'm glad about that." Camilla sighed, "Rent and utilities are my biggest expenses; you can't get cheap, decent living space here when you're competing with the students."

"I have a whole three-bedroom house with no roommates," Amy volunteered, "I'll be lonely if I don't have company. If you didn't have rent to pay, what would that do for you?"

Camilla, immobile, considered what was happening.

"You're struggling with that." It was my turn to encourage. "You think that it would be charity, and there's justifiable pride that conflicts. Consider Amy's offer, though. We can't go where you can, and we can't do what you can do there. You have gifts that we don't have. We can join you vicariously, investing in producing a physician who would benefit who knows how many people and be a boon to those treated by you. You can't deny those folks, right?

"For my part, my company replaces our computers annually. I have business in Durango this weekend, so I'll bring back a full set up for you; modem, printer, CPU, software, the whole shot. You'll need it for your studies."

Camilla finished her Barolo while she stifled tears. I pulled a box of tissue from the counter. When she reached for one, I topped our glasses, starting with hers.

"You'll consider letting us help?"

"I would; I have a lease, though."

"I might have an idea that would make that a moot point.

"Have more wine. Really. Celebrate. Enjoy," I urged. "You know, I work hard, and it rewards me exceedingly well. What am I going to do? Buy a Mercedes, live in a twelve thousand square foot home, and wear Prada and Armani? I do know a guy who can pull that off successfully. He does a lot of good things, too. But Amy and I saw a lunatic today who lives only self-indulgently. I've had a couple of mentors who have helped me make conscious decisions. They've taught me that I can determine my character and not be passive about it. My choice? I'd rather be constructive than merely impressive."

Amy jumped up with the same verve that she had lighting from the rock when we met. She pulled Camilla from her seat, defying her sudden sea leg's resistance, and wrapped her up in a huge hug.

219

"Group hug," Amy cried loudly. She looked at me in wonderment, gathering me in.

What thoughts were behind her engaging eyes? I hoped I would find out. Maybe it would happen the day when I could open up to her about my past.

"Thank you." Camilla, recovering from self-doubt. "Thank you."

"You're welcome. I'm glad you came to the party, and we got a chance to know each other better." I took a few deep breaths and looked hopefully at Amy and Camilla that they would do the same.

"Let's have a sit again," I suggested.

"Endorphins make me feel good. They're contagious, and I enjoy sharing." Much wine had loosened my lips. I'd have to stop both the wine and my expounding before it got me in trouble.

"I told Amy earlier that I preferred endorphins over adrenalin because endorphins produce unfettered thinking. Adrenalin is useful, but it shapes your choices in coping with a situation."

"Cal, thank you for inviting me and persuading me to come tonight." Amy, ever dear, at least for the past fourteen hours. "I had no idea how this day would end, but I can't say when I've felt so secure, happy, entertained, and surprised."

"Amy, I don't recall ever having a better day than today." I garnered agreeing nods.

"Cal, you did say that you started the day today at what, three this morning? Do you feel okay to take Camilla and me home?"

"Peter's uniformed friends are out, and I'm afraid that they wouldn't want me driving, or you, or Camilla."

"Should I make coffee then?" Camilla chimed helpfully.

"Thank you for offering, Camilla, though if it's all right with you two, I have two extra bedrooms, furnished, upstairs. Marv and Tex, my college renters, won't be back until next week. Sometimes, their girlfriends stay the night, so if you need any girl stuff, it'll be in the shared bathroom. You might find a change of clothes in the dressers, too. The girls are nice; they won't mind. I'll let them know when I see them and replace anything you use. I am beat, even if it is only eleven-thirty, you two can chat longer if you want. Remember we have arrangements to make tomorrow morning. I didn't mention it? We're meeting Kirkland and Ted at the café."

Camilla let loose with another flow of happy tears.

The kitchen door creaked, opening, uninvited, by the hand of a shadowy Mexican. Amy and Camilla were transfixed.

"Not twice," Amy spoke under her breath.

The Mexican, now standing in the kitchen, pointed at me, hand outstretched, and proclaimed, "That's the man who broke my finger."

I rose to my feet, and with a false limp, approached this stranger to Amy and Camilla.

I extended my hand, and with a handshake, drew him in for an over the shoulder hug.

"Bobby. I forgot you were in Denver today. These are two new friends. Camilla, Amy, meet Bobby. He's my business partner and best friend."

"Very pleased to meet you both." Bobby motioned both to stay seated. "Hope he treated you better than he did me on the first day we met."

"How so?" Amy inquired for herself and Camilla.

"The first day we met, Cal punched me, bloodied my face, tried to break my nose, then he broke my right index finger and threatened to break the left one, too."

This time, I nodded sheepishly.

"To be fair, I'd just slit open his leg with a shovel. Wasn't it ten stitches to sew it up?"

"Twenty-four, but who's counting."

"This was a construction accident, right?" Amy recoiled, recalling Judy's warning.

"No. Definitely, a serious fight," Bobby continued.

"Bobby, let me jump to the day after when I came to your house. Amy's already had a scare earlier today. Some goon wanted to slice and dice me with a stiletto because I was walking her to the bike shop." I held up my palm.

"Did you break his finger?" Bobby and I shared a laugh.

"No. You remember Peter Nori? He showed up before it crossed my mind, then it was too late. Besides, I liked this creep less than I liked you."

Amy agonized over Cal and Bobby's conversation, deciding if what we'd said was true. *What would it mean if it was? How violent was Cal?*

"I did scrape him up nicely and sent him back to Boston.

"The day after Bobby and I scuffled," returning to my story for the girls, "I spoke to a friend. He tipped me off that Bobby was a good guy in a horrible situation. Some thugs threatened his family. He had to fight me or lose his job and see his family come to serious harm."

"This is true, ladies. Cal came by my place the next day and apologized. Then he paid out of his pocket to get this finger operated on and properly set so I could point straight. My finger pointing and his limp are sort of a secret handshake, sorry if I shook you up. It was the best ever fight I've lost."

"If nothing else, today has been a diverting introduction to the West." Amy was starting to fade. "And everything else."

"Bobby, you get the Queen Murphy in the office. The girls are getting the guest beds upstairs. There are ribeyes in the fridge, salad, potato, La Bohemia Obscura, too. See you in the morning. *A che ora parti?*" (When are you leaving?)

"*Alle otto.*" (At eight o'clock.)

Amy was too tired to notice.

"You know your way around the house. I'll be up before six. We'll chat in the morning before you go. We need to talk about Telluride. Girls, let me show you to your rooms."

"Yes, please." They answered in unison.

"This way. Good night, Bobby."

§§

Chapter 40

Bobby had been efficient in restoring his last night's accommodations to presentable office space. Over early coffee in the kitchen, we discussed the logistics of running a considerable job in Telluride, more involved than any we had done previously. It was the next logical step in the growth of Smart Start.

We had questions to answer. Was Bobby's young protégé ready? What to do about offices, storage, supplies, equipment, tools, communications, and our workforces. Could we bond the project? Would Dave supply excavation and crane work?

Telluride was three hours distant and, at times, isolated from Durango in winter. It was no simple undertaking.

We hadn't thrown our hat in the ring yet, but we were excited about the prospect. As with all our previous leaps, we wanted to minimize our risks in those things we had control over.

We divided our follow up items. Equipped with a plan to proceed, Bobby had left at six-thirty.

§

The *William Tell Overture* announced much too loudly that I had fired up my home office computer, the result of a .bat file I'd installed to humor myself. As quickly as I could remember how I killed the volume and listened to hear if I had disturbed any of my sleeping guests.

All quiet.

A few clicks on the keyboard later, I found the phone number of Nations Pennsylvania Bank.

"Good morning, Gail. Would you ring Jim Shipley for me?" the early bird receptionist recognized my voice and placed me through after a few pleasantries.

"Jim, it's Cal James on the phone for you," she announced.

"It's been long enough since I've heard from you. I still haven't seen you out here in Strasburg."

Welcome banter, his family, my business. Was he hunting in upstate New York? When would he take a family vacation to southwest Colorado? Jim's bank had been my random selection to receive my parents' insurance proceeds, and now all my investment proceeds. We talked about projects the bank was supporting.

"What prompts your call at this hour?"

"Business, Jim. The last draws on the scholarships for Steve and Chelsea Chauklin, and Jill and Jack Walsh have cleared through, is that right?"

"Yes, sir."

"Have they been requested to return their stipend cards?"

"They've been surrendered. I'll send you the thank you note they sent with them, which was very touching, and signed by all four. We have the cards at the bank and the note."

"Good, I'd like to see the note. In the meantime, I want you to direct tuition money to two other schools. First, not urgent, to Berklee School of Music, in Boston, for the benefit of Ted, Theodore Commons, his scholarship will start in September next year. The other, to the University of Colorado, Boulder, for the benefit of Camilla Corrigan, we'll have her on the books for a decade. Arrange full rides for both.

"You've handled the previous presentments delicately and precisely. If you would, have the same done for these two, I'd appreciate it. No traceability to me. FedEx the stipend cards, account signature cards, and information requests. When you transfer me back to Gail, I'll have Camilla's address. Ted's I'll have later in the day.

"Cal, I'll get this done right away. Anything else."

"You're the next best thing to the Caymans, Jim. Enjoy the holidays; I may not be in touch before then."

"I'll have Gail on in a minute."

Once again, I was selfishly trying to establish meaning for my family's deaths.

§

Amy rose and dressed at the unexpected cue of the *William Tell Overture*. The jeans she found in the chest of drawers fit so well she couldn't have done better if she had shopped for them. Padding quietly down the stair treads, she heard Cal on the phone.

"Have they been requested to return their stipend cards?"

She eavesdropped, although not wanting to, spellbound. She knew she should have walked away sooner.

Having stopped short of Cal's office door and not wanting to interrupt his morning business dealings, she'd overheard all of what Cal had accomplished with his phone call, including his reference to the Cayman Islands. Amy turned, even more quietly, and tiptoed in sock feet toward the smell of coffee.

She, for so short a time, was Cal's acquaintance? Friend? What? She knew so much in the grand scheme that mattered in his character makeup. How much had she still to learn about him and his troubling incongruities.

§

"Can I pour you another cup?" Amy asked when I rounded the corner into the kitchen, "I'm getting one for myself."

"Sure, I'd love one. We have a few hours before we go over to the café. Didn't you sleep well?"

"I did, thank you, out like a light, and I slept soundly. I didn't expect to with the all commotion. It's nine o'clock at home. I never sleep past seven. Usually, I'm up at six."

"Most days, I see the sunrise. Bobby and I had to align ducks for an expansion risk this morning, and we now have a course of action.

"Bobby has a fellow, younger than me, that he is very high on. It's funny how we picked him up. He was the one laborer that kept on working at a jobsite. Everyone else stood around, watching to see if I'd win an argument with a subcontractor's foreman. I call him ProtoBobby. Bobby wants me to talk with him tomorrow to see if he's ready to oversee a huge satellite project for Smart Start Builders. I'll be back after the weekend."

"How old are you?" Amy bit her lip.

This question should be easy. I was a scared rabbit, a deer in the headlights.

"You wouldn't believe me." I withdrew my license from my wallet and, cowardly, let the document lie for me.

"Twenty-three. It's a Class A license. You can drive eighteen-wheelers? It says here any vehicle except motorcycle or bus."

"You can't believe everything you see." Godsend. The commercial certification was real, but I wasn't clarifying. "How old are you?"

"I'm twenty-one. So you delayed college?"

"Yeah, the autumn after..., a couple of years after I graduated from high school, Bobby and I started our first project together; by mid-winter, we had our own business."

"Cal, change of subject. Could you give me directions to the Marshall Horse Stables? I volunteered to help out once a month, and I start this weekend." She wanted to ask a different question. "A friend of my mom's, when we lived in Newburyport, runs them. She also owns the house I'm renting. I haven't even spent an hour there yet."

I grabbed the *Colorado Gazetteer* and quickly had her oriented and directed.

"I should call my mom, too. Could I use your phone?" She still couldn't bring herself to ask the question she wanted to.

"Use the phone in my office. Close the door if you want."

"Thanks, Cal. It's long-distance to Lenox. You're sure?"

"Absolutely."

"Can I hug you again?"

Last night her hug was an A-Frame. This morning, not so much.

I was in deep.

§

"Hi, Mom."

"Amy, hi. How are you? I thought that you would have called last night."

"I have never been better, Mom, for real. I would have called, but things got pretty loony yesterday. How are you?"

"I'm good. Missed you all day."

"Mom, this is ultra-bizarre." Amy began to speak faster in excitement. "Yesterday morning, I signed up for all my classes, no problem, right? At the edge of the quad, there was this landscaping rock in the sunshine, perfect for sitting. You know that bench in the garden at Whistler's?"

"Is this a long call, dear?"

"Make yourself comfortable, Mom. So I'm sitting on that rock, and along comes this guy, six-three, a little scruffy, good looking though, and rugged. He stooped over and picked up a piece of trash that the grounds crew missed. A good deed thing. He looked at me and said, 'Hey,' so I said, 'Hey, *lavora con questi ragazzi?*' You know, my usual Italian brush off. Then he looked me in the eyes and said, *'No, nessun non faccio.'* Then he invited me to go to a bicycle shop with him, all of it in flawless Italian without even blinking."

"Amy, so this guy is the reason you didn't call?"

"Mostly, Mom, but don't shortchange the story; it's not that simple. There are details that you want to know.

"Okay. Then we walk over to his car, conversing in English now, and we do deductions. He's very good at it; I even called him Sherlockian. He drops his stuff in his car, and we head off to the bicycle shop.

"We've known each other for, what, tops, it's fifteen minutes. We're getting ready to cross the busy main street. Lance Grimaldi is there and starts wielding a stiletto in Cal's face. His name is..., anyway, Cal waves me back. I almost threw up. But Cal starts talking to Grimaldi, knowingly, about the features and merits of his stiletto, lecturing him on how he's misusing it. Cal has a novel way of dealing with his circumstances. Somehow, Cal grabbed Grimaldi's knife hand, the knife cuts him in the process, but he drops Grimaldi face-first into the asphalt. All at once, a policeman is there, and Cal knows the officer."

"Amy, how did Grimaldi...?"

"I don't know how Grimaldi found me here. He must have minions following me, too. There's no way to tell where I would be right now if it hadn't been for Calvin."

"So, what happened to Grimaldi? Are you safe?"

"I'm very safe, Mom.

"I don't understand how he did it, but Cal arranged for the police officer to hold Grimaldi and then load him on a plane to Logan. Later, I talked to the officer; he said he waited at the airport until Grimaldi's flight left the gate.

"So you spent the day together? You and this Calvin? Can you trust him?"

"Not all day, and not so fast, Mom. When have I enjoyed telling you of a promising encounter with a guy..., ever?

"Okay, so after the fight, Cal takes me to a café. I'm so wound up, anxious, and upset. Without asking, he orders for me, bocconotto no less, and iced coffee. I calmed down and bandaged up his hand. I used butterflies, but I'll stitch him up later.

"Then we went to the bike shop, and it was as if I was nice and safe, and nothing out of the ordinary had happened to me since I was a kid. I bought another Bianchi, by the way." Amy took a short breath. "It won't be ready until Monday. Cal did pick up a new Trek that he had ordered, and we walked back to his car. You won't believe this."

"I'm already enthralled."

"So we're there with his bike, and his car has no bike rack. Oh, his car's a Corrado."

"The incredibly fast Volkswagen?"

"The same. Then, Cal says that I could do *him* a favor by taking it while he rides his bike home. He invited me to a back to school get-together he was having last night. The police officer I met will be there too, he says, and that I can use his car all I want to, to run errands. Only bring it back that evening." Amy paused for a little tee-hee. "He has a mobile phone in it, and it is speedy."

"Amy, you're a grown girl. Don't you think..."

"Mom, I'll be careful, but let me finish.

"So, I'll skip all the fantastic, high-level party chatter with unbelievably brainy folks there. Oh, the party was what Cal called a first-degree party. He knew everyone there or the person who invited them. I invited the waitress that served us at the café. Her name is Camilla. We're all good, conversing, eating steak and salad. Then this guy walks in off the street with a guitar, and Cal asked me what I thought. I think, as a purist, he would have thrown him out. I said he should consider him, and Cal *listened* to me. It turns out that this other guy, Ted, is an extraordinary musician, a guitarist. He played a couple of incredible sets for the party."

Amy lowered her voice.

"This morning, I overheard Cal on the phone do an unimaginably tremendous thing for both Ted and Camilla. Really over the top. I wasn't supposed to hear it, and I'll probably let it slip, but I don't think Cal wants it broadcast at all. Ted and Camilla don't even know about it.

"Anyway, last-night everyone had left but Camilla and me. We'd all had been drinking wine. Cal wouldn't drive us home; he wouldn't let us drive either, wisely. We all had drunk too much. He said that he had guest rooms that Camilla and I could stay in for the night. Then he brought out another bottle of wine. Can you believe it? It was Barolo. It has to be some kind of a sign, right, Mom?"

"So you stayed the night, you and Camilla, in guest beds? After a lot of wine? What about the anthropology prof that you were so anxious to meet? Was he as good looking as this Cal?"

"The anthropology prof was, yeah, really fine-looking. *Especially* fine. Boulder may have its own set of rules, but if he were on the Cape, he'd enjoy Provincetown more than Hyannis, if you know what I mean. And yes, Mom, Camilla and I, each slept in our separate guest bedroom. Alone."

Amy suddenly slowed her rapid-fire narration.

"What Cal said about your inference is interesting. You know how two people can share mutual thoughts? Anyway, Cal and I were doing that last night. The Barolo loosed his tongue. He said, and this is near quote, he 'didn't want to jeopardize the potential of a good, fun, healthy, long-lasting relationship by doing anything inappropriate or regrettable. Everything in its time.' Then he said anyway he would have to know a girl a whole year before thinking of anything resembling a marriage relationship. You know *costruire sulla roccia* (Built on the rock). This is so poetic. The rock is where we met, and he's a builder. He has his own general contracting company. Exceptionally successful by all accounts."

"Is this guy real? His name is Calvin?"

"Without a doubt, Mom, at least, I can see and touch him. He talks *and* listens and has good friends that see him, too. He has all the appearance of being real. I will confirm that he's good looking. I'm calling on his home office phone.

But, we're meeting with some people who were at his party, at the café this morning at nine."

"Be careful, Amy, and call soon. I'm happy for you, and I want *all* the details. Tell Cal that you have a mom who cares about you. He'll know what I mean."

"Sure thing, Mom. Bye for now. Love you."

"Bye, dear. Love you, too."

§

Camilla led Amy and me to a tall, round table suitable for five at the back of the café. In our wake, we gathered one of Camilla's co-workers, Susan, who brought with her five setups and water.

No sooner had she distributed them, Kirkland and Ted slipped in behind us.

"Camilla," I deferred, "you know what's good for breakfast. Leadoff, I'll finish."

Susan had stayed to take our universal order. Blueberry crepes, croissant, OJ, and coffee *du jour*, five of them.

"I don't have a whole lot. My house is committed to capacity once the semester begins. Kirkland's house is full and has the added hazard of actors rehearsing scenes and doing improvisation in any open space. Amy said that she would like to share her place with Camilla. Therefore, Ted should take over the lease on Camilla's studio apartment. If there is any landlord bickering, I'll handle it.

"Thank you, Susan." The coffee carafe had arrived.

Kirkland doctored his coffee so that it more resembled coffee ice cream, only hot. He and Ted began discussing in earnest what Kirkland's agent could do for Ted.

"When I come back from Durango," I confided to Camilla and Amy, "I'll be bringing up a couple of computers, last year's technology. Camilla, I know I'm intruding, but tell me how much you've been sending to your family in Jamaica, and I'll have my company take that over for you, then you'll be able to concentrate on your studies."

My offer took Camilla aback, astonished at my certainty but grateful. She had only generalized about her finances and hadn't yet considered "studies," as I put it. Amy nodded in affirmation with me. She had surmised the same thing.

I caught sight of Susan as she approached with our breakfast.

"I'm done. If you need help, you have a wide circle of friends."

"Who had the blueberry crepes?" Susan asked with comedic timing and set our plates down.

"I could use you in my club act. That was impeccable timing sense. Are you free tonight?" Kirkland was no Nick the Pickup Artist, but he gained himself a willing stage assistant *proprio adesso* (right then).

Good fortune had it that we were all surprisingly hungry.

"Camilla," Amy broke the silence well, "can we call you Cam?"

"Thank you for asking, and please do. My grandmother calls me Cam. If you guys don't mind, it is akin to being asked into your family."

The rest of us chuckled at the inadvertent pun.

"No, honestly, Amy, you're far away from your mom, your only family. Ted, you are a nomad. Kirkland, I don't know you. I haven't heard of mother, father, brother, or sister from you or Cal either. Me? Those who care for me are far away, and now I have all of you."

"Kirkland?" Amy interjected. She skillfully took the conversational tiller and steered away from my past. Yesterday I dismissed it as coincidental. Today, she verified it with a look. Stunning. What did she know?

"Kirkland?" Amy repeated. The playwright in him caught the change in tone. "If we call Camilla, Cam, that makes you the one thing, not like the others, see? Ted, Cal, Amy, Cam? Three letters. Right?"

"How many assistants can I take on in one day?" Kirkland laughed defensively. "I could start writing a new stage play right here and now."

"So, what do we do about you?" Amy held him on her sparkling hook.

"What do you suggest?"

Ted, Cam, and I yielded agreeably to the banter.

"To protect you from the starship jokes, we'll all take a mental trip to Wellington, New Zealand, and listen to people call you Kirk all day. Then we'll all come back speaking with the Kiwis' implied diphthong, dropping the 'r' and calling you Kik." Amy was a star.

"Masterfully spun, Miss Amy, how could I refuse?"

"Very good," Amy encouraged, "we will be known as the family of three-letter names. Very anthropological. I will have to study us."

"You're going to ask us a lot of questions?" Kik, formerly known as Kirkland, inquired.

"That *Rosencrantz and Guildenstern are Dead* bit?" Amy shifted gears again. "Will you concede that I'd win?"

"How's that?" Kik was right with her.

"Don't you know?" Before the inevitable volley of questions, Amy braked conversationally and downshifted. I could see how she would have enjoyed the Corrado. I envisioned her skillfully engaged with a Grand Prix racetrack.

"I had a friend in high school. He was a brilliant actor. At sixteen, he acted Shakespeare, *Richard III*, with a pro-am group. The Stratford Festival Theater scouted him. In Lenox, he was in all the school plays and community theater productions. You would have liked him, Kik. He taught me a lot about theater, acting, and stagecraft."

"The same guy who told you that you should dispense with math studies?" I meant it as a kind inquiry.

"Indeed, Sherlock." Mock disdain, same nostalgia, kindly taken.

§§

CHAPTER 41

"Did you get your business settled in Durango?" Amy asked as she alighted from my 4Runner's driver seat.

"Yes, I did," I assured, delighted to see her, "papers were signed, and I was able to do a site check while I was there. How about you? You found the stables in Marshall okay? How about moving into your house? Did you save me any lifting? I have computers and accessories for Camilla and you in my back seat."

"I'll have lifting for you. Thank you for the use of your 4Runner, and your friends, by the way. They did most of the work. The house looks great. Camilla and I want to have you over this evening for dinner. You can lift a fork and a glass. When you recover from your drive, we'll go over," Amy stipulated with a smirk.

"I'll have fun helping out at the stables. Oh, I got my bike this morning from Judy, it works fine, but it needs a good workout. Any ideas?"

"I'm full of ideas." I laughed, knowing that she'd guessed half of them already. "I could take you on an easy half-century tomorrow. Do you want to wait while I shower and change?"

"I'll take you up on the bike ride. But Cal, when you ask if I want to wait for you, you're implying that I have free use of your vehicles, it's that, or you want me to walk."

"Let me stop implying then, if I'm not using one of my vehicles, feel free to use it. Come on in, and I'll show you where I keep my keys. A house key is in a recess under the back stoop handrail."

We entered the house through my office, where I dropped file folders and blueprints.

"All my keys are in the top right drawer. I never lock the desk."

"Cal, stop. You and I have spent less than twelve waking hours together; you let me drive your car and entrust me with your 4Runner all weekend when you're off on business three hundred plus miles away. You are so generous and unassuming; why do you trust me so much? I almost feel like your younger sister."

"I certainly don't see you that way at all. Oh, no, no, no. Let's say that when you returned my "Hey," with such composure, I was sure that I had known you for years and was so fortunate to have crossed paths. Then, when we talked, Italian or not, there are so many connections, interests. You haven't had it easy, growing up with a single parent and all. I haven't had it easy either, but you handle yourself unlike any girl I've ever met. And, we communicate with each other, that's the main thing. I don't need a sister, and I enjoy your company. Point blank, it hasn't taken any time at all to know that I really like you. "

"Amazing. I like you, too."

"Make yourself at home, library, kitchen, sofa, stereo. I'll be down in a few." With that, I climbed the stairs and left Amy to entertain herself.

§

Amy lounged on the sofa while she waited, contemplating this new undefined relationship. She could read the minds of most guys consistently, same mentality, different guy. Cal's was, if not impossible, different, requiring thoughtfulness, not stereotyping.

She surveyed the room. The last time she was in this room, she had overheard conversations, participated in them, or been decrypting her charming host. It felt odd to observe what she had overlooked.

The room was clean, orderly, and comfortable with blonde oak flooring. Custom hooked area rugs, framed photographs of homes, presumably built by Cal's construction company even incomplete design sketches tastefully framed made it cozy. It indulged an upright piano, TV, coffee table with architectural design books, and a picture window. A bookcase contained obscure titles, among them: *Applied Imag-*

ination, Building the Timber Frame Home, Boolean Algebra, Rise of the Human Ecumene, Theory of Constraints, The Hunt for Red October, and *Introduction to Algorithms.* Amy ran her fingers down the book spines committing the titles to memory. What she didn't find was equally intriguing, no English Italian, Italian English dictionary, and no portrait or even candid photos.

§

When I descended the stairs to the living room, Amy stood poised to stroke a few keys on the piano. She turned her head and smiled irresistibly. She was wonderfully unfair.

§

Promised a light breakfast of eggs, toast, and orange juice, Amy coasted into my driveway promptly at seven. She rested her bike's back wheel against my sidewalk's lamppost. An Eddie Bauer backpack made its way to a chair in my office before Amy followed me to the kitchen. We ate breakfast slowly and discussed a campus tour in the afternoon.

A gorgeous, bracing morning, one or two wispy clouds, contrails crisscrossing high above, dazzling sun, customarily dry, and a beautiful companion, made a ride axiomatic. Nutty aroma of leaves dissipating chlorophyll drifted in the precursory autumn air, accented with dry sage. Our route, Boulder to Lyons to Longmont and back to Boulder, was on well-trafficked roads that lacked significant vertical challenge.

Squirrels scratched noisily on the rough bark of the two silver maples that occupied my front yard, asking if today was one of those lucky days that I would salt the branches and ground with raw almonds.

"Sorry, buds, not today." The nettlesome rodents scolded and shook their tails vigorously. Their message clear. "Pay up. We know where you live."

"You feed those tree rats?" Amy asked incredulously.

"On occasion. Gotta keep them in good shape for the neighborhood owls and foxes."

The squirrel chatter ceased abruptly.

We walked our bikes to the street and saddled up.

Pedaling to the end of Hawthorne Street, Amy was admirably aggressive in gear selection and crank rate. She was an accomplished rider. On the side streets, we rode side by side. There was minimal traffic, and the local drivers were mostly respectful of cyclists.

"You up for a fifty miler?"

"It'll do for a warm-up."

The leafy green foliage of the aspens and cottonwoods hinted at the coming, flash-in-the-pan color changes. I was colorless with black Lycra shorts and a white jersey with a black Trek logo. My helmet, although silver, did have blue padded sections, my one claim to color today. Amy's dark blue shorts came just shy of her knees and sported a Bianchi blue lengthwise stripe. Her jersey also boasted Bianchi in both color and script. Her helmet was white, with pony-tailed hair streaming down her back.

Amy had adapted quickly to her bike's new Look cleat system. She swiveled her foot from her pedal effortlessly, anticipating a green light at the less green, industrial end of Boulder. Traffic was casual this Wednesday morning, so it was easy to hear, in the distance behind us, the high-pitched whine of a Maxidyne, the telltale sound of a Mack truck approaching.

"You don't wear contacts, do you?"

"I'm twenty fifteen. Why do you ask?"

"That's a belly-dump tractor-trailer coming up behind us. It'll fan up a lot of dust. Rough on contacts."

Dry grasses, and sparse, short yellow pine, cloaked the mildly undulating near horizon and dotted the flat stretch beyond our three-way intersection. In the middle distance, green leafy cottonwoods rose from secluded depressions exposing only their tops. Power poles sagged with drooping power lines hanging a dozen feet higher over a lazy barbed wire fence and equally lazy wooden fence posts. A shallow grass-lined ditch paralleled the road on which we would travel.

Route 36 runs north-south along the Rocky Mountain foothills, from Boulder to Lyons. Six cyclists in a single paceline were fast approaching our intersection from the south. All six wore matching red, green, and blue colors.

"What do you think? Should we join them?" I asked.

"Let's get out ahead and let them pass us. See if they'll take us in." Amy looked over her shoulder at me.

"Sounds good." So much for mile-high elevation assimilation.

Amy and I crossed the intersection at the green light and picked up speed. For myself, and I took for granted, it was the same for Amy; we were nowhere near full speed when the paceline overtook us. We slipped into their draft with Amy in front of me. The group left us out of their first rotation, but the second time through, the lead cyclist came to the back and drafted me.

Amy had great ease working the line. When she had the lead, she kept her cadence, gauged the mild elevation gains, paid close attention to the road, and signaled road hazards to those following. She also stayed in the lead longer on the modest ascents.

Rolling hills and long turns were our traveling fare. The westward view was of ragged, upthrust foothills that obscured the mountains they had yielded up millennia ago. They exposed the jagged, ruptured ends of the flat sedimentary formations that hid below Colorado's flat eastern plains.

Conversation and pacelines mix as well as oil and vinegar, but we did manage to pry from the group that it was from Colorado Springs. It was the third day out for the two lawyers and four independent businessmen embarking on their final summer cycling adventure. Their equipment was higher end; two rode Cannondales, the other four, Specialized bikes. They were traveling beyond Lyons for the twenty-mile, two thousand foot climb to Estes Park.

Amy and I would double back in Lyons and head to Longmont on the flats.

"Antenna farm?" Amy looked over at an understated mesa, cluttered with parabolic dishes and vertical antennae.

"It's a National Oceanic and Atmospheric Administration site."

On another rotation, Amy glanced east and noticed the many retention lakes, ponds, and reservoirs. "I'm surprised that there is so much water out there."

I slipped in behind her.

Traffic was light. Few cars encroached on the group's passing routine. The RGB's, my pet name for these red-green-blue clad cyclists, were belligerent in their possession of the road. Amy and I were independent in gab, garb, gear, and enjoyment.

"I worked out a deal on seven acres up that road," I pointed, "to build a spec home on."

"Lots of horses and horse property out here." The duration between the paceline passes punctuated our conversation. "I like it."

"You're staying hydrated?" Still attentive to Amy's adjustment to high elevation. "How's your wind?"

Next time around, I overheard the Cannondale behind me invite Amy to accompany the RGB team to Estes Park. We hadn't bothered to make introductions or take the names of our companions.

On his next pass, I heard the most antagonistic road rights rider gasp out another few unintelligible words to her.

"Hey, slick, you're annoying my friend. That's dangerous. Besides, I'll let your wife know what you're doing."

"How will you do that, brainiac? You don't know me," was his antagonistic query.

Okay, he's married. I'd bet his friends were too.

Amy, on our next pass through the rotation, engaged my eyes.

"*Lui è disgustoso.*" (He's nasty.) Amy made a face, "He ick's out at 8.0."

"Next rotation, I'll hold him out."

Dirt and asphalt flashed beneath our skinny tires. Our fellow travelers mainly looked down, missing grand vistas and beauty. Amy had the presence of mind to enjoy the sights.

Our unrepressed lounge lizard had licked his lips suggestively at Amy, heedless of my warning, on his next pass.

"Hey, Cannondale, hang back. Let's talk."

§

"He apologized;" Amy, truly curious, asked, "what did you say to him?"

"Tell you when we stop. Do you want to hang with these bozos?"

"No, let's crack 'em. You up for it?"

"You betcha."

Nelson Road, midway between Boulder and Lyons, had been my bailout plan if Amy were flagging. Not her. No, she upped the pace of this mini peloton every time she had the lead. I followed suit while the Springs group attempted to throttle back. That gave Amy and me more time on point. All the chitchats had washed-out. Impossibly, she impressed me more with her cycling prowess. Amy had her own beautiful, torturous method of cutting off unwanted dialog and very capable of winding the RGB's, and I was glad to help.

"That place is amazing," Amy gushed at the horse facility on our left. It was a beautifully maintained, horse-boarding ranch. Clean grounds and freshly painted barns and stalls, accompanied by well-groomed lawns, raked paddocks, and lunging enclosures.

"Sweet," I managed before our brief side-by-side had elapsed.

Despite the intensified pace, Amy and I continued our verbal exchanges. Our breathing was heavy, not labored. Neither of us was close to tapping into our reserves.

The same rider that had gathered us into their fold begged us to lighten up. He hung out with Amy and me for a response.

"In another twenty-five hundred feet," I told him, "after that crest, we'll have a five-mile, gentle descent into Lyons."

It was relieving news for the struggling rider.

"Stay with us or drop out. This pace isn't comfortable for us. You guys can rest in Lyons before you head up the hill."

Starting on the downslope, I stood on my pedals before sitting with a higher cadence. It was a fast break from behind Amy. She held my wheel and accelerated in-chase when I passed. We had a breakaway. By the time we reached the next intersection, the RGB's had withdrawn by a couple of minutes.

"I counted three flagstone places in the last mile," Amy observed, her foot set down at the light, "what's up with that?"

"There are a lot of quarries around. It's a function of available raw materials. A quarry north of Lyons supplied a lot of rock for CU buildings. I'll take you there another time if you're interested. We'll need different bikes, though."

We had slowed to a more casual tempo, still faster than the RGB's, as we approached the small town.

Shops and restaurants of tourist appeal lined the four lanes into Lyons. Just before the town proper, a block of businesses divided the highway into a matched pair of one-way streets. The resulting island was a teardrop shape larger at the far end. A retro convenience store marked our most northern and western progress today. We looped back to a greenbelt park that included a tourist center.

"Potty stop?"

"Sure." We coasted to a stop. "First, though, what did you say to that creepy guy?"

"I told him that I'd take out a full-page ad in the *Springs Gazette* describing their team's gear, clothing, occupations, and route. I'd call out his bad behavior in the ad but not ascribe it to any one of them. I'd place a contact telephone number for questions. It would guarantee him and his team of never taking a cycling overnight again, that is if their wives kept them."

"Ah, social C4. Why didn't you say so?"

§

"Gee, eleven o'clock. Nice, brisk bike ride, and we still have half the day to kill," Amy said brightly.

The remaining part of our ride had been paced the same as the first part, but uneventful, just the two of us. I had been overindulgent in pointing out landmarks and features, while Amy had been a gracious listener. Occasionally, I would spark from her stories of Lenox, the Berkshires, Boston, and Wellesley, of friends, old haunts, favorite rides, her home, and at length about her mom.

We leaned our bikes against the back of my house. I pulled the back door key from its recess in the porch rail, emphasizing for Amy its location and availability.

"I brought a change of clothes," Amy said as we continued through the kitchen, "I thought we could get cleaned up, have lunch, and after that, you could walk me around campus before classes start tomorrow. You could show me the library, classroom buildings, and your favorite study places, so this evening, I can get myself organized."

"Have a Gatorade." I pitched a bottle from the fridge.

Amy nimbly made the catch.

"You know the shower upstairs. On second thought, you'd better use my bathroom. Marv and Tex will be returning anytime now, and you don't want that kind of surprise. Fresh towels are in my bathroom closet.

"I'll prep lunch. Turkey club, no mayo, and chips? I have gherkins or dill spears. I'll hop up for a shower of my own after we eat."

§

Miraculously, we parked the Corrado by Old Main in the space next to the one it had occupied six days ago.

"This," I referred to Old Main, "was the first and only campus building for a time."

We might have walked the three miles from my home; however, I wanted to play the tour guide and take all the time necessary to show Amy her new campus.

Amy made a beeline to the rock with me chasing.

"Hey," I greeted in imitation of our introduction just days ago, "care for a campus tour?"

"*Siamo un pò diretti, non è così?*" (We're a little forward, aren't we?) She was in a semi-reclined pose on our rock.

"*Posso fare la guida per la tua visita in Italia per maggiore convenienza.*" (I can guide your tour in Italian for extra convenience.)

"*Andiamo, mio amore.*" (Let's go, my love.) Amy bit her lip and held her breath.

"*Mio amore,*" I reassured, my arm proffered.

Amy leaped, once again, gymnastically. She placed her left hand in the crook of my elbow, covered it with her other hand, and inclined herself toward me, theatrically poised to hang on my every word.

"Let's head toward the theater group." We crossed the Norlin Quadrangle's flat green lawn on a concrete sidewalk and headed to a stone archway between two close buildings.

"Geography,... Theater," acknowledging first right, then left. I extolled the virtues of Charles Klauder's design down to the sandstone motif.

"This is Hellem Arts and Sciences. You'll have anthropology classes here."

We took to the outdoor stage behind the Hellem, unlinked arms, and made a stage presence in the three-story building's partially enclosed theater.

A dialogue might have had a promising development had it not been for the recognition applause from two separate groups of couples and a wolf whistle from a girl who sat in the center section. An audience of nine had appeared out of nowhere.

We ran down the steps into the flagstone seating to do a meet and greet. Amy greeted the wolf whistle girl. She, it turned out, was a sophomore anthropology major. The guy I approached was a sophomore business major who supported himself with summertime concrete form setting and flatwork. His girl was a premed student. We grouped up and exchanged contact information for a later get together.

The underclassmen were surprised at Amy's and my gregarious introductions. We all enjoyed a good conversation and some good laughs.

§§

Chapter 42

At the start of Christmas break, in a parking lot between Fisk Planetarium and the Koelbel Business Building, Amy's and my strides wandered a step apart to avoid a patch of snow-dusted ice. We both overcompensated, correcting; our jackets brushed with a slight swish. Our fingers intertwined comfortably, as right as rain, on roses.

On Amy's first day in Boulder, I had taken her hand, guiding her across Broadway, away from Lance Grimaldi. That time our handholding was different, urgent, and necessary.

At Tom and Judy's wedding just after Thanksgiving, we faked our way through western swing dancing. We watched at first, then imitated what we had seen. It was nearly instinctive, twirling, reliance on counterbalance, physical contact, arms around each other, swirling in complementary orbits. It was intoxicating, even aside from the adult beverages. Between songs, our fingertips did linger, begging the question, why were they not interlocked, engaged with, and enjoying each other?

Today our hands finally had their affectionate answer to that lingering question.

"My FedEx driver should bring us a new Italian movie this afternoon. It's that, or *Father of the Bride* at the mall, or we could watch *Harvey* again."

"Movie night with linguine and salad at Cal's house." Amy solidified her grasp. "Bring down your kettle popper, and I'll make us caramel corn."

Neither of us had additional finals to burden us this semester. I hadn't yet received the blueprints and specs that Bobby promised for our very involved, upscale Telluride condominium project. Perhaps he was keeping them until I came back to town.

The idling nuclear reactor of Amy's and my relationship was experiencing the withdrawal of the metaphorical graphite rods of work and diligent study. Things were heating up rapidly.

"We have all the fixings, even breadsticks if the guys haven't finished them off. *Fume Blanc* or Fat Tire?"

"*Fume Blanc* would be perfect. What's the movie?"

"*City Slickers*, parts were filmed in Durango. Billy Crystal was a big hit when he was there. I'll be able to point out some of the filming sites when we're in town."

"You won't miss Christmas with your mom too much? You're still okay, a nice Catholic girl like you, going to Purgatory for a ski vacation with me?"

"If Mom and I can talk, we'll both be okay. And, Purgatory's okay as long as we're skiing the slopes and not in the blasted place itself. Mom will have her Tea at Whistler's friends over for Christmas dinner, Mrs. Lang, Mrs. Smith, Mrs. Thomas, and Janis."

We managed a seamless segue from hand in hand to arm in arm, mutually unnoticed until we reached the Corrado. It happened smoothly, comfortably... magically.

I opened the passenger door for her.

§

The FedEx driver had been faithful in his rounds. Our movie was set just inside the windowed storm door.

I headed straight for the kitchen. Amy joined me in minutes.

I had pasta on and wrestled with a corkscrew. We were complementary in our dinner preparations. Amy procured glasses and rummaged in the fridge. Garlic, leeks, sun-dried tomatoes all arrived on the cutting board.

"There's a note on the table," pinning it with my eyes.

Amy turned the paper napkin to read the neatly printed note.

We decided to take advantage of champagne powder at Crested Butte with the girls. See you in a few days.

Marv & Tex."

My two roommates were perceptive and thoughtful.

Fume Blanc saw us through spaghetti and meat sauce, salad, and the providentially preserved breadsticks. Much the way we had become with each other during our frequent shared meals, we had a slow, casual dinner. We ate at the kitchen table and talked at length about the drive to Durango and the places I wanted to show her. If road conditions allowed, our return trip would include Ouray, with a swim in the natural hot springs pool and dinner at the Bon Ton.

I retrieved my kettle popper from the upper shelf and placed it on the stove. Amy searched for sugar. I brought out a quarter pound of butter from the refrigerator door. Amy cranked the popper while she monitored the simmering pan on the stove. I went to the living room; instead of dimmed lights, I opted for seldom-used bayberry scented candles.

Without asking, I slipped up to Amy's side, put my arm around her waist, topped off her glass, and stirred the caramel. She, for a moment, turned her attention away from the preparations and looked up at me. A single pop became a cacophony; aroma and vapor escaped from the popper lid. The caramel seethed, too, allowing no time for even the most pleasant of distractions. She turned down the heat on the two components. Quickly mixing them, she filled a baking sheet, placed it in the oven, and set a timer.

I took our glasses to the sofa. Amy sat back, relaxing with her wine while I engaged *City Slickers* in the VCR.

§§

CHAPTER 43

Adolfo was an excellent mechanic. Lance used him solely for delicate operations. Lance had many nefarious skills and connections, but they hadn't been sufficient to have Adolfo at his disposal when he wanted him. That was in September.

Adolfo had a drug problem and a resultant incarceration at Walpole State Prison until the first week of December.

Heroin was a useful tool in Lance's repertoire, a hook for the unwary client. For the last several months, heroin had worked against him, hoisted by his own petard.

The day, the hour Adolfo was released, Lance was at the prison yard eager to transport him, detoxified and newly minted.

An excellent mechanic of men, Lance offered Adolfo a new dealer and the promise of quick money for a familiar job.

Intensely fatigued caliper bolts, coupled with disc pad distress, guaranteed brake failure. His co-saboteur assured Lance that there was a very narrow window in time and space for Cecelia Farina's homeward bound BMW M6 to careen off the road.

With the front drive wheels locked up, Mrs. Farina would spin 180 degrees, skid backward across the opposite lane, then tumble down the gaping, treed, ravine embankment. The Beamer would come to its final resting place, landing in a crumpled heap, crushed. A neighbor would explore the skid marks and freshly scuffed roadside debris.

A bug in the right attending EMT's ear would have the once lovely and hopefully only near-death Cecelia Farina flown to Mass General. It would be an accurate assessment. Sweet, predictable.

§§

The phone rang as I almost sat with a trajectory that would have ended with Amy and me, once more, in warm contact.

My silent inquiry, *should I answer it,* received a corresponding nod of approval. I took the call on the office phone.

"Amy!" I shouted with urgency, "there's an Annette Smith on the phone. Your mother's been in an automobile accident.

"Let me write down your number," I followed up with the caller.

Amy whimpered, then reacted fully to the impact of my announcement with a shriek of pain, suddenly sobbing.

"Please, talk to her," I said, without necessity.

Amy grabbed the handset.

"How serious?" Amy asked and slumped at the answer.

"Tell her that you're leaving on the next flight. To Bradley? Is she at Springfield Hospital?"

Amy relayed the inquiry.

"She's being airlifted to Mass General." Panic and weakness infiltrated her voice.

"Logan, then."

"Thank you, Annette." Amy cradled the handset softly.

"Amy, I'm sorrier than you can imagine. What can I do aside from getting you to your mom?" I had to support her as she wavered on unsteady legs. "Let me know what you need to take if anything. You'll be in Boston. I'll make flight arrangements and pull some things from the dresser upstairs."

"That's okay, Cal. I have a place to stay with Janis in Wellesley."

The wine's effects, along with our enjoyable expectations for the evening, or weeklong vacation in Durango, paled and faded to nothing in the gravity of the situation. Amy listed. Making her way to the sofa, she turned off the VCR and snuffed the candles.

"Stan," I'd raised my able travel agent. "I hate to disturb you in the evening, but I have an emergency; I need a flight from Stapleton to Logan, ASAP. First-class, two seats if possible, if not, whatever you can find. Can you head down to the agency and see what you can do?

"No, don't worry about that. It just has to be right away, immediate. Yes, direct if that exists, or short circuit layovers, there won't be any luggage. I'm driving to the airport in two minutes. Call me on my mobile phone, 303-555-1414. Thank you. Thank you, Stan. I'll talk to you in a few."

In the living room, I lifted the girl who understood me so uncannily well from her sunken spot on the sofa and tried my best to return the favors she had shown me. I only knew to hold her without an inkling of what to say. My questions would wait. My shirt was soaked where she buried her face. That dark rain, I knew too well myself. The mention of Logan recalled that mournful, dispirited time of my own. I teared up for her, unable to tell her how personally I could identify.

"Let's go," I finally broke into our silent embrace, "we'll be in Boston at about one in the morning if I can fly with you. I don't know if I'll have a seat or not."

"Thank you, Cal. Hold me for a minute more. I'll tell you, on the way to the airport, about the time this happened before. It nearly killed Mom then. She told me that I was too young to be on my own. That's what got her through."

Traffic was light, and the speeds of other automobiles were temperate. I didn't cram the Corrado's speedometer or tach.

"Single cancellation? Nothing else? Okay, the ticket will be for Amy Farina. No, thank you. One more thing, though, could you get limousine service for ground transportation to Mass General? Page for Amy Canfalierri. It's *C A N F A L I E R R I.*" I winked at Amy, squeezing out an inadvertent tear. "Just let me know Stan, we'll settle up tomorrow. Have a good night."

"Unfortunately, I'm sending you off on your own. Fortunately, you'll be flying first class. I'll be on the next flight."

"I've been spun like a top. You're right, Cal. This is too much of a coincidence, same mechanical failure, same location. Yeah, I should be paranoid. Count on you to think for me when I can't think for myself. I'd love for you to come out, but let me figure out mom's condition first."

My hand found her's to administer another squeeze of reassurance. She held on until it was time for me to shift again.

Too soon, but not soon enough, we turned south onto Quebec Street to be interrupted by traffic lights on the final stretch to the airport. We parked in the short-term parking and drifted, with consoling arms around each other, across the walk bridge to the terminal.

Worry and anxiety were new expressions for me to identify on her ordinarily delightful face. Her frame of mind affected her stride.

Once we collected her ticket and boarding pass, we made our way down concourse B to the United Airlines boarding area.

"Amy, call me when you get to a phone and let me know what you find out. I don't care what time it is. I won't be doing anything except waiting for your call. Tell Cecelia I'm pulling for her and that *anything* I can do, I will. Anything at all."

We held each other again before parting for what presaged the longest time we would be apart since meeting on the rock.

§

Note to self, flowers as soon as I can raise a Boston florist.

I drove faster on the way back to Boulder. I was infuriated that Amy had to suffer these circumstances with her mom again and agitated that I had to send her on alone.

Note two, to self, get with Peter; with any luck, he's on the night shift. Have him dig up what he can on Cecelia's accidents.

§§

249

Lance Grimaldi and Glenlivet had planned this day perfectly, down to the minutest detail over the past three and a half months. He sat in silence. His living room settee's upholstery clutched at him with shades drawn; he wanted to savor his victory.

Sorry, Lance? Not so fast. It's sorry, kid. I'm better at this. The girl is my destiny.

Three flights originated from Stapleton nonstop to Logan on this fateful evening. Lance had a single first-class seat reserved on each of the reliably full aircraft.

Destiny or not, Lance was anxious, unable to sit or stand for more than a few minutes at a time, without the self-discipline to wait, and helpless to do anything else. He couldn't even bring himself to engage in stress-relieving collection calls.

He strayed to his tall, draped windows. Peering down between the maroon curtain panels, he gazed at his cross-street neighbor and his miserable Scottish Terrier out for a relief break, little yapper dog. A wrought-iron picket fence surrounded a ten by ten-foot urban lawn kept for that purpose.

Lance's own hundred square foot set-aside broached his short but wide brick walkway. He had it sensibly landscaped with crushed white quartz. The taillights of a passing car ignited the rocks, leaving an uproar of scarlet sparks.

Revere Street's streetlights, imitation gas lamps, reflected off the roof of his Fleetwood. It was halfway through its year with Lance, would soon trade it for the '92 model. He'd already picked out its replacement.

A couple that he saw frequently walked past his yard. He pried the curtains further apart. He never saw enough of them to convert them as an addition to his revenue stream.

Lance's phone rang. *Finally.*

He left the drapes, which closed of their own weight. Still troubled, he shot across to the bar, answered the ring, and picked up a couple of cashews from his nut bowl in the process.

"Half hour before the chopper lands? How good or bad?"

"Broken jaw, a couple of ribs, a lot of lacerations. The steering column caused a punctured lung. She has a damaged liver and spleen. Messed up internally."

"Great."

He hung up quickly and dialed out.

"Brown Stone Travel? Lance Grimaldi here. I have a reservation on the seven o'clock United flight out of Stapleton to Logan. Yeah, the 1102, first-class, nonstop. You made the reservation for me several weeks ago. Cancel it. I don't need it; bill me what you need to."

Lance cut the conversation short and dialed again.

"Yeah, it's Lance Grimaldi. Get a limo out to Logan set up to page Amy Farina. Get a sign, too. She's on the United 1102 from Denver. Be there at one, and when you drop her at the hospital, tell her the ride was courtesy of Lance."

The cashews disappeared, replaced by two more. *Have a Glenlivet, you winner.*

"Winner" made Lance consider himself worthy of a social visit to the Combat Zone. Once more, he dialed out.

"Yeah, send a cab to 211 Revere Street. Lance needs a ride."

§

"What do you mean she didn't get the Limo? She was on the flight. She saw you before she could hail a taxi, right? Something so simple, how could you mess it up? Idiot."

§§

CHAPTER 46

Amy's Land Rover came to a stop on the dual approach, rural driveway. Between its two prongs, a white rail fence enclosed what was, at one time, a triangular paddock where a visiting rider could corral his or her horse. The arrangement was a convenience, featuring a gentle enough turn for tractors hauling four-wheel wagons.

Amy left the Land Rover's warmth shutting the door behind her. She advanced the few steps toward the broad white gate that prevented her progress, surveying the home. It was... comfortable.

"It's been a long two months at my mom's bedside. Cal, I want to get away," Amy had confessed before leaving him at the airport, "where I won't have guests dropping in to console me on my loss, or to comment on how beautiful the funeral service had been, how eloquent the eulogy, how lovely the flowers. I've already had time to prepare myself to grieve. I'll console with friends on their loss, but it'll be my timing.

"I packed a bag, and I'll stay a few nights on the New Hampshire or Maine coast in a bed and breakfast that stays open in the winter. Or at a ski lodge without the skis. But, not Greylock."

"I know what you mean," Cal had not interrupted. "I could stay with you... but another time would be better, don't you think?"

He understood, as always. Amy could tell that his empathy was sincere and based on his own experience.

"This is where you have to go. It'll be perfect." He had opened up her *Rand and McNally Road Atlas* and marked out a route to this location.

"There's a white Cape Cod, with black shutters, a dark slate roof, and a central chimney. There are sugar maples in the front yard and a white-board fence." Cal had conjured it from thin air with his eyes closed and spoke as if he were dreaming. "There's a red barn with an attached silo and apple trees between it and the road. Open, snow-covered fields, stonewalls...

"When you meet the caretaker, tell him this, 'You waved at me behind your back.' He'll let you stay as long as you like, and it won't cost you a cent."

"Cal, how do you know about this place? And describe it so well?"

"I have a materials supplier and friends close to there. I've seen pictures of it."

Cryptic Cal, the familiar clue for Amy to interrogate cautiously or not at all.

§

A man, comfortably dressed for the crisp, late February weather, materialized from the general direction of the picturesque red barn. He was halfway down the snow-banked driveway. A corncob pipe adorned his clean-shaven face and released an occasional wisp of smoke. His mustard-colored chore coat covered a red plaid shirt with a different green plaid collar grafted to it. He wore a tan canvas baseball cap with an attached forest green band that covered his ears. From his face, Amy surmised him to be in his mid-forties. His gait was steady, not at all hurried. Leather gloved hands hung comfortably at his side.

He walked through a meager patch of shade cast by the leafless maples lining the driveway. Ice, disturbed under the man's boots, made a satisfying crunch to both their ears.

Now within earshot, the man spoke first.

"My name's Dave Harris. What can I do for you?"

"I'm Amy Farina. A friend of mine gave me directions here. He said that a caretaker, a local farmer, maintained this farm, a trust of sorts. That caretaker would be you?"

"That caretaker would be me."

"My friend also said that I could stay here if I told you this, 'You waved at me behind your back.'" Amy noticed the slightest roll of his eyes.

"Yes. It's okay. You're welcome to stay." His friendly smile returned. "Do I know your friend?"

"Probably not. He didn't say so. His name is Calvin James. He lives in Boulder..., Colorado, and goes to the university there. That's where I met him, and except for last week, he's never traveled east of the Mississippi."

"He's right about this place. Strange, he knew that he could offer it so freely."

"He's well connected. His circle of friends throws a wide net. Doesn't surprise me."

Dave smiled unlike any other smile he'd enjoyed in the last six years. Bushy salt and pepper eyebrows and the crow's feet at the corner of his eyes agreed. He drew a puff of Erinmore.

"Let me unlock the gate so you can drive up. How long will you be staying?" Dave walked a few steps to the maple nearest him, reached up to the lowest branch, and came down with a key to the gate's padlock.

"No longer than a week. I have to wrestle with transferring credits from the University of Colorado to Wellesley so I can finish up my undergraduate degree this spring. First, though, I need some time alone and quiet to think. Do many people come to stay here?"

"You're the first since I've maintained it. The house is guest-ready, always is. The only thing that I should do is set the thermostat up for you." Dave swung the gate wide open and latched it to a post. "I'll leave this open while you're here."

"So, you don't live here yourself? I'm not intruding?" She hoped, gathered that the answer would be in the negative.

"Oh, no. My wife, Betty, and I live about two miles from here. Drive your Rover up there," pointing with the stem of his pipe to the home's attached garage. He returned the key to its hiding place on the maple branch. "I'll walk."

Amy climbed into her driver's seat, glad that the upholstery was cloth, not the standard leather. Initially inching forward, she noticed that without effort, this farmer would get to the house before her, despite the hundred-yard distance. Branches of sugar maples lining the drive reminded her of Cal quoting Hawthorne, "overreaching branches created noontide twilight." If Cal were here in the summertime, he might say the same of these maples fully leafed out. But now, their rough pewter bark and unadorned branches made thin, tenuous shadows that added a chill to the air, skeletons with promise.

Several things were just beyond the periphery of her mental sight. Puzzle pieces should fit together, but she couldn't even tell what the pieces were or how many different puzzles they went. *This is why I'm here*, she reminded herself. She so welcomed the opportunity to get away to a place, not knowing anyone. Excellent for meditation. She had plenty of ink and legal pads ready to make all the pieces fit where they should.

Every subject she could think of was open for her confrontation with her self. She would consider her mom's revelation about her dad and her dad's whereabouts. What were her plans after graduation? Had she shaken off Lance? Finally, how would she handle her long-distance relationship with Cal?

Cal's letters were sustaining and supported her when she returned to Wellesley. She'd brought all dozen of them with her. One of her first to-dos would be to write Cal a thank you note to pass on to the people who made this house available. She'd call him tomorrow.

As her Land Rover crept up the drive, she absorbed the differences in sound as snow and ice crushed under her wheels, from soft and low to crisp and loud, varying with the amount of sunlight it received.

Dave tapped out the contents of his pipe on the ankle of his boot by the garage door. After emptying the bowl, he scraped its sides with a hinged nail and tapped it out again. By the time Amy rolled to a stop, he had used the same tool to tamp down a new fill of crumbled Erinmore.

"Right this way." They walked around the corner. "Here is the key. I'll grab your bags."

"That's okay. I only have one suitcase."

From the road, the house had appeared to be a traditional Cape Cod. Then she saw the extension off the backside. The front roof-ridge hid the addition, built just inches lower. The back part was narrower than the front section, shielding it from the road.

Dave had recently and conveniently shoveled the deck clear of snow. Dave stepped to the side and deposited his pipe on the flat deck rail. A nine-light door accessed the mudroom just inside. Amy fit the key to the lock and stepped in.

"I'll show you the thermostat and then leave you to yourself."

Dave slipped out of his Sorels and led the way through the family room and the kitchen. The living room stretched from the kitchen to the front door, featuring a fireplace, an older TV, and comfortable furniture. A braided rug almost entirely covered the wide pine flooring.

"A few essentials," Dave offered, "the bathroom is around the corner that way. The towels were fresh on Wednesday. Let's set the thermostat up to seventy; adjust it where you like, though. When no one is here, we keep it set to fifty-five, just warm enough to keep the pipes from freezing.

"Betty remade the beds on Wednesday, too. There are extra blankets in the cedar chests at the ends of all of them, flashlights in the side tables. I'll leave my number on the refrigerator in case you need anything. There's a phone in the kitchen.

"What am I missing? Close the gate and padlock it when you leave for home; leave it open while you're here coming and going. Cordwood is outside beside the deck. It's there if you want a fire in the fireplace or woodstove.

Amy looked around. Peaceful and homey, perfect. Leave it to Cal.

"I'll be in the barn twice a day unless you'd like some animal care therapy. No?" Another thought occurred to Dave. "There's no food in the fridge. I'll call Betty to bring a lunch over for you."

"Thank you. That would be so nice. I'll be fine, though. I want to go up to the Sunapee area. I've been to the lake in the summertime with my mom. With the skier trade, I'm sure I'll find a good restaurant. Newport looks big enough on the map to have a grocery store. I'll stop there to stock up.

"Dave, this is perfect... and lovely. Thank you."

"You're very welcome. I'll be going. I still have to finish up with my animals. Amy, it's a pleasure meeting you. Enjoy your stay." Dave made his way through the mudroom to the deck, where he donned his Sorels and retrieved and lit his pipe. He dappled the air with puffs of smoke on his return to the barn.

Amy wandered through the house and chose the bedroom upstairs over the garage, closest to where she had parked. The window overlooked her Land Rover. A colorful quilt covered the recently made bed. The interlocking circle pattern, she recognized, but the name of it was beyond her recollection. Its dominant umber and maroon colors brightened up the room, with more autumn than winter. A Lane cedar chest opened to reveal several handsome Pendleton blankets and the aroma of sweet cedar.

It was so tranquil.

The bedroom walls, pale blue, sported a few nondescript, framed prints on either side of the window. The roof angle reflected in the walls and ceiling, joining them with an angled portion of about eighteen inches. A chair and a desk sat in the corner toward the window. Amy pulled open a drawer. She wouldn't have been surprised to find Gideons' Bible. She did find stationery, pens, graph paper, legal pads, and pencils. She closed the drawer wistfully. Classics: Stevenson, Defoe, Hemingway, Tolkien, Shakespeare, and contemporary titles graced the bookcase shelves by the desk. Robert Ludlum's, Tony Hillerman's, and Douglas Adams' series were all complete to a point, and Patriot Games was Tom Clancy's only book.

The stuffed chair would make for comfortable reading.

Amy explored the closet and found hanging, heavier LL Bean shirts and a chore jacket similar to Dave Harris's. Folded on the shelves were jeans and sweatshirts. The jeans she determined would be too long for her, and boy cut anyway, and the shirts were larger and longer than what she might have worn. Not much else spoke of the previous occupant. If the clothing told her anything, it had been a boy's room.

... We... made our way... towards one of those pleasant wood paths that wound among the overarching branches. Amy remembered Hawthorne's words and thought to take the advice.

§

"Janis, *Ciao.*" Amy dialed her Wellesley roommate.

"Amy! *Dove sei?*" (Where are you?)

257

"*Al sicuro e divinamente appartato. Chiedo scusa di averti lasciato a Lenox senza riaccompagnarti a Wellesley.*" (Safe and delightfully secluded. I apologize for leaving you in Lenox without a ride back to Wellesley.)

"*Potrei chiedere ad Alan di portarmi.*" (I could ask Alan to take me.) He was Janis's on and off, special friend.

"*Spero che questo non sia inconveniente. Sai che io e mamma abbiamo rimpiazzato la vecchia e rovinata BMW. Potresti prendere la nostra Beamer e venire al campus. Te lo spiego quando arrivo lì, ma sarebbe un favore per me. Veramente.*" (I hope that this isn't inconvenient. You know that Mom and I replaced the wreaked BMW. Would you take that Beamer and drive to campus. I'll explain when I get there, but it would be a favor to me. Really.) "*Il codice per il nostro garage è uno zero zero otto e le chiavi sono nel cassetto degli utensili in cucina.*" (The key code to our garage is one zero zero eight, and the keys are in the kitchen utility drawer.)

"*Ne sarei lieto.*" (I'd be happy to.) Janis, indeed, was pleased to help.

"*Grazie, Janis. Avrò bisogno di entrambe le auto a Wellesley. Ciao per adesso.*" (Thanks, Janis. I'll need both cars in Wellesley. Bye for now.)

"*Arrivederci. Non vedo l'ora di vederti.*" (Good-bye. I can't wait to see you.)

§§

CHAPTER 47

"Snap your fingers or lose your mark; what can you knuckleheads do faster. You idiots! You fools! I could have had my grandmother or even my cat to follow that Farina girl with better results," Lance laced his outburst with profanity, flicking foam from the corners of his mouth in rabid fury. "When will you guys realize that I've got money, lots of money, the whole spitin' world invested in this project? When I want a job done, I want it done, done right, and done right now! Jeez!

"Okay, tell me again. Ms. Farina dropped the jerk from Boulder off at Bradley Field then headed north on I-91. You jackasses thought that you could stop in Springfield, toss down a couple of Johnnie Walkers, then go to your usual post outside her Wellesley apartment, and wait for her to show up. Which she doesn't do, not last night, not even today. I should let Breathless practice on you. You're *sure* that she didn't end up in Lenox?"

"We're sure, boss. We called your guy out there. She hasn't been seen."

"Idiots, idiots, idiots. Stupid. Arrgh! Get out of here. Don't come back until you have something. Don't come back until you can tell me absolutely where she is. What are you waiting for? Get out! *Get out! Now!* Don't expect to get paid."

Lance rarely called his men to his home, today he had. He started drinking early, too. Today it was Talisker. He elbowed down at his bar and tended himself with a shot.

Ms. Farina had become unpredictable. It started when she ran off to Boulder and hooked up with that cocky college kid.

Lance tossed down another shot.

His perfect plan had been to lure Amy back to New England with Cecelia's recent automobile accident. Thanks to Adolfo's work of art, a masterpiece, under Lance's direction, Amy had come back to be with her mom.

Another shot.

His men were to keep her under surveillance until he could extort her sufficiently to tie the wedding knot and respectably seal his place at the top of his own crime family. Don Grimaldi.

The surveillance part had worked flawlessly until yesterday.

Bottoms up again.

How was he to control her if he didn't even know where she was? Spit!

One more shot.

"Lance is taking his sweet DeVille for a drive." Alcohol had transformed his self-references to the third person.

Two more shots back to back.

The shot glass impacted tumultuously against the bar.

He struck his index finger against the side of a Breathsaver roll, causing it to spin and roll toward him, an ingenious bar trick he had taught himself. He fumbled clumsily as it drifted off the bar's pleasure side and slipped into his jacket pocket.

Minutes later, his DeVille roared to life. For the benefit of Lance's admiring neighbors, he revved the Cadillac's engine to a high-pitched whine before he dropped it into drive. Smoke billowed from sweetly burned rubber. The squeal reverberated up and down the narrow street and its three-story brick canyon walls.

§§

CHAPTER 48

A discomforting dream of Cal being on the other side of an unbridgeable chasm startled Amy awake. She instinctively pulled whatever sheets and blankets that were within her grasp around her. Adrenalin swarmed cold into her bloodstream. Her mind, cluttered with cobwebs in the early, dark morning, prevented her from recalling where she was or how she got there. She stroked the mattress surface next to her and found it comfortingly cool.

The only sounds she noticed were the sheets rustling on the bed, the sudden rapid increase in her breathing, and her pulse elevated by trepidation. The unfamiliar nightstand clock flipped its paddle over to the next minute, 6:32 AM.

Rational thoughts began to come together coherently.

She wanted it to be Calvin's room where she had woken up. It would be a comfort to know that he was close, but this was only a house he had made available through his obscure connections. By his own declaration, Calvin James had never been in New Hampshire, a rare glimpse into his past, even if by exclusion. He was two thousand miles away, at home in Boulder, and would be studying or working on a bid or design when it came to be 6:32 AM where he was. Maybe he was already awake.

Under the covers, she discovered her nightclothes consisted of a long flannel shirt from the closet, buttoned all the way except at the collar. The shirt reminded her that she hadn't packed pajamas for her secluded getaway. She clicked on the bedside lamp, thankful for the low wattage bulb, and found her suitcase on the cedar chest.

She selected warmer clothes for the day and headed to the bathroom downstairs.

The house layout and her previous evening's adventure were more distinct after a shower.

Bread baked at the store, and other groceries purchased the night before at Newport's IGA were still on the counter. The fridge revealed her whole bean coffee, eggs, bacon, milk, and orange juice in a carton. She found the kitchen cabinets arranged the same way she would have done. Her dry goods fell right into place as she unpacked the paper bags.

A dreadful thought occurred to her, *what if there was no coffee grinder.* She checked the under-counter lazy susan. Fears relieved; it was a Braun. Her mother had given her a Braun for her Wellesley apartment.

She felt akin to Goldie Locks, an intruder. Then abruptly, for no apparent reason, she felt at home.

§

She wanted to weave a tale from her experience last night to entertain Cal. He would be proud. She aimed to tell her story, mercilessly drawn out, on her phone call to him. Thank heavens for Sprint's flat fee long distance plan.

She'd found a delightful restaurant on the main street of Sunapee after an aimless drive of twenty-five miles that drifted toward the ski area. A neon sign announced the charming, converted Victorian. It was the "Open" Newbury Inn. In the former home's transformation, the entire ground floor became a dining area with an enclosed wraparound porch, a kitchen, and a small bar.

Waiting for a table, she sat at the bar and enjoyed a glass of wine while fighting off several would-be single duty suitors. The last one, in particular, wanting to impress his cohorts, was very pleased with himself. Rebuffed by her once, he struggled with a scant knowledge of Italian. She laughed at him then started describing the native Amazonian Yanomamo kinship system in Italian with the same inflection of a skier raving about her exciting run through the moguls. The wannabe suitor nodded, thoroughly understanding.

I will dub you Naught, Amy mulled soundlessly.

Naught had reached for the decoratively swirled sheaf of bar napkins in front of Amy, presumptuously violating her personal space. His other hand lingered around her waist for faux stability. She stood briefly and surreptitiously positioned a leg of her stool just above the top of his chic light blue deck shoe. She sprung swiftly onto her seat before Naught realized his foot was doomed. If he was a vacationing skier, she had just gutted the remainder of his trip.

She felt no qualms about her aggressive personal defense, but she wasn't emotionless, actually taking pleasure in her creativity.

She thought of Calvin again, how he had first come to her defense with Lance. *How indulgent his social criticism was when he confronted the armed, angry, combative, and dangerous jerk. How similar to that was this encounter? How influential had Calvin been to her, and how beneficial was that influence?* She intended to explore those questions this week.

All the restaurant patrons had turned from their fine dining, alcoholic beverages, and banal conversations to Naught's excessively dramatic and painful outburst. Amy offered equally melodramatic pseudo-apologies to him and the distracted patrons. Naught attempted to walk away unaffected, retreating with a magnificent limp instead.

A broken bone or bones were, no doubt, the result. His self-absorbed image had suffered as well. It would suffer again when he recalled that she had apologized in perfect English.

Amy had remained calm, as if entirely disconnected. Consequently, she had immediate solo table seating and had enjoyed a delicious lobster salad with a split of Pouilly-Fuissé. The waiter very unobtrusively topped her wineglass every time he noticed that it was only half-filled. She finally had to stop him before he started her fourth split. After black coffee and a chocolate cherry torte, she'd left the last untouched wine split as a material gratuity along with a generous monetary one.

§

The cold morning and her deep comfortable sleep piqued her appetite. She made short work of eggs, bacon, and toast with apple butter.

"Cal, Cal, Cal." She muttered in rapid succession, stepping from the kitchen to the living room. She parted the glass doors on the fireplace and poked at the ashes. A glowing bed of coals remained from the fire she'd kindled before leaving for Sunapee. Tinder nestled on the log grate took to flame quickly. The fire pleaded for a more robust fuel. Partially consumed log ends, she turned to the middle with fireplace tongs. The flames were satisfied and caught rapidly.

In the time she took to get coffee in hand, her first legal pad, and a pen, the quirky fireplace was ready to have the flames enclosed behind glass. Amy fed logs to the fire, turned the heat exchange blower to low, and made herself comfortable in the recliner.

Words never before flowed so effortlessly from her mind and heart to paper. Three cups of coffee later, she brewed another pot. She had pages filled and paragraphs upon paragraphs, categorized and devoted to remembering her mom, about Cal, about this remarkable home, what her first words to her newfound father would be, about her studies, Boulder and her circle of fast friends there, studies and friends at Wellesley, and her activities for the remainder of the week. She even detailed out new thoughts on her senior thesis. More darkly, she had written about Lance and the threat he still posed.

It was a singular work, an autobiography, and a short-term life plan. It should have taken her all week, not a mere few hours. Amy promised herself to review, modify, and add to it over the next few days while she was here.

§

Amy heard a knock at the mudroom door, the sound of a latch releasing, and a telltale creaking hinge. Alarmed for the second time this morning, she froze. She wished she could silence the percolating coffee.

"Hello, Amy? Are you decent?" It was Dave.

"Yes, Dave. I'm here in the living room." Relieved. "I've been up for a few hours."

"I saw the smoke from the chimney. Are you doing okay?" He turned into the kitchen from the mudroom, with an arm full of split maple and applewood. "I see that you figured out the fireplace."

"It works great. I lit a fire yesterday evening, and there were still live coals in the grates this morning. You said the young man who lived here designed it to draw in or have air blown in for combustion. Sounds very clever."

"He was clever. His folks had to replace a cracked chimney flue, so he convinced them to replace the whole fireplace.

He lined up the mason, mixed and carried cement, and laid bricks, too. He was always learning and thrived on hard work."

Dave let down the logs into the tinderbox by the fireplace and walked back to the kitchen, his felt liners scuffed rhythmically and lightly on the wide-pine floor.

"Dave, tell me about what happened here," Amy inquired, following him, "about the family that lived here. I'll pour you a cup of fresh coffee and help you with your girls in the barn if you would take a few minutes."

"I'll take the coffee and the help. Telling won't take long." Dave sat down at the kitchen table, an obviously familiar place for him.

Amy filled two cups with coffee, poured milk from a carton into two shot glasses, and put her raw sugar in a small bowl. These she arranged on the curious hammered-aluminum serving tray she'd discovered leaning against the counter backsplash. Grabbing paper napkins and a couple of spoons, she completed the serving and flashed back to Camilla in Boulder as she set the tray on the table.

She missed her Jamaican friend.

She handed Dave his cup and doctored her own with milk and sugar.

"Thank you, young lady. Please, though, don't buy milk that way. I'll bring you raw milk tomorrow, or you can come by the house, meet my wife, and get the good stuff this evening after milking. Much better than processed." Dave shuffled himself in his seat, took a sip of his coffee, black with a touch of sugar, and nodded approvingly. He leaned back again and began his narrative.

"This is a small community. I'll bet you never even knew Acworth existed before yesterday. Typical close-knit New England."

"I wouldn't have, but I cite Talcott Parsons in my senior thesis. He wrote his better work here." Amy interrupted.

"You're a sociologist then?"

"Anthropologist with mathematical applications."

"A genuine creative scholar. I'm very impressed."

"Thank you. Don't think me rude; I could easily get sidetracked by my thesis. But the family..."

"Not at all. I would be honored to read your finished thesis, though; I might understand some of it.

"Let me tell you about the Barton family. They owned this house, a very winsome, beautiful couple, had two sons. They bought this place in '85. They'd moved from Plaistow on the other side of the state. One son was a high school senior, the other in college. The dad and mom ran the Barton Insurance Agency down in Keene. I had all my insurance through them, still insure through the same company. A few years ago, thugs shot both the parents dead after they returned from their lunch. Thugs shot and killed the older son, Phil, too.

"The other son, Michael, had unexpectedly enlisted in the navy months previous to this, though MIT had already accepted him. He even could have gone there instead of finishing his senior year of high school, but he changed his college plans. He was exceptionally smart, his future very promising. He wanted to travel and wanted GI bill help for his studies. He had to leave the same day as the shootings. A stray bullet killed him as he was observing a live-fire drill just two days into basic training. He didn't even make it to his own family's funeral. Naval authorities investigated but didn't find any relationship of his death to his folks or his brother. Within a week, the whole family was gone."

"That is awful. Makes me want to cry." Amy's eyes moistened. She couldn't tell; was it the proximity to her mom's death or the sad story?

She thought that by Dave's facial expression, he had more that he could say but chose not to. Reading a stranger, a stoic New Englander at that, was difficult at best.

"My mom died ten days ago." Amy dabbed a tear with her napkin.

"I'm so sorry. Why didn't you say so?" Dave said, leaning forward, suddenly concerned.

"Thank you, but you needn't be sorry. She was in an auto accident two months ago and died of complications. I'd expected her to go at any time for the last two months. We had a great relationship and talked about her end a lot. I came here to get away from feigned sympathy. I'll mourn with her friends on my own time."

"So, your dad? Where is he in this picture?"

"That's part of my life that needs attention. I don't remember ever having met my dad, but that will change on Friday. My mom told me where to find him and that he would be anxious and pleased to meet me.

"I have Calvin, too; he's an incredible person. I'm sure he'd impress you; he's smart, industrious, kind, and very protective of me."

"So, what of this Calvin? Why isn't he here with you?"

"There's so much to say about him. He's very... careful about his past. He has his own successful construction company in Durango, Colorado, and a home there, but we met at the University of Colorado in Boulder. He majors in engineering, construction management, and law. Fifteen minutes after we met, he defended me from a knife-wielding freak who followed me from Massachusetts and was stalking me. Ever since meeting Cal that day, I've always felt safe. He's like a big brother... without the 'brother' part.

"He's charitable, too. That's so unusual in a guy his or my age, isn't it? He's old-fashioned in a lot of ways, even in our relationship. In some ways, I wanted him to be here. If he's not here, though, he won't skew my thinking.

"I've written down a lot of recollections and reflections already this morning, trying to get them organized so I can live right and make good decisions." Amy stared off, momentarily, into the middle distance and asked, "So how did you come to be the caretaker of this place?"

"Mind if I smoke my pipe?" Dave sipped his coffee.

"Generally, I don't like tobacco smoke, but last night when you were leaving, the aroma from your pipe was so rich, if you don't mind me saying, paternal. So, I'll give you a conditional yes." Amy laughed at herself.

"Thanks." Dave pulled out his tobacco tin, packed his corncob, tamped with his hinged nail, and lit it with a safety match snagged from his shirt pocket. "How did I get to be caretaker here? This is what I know, I've mowed hay on the Barton farm, trimmed pasture and fence lines, pastured cows, repaired fences, and wintered dry cows in the barn, even before the Bartons bought the place. A month after the family passed away, I received a letter. It said that there was a checking account at the Walpole Savings Bank, for which I would sign a signature card. Annually, a specific amount would be deposited for me to use for any purpose, be it property maintenance or personal. The understanding was that I would continue to use this property and that I would maintain it as if occupied, those words exactly. Six years later, here I am."

"Well," Amy's high-octane curiosity had a welcome distraction to engage with; she would watch Dave's response closely, "did the letter include a passphrase for using this place? Like, if anyone shows up and says you waved at them behind your back, they can stay here without limit?"

"Young lady, your inquiry does you proud. Are you studying journalism, too? Or just a good detective?" A small puff of sweet smoke escaped from Dave's lips. "No, that wasn't in the letter. The letter was strictly business, short and direct."

A tip and swallow of Dave's coffee punctuated his answer.

"Here's the thing, along with the letter was a photograph of me on my John Deere B with the cutter bar on as I drove up the road between my farm and here. You could see the smoke from my pipe. Taken from behind; my right hand was waving behind my back, for the life of me; I don't recall ever having a good reason to have done such a thing. As a matter of fact, who would have the opportunity to take it? Written on the backside was, 'You waved at me behind your back.' The next line was, 'Yes, it's okay.' Two lines of a script. I considered it curious at the time, peculiar. It took me aback when you said those words yesterday. Although I meant what I said, you see I had my scripted reply, 'Yes, it's okay.' from the photo."

Dave pondered aloud, "Food for thought, isn't it?" Another wisp of smoke rose.

§

"Amy, you don't have to help out in the barn. It can be aromatically challenging, but it's not that much work." Dave said in semi-apology for having made the suggestion."

"Rhetorical or not, let me help. Work is good therapy. It'll help me out. You go. I'll be along in a few minutes."

"Okay, Amy, I hope you know what you're in for. Come in through the door on the lower level." Dave stood to leave.

Smoke billows bread-crumbed his trail to the barn.

Amy skipped up the stairs, two at a time, to her bedroom. After twenty hours, she now thought of it as her own.

It dawned on her that she never had this accelerated, if selective, sense of ownership until she had met her Cal. Thoughts to put to her legal pads.

She quickly recovered a flannel shirt and jeans, without regard for their boy cut and length, from the closet and made short work of changing. She rolled up the pant legs less than she thought she might. In the chore coat pocket, she found a rolled-up, R. N. Johnson, John Deere hat, and put it on, tucking her ponytail up protectively under it. Downstairs, in the mudroom cabinet, she found a pair of nearly new Sorels nearly her size. She ran out the deck door while she pulled her coat around her and trotted to the barn.

§

Dave looked up to see Amy at the end of the stable. He gasped and almost dropped his pipe. "Lord, Amy. Dressed like that, for a fleeting second, I thought you were the ghost of Michael Barton standing there."

§

"I'd be happy to tend to your girls for the next couple of days if this is all it takes."

"That's all there is. They get hay and silage in the front, and the water bowls need to work. Muck out the end result and put down clean wood shavings, morning and evening." Dave was thankful for the offer. "You're on vacation, though."

"Not really, I'm here therapeutically. For me, it's a week of mental health recovery and planning. I can't be idle for long. Activity will do me good," Amy reassured, then remembering her need for exercise. "So, what would be a good hike from here? And, what would be a good time to stop by this evening to meet Betty and to pick up a quart of genuine milk?"

"There aren't many open trails close by at this time of year. There's a pair of Tubbs modified bear paw…, they're snowshoes, in the mudroom closet, and the Barton boys used to Nordic ski…" Dave left the suggestion in the air, right next to a wisp of smoke.

"The Tubbs aren't complicated," Amy interjected.

"At the corner of the field, over that way, you'll find two stonewalls that parallel a small stream. The space between them is grown up with trees now. Used to be, farmers moved

269

animals from pasture to pasture that way. If you hiked far enough, those walls would take you close to Acworth Village.

"Stop by the Harris house around six tonight. Call us if you won't make it, or we'll be out on snowmobiles hunting for you. Turn right, before the river, at the foot of the hill. First house on the right, come hungry. I'll have Betty set an extra place."

§

"Dave, Betty, thank you both so much. This week has just flown by. You've made me feel profusely welcome. I want to do something lovely for you. I know that you'd refuse, so I'll have to be resourceful. And I'll have to come back."

Amy was leaving her outstanding refuge, the place, and these lovely people, reluctantly. She had stopped by the Harris home to make her goodbyes. Their welcoming farmhouse kitchen, where she had dined with them for dinner three times, was now the scene of mutual affection. It smelled of warm bread and gingersnap cookies. Happily coerced, Amy took offerings of both.

"Amy, you've done us a world of good, too, more than you can know." Betty was effusive. "It was heartwarming to see smoke coming from the Bartons' chimney and to know that you were staying there."

"Come back soon and often. You know where the keys hide. We'll know you're here if we see your Rover."

"You're sure you have to leave so early?" Betty was earnest. She would have had Amy stay longer, having found a fast friend.

"This is my third home. I have Lenox, Boulder, and now, here. I do have to go. I need a slow drive to prepare to meet my dad. I've called ahead. I know I shouldn't be, but I'm really, really nervous." She knew that these great people were concerned. "I'm headed cross country; Marlow, Stoddard, Hancock, Peterborough. They must be lovely places."

"Take care, Amy." Dave and Betty waved goodbye to the girl they now considered as family.

§§

CHAPTER 49

Easter Sunday evening, I set out to pen my regular four-day update to Amy.

Dearest Amy,

I woke up before sunrise today, thinking of a Shakespearean Puck. "I am that merry wanderer of the night. I jest to Oberon and make him smile." I had been dreaming of your smile. If a benevolent Puck were to blow out our candles, how bold or mischievous would I be? (Last Christmas would have been too soon.)

Today being Easter Sunday. I thought of Harvey. Maybe a genial six-foot-tall rabbit might stop time for us. I would share those occasional eternities with you. (I hope that you won't get tired of me saying I wish you were here with me, or I were there with you.)

Could I amuse you with a twisted approach to the Easter Bunny? I've enclosed a copy of what I've done so far with a monograph entitled The Monotreme Lagomorph, Nocturnal or Crepuscular. It starts with lineage from the Minorcan Giant Lagomorph. Perhaps you would like to co-author in your spare time.

It seemed that the downtown cemetery was an ideal place to think about the question of nocturnal or crepuscular. So, I biked over and parked at that ornamental iron arch by Pleasant and Ninth. Do you recall it? We've walked and biked past it many times on the way to your house.

The lilacs were budded and ready to open when the sun shone on them. Normally my allergies would wreak havoc on my sinuses. I'm attributing their lack of success this year to you.

I put the letter aside while I thought about how to write down my cemetery encounter. After sitting on the back steps staring at our empty Adirondack chairs for a few minutes, I brought the letter from my office to continue it at our kitchen table. Despite our long-distance relationship, I curiously considered the places we spent time together as cooperatively owned.

You may be able to help me make sense of my cemetery adventure.

I noticed a small gathering of people in the distance among the stones and monuments, all dressed for chilly weather.

A man was walking up behind me only slightly faster. He was about five-eleven, gold-rimmed glasses, oval face, not quite clean-shaven. He had an olive complexion, black hair, cut short, with a voice that invited attention. We never exchanged names.

This is the rather long version. I don't know what, if anything, to make of it.

TG (The Guy): You here for the sunrise service?

Me, perplexed: You mean those guys over there?

TG: It's a Resurrection Day Sunrise Service. Anybody can go.

Me: So, what's it about?

TG: We're celebrating the first visits to Jesus' empty tomb.

Me: Isn't that a little archaic? I mean, respectfully, do you believe that?

TG: What's not to believe?

Me: I think that it's a myth. I'm here answering a tongue-in-cheek research question for an anthropologist friend of mine, Monotreme Lagomorph, Nocturnal or Crepuscular?

TG, laughing: Funny. I'd go with crepuscular. Your egg-laying bunny, that's mythical, but not so the empty tomb.

TG talked about real centurions who guarded the tomb where Nicodemus laid the body of Jesus. He said the penalty for them letting their guard down for even a moment was death. Sleep, which was the excuse the centurions used when the body went missing, should have resulted in their execution, even crucifixion, which didn't happen to them.

Also, in Jewish culture, he said, false testimony was punishable by death. The occupying Romans took that penalty away so the Jews couldn't administer capital punishment. False witnesses could only receive from the Jews lashings or shunning. He said Jesus' disciples testified that Jesus had risen from the dead. After that, Jesus showed himself to over five hundred people who testified to seeing Him, but none of those were killed or punished.

My companion did a little "Hm?" when he finished a challenging statement.

Me, flatfooted: Okay. You're saying that Jesus actually died and then wasn't dead?

TG reminded me of Nixon's inner circle, Colson, Liddy, Magruder, Mitchell, Halderman, the world's most powerful men at the time. How long and under what penalty did they crack and speak the truth? Then he asked how likely was it that Jesus' inner circle would never contradict their initial account? They were a ragtag bunch, uneducated, but steadfast in their profession of Jesus, even when facing excruciating deaths.

I'd never thought about it that way. He was talking God stuff as if it was real.

He said that, across time and space, the laws of physics are constant. Why would you expect that to be true when even your next-door neighbor will turn the pages of a book differently than you do? Then he reminded me that Einstein pursued a universal theory.

He also asked, "have you ever heard what Heinrich Hertz said, 'We can not study the theory without feeling that mathematical formulas have a life of their own, and that they appear sometimes more intelligent than we ourselves, and even than the master who established them, giving out more than he looked for in them."

I admitted that I had.

While we continued walking, TG provoked me with more questions like, can you tell the difference between a manufactured item and a product of nature? When you look at a watch, you know it didn't grow in a vegetable garden.

You wouldn't wait in a junkyard until a Volkswagen assembled itself. Think about the beautiful intricacies of DNA reproduction, that's much more complex than an automobile. How long would you have to wait for that?

He proposed that discovering elements of design is a valid inquiry. He said SETI's Carl Sagan thinks it's a legitimate undertaking when it involves searching for extraterrestrial intelligence, looking for evidence of design among celestial radio signal noise. Is a thing or signal designed, or is it a product of chance? Which direction does the evidence point? Though Sagan, he said, doesn't extend that courtesy to any spiritual results to those inquiries.

I laughed.

TG asked that if you have evidence of design in the origins of life like DNA reproduction..., A builder knows that specifications for a construction project are written by...? He punctuated with his Hm.

Four times he hit me with my own experiences, physics, my VW, Hertz, and construction. He couldn't have known about the Hertz quote.

I asked, "do I know you?"

He said he just liked to talk and asked again, "so, who gets to write up the specs?" then added, after a moment's pause, that I could purchase those Designer's specs for reality at Barnes and Noble for about $12 in the form of a Bible.

"Help me out here. You're kidding me. What am I missing?" I asked.

He backed off, saying if he'd gotten me to consider the reality of God, of Jesus, he'd be happy.

I did mingle with the group that had gathered. A generator, barely audible, powered a small sound system. A poor guitarist bent his cold fingers to strum an acoustic guitar and played songs I didn't recognize. The group sang along. I kept the program booklet they handed out. It had the song lyrics and the Bible verses that they read.

There were several younger families with kids, a couple of empty nesters. Most, I guessed, were CU students judging by their ages. When the guitarist finished, the sun broke above the horizon toward the campus. Folks shifted to take advantage of its minuscule additional warmth.

A person stepped up to the microphone. He said; the Psalms were dated hundreds of years before Christ and predicted the method of death Jesus suffered. He said, too, that when the Psalms were written, crucifixion hadn't been invented. He combined his Psalm reading with excerpts from an article in the Journal of the American Medical Association that described the physiology of crucifixion. JAMA and the Psalm were remarkably similar, and both told of how efficient and torturous a form of execution it was.

Another person read the Gospel accounts of the empty tomb. The same as I'd heard from TG.

Another speaker read, "Greater love has no one than this, than to lay down one's life for his friends," and, "For God so loved the world that He gave His only begotten Son that whoever believes on Him should not perish but have everlasting life.

"If there is no resurrection of the dead then Christ is not risen," he continued, "and if Christ is not risen, our preaching is empty and your faith is also empty, your faith is futile; you are still in your sins! If in this life only we have hope in Christ, we are of all men the most pitiable."

Nicely syllogistic. Straight from the handout.

The people were shivery, but they looked anything but pitiable. Amy, you're Catholic. Does this ring familiar?

The frosty guitar player sang another song. Then the last speaker said, "in a gathering of this size, I don't recognize everyone. You," glancing off to my left.

"Or, you," looking straight at me.

"I want to invite you to our traditional Resurrection Service. We meet in the gymnasium of that school right behind you at ten every Sunday morning. I hope to see you all there. If you show up this morning at eight-thirty, we'll serve you breakfast; pancakes, maple syrup, bacon, sausage, eggs, OJ, coffee."

Why not, that little voice inside me said, you're always treating other folks?

"The Lord bless you and keep you; the Lord make His face shine upon you, and be gracious to you; the Lord lift up His countenance upon you, and give you peace. Now, and forever, amen."

That was it, TG was nowhere around, and the people were leaving.

My dear Catholic anthropologist, what do you think about this? I still don't know what, if anything, to make of it.

Now that I've monopolized the first part of my letter, how are you? Have you gone back to that house in Acworth or heard from the caretakers?

Thanks for sending me your thesis draft. That was an excellent treatment of morays and folkways. You have them excellently elaborated with Venn Diagrams and set theory implications. I'm sure that ANDs, NANDs, ORs, NORs, and IF ELSEs are not too far off in developing associated algorithms. (Do you want me to send my algorithm book?) Will your colleagues allow your work to remain diagnostic only and not predictive? Might be wise to mention. Regardless, you're on the verge of single-handedly resurrecting the respect of anthropology in the academic community.

I invariably hear your voice when I read your work (like I hear you when I read, and reread, your letters.)

How is your relationship with your dad progressing? We haven't talked or written about him much. I'm glad that you're able to reconcile with him.

You'll have to tell me the deal behind switching your Rover with your mom's Beamer in Southborough when you go to see him; sounds thoroughly clandestine. I can't wait. I like it already.

When the timing is right, I want to meet your dad and to get to know him. You know my regrets about only talking to your mom over the phone.

Cam, Kik, Sue, Ted, Peter, and Marcia all say, "Hi."

Tell Janis and your dad, I said, "Hello."

Thanks for putting up with me and the many miles between us.

I hope that I'll be able to come out for a visit soon. We should visit that bakery that you frequent in Southborough, take some time in Lenox, and maybe visit that homestead in Acworth.

I still want to get us to Durango, too, when you're okay to take a break. It's too late for skiing, but always lots of fun stuff to do. You know Smart Start closes down the second week of June.

With much Love and missing you, Cal.

§§

CHAPTER 50

Amy's question, the one I had been expecting since I first met my phenomenal companion, arrived in letter form, with an indelible red ink postmark of June 4, 1992, Southborough, MA. I found it Sunday morning on my desk where Marv or Tex had left it.

The distance between us was not the issue; her dad now anchored Amy in New England. She had little to offer about him, though. I knew that she made time to visit him every Monday. What could I say? My past was a closed book to everyone; no quid pro quo.

Amy began her missive appreciating our mutual respect of persons, our need to devote time to our studies., and describing at length how each of our many outings affected her. She wrote about my surprise horseback picnic near the Caribou Ranch, our all-day hike up Mount Elbert, relaxing at the Glenwood Hot Springs public pool, the bicycle ride when we took shelter from the rain in a gazebo in Estes Park, seeing Kik and Sue perform at the comedy club in LoDo Denver, the Sun's basketball game against the Denver Nuggets, the afternoon drive to Fort Collins with a late evening, dancing to rock and roll music at the Starlight, and on. She did say that she missed me and signed off with her usual "Love, Amy," but... Amy had summed up this affirmative letter with the question that would forever determine our relationship's direction.

"Who are you, Cal, and what does that mean for us?" The question I most feared brought the dread of unplumbed loss upon me. I couldn't answer the latter part of her query without answering the first. Without a change, the first part was impossible. I couldn't be truthful even about my place of birth. *How simple was that? How devoid of trust did I appear? How devoid of answers.*

For all our time together in Boulder, I sensed that Amy protected me from that same inquiry. Now she wanted to know, to understand, just what she helped me to hide.

Even at the outset, with my very forward, "Hey." I knew, inevitably, this day, this question would come, no matter the provocation. I'd even asked myself the question, *how long?* If there were any move forward in Amy's and my relationship, I would have to respond. Otherwise, there was nothing to build upon. *But how could I?*

I set her letter next to the phone. I needed the wisdom to place in the scales, life in witness protection with love lost, and a conceivably abbreviated life, with love gained. Admittedly, it was unconfessed, perhaps unilateral love.

Unilateral? I don't think so.

§

Peter Nori had been adamant, discouraging me from opting out of WITSEC. I'd never seen him angrier. My handler in Durango echoed the same argument. Stepping outside the US Marshals' protection would be suicidal.

Deception versus truth had come up over coffee with the pastor of a church that met in a close-by school gymnasium. His advice came down on the side of truth.

"The time for truth," he said, "usually comes well before events which cause a choice to be based on situational ethics. Truth anticipates difficulties. Deception reacts to them."

I reasoned that Amy's question was rooted in her father's concern for his daughter. A man who was as mysterious to me as my past was to both of them.

It was a father's thoughts and advice I craved. I had mentors, but I knew of only one living person who had exhibited a paternal concern for me. What would that man's counsel be? Would he give it if I asked? Wasn't it the sparsely counseled decision to enter the witness protection program that created this dilemma?

If I saw him, could I convince Petros Belluno to provide me a reprieve from those contracted to kill me? Doing so would be to expose Michael Barton. He would no longer be dead; only his whereabouts would be unknown. How long could I hide that?

I would have love or die trying.

§

Serendipity, I hadn't scheduled it. Who, I wondered, *put it there?*

My plan was a Sunday flight to Boston, then Monday, have a short discussion with the man who might have the influence necessary to set Calvin James free. Free him to talk about his past and remove the barrier to a much closer Calvin James, Amy Farina bond. I sought release from the belayed, suspended life of Michael Barton. Petros Belluno, from whom I'd received my last look of fatherly concern, might do that for me.

Serendipity basks in slipping in unannounced. Today it sashayed with panache.

§

The anticipation of my encounter with Mr. Belluno was nerve-racking, not helped by my Sunday evening flight transforming into a Monday morning red-eye.

Blue skies with clouds, leafed out trees, narrow roads, and the green grass of New England intruded on my attempts to be at peace with my decision.

Inside the ordinary-looking steel building, prison was prison, bars, locks, stripes in the hallways, clean and linear. Mr. Belluno appeared, except for his prison orange, as I had seen him in the courtroom six years ago.

He greeted me warmly across a cafeteria table. He was rested, resolute, and at peace. His easy recognition and graceful greeting put me at ease.

"Michael Barton!" His handshake was firm and affirming. "Son, you look good, I'm glad. I never had a chance to say how very, very sorry I was that you were tragically involved in that Boyle mess. I never had the chance to offer condolences on the loss of your parents and your brother. It wasn't appropriate, at the time, to contact the Taylor family about your brother's girlfriend, either. I didn't foresee or have the slightest control over that. I'm *so* glad that you are among the living."

"Mr. Belluno, thank you. I saw the shock on your face and concern for me as I went to the judge's chambers. Your expression looked to me as if you wanted to protect me as a father might." As I searched his face, our meeting eyes confirmed that his care was still there. "That look caused me to believe you then. I believe you now."

"Call me, Pete, Michael. You know that you shouldn't be here of all places, especially as a requested addition to my visitor list. But I am relieved and overjoyed to see you."

"Sir, Pete, I mean, I've already concluded that Tom Boyle's death was an accident, the regrettable result of ferreting out a subversive in your organization. My family's fate was, no doubt, the action of that same person."

Pete marveled at the depth and correctness of my insight.

"My hope in coming here was to ask you for advice and relief. The advice I'm asking for is, do I fear or trust?"

Except for Amy Farina, I rarely felt the need or desire to seek wisdom from others. I shifted uncomfortably.

"Do I fear for my life, or do I open my past in favor of trust and love? It's a question I'd ask my dad if I could. But I'm desperate to get out from these prison walls of witness protection. So, I'm also asking you to do whatever you could to remove any cause I might have to remain in witness protection. Is my being here a mistake? Please tell me it isn't."

"No mistake. No misadventure. I'm certain that your being here is by divine appointment." Once again, Petros Belluno's eyes spoke volumes of sincerity and certainty.

I thought "divine appointment" a curious statement, but I had an agenda of my own. "I don't want to deceive anyone or hide my past anymore. I have a very dear friend..."

"Wanting to pursue honesty says a lot about you preserving your character. My advice, be truthful," Pete preempted. "I still have contact with the better people who were in the family business. I can put the word out to them, but I'm sure they wouldn't ever harm you. Lance Grimaldi is the man who now has control over the business. You want to be concerned about him. I don't have any influence there."

Pete took a glance at the industrial wall clock, a sliver of apology for cutting me off.

"Right now, son, I'm concerned about my daughter. She's late and hasn't missed our time together on Mondays since we started in February. It was she that I expected to see today. Although, she may have gone to Colorado to pick up her belongings. She left them in Boulder, and she wanted to talk to her special friend...,

"Michael, what's the matter?" Pete reacted to my look of incredulity.

"Your daughter is Amy Farina?" I observed abruptly.

Pete, startled, jumped from his seat and stood, catching the guard's attention. He reseated himself quickly and uneasily.

"How do you know that?" His smile dissolved into a tightened jaw, compressed lips, and narrowed eyes. "Only a few people know that she's my daughter, treacherous people I once trusted."

Words formed in my mouth. *Should I say them?* Trust the truth was my slow realization.

Pete watched my conflicted struggle, furious at what I might say.

"Pete, I'm the one that she would be visiting in Boulder! I'm Calvin James!"

A thoughtful, collaborative, collective pause ensued.

"You trust *me* with your changed name?"

I affirmed with a nod.

Pete composed himself more quickly than I did.

I reeled, knowing Amy's dad sat across the table. Doubling down, I'd given a former crime family boss, whom the courts and law enforcement thought I needed protection from, my legally changed name.

Pete had already moved on to the implications of my confession.

"You've already brawled with Lance Grimaldi," Pete weighed that fact. "He's the one who would have a contract out on Michael Barton, maybe Calvin James, too. You've delivered Amy from him once before. She told me of that fight several times. Beautifully done, belittling him so well. That was you. It's no wonder that she couldn't tell me anything about Calvin James' past."

I was dumbfounded.

Pete smiled, enjoying the presence of the one his daughter thought of so highly and who treated her so well. He savored the moment before becoming serious again.

"If you're here and Amy is on her way to Colorado," Pete continued his thought, explaining for my benefit, the motivation of our nemesis, "she is in danger. Lance is obsessed with marrying her, claiming it's his destiny. He wants that relationship because it lends absolute credibility to his 100 percent family business takeover. He'll snag her and leverage me, my well being in prison, to coerce her to marry him. He plagues me with that scenario regularly. You know, only in part, how ruthless he is."

It had been years since I raged at the unwarranted death of my parents. I'd never expected to feel that way again, but that dolorous anger threatened to surface. I could see the same fires burning in Pete. I had to admire the man once more. Although his emotions were in turmoil, his mind regained control, and his posture straightened in resolve.

"Sir, Pete, I can't, I will not allow that to happen." I found in Pete's example the courage to exercise the same self-control and resolve to act. "I came to meet with you because I wanted to be honest with your daughter. Under the US Marshals, it wasn't something I could do. You can be sure I'll have them all over me for pulling my little stunt here today. That pales in comparison to Amy's safety. Amy is the most fantastic, fun, intelligent, very perfection of a girl I've ever known, and she is precious to me.

"Grimaldi and I have conflicting destinies," then suddenly, I reflected on Pete's similar suffering and knew we had that anger in common, "I would very much have liked to have met Cecelia. I'd only talked to her over the phone a few times. Even still, I knew of her motherly concern for Amy. I see now that her concern extended to protect both you and her. She did such wonderful work, bringing her up. I'm sorry for your loss. I came out for Cecelia's funeral."

"Then you sent Amy to your old home for peaceful reflection in safety," Pete propelled the conversation forward, not dwelling on his loss. The apple doesn't land too far from the tree.

"Afraid so," I confirmed, "I knew that she would be secure and comfortable there."

"Tell you what, Cal, aside from her time in Boulder adventuring with you, and she never tires of telling me all the things you did together, she had the best time at that country house. It's obvious that it's still a home; you chose your caretaker well."

Pete's connection of Dave Harris to me struck me as extraordinarily intuitive and a complement to Dave's character.

"Do you have any idea what Lance might do?" Could I, could we capitalize on Pete's intuition? Could we come up with an actionable plan? There was no question; we had to.

"I heard yesterday... I hear things..., Grimaldi wanted a marriage certificate signed before meeting with criminal counterparts in New York this Wednesday. And Amy was finished with college. I was ready to send her to your Acworth home for protection this afternoon. If she's headed back to Colorado..., she's become quite adept at eluding him. He'd find out too late that she'd left the state to stop her, so he'd arrange to intercept her at Stapleton International. A limo page..., Have the limo drive her toward Boulder, then lock down the doors and windows, and circle back to the airport to pick up him and his crew. That's the way I would have done it." He reasoned well under stress.

"Well, I can clear up if she's on her way to Colorado with a call to her Boulder roommate. Amy would call Cam, and she'd leave a message on my phone. What would Grimaldi do next?"

"He couldn't realistically transport her back to Massachusetts." Pete shifted his posture as he fathomed Lance Grimaldi's mind. "He would take her to the place I had him scout out for me a year ago. It was to be my getaway retirement home in Colorado. Durango. Beautiful from the pictures I've seen, secure as all get out. You know Durango. You live there. You were going there with Amy for a ski week before Cecelia's accident. Grimaldi arranged both of Cecelia's accidents..."

Pete stopped midsentence as I slowly turned my head from side to side. I spread my hands flat on the table, smiling.

"Is there something else, Cal?"

"I know Jeff Teller,... of Bell and Teller. I designed that house! That's *your* house? *Ha! My construction company built it!*"

"*Sbalorditivi!* Could you have imagined it?" Pete stood enthusiastically. Then he sat again and sighed, "I can't do anything to help you from here."

"I'll take care of it," I waxed confidently.

"Knowing Grimaldi, you have forty-eight hours. If you stop him, you won't need any help from me or anyone else to regain your past. You'll have proved that you'll prevail no matter what, inside or outside the program. You'll have a reputation that demands respect from *every* element, far superior to the considerable resources the Marshals have exercised for you."

"Pete, let's take advantage of that forty-eight-hour pressure on Grimaldi. Is there a telephone available for you to use if I can arrange it? If so, I have a role for you to play. We can challenge him, realign his thoughts and emotions to our advantage, and direct his actions. Let's talk some more."

§§

Chapter 51

Pete suggested two tasks while I waited for my mid-afternoon flight out of Logan. First, revisit the Agassiz Bridge, where I had witnessed Tom Boyle's murder. He wanted me to confirm the distance to apartments across from that site; then, he suggested I compare what I found to the analysis I gave so convincingly to the courtroom and jury.

"I have all confidence in your recalling the gunshot echo's delay and in your calculations at the trial; I'm just as confident that you'll figure out the same thing as I have. You'll be more effectively persuaded if you make the discovery yourself. Then you'll be able to act on it." He had said this with a sincere smile and affirmation.

With Grimaldi away in Colorado, Pete also wanted me to visit the inside of Grimaldi's residence.

§

Grimaldi's house was on the two hundred block of Revere Street. Joining me was a young, skilled locksmith who confided in me that if it weren't for Mr. Belluno's personal request, he would not, for a moment, consider doing what we were about to do. It was a favor owed and one gladly and respectfully repaid.

The young man, Jack, was able to find us generic service uniform coveralls and an aluminum box clipboard. My cab picked him up on Mass Ave.

After just a few minutes, we left our ride with an In-Service metered wait. We walked deliberately around the corner onto the narrow, one-way, Revere Street. It was an appealing locale, lined with nostalgic, clean, brick row houses and all cars parked facing us. Concrete sidewalks were generously wide.

Grimaldi's row house, well maintained, was a third of the way down the block.

Trees: maple, ash, and oak were greener and brighter now than they would be in August. The City of Boston, as with all the regularly spaced, individual trees lining the street, protected their roots with a cast-iron sidewalk grating. I observed, hidden below Grimaldi's grating, a camera that would record us as we made our way to Lance's door. It wasn't Grimaldi's security service.

Distinctive variations in similar architectural themes distinguished the individual brick houses. The stoops were brick, concrete, or granite. Little, postage stamp lawns with shrubs, gardens, or crushed rock, graced their fronts. The window and bay window arrangements varied with materials and styles of sills and lintels up through their third floors. Parapets, dormers in various combinations topped the three or four-floor structures. Front doors, too, reflected individuality.

Since surprise was the order of the day now, I was surprised at the comfort I felt in conducting a conversation with the imaginary Lance Grimaldi, while Jack charmed the lock. A skilled practitioner, he had us in the door in moments, at an apparent Grimaldi invitation.

Grimaldi's home vexed me. His place was full of expensive, tasteful things but devoid of character. Oriental rugs no more appreciated than a welcome mat, leather sofa that had never seated more than one, and drapes, thick for isolation.

The bar declared Grimaldi's affinity for Scotch.

"The king o'drinks as I conceive it, Talisker, Islay, and Glenlivet." A glint of curiosity directed at me from Jack told me that I had spoken aloud.

"A pair of lines from Robert Lewis Stevenson I memorized in high school. No chance that Grimaldi made that connection. He doesn't have any class at all." I waved my hand dismissively at the room's contents.

Bookcases located next to the wet bar were incongruous. Lance seldom visited his books, dusted but otherwise ignored. There, on a shelf, a before and after picture of Grimaldi's living room remodel caught my eye, beckoning me. It showed a diminished living room area without any corresponding gain in the other rooms. A panic room, storage room, hiding place..., The newly relocated walls would necessarily have required structurally engineered modifications.

Pete B. knew this existed, having never seen it. I knew the reason; Lance Grimaldi had told me himself. Undisputably, Pete would have been a formidable don.

"How considerate, the interior decorator and the contractor left business cards on the back of their commemorative photo." I held the framed picture up for Jack to see. He remained motionless by the front door, anxious to depart.

My legal pad had the business cards' contact information promptly jotted down. I wiped the frame edges with a napkin from the bar, which I pocketed.

"That's all I need."

Jack was relieved that this intrusion was so short-lived. If we had been inside for more than two minutes, I would be surprised.

As we left, I turned and bid farewell to our absent host.

Jack and I also tipped our hats to a couple walking leisurely toward us as we headed back to our taxi.

"That didn't take any time at all." One whispered.

"But will they share?" Whispered the other.

§

"Jack, thanks for your help. Although, even now, we've never met, and Jack's not your name, is it? That's rhetorical, don't answer."

As I had requested, our cab driver had summoned another cab for Jack's ride elsewhere. I paid Jack's fare, in advance, with a gratuity sufficiently large to induce amnesia.

My cabbie took me to Logan International Airport. I found the United Airlines frequent flier lounge and began making telephone calls from the courtesy phone.

§

"Hey, Cam. Cal here."

"Cal, how are you? I'm glad you called. Amy left a message on our answering machine hours ago that said she was at Stapleton and was coming in to pick up her odds and ends and to say hello, but she never showed up."

"That's why I called, Cam. I'm worried sick that she's in trouble, and I'm already involved. I'm in Boston right now and flying west shortly. Would you get a notepad to take some notes? I need your help. Ah, Cam, this is clumsy timing, but I have a confession to make. I'm the guy who set up your college funding."

"I know," Cam replied matter of factly, "If you need help, I'll help regardless."

"You know?" I was surprised that Cam wasn't surprised. I hadn't told Amy, although she was the likeliest person to relay that information. "I hadn't wanted you to know that. Oh, ah..., No. I'm not asking for any of it back. No. I transferred twenty-five thousand onto your stipend card this afternoon to cover whatever you need to help me. That's why I had to tell you."

§

Leaving Boston, my flight banked eastward and rose over the elegant luxury hotel I had emerged from as the newly coined Calvin James years ago. Multi-masted yachts filled the docks' slips, and tiny people mingled on the floating gazebo.

Twice I'd left that hotel behind. Both times, I had recently departed from Petros Belluno as well.

The 747 banked again and flew along the coast before it banked once more. I thought of John and Martha's Bakery.

§§

Chapter 52

Dick Mason of Mason's Helicopter Service was Smart Start Builders' go-to guy when we had vertical cargo transport needs. Bobby and I had bid on a communication tower for the Western Area Power Administration, located on a difficult to access mesa top between Mancos and Durango; the bid process included submitting an injured worker evacuation plan. Dick Mason was ideally suited. He'd flown medivac in Vietnam.

He subsequently piloted equipment delivery and bucketed concrete for us when we installed lift towers for the Purgatory Ski area. During a remote San Juan National Forest cabin remodel, a short distance but hours away by road from town, he was our gofer.

Naturally, he was the guy that I called from Boston for tonight's flight requirements.

§

My familiar Silver Restaurant and Lodge was on the last civilized road I'd drive my gently used Previa on tonight. I had taken a room at the lodge for a week, only to park in it a brand new Trek, an equally new Bianchi road bike, and riding togs. With good fortune, I'd scored Trek and Bianchi shorts and shirts, the same gear that Amy and I usually wore in Boulder. The bicycle sales clerk had also favored my shopping helpers with matching helmets to join the stash.

Ten miles and forty minutes later, between the tines of a fork in the rough, potholed, and only access road into La Plata Canyon, was a decently maintained picnic area, and Mason's and my designated rendezvous. One of the forks led to Columbus and Cumberland basins, the other to Eagle Pass. I unloaded and parsed out my remotely accomplished purchases. Remarkably, everything I had asked for, an auto detailing crew in Albuquerque, successfully scavenged and packed, ready now for me to strategically distributed. My agents had earned their reward.

Growing louder was the distinctive rotor thwack of a demilitarized Huey 204, Mason's preference for light lifting and night flying. Acquired from army surplus, it maintained its original olive drab exterior. He'd been restoring it for the past five years with a new paint job to be the last stage. Still his pet, it was the model favored by his favorite starship pilot.

9:32 PM. Prompt as the proverbial bus driver, Dick lit up the grassy area next to the weathered picnic tables and set down. In seconds, my three individually netted cargo bags were carabinered to the Huey's lading hooks. Dick unlatched the cabin's passenger door. I levered off the runner step and settled into the high-backed, starboard seat, careful not to knock the cyclical. I strapped in and grabbed the headphone set from its bulkhead mooring.

"I see you finally fixed your windscreen wiper," I pointed out, "no need to hide little Ricky on the skids to make it work." My little jab prompted a laugh from the usually unflappable, avid sci-fi fan.

"And you're going to have a little downhill joyride. Mountain bikes, I see, and unless those are party tents, hang gliders, pack frame, and a couple of mystery duffels. Intriguing." A complimentary jab at my deductive habits.

"I'd engage you for a snatch and grab, Dick, but there would be a high risk of lead poisoning, personal injury, and mechanical damage. Both of us could do without that; nice to have a little fun instead." Noise-canceling headphones made our conversation clear and effortless.

"There *are* guests at that house over by Junction Creek, Cal, a bunch of them by the looks, lights blazing, but no smoke. A limo and a sedan of some sort were there. Good call." Dick knew expressly what to look for; a three thousand square-foot footprint, lighted home, with a forest green metal roof, which bordered on the National Forest, with possible smoke from the chimney, automobiles in the loop drive, and maybe some milling people.

"I'll be standing by at the airport in case you change your mind."

"Dick, I'm willing to wager that you'll get called into service from that house before noon tomorrow, and the guy will be PO'd. If you offer to get there the fastest, the job's yours. If he does call, take the Jet Ranger and sell him on limited elevation, right?"

"Okay. Any places I should avoid?"

"Be a good safety-conscious tour guide. I've lined up my caches enough off the beaten path so a capable tour guide won't interfere. Charge him double your hourly rate and take him for a good ride." I chuckled.

§

Skillfully, Dick landed the cargo net then slid to the side to avoid setting the landing strut on it for my final disembarking.

"Spin her up," I mouthed while I signaled with my index finger after detaching my remaining cargo bundle.

Dick tapped his chest above his heart in a mock effort to activate an insignia communicator; he then reverted to a thumbs-up and was away.

The clear night was temperate, and unmixed pockets of warm air drifted through the meadow. I stood still.

In the distance, the whine of Dick's Lycoming turbine yielded to the Huey's distinctive cavitating rotors. Deeper on departure than when approaching, the rotor would be heard for miles. The Belluno household would hear it.

Minutes later, the sound was lost in the soft mountain downdraft. Insects sang, intent on mutual attraction, replacing the mechanical noises. Nighthawks or owls were halo diving for their evening meals. The rustling of leaves and small twigs breaking disclosed other night creatures as they assumed their station in the food chain.

A whiff of pine rode on warm wafts while other nocturnal air currents coolly floated the earthy aroma of decayed leaves or a faint sweet floral scent of wildflowers.

Unbridled by urban glow, the stars were sensational. The Milky Way, incredibly inspiring, rose from the southern horizon, banded across the lower eastern sky, and dropped down in the north, highlighting the ragged San Juan Mountains. Antares, the heart of Scorpio, just rising, was brilliant. Polaris, even in the crowded wilderness sky, was easy to spot. At almost forty degrees in elevation, it would be my companion while I traversed north. I had a compass with me, but the stars would aid my foray into nighttime orienteering.

The terrain would start as a grassy meadow, through which I would have to look out for yawning, rain cut gullies. Otherwise, I would be hiking through yellow pine and spruce forest, free of undergrowth. The three-mile hike consisted of a gradual ascent to the Skunk Creek drainage. It would be challenging. Starlight was the only illumination I'd use aside from my laser pointer.

The waning moon would be rising when I reached Skunk Creek's rim. If I arrived earlier, I would wait for the lunar assistance to see my way to the creek bottom.

Occupied with plans for this evening and tomorrow, I couldn't allow myself to imagine the challenges that Amy might have with her demented kidnapper.

§

Overlooking Skunk Creek, I checked my watch, although I didn't need to. It was 11:37 PM. If good omen wasn't appropriate, then bade well was better. Best, providential.

Silhouetted on the enormous, rising coral moon, Baldy Mountain was a noticeable jag. I was able to look over Animas City Mountain and into the eastern San Juan National Forest.

Pete's summer retreat remained out of sight, at a distance of about a thousand yards. The straight vertical rise on the creek's north side was impressive and rose somewhat higher in elevation, blocking my view.

I couldn't tell how far, east or west, I was from being due south of the retreat. So, I did what anyone would imagine doing at eleven-thirty on a moonlit night in the forest, though I could not remember once having the desire to climb a tree at night. I selected a tall pine with sturdy branches.

From a solid branch, about twenty feet up, I was able to see the house, my first time personally viewing Smart Start Builders' finished product. The commanding south-facing glass wall glowed warmly from the lights within.

§

The same challenges that made the property so defensible also severely limited the routes of escape. If the flatlanders who occupied the Belluno house expected any intrusion, they would think about vehicles, either road or air, and the

293

the use of armed force. Unwanted approach or departure, on foot, would violate their preconceptions, involving effort far beyond their experience or imagination.

Perins Peak State Wildlife Area, directly behind me, Mason and I had skirted it, was a no-fly, no-drive zone at this time of year. It would have escape appeal to a thinking mind; it could be that Grimaldi would waste time and resources there.

Escaping higher into the La Plata Mountains would broaden the inevitable search's scope following Amy's disappearance. The longer we traveled undetected would exponentially increase the area Grimaldi would have to search.

§

Petros' southeast property line eased from cliffs into a merely steep incline for a limited span along the creek. Covered with oak brush, it sloped precipitously to the creek bottom, that sole avenue allowed foot, hoof, or paw traffic into or out from the creek. Centuries-old game trails of deer, elk, bears, foxes, mountain lions, and an assortment of other animals made access to or egress from the creek bottom possible. The only other methods were rappelling or technical climbing.

For my camp, I settled on a flat area, creekside, well padded with pine needles. Duct tape, tie wire, monofilament, gold panning gear still in the box, a tarp, cheap sleeping bag, two hundred yards of climbing rope, a Sharpie marker, and two bicycle tire tubes were my resources for MacGyvering. Those, along with energy bars, bottled water, a change of clothes, and shoes for Amy, were what I had on hand to implement my rescue effort.

The moon was now high enough to trickle light through the tall yellow pine and spruce. I labored silently, wanting nothing to give away my presence until I was entirely ready. With my makeshift camp rigged, I clambered up the game trail to where I could fix my binoculars on the house.

Radiance spilled from the living area's high glass wall. I made out two men who stood in the great room, guessing Grimaldi to be the taller.

They'd kindled a fire. I was surprised they figured out how. Smoke drifted up from the chimney; ten feet above the roofline, it formed a lazy finger that pointed east.

The silence was neither a positive sign nor a negative sign. I could count on Amy to make incendiary complaints if required, but by the sounds, she was still in control of herself. On the other hand, the ears of these city dwellers would be extra sensitive.

A sudden spray of light swept past. A flashlight lit up the field, then flicked off.

I checked my watch. 2:15 AM.

Arranged perimeter patrols, timed from the top of the hour. Fifteen minutes to get around to here, savory, predictable.

Lance's lackey tramped by, not noticing me laid low in the bushes. I stalked him on his return to the house to have a closer look.

The asphalt Neanderthal stopped to light a cigarette, a real Marlboro Man; fire was always a danger this close to the forest. Clean white light beamed from the house, transfixing the smoker accusingly in its swath. The wasted cigarette hit the ground, immediately snuffed, crushed under the soles of cheap tennis shoes.

Throughout my planning, I knew much could go wrong. To prepare for rational actions was one thing, but how hard it was to plan around stupidity, Marlboro Man, case in point.

The perimeter patrolman swept the field with two more flashlight passes along his remaining circuit. He thoroughly ignored the forested edge, so it was unlikely that any inspection accompanied the sweeps. Ten minutes later, he reached the deck, where his superior scolded him well. I took satisfaction in the sight and sound of a well-placed cuff on the back of his head.

Near the landscaped grounds, I stumbled upon a tremendous find. It meant additional work for me, though Amy's vanishing would be much more elegant as a result. I silently lugged several dozen two by twelve scaffold planks left by the stonemasons, making multiple trips to the upper end of the abandoned irrigation ditch.

A few minutes after four, I took a restful moment to admire the night sky. The Red Planet had just shown above the horizon, north of Baldy Mountain, the god of war, and Pegasus had finally gotten to his feet.

My work resumed after the perimeter guy passed me by, unnoticed, once more. Another half hour and I vanished with the moonlight.

At camp, I drew up an A. Canfalierri chauffeur's paging sign and took a nap.

§

"Hey, what are you doin' down there?" hurled the nasal Bostonian. His question battled the tone of Colorado and the National Forest. Smoke from my campfire had alerted him.

"This is National Forest," I answered in my best Mexican accent. "I can camp here, and I can pan for gold, too, unless you have a claim. *Si?*"

I remained purposely out of his sight, blending with the undergrowth.

"You can't be here. Get out." He threatened over the steep embankment. Again, his heavy accent racked the forest.

"But this is my camp, and I found a heavy gold nugget this morning already." My Mexican accent fought back. In truth, the nugget was about five-eighths of an inch around. Exceptionally fortunate, I figured a little over $300 worth.

"You found gold?"

"It is what I come for. *Si, señor.* Come see."

"I'll come down, but you still have to leave."

The lure of gold, infallible.

I didn't want to see his gun come out, but it did. It was an ugly snub .38. I hoped the safety was on. I didn't need a gunshot to announce my presence to the whole enclave.

"If you slip, *su pistola* could get you hurt." Sincerity, Mexican style, hard to resist. He reholstered his weapon but didn't secure it.

Furtively, I hid while going through panning motions, digging in the streambed, scooping gravel into the pan, circulating, all the while narrating in my phony accent. I could hear him stumble closer. *One step, two steps...,*

"Aghaa!"

Tie wire, placed hours ago, had snagged its first victim by the shoe tops. Low, close to the creek bed, he was out of anyone's hearing but mine. Grunts and groans, along with obscenities expertly roared, attended his tumble.

My new, rotund, gold panning pupil belly-bounced his way to a stop, hands outstretched.

In a flash, I gathered his right and left hands together. With one knee on his back, I was careful not to let him roll, effortlessly dispensing duct tape. When I arched his back, he bent his knees for balance, facilitating a quick tape wrap of his ankles. Hog-tied. I shot both hands in the air to imaginary rodeo fans. I had imaginary audiences everywhere. His face wound up only inches from the stream surface, making any struggle unwise.

"You can't do this. The guys at the house will kill you if you don't let me go."

More duct tape cut off his passionate, futile argument. Consequences, he hadn't shaved either. I chastised myself for the thought.

"Tell me about the *gringos* at the house; I begin at *dos*. You grunt when I say the number of *hombres* there." Temporarily addicted to my assumed accent, "*dos, tres, cuatro…*"

I stopped at "*doce.*"

"Let me give you incentive, eh, *señor?*" I raised his feet, submerging his face in the icy, snow-fed creek. He thrashed desperately until I lowered his feet thirty seconds later.

"I'll count again for you, *señor.* You have much to tell me, no? And, so much time."

§

His chest was wet. If it weren't for the icy stream, he would have been wet from sweat. I dragged him across the creek, dousing him and scratching him up. I taped his knees together and cut the tape that connected his hands to his feet. With a rope over a pine branch and encircled under his armpits, I raised him to his feet. More tape affixed his legs to the tree base. With even more tape, I pulled the side of his head to the tree as well.

"Listen, the tree is saying, go home, Yankee." My feigned accent remained. "*¿Oyes?* Can you hear it?"

Removing his tape would cause painful hair loss, a huge entertainment value. I cut free his hands so that I could remove his coat.

"I'll need this. *¿Hace frio? ¿Si? Gracias.*" (It's cold, yes? Thank you.)

Even though this unfortunate associate of Grimaldi flailed his arms, additional coils of tape soon made him a cocoon.

"*Consejos de mi, señor*. (My advice, mister.) I pull this tape from your mouth. You don't yell until you hear *sus amigos* call you. You don't want to be hoarse when they go by, and then they miss you. *Tendrás una hora, más o menos.*" (You'll have an hour, more or less.) I pulled the tape off at a compassionate speed.

"Help! Hey! Down here!" he hollered with all the volume he could muster.

"Suit yourself, *señor*," I interjected when he took a breath. I donned his coat and grabbed my sign, corralling his scattered baseball cap and gun. I pitched the weapon into the stream and scrambled to the pasture above.

Among the tidbits shared by my gracious informant, Amy had run of the house and grounds. One less worry in trying to contact her in the hour that I had budgeted. The sixty-four thousand dollar question was, *how I would make that contact?*"

7:20 AM. My perimeter guard was a little behind schedule, not yet enough to draw attention. Even flatlanders need to occasion the woods.

§

Never would the original homestead's builders have ever imagined the seemingly palatial, post and beam second home that now replaced it. The open field provided me with a clear view. The new house dominated the hayfield they had undertaken to clear and cultivate.

Bobby told me that the architect incorporated all the design elements I had suggested. The exterior spoke to all of them, confirmed by Bobby's photos and my compensation check. In a gentlemanly agreement, Jeff Teller's architectural team was to pay Smart Start, on a prorated basis, according to the features of my design that they used. I received full payment.

I kept close to the perimeter and walked along the forest edge the way Grimaldi's wayward guard had the night before. His coat was too large, not comfortable, and reeked of tobacco smoke, but the baseball cap adjusted to fit. I jogged several intervals in case there was a set timetable for clearing the circumference.

It was almost seven-thirty. If Amy had any freedom to wander, I would expect to see her on the deck in moments. I didn't have any realistic expectation of such good fortune. I did have my paging sign prepared to initiate our communication.

The dimwitted guards were out early, a harbinger of good things to come.

Time was in my favor. Grimaldi had not yet set up tight security. He would wait until he had placed a call to Pete to announce his intentions.

I knew the schedule to be different; by agreement with Pete, Amy and I would have until 11:00 AM, 1:00 PM eastern. Pete would call Lance. For Pete to have telephone privileges at Fort Devens, Peter Nori had leveraged federal law enforcement's interest in Grimaldi's living room remodel.

I focused on the forest to keep my face turned away from the house. My eyes did shift toward the ground and behind occasionally for good measure. In the neatly landscaped yard, just beyond where the scaffold planks had been, a motion in my periphery startled me.

Amy was reclining on an attractively situated rock. She was wearing heels, a skirt, a sweater, and a blouse, her self-prescribed airline attire. Garnering from her a casual glance, I bent down and pretended to pick up something off the ground.

"Hey." I tried to mimic the inflection that I had used ten months ago. I turned so she could see my face.

"Hey." She returned the same inflection. I had anticipated a startled look that didn't materialize. "*Lavori con questi ragazzi?*" (Do you work with these guys?)

"*No..., non lavoro con loro.*" (No, no, I don't.) *Déjà vu*, all over again.

"*Bene, per chi caspita lavori?*" (Well, who the heck do you work for?) She raised her voice, irritated that she genuinely didn't know and worried that she might not want to.

"*Sono lavoratore autonomo.*" (I'm self-employed.)

"I'm glad to hear that," Amy replied, with less exasperation.

"I'm sure you are." I smiled my most reassuring smile. *"Sto andando al aeroporto. Ti interessa venire con me?"* (I'm going to the airport. Would you like to join me?)

"Sure. Can we avoid any knife fights on the way? I hear that you have a mysterious, intense, combative dark side." Her dismount from the rock hindered by her skirt and heels was no less pleasurable nor less gymnastic than at our first Boulder meeting.

"I'm not expecting any if all goes well."

Instantly panicked, Amy clutched at her conservatively bared collarbone. "My mom's locket, it's inside. I can't lose that. I can't leave it here."

"Don't look at the house, but what room are you in?"

I pulled out the cigarettes dill wit had in his jacket pocket, not that I could bring myself to light one up. I wondered if he craved one. I fumbled with the pack, fumbled for a lighter, dropped the cigarette, and fumbled with the pack again.

"The master suite was all mine last night." Stress choked out Amy's laugh even though the cigarette business amused her. "But I don't know what's on the lunatic's mind."

"He hears wedding bells for you and him. We'll have time to talk about that later. I wanted you to go back into that very room, very obviously, anyway."

"You know, Cal, when I got here, this was the same as the house you described to me while we were in Boulder. The one that you designed and Bobby built without you. I looked for a panic route and found the false wall panel in the closet. There was a catwalk over the garage and a trapdoor through the garage ceiling. I thought, *how weird is that; Cal designed this place, and Jerknoid brought me here.* Then you show up.

"Grimaldi has his guy in the garage guarding the automobiles. If I go in now, I may not get out again this morning."

"Do you remember a loft in your bedroom toward the stairs, over the door?"

"Sure, there's a bunch of interior decorating crap up there, dried flowers and some ceramic pots. There's a library ladder on a rail between the two bookcases."

"Perfect. That's the portal to the sworn-to-secrecy rabbit hole. Get up there, and find the release, a book pull, or a vase turn. You'll have to discover it. It will trigger the loft floor to drop two feet at one end, opening into a playground tube slide. Once you're in the tube, the shelf is rigged to spring back to its level position. It's dampened, so no one will hear it.

"If you want to go back to get your mom's locket, now's the time. We have until eleven before Lance puts a heavy lockdown on this place."

Now there was puzzlement on Amy's face.

"Don't tell me now, I'll ask later. You have a bunch of explaining to do, young man." She wagged her finger at me. "It's so, so good to see you. But Cal, I don't have anything less stylish than this to travel in if we're making a run for it."

"When you say run for it, you make it sound so flighty. I have copious fun activities planned for us today." I sent her off with a knowing wink.

"You haven't changed, Cal. I'll meet you in a few minutes."

"Do you know where?"

"Where else?" Amy nailed me again with the obvious, grinning at her point scored.

"Take your time." A glance at my watch revealed my apprehension. "I'll be waiting."

Amy was bold and confident. Very different from how I had seen her react during our previous Grimaldi encounter. Today she was ready to rock, to slip from his grasp or fight trying. In minutes, she would walk right past his face into his prison, trusting me as I sent her there.

§§

CHAPTER 53

Amy took her time, puttering back to the house, making it apparent to anyone who watched that high heels were not designed for field walking, with an ankle wobble here and a stumble there. Deck steps, she demonstrated, were not favorable for heels, either, and in disgust, she artfully removed her shoes. Not used to flaunting; nonetheless, she effortlessly enthralled her overseers.

Rather than enter the house at the more convenient south entrance, she drew all attention to the main entrance. She casually observed the beautiful scenery toward Durango, stretched, yawned, and held her captors' attention captive.

Earlier, she had considered slipping out at night to signal an SOS, futile as it might prove. She knew that neither she nor Cal was invincible, but she did now have her trusted ally. Separately, or when together, Cal had built up her confidence in studies, cycling, socially, dealing with unexpected circumstances, and even preparing her to meet her dad.

So far, she had delayed telling Cal many details about her dad, unfairly holding that information as a bargaining chip to pry into Cal's undisclosed past; today, she would spill it all and let the chips fall.

As she entered the front door, Lance attempted conversation from the library.

"Kind of chilly for a morning outing." Ice-breaking, not Lance's forte.

"You'll know damn cold if you don't stop this stupidity. You'd be better off sleeping in the freezer." Amy neared the top of the stairs to the master suite.

Lance, in slow pursuit, looked up at Amy and laughed. *She can't not come around.* He hadn't yet played the threat card over her father, and his prison was a short reach. Besides, he was irresistible. Lacoste, Breath Savers, and lots of money would warm her up.

She blasted the bedroom door shut and quickly locked and bolted it behind her. She thought that the interior lock would only provide minimal security. Anyone determined enough would be able to bull their way through it.

She hadn't had the designer's full input; she only had confidence in the designer and his plan. Had she known, behind the external drywall was galvanized steel sheeting. The doorframe was steel also, well disguised with wood trim. The oak-laminated steel door only appeared to be solid wood. Its lock had multiple bolts, and heavy-duty hinge plates interlocked when the door closed. Not a fortress, it did offer additional protection against unwanted entry. Cal had placed her in the house's most secure room.

Her mom's locket was Amy's most cherished physical possession. Her heart sank when she didn't see it on her dresser but settled back into resolve when she found it on the nightstand.

She went to the library ladder that she had considered an extravagance and slid it over to the knickknack loft. She thought better of throwing off a few pieces. The less noise, the less attention she would receive. Don't overact the part.

Items in the decorative alcove, she found, were fixed in place. She pulled at the vase that she most wanted to shatter. A cable attached through its base offered resistance. The loft dropped down, revealing the Rabbit Hole's illuminated round opening.

§

My alternate escape scheme was the result of an endorphin-inspired brainstorm in Barnes and Noble. I'd overheard, "down the rabbit hole," a reference to *Alice in Wonderland*, spoken to a stroller-secured youngster. The youngster made me think playground, and I'd seen the design at once. A playground slide within the walls, twisting and turning to hide its existence, backlit with triggered lighting, a refined solution, and true to name.

Only Dave, Bobby, and ProtoBobby were involved with its construction. Jeff Teller was the only one on the design team who knew the reason for the voids within the building. Bobby changed crews on this job often. Walls had been intentionally framed and drywalled only to have Bobby remove and then replace them. Dave lifted the yellow slide tube pieces through vacated window openings with a light crane. Bobby ingeniously used plywood, planks, Hi-Lift jacks, Come-A-Longs, and ratchet lever hoists to lower, assemble, and affix the tubes sturdily to their supports from the bottom up. Longer than a weekend project, Bobby had accomplished it without questions and risky though it was, without county building inspectors.

To finish the escape, Bobby ordered prefabricated concrete box culvert sections. He made sure that the loads were tarped before they arrived on flatbeds. Dave masterfully used his own custom turf striping device to curl back the sod, then excavated the subterranean escape route. He camouflaged the copious amounts of dirt as the landscaping's protective berms. They placed the box culvert pieces, joined, caulked, sealed, and backfilled them so skillfully that there was no hint of subterranean disturbance.

§

Amy sat on the slight staging platform, primped her hair, and kept her laughter within. She touched the luminous tubing in wonder then pushed the ladder back over to the bookcases.

Sans operating instructions, she gathered her floral skirt at her knees, trying to hold the folds and her shoes. She found it much too awkward to enter the chute sitting upright. When she leaned back, she was unable to maintain a grip on her skirt. She regrouped, put her shoes on the shelf behind her, rolled her skirt thigh-high, and tested her revised configuration by leaning back once again. Her correction was a much better attack plan; her shoes fell to the floor as she launched prematurely down the slide. The loft floor abruptly sprang up and locked.

She suppressed a schoolgirl scream of joy; instead of being terrified, she laughed. This was so Calvin.

The slide was much longer than she expected, and the windup much tamer. Amy slowed to a stop with her knees just bent over the slide's run-out. She inched forward; her bare feet touched the cooler, epoxy-coated concrete floor. Not knowing how long her lighting would remain in the chilled gallery, she jogged its full length.

Happily, she reveled in running toward this unknown.

§

Amy popped into the sunlight, concealed by an alcove outside the outdoor room. I'd intended this detached structure for clandestine conversations. Away from the residence, it was closer to the National Forest. Its front deck offered a gorgeous view of Durango.

"Cal, that,... that was inspired. This is inspired." She waved her hand toward the house but wisely used her library voice.

"I'm glad that you enjoyed your adventure down the rabbit hole. We can try it again another time." I eyed Amy's bare feet.

"Can we stop by the shoe store before we get to the airport? I slipped up."

The best plans have leeway for unanticipated events, the same way a skyscraper will flex instead of snap. The duffel I had assembled for her was at the bottom of Skunk Creek. Size eight and a half Merrells were in it, with the outdoor wear I'd picked up.

I dropped my borrowed jacket.

"I don't think that we've piggybacked yet. Hop on."

"More playground stuff? Where do you get this hooey?"

"I practice endorphin production, remember?"

Amy jumped onto my back. I huffed.

"Where to Endorphin Man?"

"Along this retired irrigation ditch. It'll give us a lower profile. The outdoor room will screen us from your stalker for all but the last few yards. Then we take the invisible walkway to the bottom of Skunk Creek. We'll pause there to catch up on the rest of our outing. Any questions?"

"More questions than you have endorphins, *Signore*."

I began our trot across the old pasture. It was not comfortable for Amy. She was snug, plastered across my back, and held tightly for the least jarring ride.

In the middle of our jaunt, Amy tried to ask a question, but when a bounce gave her little volume control, she stopped. When I set her down, she clung longer than was necessary.

"We'll have to go one by one here." I kept the conversation quiet. "I walked back and forth through here last night quite a bit. There shouldn't be anything to poke your feet. Don't look back, and don't scuff your feet on the planks; you could end up with a sliver."

"What planks? You've been here since last *night?* I only got here yesterday afternoon." Amy whispered fiercely.

"It's the invisible walkway, trust me."

We were just yards from the cliff's edge; bushes obscured the way forward.

"You're a fun-loving guy. What's not to trust?"

"I won't be but a few seconds behind."

With that, Amy crouched low, scooted across the exposed distance, and was gone.

"Whoa!" a muffled peep came back from the spot where Amy had disappeared through the bushes.

§

"Calvin. What is this? You couldn't have done *all* this last night." Amy was incredulous.

Few who had seen the engineering accomplishment that I had taken advantage of even realized what it was. She regarded the weathered, and rusted iron brackets securely bolted to the cliff wall, spaced less than eight feet apart, and nearly level from one to the next. The original homesteaders installed them decades before. I'd straddled the brackets with the stonemasons' scaffold planks.

By optical illusion, it appeared that we descended, even though we walked gradually uphill. With a rope, I lowered each plank behind us, leaving no visible trace of our escape route.

"Inventive engineering. These brackets held a wooden sluice. Years ago, the folks who owned this property built an aqueduct from Skunk Creek to that irrigation ditch we just piggybacked through. Us Easterners aren't that used to irrigation; out here, it's a way of life.

"The planks were left by masons who worked on your house. If it hadn't been for their planks, we'd have walked on a rope bridge.

"We can forget our library voices for now. A waterfall downstream prevents anyone from coming straight up the creek after us. This cliff will separate us from any approach from the upside. We're hiking to the top of Lewis Mountain. It'll be a challenge."

"I thought you said that we were going to the airport, and let's be clear, this walkway is not invisible; it's merely disappearing."

"It's invisible now, and we are headed to the airport," I said with an undertone that told her that there was a scrap of truth there if she could find it. "When we have our feet on the ground, we'll talk about our situation and my whole story."

Amy became quiet and thoughtful.

§

"If you want to change into more comfortable clothes, I packed a duffel for you. I promise not to look. There's a long sleeve t-shirt, a sweatshirt, jeans, a cotton shirt, a windbreaker, and some other stuff."

"This is why bears come to the woods?" Amy hung on to the banter. "And look, here's our ubiquitous rock. When I got your answering machine in Boulder, I figured that you were in Durango, so it was odd when I was paged at Stapleton, creepy when the limo turned back for Lance and his crew."

"Yesterday, I was in Boston. I didn't get here until about midnight."

Amy muffled an exasperated scream, unable to grasp what I was doing in Boston and how I had arrived at this Durango homestead only a few hours after her arrival, knowing of her imminent danger, and rescuing her from it.

"So, here's the thing. Lance had you here for the two of you to be married. He is serious, seriously demented, and merciless.

"He has a few perimeter guards patrolling the property. It's eight twenty right now. At eleven o'clock, he'll want to confirm that you're in the house and eventually find out that you're not.

"This is a treacherous game. Questions so far?"

"Better than a dozen. What are these? Calvin?" she said in mock, nearly parental tone. She'd found some specific accessories that I had packed for her. "I'll start with, how did you know my..."

"If we were in Boulder, this would be your weekend to help out at the stables, I extrapolated. I didn't think it would hurt for me to be wrong."

"Sports bra, perfect size?" A happy voice betrayed the fondness behind her affront.

"I'm pretty good with visual estimations, professional perk."

"I thought you were always looking into my eyes. I should have known better when you spied my Yale house key hanging from my back pocket that first day," she teased comfortably. "I'm going to kick you in the..., nicest way possible. Cal, will you ever stop being such a dear? How do you know that Grimaldi is planning to marry me? That's a ten ick, by the way."

"Your dad told me, I talked to him yesterday at the prison."

"Seriously? My *dad* told you?" Amy asked incredulously, "you know my dad?"

"Seriously. That's why I was in Boston. I'll tell you how I know him on our hike. It's complicated. Let's put more distance between Grimaldi's crew and us before we get into that."

"How are you certain of how much time we've got before I'm discovered missing?"

"Pete, is that weird, calling your dad, Pete? Pete will make a call at one o'clock his time to Grimaldi; he'll say that he knows that Lance kidnapped you and that you have vanished. We agreed on the timing. Your dad is a very astute person."

"So, we've got two and a half hours of lead time?"

"Right. Minimum. Grimaldi's lackeys will spend some time breaking into the master suite. I also have one of Lance's perimeter sentries duct-taped to a tree downstream. When they find him, they might be distracted for a while."

"What's the plan?"

"Well, there are contingencies, but the preferred plan is we hike to the top of Lewis Mountain, hang glide over the Indian Ridge Pass and continue down the Bear Creek drainage. The road distance from your house, where Grimaldi is, to the meadow where Bear Creek joins the Dolores River, is about eighty miles and two hours. We'll make it from here in four and a half hours, three and a half up, and an hour's glide time. It's only fourteen miles as the crow flies."

"Hang gliding? Calvin?"

"I said that I have a fun day of activities for us. So, we land in a meadow and join up with a horse pack trip returning to the Priest Gulch Camp Ground. They'll have a couple of mounts for us, so we'll blend right in. At Priest Gulch, a reserved rental Jeep is there for us to drive to the Telluride Airport, where we have reservations to fly through to a Nantucket bed and breakfast. Tomorrow a commuter flight to Hyannis, a drive over to Devens, and then we play a little shell game to get you in to see Pete..., your dad, I mean."

"That's your plan? Sounds exactly like a Calvin James plan." Amy put on a warm, contemplative smile. "You can turn around. I've been dressed for five minutes. How come you haven't called in any help from your Durango friends?"

"No one's in town. It's our company's week off. Dick Mason did help with chopper flying last night, but he's had over his quota of flying in gunfire. Boulder's five hours away, and Peter's out of town anyway, a Chicago convention."

"Contingencies?"

"Same amount of fun, a little more work. Maybe another couple of clothing changes."

§

Amy and I shouldered our daypacks that held water, snacks, cautionary items, and extra layers of clothing.

"So, Cal, your story? I get to know who you are, your past, and everything?" Amy spoke from behind as we trod upstream on a well-worn game trail.

"Who are you?" I answered over my shoulder, "that was your question to me in your last letter. Opening up to you, who I am, my family, my history, everything about me, is why I'm right here with you right now. That question has haunted me since my saying "Hey," at the rock. Your asking it was what I needed. Since one of the possible outcomes in the next forty-eight hours is me dead, Pete dead, and you married to a demon schmuck who can make your skin crawl even when you don't know he's around. Another outcome is we go on, and I'll be able to talk about anything and everything. I want to thank you, Amy, too; I love the fact that you never pressed me until last week."

I ducked for a low branch that I almost didn't see.

"Cal, I got advice from several people, early and often, to not probe your past. I respected their advice because I respect you. You can imagine, knowing my dad, he would wonder about you. You were a part of most of our talks, but I couldn't answer his questions about you. That made him nervous."

"Last week, I researched Pete's whereabouts." I inclined toward Amy. "Did you know that there's a Federal Prison Inmate Locator Service? Peter Nori helped me, very reluctantly because he knows about my witness protection. With Peter's referral, I went to see your dad yesterday to get my past back. My name was Michael James Barton; my testimony put Pete behind bars."

Amy ran up and pulled my sleeve to turn me around to face her. She looked very intently at me, accusatorily, an emotional response from my beautiful sidekick. I expected it and looked back sorrowfully.

"My parents and my brother were shot and killed at the same time I was giving testimony, so the Feds put me in WITSEC. There I became Calvin James and was stripped of my past."

"My dad told me about his trial and the kid witness. Dad said that he was innocent of Tom Boyle's murder and the murders of that boy's parents. You're the one Dave Harris told me about. Your family was executed, and your testimony convicted my dad. Cal, this is so twisted. I'm so sorry about your parents and your brother. But I'm angry about my dad being in prison."

"I didn't believe that he was guilty at the trial when I saw his reaction to all that was happening in the courtroom." I turned to move on with our hike. "We were talking, your dad and I, and I told him I wanted to get out of WITSEC and get my name and life back, primarily to open up to you and all my friends. I thought that he would be the most able to counsel me on any outstanding threats.

"He explained, first, that Grimaldi was the one who put a contract on Michael Barton and his family. Second, when he came to the visitors' area at Fort Devens yesterday, he expected to see his daughter. He was concerned about her. She had come so regularly to visit him every week since his wife had died back in February. When I said, 'your daughter is Amy Farina,' we both nearly fell off our seats."

"You mean..., *hey*, stop. You mean you didn't know that he was my dad when you went to see him?"

I pointed to a clearing ahead of us where we could pause a minute.

We scrambled through the oak brush, ducked low under a spruce bough, and balanced on a log to cross the babbling stream. The creek embankments remained steep, but the canopy opened up to more sunshine. Aspens, yellow pine, spruce, scrub oak, and berry bushes with prickly thorns lined both banks should we get off track. Birds chirped and flitted. Softer footing on the trail was impressed with tracks of wild animals, deer, bear, raccoon, and skunk.

Amy ran up and pulled my sleeve as soon as we cleared the thicket, turning me to face her, wanting me to answer her question.

"*Caduto dalle nuvole.* (It fell from the clouds.) Wholely unaware. He talked on about your guy in Boulder. I confessed that your guy was me. We were both astonished. He continued, saying that if you weren't there to see him, you said you were going to Colorado to pick up the rest of your belongings and arrange to have them sent back to Lenox. You wanted to meet your guy friend from Boulder at Stapleton. If I were at Devens with him, he knew beyond a shadow of a doubt that Lance would proceed with his plans for your abduction and coerced marriage."

The deteriorated dam that supplied water for the cliffside aqueduct was off to our right. I pointed out the ruin.

"Your dad is extremely perceptive. It must be genetic, right? Grimaldi had boasted of his intentions regarding you immediately and consistently to Pete after he had been imprisoned. Of course, your dada wouldn't burden you with that."

"Pause button." Amy put up her hand and looked back and forth between two different locations in the middle distance. "I need a minute to process."

"Take your time. We've got more hiking yet."

"Lead on, only quietly."

We continued upward on the south embankment, leaving the Skunk Creek drainage. Amy followed, just far enough to avoid whipping aspen or spruce branches. The trail widened, padded with evergreen needles and decayed leaves. Soon Amy was beside me, reconciled with all that I had told her so far.

"Tell me, is there a hang glider shop on Lewis Peak?"

"That's where our gliders are waiting."

"Did you push a button?"

"Straight up. I called from Boston to the Toyota dealership in Albuquerque, where I bought my 4Runner. I told my sales guy, Jim, that I would pay handsomely, he knows that I can, if he would get me a four-wheel drive and a laundry list of other things when I came in last night. I had to settle for a used Previa van. He sent out his detailing crew to get me ropes, packs, bicycles, and all the stuff I thought I would need. I had to call him back to get the pair of hang gliders. A shop in Albuquerque does parasails, hang gliders, pterodactyls, and ultralights. His crew got everything I asked for."

"You didn't send the crew for my..., personal needs?" Another reproach.

"No, I stopped at J. C. Penney at the Coronado Mall in Albuquerque to get your clothes. Those other accessories I got at Rite Aid, along with insect repellent and sunscreen.

"I'd given Dick Mason a heads up from Boston that I'd call him for nighttime helicopter support and called again from The Silver Restaurant and Lodge, which is about eight miles from here. He met me on the other side of the mountain, then we flew to Lewis Peak, where I dropped off the gliders. He dropped me off south of Perins Peak Wildlife Area so I could hike over to your place in relative quiet."

"Cal, let's take a break."

The ridge between Skunk Creek and Deep Creek was without the cloaking of hardy spruce. Scrub oak was becoming more prominent, aspen groves, less so. On the Deep Creek side was a much-used game trail that followed high along the divide, affording the fastest travel.

We turned to evaluate our progress and to enjoy the scenery. Tucked in the Animas River valley below the San

Juans' ragged horizon was Durango; it was an extraordinary panorama.

Talus covered the steep slope into Deep Creek. A rock, gray and lustrous, was a perfect flat-topped bench. We sat and watched as four deer appeared in the grassy meadow far below us in what would be the Deep Creek's headwater drainage. I pointed out their slow procession.

Once again, comfortable with each other, we sat side by side.

"In about ten to fifteen minutes, their buck will come out from the scrub oak to join his little harem. They've developed street smarts out here in the woods. We should leave when he shows up, but if they all run, we'd better do the same."

Affectionately, and without a word, Amy rested her head on my shoulder. "How did you know where you'd find me?"

"Your dad commissioned that house and was confident that Grimaldi would bring you here. That was before we discovered that I'd designed the place.

"Amy, I've seen Grimaldi several times, but I never connected the dots. I'm sure *he* murdered Tom Boyle when he stood next to your dad that night in Boston. I never got a good look at him then. I saw him in the courtroom at your dad's trial for a split second. Once again, here in Durango, Grimaldi evaluated your dad's property, but I only saw him walking away from me to relieve himself in the woods.

"The next time, in Boulder, was the first time I saw him face to face. The day you and I met, Peter Nori in one phone call, sounded out all this connection with Grimaldi, with your dad, and my WITSEC, but not your link in all this.

"Lance is a trophy collector; remember what he said about his stiletto? 'I'll put this in my trophy room right after I gut you with it.' What better way to put his stamp on the business than to marry you in the family home.

"Are you okay?" I steadied Amy with my hand on her shoulder.

"Sure. Maybe," sinking into my support, "I'm not used to the altitude. The mental stuff is the hardest, untwisting it all. How did we end up so raveled, and neither one of us knew? We're supposed to be good at this."

"We are good at this. For example, tell me, my anthropologist, what's strange about our bench."

"Nice deflection." Amy, with a small laugh, compiled her observations. "This rock was brought here. It's larger and darker gray than the talus rocks. There's an abundance of flint chips. A Ute or Anasazi chose this spot to make arrowheads or spearheads. There's the hunting ground, rife with game."

"Good observations; what's your conjecture?"

"Hauling the rock here for a bench was an initiation, poor kid. Finding the flint was the kid's task too. His mentor sat right here with him, demonstrating how to use an antler to flake and shape his future weapons. When hunting, after reconnaissance from this spot, brush beaters would come noisily from below, up..., that's Deep Creek, right..., drive the deer or elk upward. The valley would funnel them." Amy was engaged in her synthesis and enjoyed the unfolding activities of hundreds of years ago. "Downdraft from the peak would alert the animals to scatter or bolt for another less viable trail if there were any hunters upslope. The hunters would set an ambush..., by those rocks, where their scent would drift away from the deer's natural escape route. For confirmation, we'd find a mess of arrowheads around that open area."

A four-point buck meandered to his herd in the meadow. I offered both hands to lift Amy.

"Let's come back later to check it out."

Amy, energized, took the lead up the game trail but kept her eye on the scene, still developing it in her mind and imposing it on the topography below. *An anthropological monograph was forming.*

"I heard that. Telepath." Amy said, laughing.

§§

CHAPTER 54

"I'm missing a perimeter guard. Who is it?" Lance was visibly upset.

Before his entourage was able to answer, the phone jangled.

"No one knows this number; leave it," Lance growled, adamant.

Closest to the phone, the man most startled, was too swift in reacting to the phone and too slow to react to Lance's demand.

"Hello?" Confused, the man wrote a telephone number on a scratch pad, then held the receiver out toward Lance. "He asked for Lance Grimaldi."

"*What?*" Lance was white-hot. "No one knows I'm here. Gimme that."

"Lance, this is Petros." Pete Belluno used his parental tone.

"Pete, I'm surprised you rang me here; I only got in last night." Lance was, indeed, miles beyond being surprised. Lance was to call Petros for his "blessing" on the marriage, not the other way around, and he planned to keep his location secret to eliminate any potential interruptions. "Are you coming to the wedding? The father should give the bride away. I know it's short notice. What's that? Can't get away? Heh, heh."

"Grimaldi, there will be no wedding tomorrow. A bride, willing or not, is an indispensable component. Am I missing the whole point, or are you? My gut tells me that you're absent one person, maybe two?"

"Oh, your Amy's here with me."

"I've heard that house of mine is built on an old Indian burial ground," part of Pete's and my script. "Things can disappear in one room and reappear in another. It happened all the time to the construction crews who built it, chasing tools they'd put down just minutes before. My daughter isn't where you think she is. Four walls that appear so solid are porous to the pure and good and solid to those who are not. Um, um, no. Amy's not there anymore."

"Nice, Pete," Lance said, then covered the phone, whispered loudly over his shoulder to an underling, and nodded vigorously toward the master bedroom. "Go. Make sure the girl's up there."

"No, really, Lance. I'm confident she's not there; you can't keep water in a sieve. One of your flaws, Grimaldi, is you lack vision. It's why your grand plan isn't going to work. It's why your grasping at straws is coming to nothing."

"The door's locked from the inside; she has to be in there." The underling returned with the non-news.

"Come on, Pete, I'm your hand-picked guy."

"I've seen beyond that. You lack the ability to see all that's in front of your eyes or hear all that reaches your ears. You've never had it. No, I have someone else in mind, better suited to my vision for the family's future, smarter, much more successful, able to conceive a waterfall, or an ocean, from a single drop of water. Someone who will grasp the nettle, who will deal with difficult situations when they come up," Pete ad-libbed with a smile in his voice.

"Too little, too late." Lance, unsettled. "Tomorrow, you're my father in law, Dad."

"Grimaldi... boy... man wannabe, don't boast about your tomorrow. You haven't a clue. Oh..., you can't confirm it, can you? Your boys can't even tell you that she's not there. Your drones checked, but you still don't know. Smell the coffee, smell the roses, face the music, wake up, get real, cup check." Petros followed the script. Cal had wanted Grimaldi wound up tighter than a clock spring. Pete was enthusiastic about his role.

Once again, Lance covered the phone and made a sly, futile search for cameras.

"Get your butt back up there. Get in that room and tell me that girl is in there. *Now!*"

Returning to the phone, "Petros, a question for you, how did you guess I was coming here?" turmoil found traction in Lance's voice.

"It's not a guess Grimaldi, you ignorant miscreant. What else would you be doing, and where else would you go?"

"Don't get far from that phone, Petros. I'll call you back in minutes with the happy news that you'll be able to call me 'son.'"

"The happy news, you two-legged swine, is that I'll talk to Amy at this time tomorrow, face to face when you thought you'd be tying the knot. You are a pathetic, degenerate, stupid excuse of a clown. If you were smart enough, you'd have delusions in your head; instead, you have rocks. There's no hope for you. The Commission isn't going to let you into their shed with the sharp tools. They'll make your life a pit of despair if you get that far.

"Tomorrow, twenty-four hours from now, Amy will be here with me."

Ashen, blood pounding in his ears, Lance slammed the receiver into its cradle with the extra assist of jumping to his feet. Infuriated, aggravated, and enraged were too mild to describe the futility and grasping of this posing crime lord. Sweat beaded on his forehead, and despite his antiperspirant, it showed dark in his shirt's underarms. Having never witnessed this level of fury, those close to him, those who had murdered cruelly and in cold blood, cringed, avoiding even his slightest glance.

"You. Blister." Lance shrieked the first of several orders that would strike as hard and fast as hammer blows. "Tell the men at the gate to let in a guy by the name of Jamie. Do that on your way to the hardware store to get me a sledgehammer. Go! Now!

"Whatever your name is," Lance pointed indiscriminately with a worn business card toward his group of men, "call this number. Get this guy, Jamie, over here ASAP or faster. No excuses.

"You. Go. Make sure that Cliff didn't let anyone out through the garage.

"Get your pistol. Yes, you, you idiot. Go outside. If I'm not at that bedroom window in five minutes," Lance jabbed furiously in the master suite's direction, "shoot it out. Look at your watch, brilliantine. How are you going to tell if it's been five minutes?

"The rest of you, upstairs with me."

§

The sturdy door did not give way to the Bostonians' burly shoulders, now sorely bruised from their efforts. The bedroom's fractured ballistic glass window, no longer transparent, didn't yield to .38 caliber bullets either.

In the garage, Cliff reeled backward from Lance's resounding backhand, demonstrating the importance of his answer.

"Boss, she couldn't have gotten out this way. I couldn't help but see her. Foot noise wouldn't matter either. Opening the overhead doors would have made too much noise, even if she did come out this way." Cliff nodded to the corner of the garage; all of them knew it to be an escape from the master suite. "She wouldn't have taken the time to close them."

Cliff's logic crept past Lance's rage. Fortunately for Cliff, it registered. He dabbed the blood at the corner of his mouth with the knuckle of his index finger.

§

Jamie arrived just ahead of Blister and the sledgehammer.

"What's happening? Armageddon?" Jamie, with his signature head toss, flipped back his flaxen hair. The scent of banana traveled with him. "I rang the doorbell; no one answered, so I just came in."

"Lance's bride for tomorrow locked herself in the master suite," Blister confided, swinging his new eight-pound sledge.

"Was it something you said?" Directed at Lance and intended to be humorous, Jamie regretted the comment instantly.

"I'll rip your throat out, and you'll be talking through your butt with another smart remark like that." Impossibly, Lance's fury had compounded over the previous twenty-five minutes.

"If this is that kind of party, I'll go home and finish cleaning my guns." Jamie turned away.

"Like spit, you will. I need to get into that room."

"Put your hammer down, John Henry, no sense in getting hurt." Jamie, not accustom to ratcheting down the rhetoric, did precisely that. "Let me take a look."

"You can't force it," Lance offered expertly.

"Eh." Jamie took the lead up the stairs; his eye roved appreciatively over the craftsmanship and design. He scrutinized the doorknob. "Industrial. Steel door, veneered with oak. The doorframe is steel, too. A circular saw with an abrasive blade could get you access to turn the knob from the inside in a half-hour if there aren't any other tricks."

"Get to it then." Lance irate at Jamie's comments, knowing them to be right.

"Patience, professor." Jamie turned and looked out into the foyer below. Taking his time, he strolled across the balcony to the reading room. His hand glided across the oak rail. He inspected the trim above the reading room door, then exclaimed, "Oh, yeah!"

From a slot in the railing's underside, Jamie extracted a key and held it up for all to see.

"I hate the guy who designed and built this place with a passion, but he's a certified genius. Townies call him a magician. In a house designed by Cal James, you expect this."

Lance already squeaked a register above normal. At the mention of Cal James, he exploded.

"What?" Lance, nuclear, with now stressed vocal cords reverberating in the upper range of audible frequency levels. He hissed out with the whistled release of a pressure cooker valve, "Calvin James was Farina's guy in Boulder!"

"Right, he should have graduated from CU this spring," Jamie said, matter-of-factly, fitting the key into the lock. As he turned the knob, the phenomenally harried Lance shoved him aside.

"Shoes for a door wedge, fat chance that works." Lance kicked Amy's high heels aside and barked out orders to search every inch. "I don't want that Farina to be able to hide under a postage stamp."

In less than five minutes, they thoroughly searched every place in the suite that was bigger than a breadbox. A quick search excluded anywhere along the garage escape catwalk as a hiding place.

"Blister, you sit in that chair and wait for the little witch to show herself.

"Hey bride, I know that you're in here. Come on out, or your dad will suffer." Petros' words about the Indian burial ground teased around the edges of Lance's mind.

"Jamo." With his theme glance, Lance focused on Jamie, "Any chance this place was built on an Indian burial ground?"

"Jamo? Really? You're calling me Jamo? Let me say this about Indian burial grounds. If you build a home around here and report that you ran across even a couple of pottery shards, you're shut down for an archeological survey on your site, on your tab. If you're stuck with a dig, you should give up on ever building on that site. That's why most houses around here since the mid-eighties don't have full basements. They're built 'slab on grade' to avoid discoveries through excavation." He tossed his flaxen locks again. "So, No."

A thought crossed Jamie's mind and showed plainly on his face. Already headed out to the balcony and stairway, he turned quickly back into the master suite.

Lance wrenched a turnabout to follow him, "What?" His fury undampened.

"Where's the laundry room?" Jamie inquired.

"Downstairs behind the kitchen." Lance caught on and entertained the idea of a quick resolution. "Laundry chute?"

"Sure enough."

After a brief secondary search, the linen closet floor revealed a finger hole for a trap door. Pulling, Jamie released its pressured roller latch. Spring hinged, the door flipped open. Sudden fervor yielded to abrupt disappointment. The laundry chute was a twelve-inch diameter PVC pipe, much too narrow for Amy's shoulders or hips. Jamie used his fist to dislodge the aqua pipe in any direction that it might give, to no avail.

"Who missed that?" Lance lashed out again. He gave a double-handed shove aside to the assembled group in disgust. "Everybody but Blister, downstairs."

§

Lance had scheduled his upper-tier personnel to arrive from Boston early that afternoon, his A-team, for added security. He assembled his available manpower in the foyer. His thoughts

320

were difficult to gather. One by one, he delegated, not neatly, not precisely, not Lance-like.

"Trim, head to the airport with the limo to pick up the first string. There should be four on a flight from Dallas - Fort Worth. Get 'em here fast..., Scratch that. When they call in, you go get 'em. No, go now and tell them to drive back here. You stay there. Make sure the girl doesn't get on a plane.

"While you're at it, find out what helicopter service there is. I heard one last night. Get someone on the phone ASAP.

"Who is it that I'm still missing. It's Cliff's brother, where is he? He's on perimeter duty. How long has he been out?" Lance examined the faces of his cringing help. "When was he supposed to be back? Who's checking on that? You idiots. Get out there. Find him. Jamo, I need them to have brains. Go with 'em," and through clenched teeth added, "please."

"One person! One person. Who'll volunteer to go into town and get maps?" Lance stepped up his belittling.

"You'll need a San Juan National Forest map, a Colorado road map, and a Durango West quadrangle topographical map." Jamie piped in with a nod to Lance to demonstrate his expertise. "Pine Needle Mountaineering on Main will have the topo and Forest Service map. A convenience store will have a roadmap."

Jamie led his party of two outside.

"He's a little testy today, hey?" Jamie's hair took another confident toss. "You two go clockwise, I'll go counter. If you see anything weird, holler."

§

"Trim, get Belluno on the phone."

Lance had only himself to intelligently converse with. *How in blazes did he do that? I've hardly gotten a few hours sleep and my first cup of coffee, and he knows..., Belluno knows my bride, who I snatched yesterday, has vanished, and I'm missing one of my men. Not even my guys knew that.*

He reviewed his informed cohorts for a rat and came up empty. *Was Petros honestly that stupid smart?* Lance had gotten him once, and good. However, Petros' wheels churned in overdrive at the trial and had ever since.

Petros Belluno's preemptory phone call flushed out all of Lance's advantages, surprise, location, and purpose. From prison, Pete was seeing and harassing him, infuriatingly. His every pulse excruciatingly pounded his temples. Belluno had called Lance at a place he couldn't have known Lance would be, at a phone number he didn't know, with information he couldn't conceivably possess, from a phone inaccessible to him. *How could this possibly be? There's no way in Hell this could be happening.*

§§

CHAPTER 55

Leveche is the Spanish name for winds off the Sahara and called Sirocco in other parts of Europe. Khamsin is the hot southerly wind affecting Egypt and Israel. Winds from the Arabian desert, Simoom. Loo is the dangerously hot westerly wind of India and Pakistan.

For the Diné, the wind is Nitch'i. It is qualified with adjectives like dil kohn for smooth or itsoh for great. Winds, according to Diné mythology, hold up the earth. Shamans offer prayers on certain occasions to assist the winds. So prevalent is wind over the desert southwest; its absence is a notable occasion.

When sunshine heats the ground, the air close to the surface warms and rises, cooler air replaces it, and the cycle repeats. This eddy production continues, and more extensive rotations of air combine above these surface microsystems as wind. Surface wind with its airborne particles compresses when it encounters a barrier, be it twig or pebble, then increases velocity when it pushes over. Decompression follows on the downslope, velocity decreases, and heavier particles drop, adding to the barrier.

This ripple-dynamic scales up when an established wind, say Nitch'i itsoh, encounters a range of mountains such as the La Platas. Air pressure builds on the upslope and increases velocity along mountain ridges, up to double its initial speed. A Venturi effect occurs when wind forces its way through the narrower gaps of mountain passes adding even more force and velocity.

Cap clouds form when the energy required to retain airborne moisture is used instead to lift air over mountains. Water vapor condenses, and precipitation results at a distance downwind, depriving the mountain of that rain or snow, a rain shadow. Roll clouds form close to the earth's surface within the rain shadow, lens-shaped, lenticular clouds layer above the roll cloud. Between cap clouds and their lenticular counterparts is a wave trough, a downward bent in airflow.

These clouds, Altocumulus Standing Lenticularis, ASLs, are tells for the experienced mountain pilot..., but not for Calvin James.

§

Nitch'i itsoh awoke with the dawn, Tuesday morning. Dust bothered Lake Powell, Tuba City, Chinle, Kayenta, and Tec Nos Pos, and the litter in these Arizona towns aspired to a kite's airborne lifestyle. Area natives considered these winds pesky at best, with only a slim chance that dust particles might seed the clouds. Less happily, during long arid spells, dust seeding resulted in virga; rain that leaves the clouds, but sublimates, never connecting with the thirsty ground, a hope unfulfilled.

This Tuesday morning, Nitch'i itsoh flowed freely over flat agricultural fields and scrub oak in eastern Utah and very westernmost Colorado. It channeled agreeably up the Canyons of the Ancients, over the vineyards of McElmo, and Yellow Jacket Canyons, it gained elevation over the piñon and yellow pine of Haycamp Mesa. Then Nitch'i itsoh encountered the aspen-covered western La Plata Mountains' upslope, slipping through a narrow pass in Indian Ridge.

§§

CHAPTER 56

Jamie whistled a low heads-up and motioned to his two subordinates, who rushed to him in response. Extra scuffing on the steep game trail attracted Jamie's attention. Should Lance's girl have attempted to navigate her way down the treacherous slope, he wanted quiet. Clever of her to find the only way down to Skunk Creek.

"Okay, Slick, head back to the house, and tell Lance we've got something over here." Jamie was quiet and forceful. "Your friend and me'll head down to see what we're onto. What's your name, friend?"

"It's Joe."

"Watch your step Joe, I'll follow."

An enraged outburst rose from the creek bottom.

"It's Cliff's brother," Joe shouted.

Quick to the rescue, Joe tripped on the tie wire that had snared his coworker. Rocks and dirt did their abrasive work once again. Jamie neared more cautiously and snickered quietly at the duct tape restraints that held Cliff's brother.

§

"Hey, Lance, watch your step," Jamie shouted from the small encampment toward the pasture above, "I thought *you* might want to free your tree-hugging helper."

Lance's shoes and wardrobe would suffer, and he was in no mood to learn to ground surf on his smooth leather soles. He had not found himself so out of control in any situation since junior high school except for his clash with Calvin James in Boulder.

"What happened here?" An unruly and uncomfortably dirty Lance began questioning his still bound guard.

"He was Mexican, I told him to get out, but he wanted to bribe me with the gold that he'd found. I tripped over a freaking root, and when I was down, he taped me up. He would have drowned me if I didn't tell him how many people were at the house. He took my hat and jacket," omitting the loss of his firearm.

"Let me interpret," Jamie jumped in before Lance could ask what he was talking about, "the guy's not Mexican; he's Calvin James."

Shaken, Lance, for the first time in his life, found that anger had taken his breath away.

"There's no root to trip over," Jamie continued, "it was tie wire. This camp was a trap to get information. Duct tape? That's not gold panning gear. He took TreeHugger's jacket and hat for a disguise to get close to your house. James is the only guy that could get your girl out of that place without your crew knowing it."

"It couldn't be James," Lance countered vehemently, "Farina didn't tell him that she was coming, phone or mail. He couldn't know that we were here, and he couldn't get to this hellhole faster than we did."

"This is all new trappings, Lance; gold pan, tape rolls, the tie wire is off a new role, sleeping bag, tent. This guy ain't no Mexican." Jamie turned to the watchman. "TreeHugger, describe the guy."

"Over six foot, a hundred seventy, muscular build, and short light brown hair. I never saw his face."

"Cut him down, Jamo. I might slip with a knife." Lance's eyes bulged. Just when he thought that he had reached anger's elastic limit, it raced beyond. "So what does this mean for me, this Calvin James?"

"He's super smart, unpredictable, and, like me, he's an expert on the area." Jamie gestured toward the mountains, then to the north, east, and south. "Two words, 'worst nightmare.' I'd say they're gone for good."

"You won't let 'Gone for good' happen. Will you?" Lance threatened.

Jamie sliced through the duct tape. A hundred yards up the hill, a fox scattered up twigs and leaves, racing away from the fractious humans below.

"That's them. Get 'em." Lance screeched.

"Slick, Joe, TreeHugger," Jamie countermanded. "no one's there. The only way down here is that game trail you all just came down. TreeHugger would have seen or heard anyone who came this way."

§

"Jamo, tell me everything you know about Calvin James." Lance rushed the five of them through the open field toward the house, attempting desperately to regain control and composure.

§

Lance paced all the faster when he heard the Bell Jet Ranger, to speed its arrival. He was none too happy about the charges. Although Mason's Helicopter Service was more expensive than the others, Dick Mason was the one with the shortest availability to fly time and shortest commute. Lance had taken pleasure in speaking directly to the company owner. Even here, Lance had pull. The owner, in turn, had taken the initiative to ask what arrival times his competitors had quoted, once Lance had described the urgency of his request. Mason had assured him he could knock off fifteen minutes from any other provider.

Lance watched warily as the turquoise and white passenger helicopter approached. He bobbled his Breath Savers, then launched one past his teeth.

Dick Mason selected a suitable landing spot, slowed his descent, and rotated the Jet Ranger expertly onto the most level piece of ground. While on the phone with Mason, Lance was instructed to wait until the rotors idled before approaching the aircraft. Under Dick Mason's hand, this took an unusually long time, after which Dick gave his thumbs up and his beckon to board.

Dick proffered headphones for Lance to wear. He put them on uneasily.

"Sorry about the door, sir; I thought that I'd unlocked it. By the way, there's a step on the strut that makes boarding easier." Dick was 100 percent business and apologized for his time-consuming error. "What's our destination?"

"I told you over the phone. I'm looking for my friends. They wandered off from the house earlier this morning. One of them is in urgent need of medicine. I want to find them right away." Lance fidgeted. He wanted to get in the air but knew he would have to answer his pilot's questions for that to happen.

"What are your thoughts on where they may have gone?"

"Another friend said that I should concentrate on the ridge. He thinks that they might try to cross over it once they realize that they don't have any medicine."

"How did your friend arrive at that conclusion?" Dick continued to stall.

"He thinks that they may have gone into the woods by the forest service road." Lance's nerves, still jagged, spiced his aggravated tone beyond the peppermint Breathsaver. "I'm paying you to be in the air, not to talk, so let's get going."

"Don't be testy. I need to know where you want to go. Unless you merely wanted a vertical takeoff and hover." Dick wound up the turboshaft engine. It whined loudly while the rotors commenced their spin.

The Jet Ranger gave a slight lurch as Mason lifted them slowly away from terra ferma. Rotor wash flattened the tall grass in waves. Lance, who implied that he was an experienced passenger, made an involuntary grasp toward anything that appeared stationary.

"How long have these folks been gone?" Mason again probed.

"Maybe an hour, maybe two." Lance gave it up reluctantly.

"What about footwear? Suitable for hiking?"

"You're asking a lot of questions, seeing as you're my hired pilot." The recollection of Amy's dress shoes on the master bedroom floor rattled Lance's consciousness.

"You're not very forthcoming with information, considering your concerns with my expense and the girl's or guy's need for medication." Dick properly ordered Lance's concerns, annoying Lance and detracting from the search. "If they've been gone two hours in hiking shoes in the direction that you suggest, they could be fifty yards from your fine home or five miles distant. If he's in a tux and she's dressed for the prom, they could be just returning, but their maximum outlying distance would be much less, say two miles. All I'm saying is that I can give you the best coverage with the best information. If all you wanted was a first helicopter ride, you could have said so."

"One of them may be outfitted for hiking. The other one, the girl, the one that I need to get a hold of... barefoot and in a dress."

"Well then, we should spot them in no time; pretty narrow search area, considering. I'd say that barefoot means they're not far at all. Guy and girl. Did they take wine and a blanket?" Mason followed with a suggestive eyebrow inquiry.

"Just find them." Lance was developing a severe headache, a side effect of sustained rage. "I have you as long as I need you, right?"

"I'm topped off fuel wise. No worries there," Mason offered helpfully. He began to narrate and point with the chopper nose, "I think your friend's guess is good. The ridge will hinder any travel that way."

The tail swung quickly around to a view toward the game trail that proved so treacherous for Lance's crew.

"Getting into Skunk Creek is near impossible, so is traveling alongside it, upstream or downstream. We'll head west about a mile over the service road; then, we'll spiral out from there.

"It's almost an involuntary reaction to wave at a low flying whirlybird. The mountain weather is tricky today, so you'll have to spot. Let me know if you see them."

An expert rotary-wing pilot, Mason dropped the Jet Ranger on its side and pivoted over his previous landing spot. The sinking sensation was adequate to produce a grayer quality to Lance's, once red, now pallid face. They flew slightly better than treetop high, the better to appreciate their excellent velocity.

§

"Do you have any aspirin?" Lance's request came after half an hour of spiraling out over a widening area.

"There should be a small bottle in the first aid kit." Dick nodded toward the box latched on the slim amount of floorboard between them. "No water, though. Hey, the couple, are they just visiting?"

"The girl and I are supposed to be married this afternoon."

"Butterflies. Or a better offer." Mason muttered, apparently to himself, unhelpfully.

"Shut up," Lance snarled, "broaden the search. What's the next scenario?"

"They could have made it over to Junction Creek Road. We'll do a flyover." Mason lurched the chopper very uncomfortably for his discomforted passenger, then took on more altitude. "If they are on Junction Creek, they would head to town or head further north to pick up the Colorado Trail, but that's not as likely."

The scouring of Junction Creek Road proved unfruitful.

"They might also have dropped into Skunk Creek and climbed up the other embankment. I have to be careful of a no-fly zone over the Wildlife Preserve. We can check the roads."

"Somebody was watching over there."

"Maybe your guests hid until your watchman left." Mason became increasingly aggressive in reorienting their search.

"Slow down. I can't see anything on the ground." Lance threw in a few select profanities.

"You don't look down. You look out ahead and to the side. Keep your focus. We need to cover ground." Mason had already had his fill of Boston instructing him. "If you paid attention, you'd see that couple walking on the road right there."

The young couple walked hand in hand on a lightly used, unpaved road below. When they heard the low flying helicopter, they waved with their free hands. A blue merle Australian Shepherd leaped from the brush, ran up to their sides, and barked. If it had wings, it would have herded the machine away from its masters.

Mason wheeled the chopper in a tight circle over the two and waved. They lived next door to Dick and his wife.

"Not your people?"

"No." Lance had never had such a pisser of a day. "I want to go up there over the mountain. What's on the other side?"

330

"I thought you said one of them was barefoot."

"Maybe she was barefoot! Just go!"

Dick Mason practiced the utmost patience to explain why it was necessary to fly south and then up through La Plata Canyon. He promised, later, to demonstrate the flight dynamics, taking into account today's weather. Dick was now into Lance Grimaldi's American Express Card for nearly five large.

Lance was not at all interested in the details of mountain flying. He did pay close attention to the road below. Mason explained that it was the only wheeled access into La Plata Canyon.

Jeeps and other large-tired four-wheel drive vehicles parked in groups at hiking trailheads. Lance laughed out loud when he saw a sedan and its three occupants in a passionate argument over its stationary state. That trio was having a bad day; his day was worse.

Dick Mason and Lance both spotted the delta wing fabric on hang glider frames high above the Jet Ranger, resting on Lewis Peak. Barely discernible were the solid colors of turquoise and coral.

"Don't see many doing that out here." Mason banked away, yielding the right of way to the unpowered craft should they launch. He hugged the great bowl on its east side, allowing his passenger to scourer the rocky rubble for signs of recent travel.

"Get close enough to see them."

"*A.* No. *B.* I'm not risking my license. *C.* You're desperately seeking your sick fiancée, and you want to take time to gawk at a couple of hang gliders?

"I said I'd demonstrate mountain turbulence for you. Here we go, hang on." Mason maneuvered around to the western rim.

"That's Cumberland Basin behind us. That's Diorite Peak. Highline Trail runs across it. Watch the control. If I pull up on the collective, it takes us up. I'm not moving the cyclical, so I'm not going to tilt us at all." He began a straight vertical climb.

The Jet Ranger rose straight up then without warning; it tipped backward as Nitch'i itsoh batted it away, a crumpled paper ball boxed by a cat's paw. Lance jerked forward, his seat restraint bruising him. His squeal pained and amused Mason.

A less skilled pilot could have stalled and spun out. Dick brought the tail around and used the potent blow to propel them above the strong turbulence. A quick timberline skim sufficed for Lance that he had wasted seventy-five hundred dollars.

"Take me to La Plata Airport." Lance barely collected himself.

Petros' words echoed in Lance's thoughts; *I'll be talking to Amy, face-to-face, tomorrow.*

He would have to head them off in his own country to save face before The Commission in New York.

"Stop by the house first."

§§

"I thought a lot about what you and I have done for fun, activities that would make our trek today more entertaining."

A crimson thread stretched over the gray, lifeless rock debris twenty feet above our seldom-used game trail. It vanished in the distance toward the very near summit of Lewis Peak. The final slope to the peak was much steeper here, and the loose rock was treacherous.

"The upper end of that rope is corkscrew anchored at the peak. I rolled it out it last night." It seemed so long ago, days, not hours.

With the rope's aid, Amy helped herself over the last hundred yards of unstable footing. She made the peak, panting from exertion, the near thirteen thousand foot altitude, and the breathtaking, top of the world 360-degree view. I followed, threading the loose rope end through my belt loop, pulling it up behind me.

"Higher still?" Amy gazed at the long ripstop bags that contained our gliders.

"That's the idea. Let's take ten before we assemble 'em."

The sun gained on directly overhead. Clouds gathered behind us, but to the west, the skies were clear. We would fly away from any weather disturbances.

We both finished off a Powerbar with a water chaser.

Seated again, I described the incredible vista before us in every direction.

"We'll be jumping off into Columbus Basin. The air's thinner, so you'll need to adjust your flair on takeoff."

"If you were heading east to Colorado from Utah or Arizona, these are the beginning of the Rockies. Those are the San Juans, all those ragged peaks north and around to the east. Purgatory Ski area is only twenty or so miles away, so we may see the ski runs if we get enough altitude.

"Your dad's house is between Durango and here. In front of us, down there, is La Plata Canyon; from its open end, sixty miles to the south is Farmington. At night, we'd see the airport lights for both Durango and Farmington. Shiprock is there, that dark triangle. You can see the Sleeping Ute, and Mesa Verde, toward Cortez, and further into Tony Hillerman country."

"I love Tony Hillerman," Amy interjected, "he's great reading for an anthropologist. More than once, I've picked up his books to revive my interest."

"Tell me about it. I read him for fun. Tribal police, romance, skinwalkers, medicine men, murder mysteries... wasn't Hillerman on my bookshelves in Boulder?" I wondered how we hadn't discussed him before.

"He can beat up on cultural anthropologists. We're too theoretical for him. I doubt that he'd appreciate my point of view."

"Too bad for him.

"Over that ridge are the Blue Mountains, the La Sal's, and all of Utah. That's Edward Abbey country. He's the only guy that can describe smoking a cigarette that almost makes me want to try it."

"No *Desert Solitaire* for you."

"I thank you very much, no worries, though." I wriggled my nose at the thought of reeking cigarette smoke. "When we gain enough altitude to see the Blues, we'll have glide ratio enough to clear Indian Ridge, so we'll need to ride thermals. Bummer."

Amy smiled at the understated humor. Her smile, as always, reinforced mine.

"That spire over there is Lizard Head. It used to be taller and have a beak, but it collapsed eighty years ago." I completed the circle.

"Where'd you pick up our gliders?"

"High Desert Hang Gliders in Albuquerque. When I was pulling all this together from Logan, in Boston, I called Wills Wings out in California to see if they had any distributors in Southwest Colorado. After I explained that Aspen was inconveniently out of my way, they were nice enough to volunteer High Desert. High Desert had just received two of these 153's for a special order, but the pick-up date is two weeks from now. Wills Wings said they would have plenty of time to replace them out of their stock, and they even made a call to Albuquerque to confirm the deal."

"Picky down to the brand and model, even with your time constraints. Humph." Amy was still in good spirits.

"I'd read in an airline magazine that they just broke a distance record for a flight over three hundred miles. Seemed a good bet."

Amy and I each assembled our unexpectedly colorful, squash-blossom-palette sails. Twice we checked each other's work. With our gliders roped nose down into the breeze, we sat in their shade.

"Over there, that notch," I pointed across the basin we would soon jump into, "that's where we'll slip over the ridge. We'll follow the creek until it opens up into meadows, then we wait for the horses.

"Look at us up here in the middle of everywhere. It's a long way down, about fifteen hundred feet right from takeoff."

"Mixing adrenalin with your endorphins?" Amy teased, "nothing the matter with that strange brew when dealing with heavier than air, unpowered flight. You said there's a plan B?"

Suddenly, the clatter of Dick Mason's Bell Jet intruded on our windswept silence from the south in the canyon. He stayed lower, between the twin ranges of peaks. Similar to the route he and I had flown last night. It was an unexpected perspective looking down on his helicopter in flight.

"That's Dick Mason. I thought we would be in the air before he showed up, and he should have come from over the ridge north of here, hired by Grimaldi."

We geared up while we watched, double-checking everything.

Dick circled through Columbus Basin. Occasionally, the chopper would dodge here or there or drop abruptly for a close-up view of wary hikers. For a few minutes, he disappeared behind Storm Peak.

Dick would have Grimaldi intrigued with the man-made notch at Kennebec Pass, out of sight from our location. Almost identical to the notch in the ridge near Pete's home with a traversable road, it posed a definite attraction. We saw the chopper again, far away, flying along the Colorado Trail in the northern basin.

The Bell Jet then settled lower than the lowest point in Indian Ridge, the critical point in Amy's and my prospective flight path. Mason commenced a slow vertical rise. When he was level with the ridge top, the Bell Jet tilted back. The rotor disc flexed upward in the shape of a half bowl, pressed by an unseen force, standing the Bell Jet on its tail. With no lift in that position, the chopper plummeted in reverse, stalled. Mason increased the pitch of his tail rotor and banked, the equivalent of a half-barrel roll. Otherwise, we might have watched helicopter debris litter the canyon floor. We would find out later; he caused Grimaldi to scream like a baby and nearly soil himself.

Dick and his passenger rocketed out of sight, headed home over Kennebec Pass.

Amy was aghast. So was I.

"What, in the great name of heaven, was that?" She cried out.

"That, my dear, was a friend's friendly warning. We might have a breeze right here, but there is a powerful wind blowing through that pass. You asked about Plan B; it's now our current plan. We still get to fly, though.

"So now we're going to head around to where the chopper disappeared. There will be thermal lift and ridge lift off Storm Peak; we'll need that. Around the peak, we'll see a weathered ore mill in ruins. Two hundred yards from that, we'll set down, stash the kites, and grab our mountain bikes."

"Of course we will, Cal." Amy's upbeat eyes rolled up as she tried to imagine my activities over the past two days. "Mountain bikes. Bike shop. Right. Let's hit it."

"After you" wasn't required. Amy was already the first step into a three-step launch. Perfectly, flawlessly, turquoise and coral fluttered, filled, and flew.

I hadn't realized how terrified I would be seeing her out there. It brought a new awareness I hadn't thought-out, the collateral damage that association with me could entail when Lance Grimaldi was involved. I remembered my brother Phil's girlfriend, Jill Taylor.

Seconds later, I was off. With a slightly different trajectory, I was higher and soon out in front, where Amy could follow.

§§

CHAPTER 58

Lance took stock of his personnel. Several of his best help, recently arrived, were still out and unaccounted for, scouring roads and watching the airport. As they dribbled in, Cliff's brother would relay Lance's message that all would have to make their way back to Boston on their own.

Dick Mason stood by at his liberal hourly rate to transport Lance to the airport.

For his ego, pride, and destiny, Lance had to keep Amy from her dad. Time was critical.

Petros Belluno was crystal clear and 100 percent convinced that he would talk with his daughter tomorrow despite Lance's efforts to prevent it. It was Petros' fantasy. Lance had assets in Boston ready to do his bidding, no less than the assassins he'd used to destroy the Barton family.

Calvin James was a ghost, always in Lance's way at the supremely worst moment. He had spirited away Lance's bride-to-be, again, this time without a trace.

It had to be him. Was he a magician? Jamie said Durango townies called him that. What right had he to cheat Lance of his destiny? If this James contracted with Petros Belluno, Lance would have known, wouldn't he? If there was a connection, what was it? How had Lance missed it? Was it just Petros' family protection instinct that caused him to be so suddenly empowered?

What, in the blazes, was he dealing with?

Thoughts raced and hammered his mind until his head begged for more aspirin, a tormenting reminder of his last humiliating flight from Colorado and his previous loss to Calvin James.

§§

CHAPTER 59

A desolate landscape of rocks was our Plan B landing site, rough mine tailings in dichromatic tones of rust and sulfur. Close by, a copse of pine and aspen engaged in a last battle for timberline. I lamented the stark contrast between this barren, afflicted ground and the lush green meadows of Bear Creek.

Amy proved to be an excellent pilot, the payoff from her weekend and summer hang gliding around New England. So fantastic was our highflying experience that whoops, hollers, and not a few woo-hoo's, punctuated our flight without regard for the earthbound nature lovers far below. She was now on a glide path a few hundred yards behind me.

Parallel to, and about five feet above, the flat mill tailings pile, I flared out, stalled, and landed a very decent landing with minimal runout. I unhitched and slipped out of my harness in time to watch Amy land.

Her approach looked too fast and too low to the ground. I wanted to wave her off, fearful she might whack, but she appeared so confident and peaceful. Her glide line, so fluid, so smooth, mesmerized me. I expected to watch a touch and go, a fly by. Instead, she stood with her kite right in front of me.

"What was that?"

"A landing, of course." Very pleased with upstaging me. "I saw guys do this off Mt. Greylock where mom and I used to fly. It looked cool. So there you have it. Sweet, huh?"

"Even the German judges gave you a 9.9."

Glider breakdowns were nominal. We wrapped and stashed them in the trees next to the cloaked bikes, where they would be safe.

"Cal, I know you wished we were airborne longer. We have to do this again sometime."

True. The all-encompassing vertical and horizontal vista was unbelievable, a lifetime memory. I hadn't accounted for the vicious wind blasting our intended flight path; still, mountain bikes were fast downhill transportation. And, so far, we'd racked up three repeat activities.

"Check these out!" Amy's enthusiasm sweetly pushed our pursuers into oblivion.

We kept our helmets. Our Specialized bikes passed routine inspection, only requiring a cam latch seat adjustment.

A narrow, unfrequented trail connected us to the rough and riven basin access road. The brakes and tires, well adjusted, kept us from injurious speed. Amy adeptly avoided the potato-sized rocks in much of our path.

We rode side by side to avoid each other's dust, enjoying riding together again. The alpine element suited her well, helmeted, relaxed, and alert. She smiled, frequently, in my direction, which proved constructive in warding off my fatigue. The only changes from our gliding gear were bike shoes, pant leg clips, and bike repair kits to add to our backpacks. Perfectly casual.

Each minute was precious; otherwise, we would be taking pictures or be in rapturous awe of the transcendent peaks where cirques above the tree line still contained snow.

Notwithstanding precious minutes, when the tree-lined road finally opened up to alpine meadows, I rode a little ahead, pulling off the road, uphill. With one foot freed, I assured my trailing Amy that this was not a cyclist's natural, a European rest stop.

"Thimble sized ripe strawberries." I pointed and salivated.

"Mmmm! couldn't you graze here all afternoon?" Amy unfairly incorporated the strawberry coloring on her lips.

Alluring. I fancied a time when I might follow up with a taste of the strawberry that lingered there.

Back on the road, in the trees once more, I did a near repeat maneuver. "Blueberry break." We savored our mutual indulgence.

"You know, no one should have this much fun when there are brutes not far away, who want you dead, and me...

not well treated. How can we enjoy this when the chase is on?" Her eyes shaped her inquiry with seriousness.

"We're not escapees; we're just taking a few days off together, so enjoy," I teased reassuringly, meeting her gaze.

In a mercurial mood shift, Amy's face beamed.

"I will! Thank you. I've heard a rant like that before. Have I told you I've missed you, Cal?"

§

The rocky, cliff-lined creek on our left, far below, converged with the high rocky ledge that bound the road's right side. The grass median between the paired tire tracks became more lush as the confines constricted the pathway of all four-wheeled traffic that braved the climb or descent. Moss, low flora, and clinging shrubs superficially hid the gray rock wall and the rocky plummet that funneled all travel here. Be it rock, wood, animal, water, four-wheeler, or a pair of mountain bikers, all passed through these narrow straits.

A younger, dark-complected man ahead startled us. He appeared from a recessed nook in the sheer embankment. He waved his hands over his head, gesturing us to stop. If he needed help, my Previa was not far down the road.

"¿Qué pasa?" (What's happening?) I slid my back tire around to stop more quickly and to avoid him, a hockey stop.

Amy followed suit in parallel.

"Calvin James," the young man addressed me, dripped in a Mexican accent much more authentic than my poor attempt earlier in the day. That he knew me by name raised my hackles and Amy's. "You were not with such a pretty lady when you came up here last night. You will have to share with me your amazing pickup line."

Amy and I both adopted poker faces. This man doesn't know who Amy is, eliminating Grimaldi from the threat matrix.

The young Mexican drew a Ruger pistol from the waistband behind his back.

New threat matrix.

"How is it that you know me? Or, better, let's start with who you are, to keep things friendly." Amy had seen this conversational approach before.

The creek rushed with power over the rocks twenty-five to thirty feet below. Its white-noise could be a compelling sleep aid in the right environment. Here it elevated the volume of our voices. It was not loud enough to disguise the approach of a motor vehicle, for which Amy and I vainly listened.

"*Cosa segura, me llamo Juan.* I picked up the bicycles you are now enjoying in Albuquerque. I even placed them, personally, in your nice van, which is also new. It was a pretty price tag, but no one questioned me at all. Hang gliders, back-packs, these and your other bicycles, all this with just a phone call. How much did all this and a flight from Boston cost you? You made of money, Calvin?" The brandished pistol and the Mexican accent was nearly laughable, an endorphin thing.

I sensed Amy's relief.

"Amy, let's dismount and be sociable to our friend, Juan. Juan, please call me Cal. And please don't say anything about badges or badgers."

"You make a joke, Cal, but Angelo and Jorge will join us in a minute." Juan maintained a mean demeanor.

"The more, the merrier. What is it that you have in mind?"

"My friends are not very good drivers on these kinds of roads. Even with air shocks, Angelo high centered our New Yorker. We need your bikes, and for us to contact your money sources, so they give us money, *dinero* that you spend so freely. We'll keep you tied up in our car until they do. You are a trust funder, no?"

From the creek-side, another similarly clothed Mexican emerged. I looked at Amy. She looked back and simply said, "*Ripetere?*" (Repeat?)

"Juan, I'm not a trust funder." Then I greeted heartily, "Angelo!"

"How did you know he is Angelo?" Juan, suspicious, squinted, waving his pistol again.

"Low man on the totem pole drives," alluding to his low hiding place. "Really, it was a fifty-fifty guess. Let me ask you another question. You've been waiting to stop me on this road and counted on recognizing our bikes to do that?"

"Yeah. We're part of an organization that has many sources of income. We welcome your contribution." Posturing to impress and menace.

Tumbling rocks from above on our right, accompanied by an inarticulate shout of anticipated pain, attracted our collective attention. The thud and crunch of a body landing gracelessly across a barkless, sun-bleached, aspen log followed.

Jorge's upper body landed on the downhill side of the long-dead aspen. His right leg rose, remaining in line with his torso. His left foot lodged in the crotch of a branch on the tree's upside. A new bend immediately emerged between the man's existing knee and hip. It resembled a second left knee where it bucked the tree trunk.

We, the four spectators, had the impression of silence. There was no rushing water, no chip of birds. Dislodged rocks tumbled on and around the new arrival, knocking together silently. There was no sound, no voice,... until the scream.

The scream. I linked it with broken bones. My business partner had screamed the same scream when I disgracefully and abusively broke his finger.

Without hesitation, but hindered by the stiffness of our cycling shoes, Amy and I launched toward the downed Jorge, who hung helplessly in a painful stop three feet above the roadway. I lifted his torso while Amy carefully dislodged his foot and stabilized his leg. We turned together, with intertwined movements. I kicked a few hefty rocks from a convenient resting place on the grassy median, where we laid Jorge there with his head uphill.

So swift and sure was our response to Jorge's predicament that Juan and Angelo's frozen postures only thawed when Jorge was on the ground, writhing. Juan's gun aim waned.

"Juan," Amy shouted over Jorge's whine of pain, commandingly, "you said that your organization had many sources of income, is one of those sources, drugs?"

"*Si.*" Juan astounded himself at the ease of his admission to a complete stranger.

"Is one of those drugs cocaine?"

343

"*Si.*" Again, Amy had extracted from Juan more than he was willing to admit.

"Don't just stand there, go get a gram. This man is in pain."

Considering the seriousness, medically and situationally, I was proud of Amy suddenly being in command.

"She's an EMT," I informed Juan.

I knew she disdained recreational cocaine use, but it was a pragmatic means to an end. She continued a cursory check down of Jorge's condition, airway obstruction, venomous bites, lacerations, other breaks, or concussion.

"Angelo." Juan gave a commanding look of his own along with his bark. Angelo disappeared, running for all he was worth up the hill.

Juan kept his pistol at the ready, following my every motion as I stood. I glimpsed, to my right, a darting chipmunk. Juan looked too, distracted by the same movement.

Like swatting a fly, I batted down the barrel of Juan's Ruger and clapped both my hands together over his hand to keep his fingers from curling back around the pistol grip. My right hand found and gripped the gun.

Juan articulated, "Aahhgg."

In a jiff, I had the pistol pointed at Juan. Shock and fear replaced swagger.

I ejected the clip, swung the pistol toward the now-vanished chipmunk, and pulled the trigger to confirm an empty chamber.

"Let's put that back where it belongs." I handed the pistol back grip first. "You know, just to keep things friendly."

Curiosity, fear, dejection, and failure joined Juan's slumped shoulders; these were all he could muster after the transition of control. He didn't attempt to fight.

Where have I seen that before? Amy pondered to herself over the continued moaning of Jorge. "Was that a Kik fight choreography exercise?"

"No, that was Peter Nori's doing, but we have to something with Jorge, right. We can't leave him like this." I asked Amy seriously.

Juan stepped closer to gauge Jorge's injuries.

"Cal, look around for four straight strong branches.
See if you can find one with a fork, like a crutch. All three to
four feet long, please." Amy, dominant. "Juan, please take off
Jorge's left sneaker, carefully.

Amy winked at me, coupled with earnestness. Scram-
bling to comply, I began on the steep easement to the creek
and scavenged for splint material.

"Here's the deal, Juan," I heard Amy explain, "Jorge
is lucky that this isn't a compound fracture; in other words,
the fractured bone ends are still inside his skin. He's unlucky
because this type of fracture can cause a lot of blood loss into
the muscle tissue around it. He could go into shock, and he
could die if he doesn't get medical attention in the next three
to four hours. Do you understand? Do you have his shoe off?"

"*Sí. Comprendo.*" (Yes. I understand.)

"Get busy with his shoe!"

Juan had Jorge's Nike removed swiftly.

"Okay, Juan, do you have a knife?"

Juan's head nodded with the recognition that, yes, he
did

"Jorge! Stay with us! You'll be okay," Amy encouraged.

"Juan, I need you to cut the toe covering off that sneaker.
Then," Amy reached across Jorge's body to point to spots in
the sneaker's sole just in front of the heel, "cut two wide holes
in the sole, both sides, and in the sides just above. Tell me
when you're done."

Angelo's heavy panting announced his arrival well in
advance.

"Angelo, put some of that stuff under his tongue."

Angelo looked at Juan.

"Juan doesn't know what he's doing. Do what I say."

I returned with excellent, sturdy branches and noticed
that Amy had all three in submission to her will. She could do
that to me with just a wink and a smile.

"Cal, inner tubes," Amy implored, "can we take two of
them to bind the splints, please?

"Jorge, how are you feeling?" Amy nurtured.

"*Maldito doloroso, pero mejor. Gracias señorita.*" (Damn
painful, but better.)

"Good job. We are about to give you a painful jolt, though. This is my fair warning."

"Juan, cut Jorge's jeans legs off below the knee. Make them into shorts. We'll need the cloth for padding and tie strips. Use some denim to pad that branch's fork, put the fork in his crotch, align the branch down the inside of his leg, and be careful not to pinch his equipment."

This last concern earned a laugh even from Jorge.

With the forked branch placed, another gently worked under his leg, and another along the outside, Amy stood to revive her circulation.

"Juan, thread the denim strips through those holes you made, then lace the sneaker up back on his foot. Quickly!"

Jorge soon wore an inner tube tightly around his waist, holding the outside branch. Another inner tube secured his upper thigh to all three branches. The branches' lower ends extended below Jorge's re-sneakered foot. Thongs of cloth draped from the slots in Jorge's sneaker. All were consistent with Amy's instructions.

"When I tell Juan and Angelo to stop, Cal, tie those three branches together just above the ankle and tie off the denim strips, firmly, to the splints.

"Juan, Angelo, come here." She stood a little off from Jorge, whispering to them both. They bent toward her to listen, nodded, then knelt close to Jorge's feet. Amy knelt above Jorge's head, put her right hand on his shoulder, and leaned forward.

"Okay, Jorge, this is the jolt I promised. You with me?"

"*Me gustaría seguir en cualquier lugar con tu.*" (I would be happy to go anywhere with you.)

"On the count of three, Juan and Angelo are going to pull on your foot. It will feel like agony from Hell, and then it will feel a whole lot better. Do you understand? Are you ready?" Amy didn't wait for answers. She leaned even more forward to place her hand lightly on the elevated mass that was Jorge's skin covered bone end. She cued Juan and Angelo. "One..."

Jorge screamed out again as Juan and Angelo, on cue, jumped the gun. They smoothly and carefully stretched out Jorge's leg until Amy signaled them to stop. I brought the three branches up against Jorge's ankle, bound them with a prepared portion of the inner tube, then speedily tied off the loose denim ends from the modified Nike. The improvised traction splint secured Jorge's leg fast.

"You know, that 'action before the count is finished' routine is so cliché," I observed appreciatively.

"True, but I had Jorge focusing on a couple of other things," Amy said with a tinge of embarrassed color rising in her cheeks.

"What happened?" Jorge inquired in English. His pain had significantly diminished.

"Your thigh bone is back almost where it should be." Amy picked up Jorge's hand and held it for a moment. "We straightened the sharp bone ends so they aren't piercing or pinching your muscles, so try to relax, and try not to move your leg. On a scale of one to ten, with ten as the worst, what is your pain level?"

Amy ascertained the effectiveness of Jorge's splint, made another evaluation for shock and checked his vital signs.

Juan and I stepped up the road a few paces and faced each other. I spoke first, "So, where were we before we were interrupted by your party crasher?"

I handed Juan the Ruger's clip. He reluctantly met my stare.

"*Preguntarle la pequeña dama jefe..*" (Ask the little boss lady.) Juan knew that there was no honor in continuing his kidnapping attempt. "I don't know, *jefe*." (Chief.)

"Juan, here's the situation. *La jefe dama* is practically that. She didn't know until about six months ago, but her dad was the boss of a major Italian crime family in Boston. A while ago, this dirtbag kind of guy did a *coup d'état* and framed her dad for murder. The slime's name is Grimaldi. He's determined to marry Amy here to establish his position as head of the family's business. Happens all the time, right?"

Juan's expression changed to dread. He feared that he might have antagonized two organized crime factions. His plans had gone incredibly wrong.

"Me, I'm a general contractor in Durango. I build houses and condominiums. Right now, the dirtbag guy is directing a search for us from a house not ten miles over that mountain. If he finds me, *yo soy un hombre muerto.* (I'm a dead man.) Seriously.

"That, in a nutshell, is where Amy and I are, so we are in a big hurry to move on."

Juan nodded thoughtfully, revealing the intelligence masked by his gang persona.

"Here is how I see your situation, Juan. You have a man down in an improvised traction splint. He could wind up dead without medical attention. You also have a gun and a useless car. Amy and I have mountain bikes." I paused to let him think. "I have the solution. It even saves you face when you get back to Albuquerque.

"Juan, you followed me, if I get this straight," I guided him to look at Jorge again, "you followed me up here. You thought that moneywise where there's smoke, there's fire. You also know that if I'm here, there's a Previa van out there. Do you have a dollar?"

"What?"

"Do you have a dollar?"

"Sure."

"I'm selling you that new Previa for a dollar. I'll write a bill of sale for you while Angelo goes to get it."

"Why would you do that?" It was inconceivable to Juan, and he expressed his feeling freely.

"You're in trouble; we're in trouble. Money is irrelevant because our collective issues are life and death. You see that." I implored. "My solution gets Amy and me on our way. It gets you reliable, legal, needed transportation for you and your guys. There's also an expensive vehicle to show for your kidnapping efforts and to cover Jorge's cocaine usage when you get back. Of course, your absolute best course of action would be to get on the right side of the law with your product and your life. I can help with that if you would like. I'll write my number on the bill of sale. The Previa cost me twenty grand. Deal?"

"Deal. The New Yorker we brought up was jacked anyway."

"Friends? You and I don't need more enemies, right?" I extended my hand for a handshake.

Juan backhanded my hand with the back of his, slapped my hand with his forehand, and drew back; our fingertips touch the other's knuckles, then he curled his fingers to grab mine. His sign of sincere agreement happened in a second.

"And Juan, you asked me about my amazing pickup line. It's 'Hey.'

"Angelo, time for you to run again, man," I directed.

Juan nodded.

Angelo looked at me, unbelieving, still out of breath.

"It's downhill this time, and you get to drive back."

His expression brightened.

"A half-mile down is a picnic table in a creek-side clearing. Walk over toward the creek; you'll see a mine access road that crosses the creek. Fifty yards down that road, out of sight is my..., Juan's new Previa. Listen, Angelo, close to the passenger side, is a pine tree. The key is resting on the lowest branch. Got it?"

"Uh, huh?"

"Go get it."

Angelo glanced at Juan, who, in return, shooed him away with the back of his hand.

"Amy, we had better motivate."

She paused to assure Jorge that everything would turn out okay and briefed him on what to expect in the emergency room.

Amy and I mounted our bikes; simultaneously, we clicked into our pedals.

We rode past Angelo as he trotted to the picnic table in the turnout. We waved and shouted, "*Adios!*"

Angelo bent over at the waist with his hands on his knees. He looked in our direction and waved back.

§§

CHAPTER 60

After a quick change at The Silver Lodge, Amy and I were reoutfitted for road riding with new helmets, road bike togs, and the new Bianchi and Trek that I had dropped off the night before.

§

Cal and Amy had just crossed the Colorado, New Mexico border heading to Farmington when a metallic maroon Olds '88 cut hard into the narrow gravel and asphalt strewed shoulder in front of them. The wayward automobile missed the Trek's front wheel by fractions. Cal's reactions were spot on; he freed his shoe cleats, applied both brakes, and steered where he must, off the pavement and into the shoulder. Unable to straighten himself up sufficiently, he dumped his bike on its friendly side. Still, the crash deeply abraded his skin, embedding sand, dirt, and gravel into his left forearm, thigh, and knee. The pain was instantaneous and acute but not sufficient to keep him from a jack-in-the-box leap to his feet.

Amy, drafting Cal by milliseconds, swerved left and remained in the roadway. Her tires skidded, briefly skipping, washboard style, until her Bianchi was upright against the halted Oldsmobile. She sprang from her seat, searching for Calvin James, her anchor in time of trouble.

Both car doors flew open, exposing two quick moving passengers. A swarthy but well-dressed man, who had been riding shotgun, walked swiftly toward the not yet stable Cal. Amy screamed when she recognized the driver who closed in on her, his prey.

"Sam Wilson!" Amy hissed with unbridled ferocity and hatred. All she knew of Sam six years ago and her current plight engulfed her thinking. Sam was one of Lance's minions. This was deadly serious. Amy turned to Cal only to see him injured and facing a man confident in his fighting ability, even against a fit foe.

Stunned, Amy delayed her physical response.

Dust was still settling from the disturbed gravel.

Sam grabbed her in a bear hug from behind, immobilizing her arms. In the open country, no houses were close by or people close enough to hear her. Regardless, she screamed long and loud. She tried to bring her weight to bear for an arch stomp, the way she had done a half dozen years earlier. Sam's feet were out of range, spread apart.

Cal glanced briefly in Amy's direction then at his assailant. He raised both hands in surrender, erroneously hoping that he could buy time. The approaching man paused in a double-take.

"Cal! No!" Amy tried to convey that it was a mistake. She struggled to gather enough breath.

"So, this must be your best friend, Calvin James," Sam ridiculed. He was breathing heavily from resisting Amy's efforts to free herself.

"These are the same bikes you rode and gear you wore in Boulder. I've seen Lance's photos.

"Since I know everyone here, let me make introductions. Breathless, this is Calvin James. Calvin, this is Breathless. You're both contractors. Breathless said that if we met up with you, he would give me a lesson in what he does best."

"I did, didn't I?" Breathless' tone was bucolic and not rushed but modulated with a thick accent, "Amy Farina, you can learn from this too."

"Look," Calvin offered, "were not unreasonable. What can we do to ratchet down the tension here?"

"Watch and learn." Breathless walked up to Calvin's side, ignoring him, facing Amy and Sam.

Amy was fatiguing but not willing to give up.

"First," Breathless wound up a clenched fist and drove it hard into Cal's solar plexus, "you want to disable the diaphragm. The loss of breathing ability creates an involuntary, primary focus on regaining it. It takes the highest priority over any reaction to any other threat. That reaction can be trained out, but very few do it."

Calvin bent forward and teetered back, unable to react quickly enough to get his hands from their raised surrender position to a defensible one.

"Second, you want to place your subject in a defenseless position." As if practicing on a manikin, Breathless struck his leg against Cal's calves, sweeping leg support from him while he beat his forearm across Cal's chest. Calvin landed prone on his back. "See, he has very little leverage to right himself. And now, with me sitting on his chest, he has no chance of breathing, and he weakens with each passing second. I call it a half Burke. The proper Burke involves holding your hand over the mouth while maintaining chest compression with the knee."

"Stop it! Stop it!" Amy let loose her plea with all that she had left in her. "I'll do anything!"

"You will, anyway. Not much of a bargaining chip, sweetie."

"But you're killing him."

"Grasp of the obvious, a good quality in a boss's wife." Breathless mocked.

"But you're interrupting," he pulled a Bic lighter from his pocket, "I wasn't finished with my lesson. Finally, to seal the deal, that's a joke, by the way. Ha! Ha! See, I can control his inhale and exhale. I think he's toast anyway."

Cal realized that he had lost his battle, no longer able to put up a physical struggle. He had failed Amy and committed her to a life of misery and worse. Lance was going to have his way. Cal's final thoughts were ribbons, once again, in slow time. He knew this too late; it hadn't been his life in suspension; it had been his identity. Now, his life *was* in suspense. Its tenuous threads were unraveling, threads of character, threads of aspirations, and of dreams. He was powerless. The distinction between identity and life was irrelevant. His attachments to the world were dimming. Even pain had lapsed.

Amy let out another elongated scream, draining her last reserves of air. It was the last sound Cal was aware of.

Breathless' eyes gleamed with joy in a job well done.

"So you grant his next to last inhale, lace it liberally with unlit butane from the lighter. Then with his last gasp, you ignite the butane in his lungs. Seals 'em shut."

Breathless looked up at Sam and Amy to complete his demonstration. Instead, he flew off Cal's chest with a startling backward flip, wheeling down the embankment away from the road until he slid onto his side and then lay flat.

The gunshot registered for Sam and Amy simultaneously. Sam pivoted, presenting his profile to the green Previa that had stopped in the road behind them.

Sam was staring into the barrel of a 9 mm Ruger. Distracted, his diminished grip allowed Amy to deal a crushing blow to his instep. In pain and recalling her kick that previously blew out his knee, he lifted his slightly gimpy leg to avoid the impact he knew was coming. Amy also had time in the last minutes to recall that incident. With a roundhouse left leg kick, and with every ounce of her fiber, she collapsed Sam's right knee instead. She achieved a more distended unnatural bend than she had on his other knee years earlier. Without hesitation, when Sam shifted his weight, Amy kept low and returned a swift blow to his left knee as well.

"Juan, Angelo! *Lode a Deo*! Help! Quick! Cal's not breathing," Amy cried desperately.

"*Jefe dama*! It's up to you! Do your EMT thing for him, whatever it is!" Angelo pleaded, and pointing at Sam, asked, "what do you want to do with this guy?"

"Pull his shirt over his head, and shove him, head first, under the Olds, then tie his shoelaces together."

"*Si, jefe dama*." The howls of pain from Sam went unabated.

No time elapsed for Amy to kneel next to Cal's limp and breathless body. She understood and embraced the rage that she now knew to be the source of Calvin James' violence.

Aka, Michael James Barton, she dreaded, would be the footnote on his epitaph. She cast that thought into a mental trashcan even as his pulse was undetectable. She pinched Cal's nose, applied her lips to his, and inflated Cal's lungs, not a first kiss, not another affectionate peck on the cheeks. Not now. In New England, Amy had begun to doubt a future for her relationship with Cal. And yet, he had done so much with and for her.

Inflate. Exhale. Inflate. Exhale. Ear to the chest. Checking first to see that she would do no worse harm, she began chest compressions.

"This is simple iteration, Cal. You breathe in, then out, and repeat. We call it breathing. You can do it. You've done it all your life."

Inflate. Exhale. Inflate. Exhale. Ear to the chest. Chest compressions.

"Come on, Cal, wherever you are, fight! Remember? *Per rifinire è di vincere!*" (To finish is to win!)

Inflate. Exhale. Ear to the chest. Inflate. Exhale. Ear to the chest. Chest compressions.

"God, if you're listening, I need him! Tell him he's not finished here yet!"

Inflate. Exhale. Ear to the chest. Inflate. Exhale. Ear to the chest. Chest compressions.

Inflate. Exhale. Ear to the chest. Inflate. Exhale. Ear to the chest.

"Calvin James. You come back here right now!" Amy commanding, as she did very infrequently with Cal. Tears of loss and fear streamed over her cheeks.

Cal's body convulsed with a gasp, a wolf howl on the inhale. It overpowered Sam's shrieks of pain.

"Hu waah!" Calvin opened his eyes involuntarily. "Hu waah!"

In an uncoordinated effort, he sat up and awkwardly sized up his situation, preparing to fight again.

Rebel yells rose from the van.

"Thank you!" Cal rasped, straining at speech. He held up his index finger and took a few deep breaths. "Amy, I heard you when you said... 'Come back here right now'! But I didn't know where I was or how to get to you."

Cal took a couple more catch breaths. "Oh, man. My lungs are on fire."

Amy was horrified at the near truth of Cal's complaint.

"Cal, maybe you ought to sit in the van. Juan, pull up behind the Olds, and could I borrow your knife?

"*Por supuesto.*" (Of course.)

"Angelo, you only fired once, right?"

"*Si. Sólo una vez.*" (Yes. Only once.)

"Check the clip to be sure, okay? Ooh, Buck Ranger, nice!" Amy's comment contrasted with her clenching teeth and determined facial set. "I might need muscle help out here. It won't take but a minute; I didn't see an exit wound..."

Amy looked up at Cal, seated in the Previa next to Jorge. She watched as color return to his cheeks, took several deep, slow breaths herself, then disappeared through the oak brush and sumac, down the slope toward the hayfield below. Breathless laid motionless in the shrubs.

"Do we have a rope that you could throw down?"

Angelo tossed a spare skein of climbing rope over the embankment.

"And duct tape?"

The duct tape followed the rope.

"Thank you, Angelo, I appreciate it."

An extended baritone scream announced that an immobilized Breathless still had breath and life left in him.

Amy came back to the van with the rope and the roll of duct tape. She showed the nine-millimeter slug to all.

"This was lodged under his shoulder blade. That's what pushed him backward off Cal. Who wants it?"

If there had been any lack of respect remaining from the Mexican contingent toward Amy, there never would be again. Everything would be "*Si, jefe dama.*" from now on.

"Let's get the bikes in the van and go."

"What about those guys?" Angelo asked.

"What guys?" Amy asked sternly.

"*Si, jefe dama. ¿Qué chicos?*" (What guys.)

The Previa moved slowly away from the Olds. Cal gazed at Amy, still catching his breath.

"What?" Amy questioned Cal indignantly. "They murdered you. Murdered! Tell me you wouldn't have done the same if it were me. I didn't kill either one of them. I just took what belonged to Angelo."

"Amy, I would have done the same. I would have been all over it, with more icy fury, though." A small laugh was all that Cal could muster. It still hurt to breathe. "Amy *y amigos*, thank you all. Amy, thanks for watching our friends' backs, too. Pulling that slug was good thinking. We still need to get Jorge's leg doctored. Juan, you can drop us at the Holiday Inn Express after we get him to the Farmington hospital. The motel will have a shuttle that'll take us up the hill to the airport."

"What about you, *Jefe*?" Juan drove. "Are you really all recovered now? You were dead, *amigo. Si?*"

"I'll be okay. A shower at the motel, a change of clothes, and I'll be fine. I *had* thought that this was my final chapter; besides, I'm not finished here yet." Cal didn't say if his sniffling and the tears he wiped away with his shirtsleeve were from anything other than respiratory irritation. "I can rest on our flight back to New England. If I need a doctor, I should be okay until we touch down."

"What do you say, *jefe dama*?" Juan inquired.

"If I hadn't seen how deadly and ruthless those beasts were just now, I'd say medical attention, stat, but what Cal and I need to do is get in the air and far away from here. Thank you, guys."

"*Como bien dices, jefe dama.*" (Whatever you say, little boss lady.)

§§

CHAPTER 61

Mildly astringent, the salt air revived both Amy and me, literal smelling salts.

We crossed the tarmac to the concourses, both of us exhausted and wanting a nice dinner and sleep. All the other passengers on the Delta flight from LaGuardia only paid attention enough to avoid bumping into one another. Intently, they engaged in conversation with their traveling partners.

Whaling, beach, and sailing motifs, tastefully differentiated the Nantucket Airport from other small airports. Once outside, the weathered gray cedar shakes, white trim windows, the roof bristling with antenna, the glass-walled control tower affixed as a widow's walk on the otherwise contemporary Cape Cod structure; all confirmed that we were on the set of *Wings*.

"Cal, why Nantucket?" Amy inquired of our stay over.

"Exactly." Even my attempt at good humor was tired. "It's because Fort Devens is equally distant from Boston and Manchester, New Hampshire. If our dill weed has access to flight manifests at those airports, let's give him a couple of places to waste his watchful assets. He can't have eyes everywhere."

"I've lived in Massachusetts for all but four months of my life, but I've never been to Nantucket or Martha's Vineyard. So, Cal, did you buy airline tickets to both Boston and Manchester, and yet we came here?"

"Of course. I've never been here, as either Michael Barton or Calvin James. And, yes, we had multiple air routes reserved for us to get here."

"You've done all this. How?"

"I called Cam for help. She misses you, by the way. She was concerned when you didn't show up from Stapleton. For our itinerary, I gave her a list of departure locations and times, all of which to end us up here and avoid Boston, Manchester, and Bradley. Then there were the decoy flights. Cam made all those calls. Our route was a mystery to me until we picked up our tickets in Farmington. It would have been the same if we'd left from Telluride. She's the only one I knew who I could pin down and who I could disburse expenses to with a phone call. She did a fine job. We'll have to thank her later."

"You've never said where we're staying tonight."

"Mystery again, I told Cam to find lodging for us that had an airport pick up. I would be out of pocket, so I had her instruct our driver to put up a sign for Dave and Betty Harris. I didn't think they would mind us adopting their names. It makes me think that they might enjoy a week off down here. You up to spelling them on the farm?"

"They never get any extended time off. That's true, let's do that. I don't think that Dave or Betty will be shocked to find out that you're alive and well. The questions they asked me make a lot more sense in light of your second life; I never caught on." Amy sighed tiredly. "You always said until Mom's funeral, you, Calvin James, had never traveled to the eastern United States. That unpacks so nicely. Deceptive but not lying. You left Boston as Calvin James but traveled west and never came back until mom's funeral."

A short black Cadillac limo pulled up, gleaming with orange highlights under the mercury vapor lamps. The driver stepped out, holding a small white dry erase board with "Harris" written on it. Before he had the possibility of calling out their names, Amy and I waved in acknowledgment.

§

The Country Club Resort was sheltered from a mild breeze by the bluff behind it; the native islanders called it a cliff. Low bushes and stunted trees, scrub oaks like those in Colorado, fluttered their leaves. They succumbed to the beach-blend, white-noise coming from the Atlantic surf.

I gawked at the reception area's open truss system. What I knew to be post and beam incorporated smooth nautical curves and finishes. Artful. Not what I had anticipated.

They intimated a wooden ship's hull lines. Whether the wood was cherry or cherry stained, I was too weary to ponder.

"You just can't help yourself, can you?" Amy, mirthful because I still analyzed the design details.

The maritime theme was tasteful.

"Mr. and Mrs. Harris, I presume." The clerk rose from his chair, interrupting his early night audit duties.

Amy and I nodded in assent.

"You are most fortunate." The man's accent was faint, suggesting a continental French origin. "Your secretary, whom, may I say, was very charming on the phone, called not five minutes after another guest canceled. When fully booked, it isn't our policy to maintain a reservation list; but to your good fortune, the previous party withdrew so late, and your reservation fit so well, we were able to accommodate you.

"I doubt that unless you brought your tent, you would not find any other lodging on the island." Etienne, as his embossed shirt identified him, sniggered at his joke. "We have you in room 10. It's a single bed luxury suite with a stunning ocean view. The deck opens onto the beach."

Before I could speak, Amy put her index finger to my lips.

"We can figure it out when we see the room," Amy said quietly, her fatigue noticeable.

"When we sent our driver out, we also started your dinner order. Let me show you to the dining area," Etienne offered.

I reached for my wallet for a gratuity.

"Oh, no sir, your Camilla has already arranged for a percentage gratuity. And, sir, madam, some packages have arrived from Eddie Bauer in your room." Etienne exited the counter confines and excitedly joined us in the lobby. "Right this way."

"What are we having?" I asked in our escort's wake; not that cost had any bearing. I'd given Camilla carte blanche. I was amazed at the thoroughness and consideration she took in our arrangements. The single room was no fault of hers, given the tight accommodation market, but ordering our dinner ahead was very thoughtful.

"A cold lobster salad, testaroli with a basil pesto, lemon water, and a *Pouilly-Fuissé* split. We can add a dessert. She said, though, that you might be exhausted."

"Thank you, Etienne, you've been very accommodating."

§

Room 10 was, indeed, luxurious, and there was enough floor space for me to sleep on and blankets enough. Hooked area rugs depicting tall-masted ships at sea suggested a more cushioned sleeping arrangement than I'd experienced in the creek bottom.

Amy cracked open the sliding glass door; the presence of wind and the proximity of the waves intensified through the screens. Then she turned her attention to the shipped packages stacked by the luggage rack.

A straight-backed chair fairly begged me to sit in it. It then defied me to relax.

Camilla's Eddie Bauer package included a full change of clothing complete with a sports jacket, slacks, light green dress shirt, solid blue tie, shiny lace-up shoes. It's what I had asked for, outfitting for the show-and-tell tomorrow at Fort Devens. Demonstrating her complete understanding of Amy and me, she included cotton pajamas.

Amy's change of apparel was a conservative blue jacket and slacks combination, a plain white round-collared blouse, with low heeled, sensible shoes.

"It's almost like Christmas only warm, and by the ocean, and you're here, with no chimney or fireplace, and no tree, no ornaments, no ribbons on the boxes..." Amy trailed off and contemplated a Christmas happier than her most recent one. "You stay put; I'm showering. Then it's your turn. Just saying, if you know what I mean."

Amy ducked into the bathroom before I had a chance to acknowledge that I did know what she meant. Aromatic unpleasantness would follow me if I didn't clean up.

§

I slogged from showering, refreshingly clean but entirely played out. Amy's and my pajamas were matching nautical blue and conservative, another of Camilla's subtle encouragements. Amy sat with her feet curled under her on the chair but hadn't laid out blankets on the floor for me. She watched for my reaction.

"Cal, just because we're careful doesn't mean we're stupid." Amy laughed the lovable way she does when she thinks that she might have gone too far, but she spoke on. "We should both sleep on the bed. It's vast enough for us to keep our distance. It's not about sex; it's about security. You sleep above the upper sheet, and I'll sleep below. Besides, it's a king; we'd need walkie-talkies if we were going to talk to each other. Can we do that?"

"We can," I yielded in weariness, "when I get horizontal, I'll be out like a light anyway."

"What, Cal? You've been up for sixty hours with less than two hours of sleep and that on cold damp ground, climbed a mountain from six thousand to thirteen thousand feet, flown six thousand miles, driven two hundred miles, bicycled seventy, been dead for two minutes, and who knows what you've had to eat. Are you sure you don't want to party now?"

"Since you put it that way..." I peeled back the blanket layer on the beachside of the bed and lay down. The pillow tag, Fretta Classic Linens, 100% Egyptian Cotton Percale, pricked my neck. Classy. I folded it away. "Good night, Amy."

Minutes later, in the twilight existence between my waking and sleeping, Amy made her way to the bed. She'd watched me from the chair, entertained, as I nodded off. When she slipped between the sheets, I was turned away from her. She faced my back and placed her arm around my waist in a half hug, hand on my chest, and held it there firmly. So much for distance and walkie-talkies, but I was dead to the world.

§

Painfully awakened from oblivion at four-thirty, I could hear a bell buoy in the distance through the screen door. The floor-length curtain swayed softly, ghostly in the ambient illumination. The room was dark and brisk.

Amy was gone.

"Amy," I spoke in my normal indoor voice, then disoriented and panicked, I hollered loud enough to raise the neighbors. "Amy?"

"Cal, what is it?" Amy spoke quietly, from the slightest of gaps in the bathroom door.

"Oh, Lord,... when you come back to bed, I'll tell you." Relief packed every syllable. And I was very conscious of how "When you come back to bed" sounded.

§

"So?" Amy crawled back under the covers, maintaining the tenuous top sheet separation. "That was loud."

"I'm sorry, Amy. Nutshell, I missed you just now like I never want to have happen again.

"The day my family was killed, the US Marshals took me to a hotel. The room was right on Boston Harbor, and that night, I remember the pillow tag irritated my neck. I was alone and cried a lot that night. I wanted to call my family, but they weren't anymore. I remember, too, I didn't sleep well that night. I heard bell buoys ring in the wake of ocean freighters coming into the harbor.

"I heard the bell buoys tonight, and you weren't here. It all added up in my sleep-deprived brain. I don't scare easily; in truth, I was frightened I'd lost you. Second time today."

"Thank you, Cal, for thinking of me that way." Amy genuinely understood, emphasized with a quick kiss on my temple. "You're sweet. It's okay. Sleep for another hour, and then we've got to head for the mainland."

We did just that after I managed to slip out the words, "Your hair smells like roses."

"Cam had my favorite shampoo and conditioner sent FedEx," Amy explained.

I didn't hear a word of it. I dreamt, instead, of her smile.

§

Amy and I dressed for the day's adventure. I wore my new outfit; Amy was also in business attire.

Deck dining, upright Perrier umbrella, sun streaming in from the east, the beach and ocean lapping up with the waxing tide made breakfast at six-thirty, delicious in ambiance alone. Camilla's humor shone through. She had it in for us. She had specified that we should be served promptly at six-thirty, blueberry crepes, with a full city roast Jamaica Blue Mountain coffee and orange juice.

§

After our short hop to Hyannis, we picked up our nondescript silver-gray Chevy Impala. On Monday, I'd had sparse opportunity to appreciate the stonewalls' nostalgic charm bordering these narrow New England roadways. I hadn't always thought of them as charming. Maples, elms, and oaks edged the streets, shading, covering, and protecting. The houses were impressive, Colonials, Greek Revivals, Federals, Capes, and Victorians white with black or dark green storm shutters.

We stopped at Doe's Bakery in Southborough. Amy frequented here on her way to Fort Devens, where she practiced spycraft to shake off would be tails, real or imagined. Amy and I were ready for a break before we finished our journey.

"Coffees, two, and two bocconotto, please," I ordered for us at the counter. Amy sat at a table set for two.

"You know, Cal, I did Breathless a favor by extracting that slug. It was close to coming through his scapula anyway. It didn't take a lot of prying, and I got it clean.

"I was terrified, once upon a time, of you having a hidden, dark, violent side. I'm now aghast at my own, not only the way I pulled that slug, but I've probably crippled Sam for life. There's the Sunapee skier, too. The thing is, I don't feel bad; I feel justified. I understand that about you so much better."

"I'm glad. We're not perfect, but 'us,' we'll be okay. I'm sure of it."

We spoke about our next steps. I imagined the pleasure and relief that Pete would have when Amy arrived. I would have my past back and with it, a future unburdened by lies.

Vivaldi was playing low enough to talk over. When the violin piece that Ted had performed on guitar came over the speakers, we were quiet, smiling, and reminiscing.

We had been sitting for about fifteen minutes when Eileen entered the bakery. Eileen was a clerical worker at Fort Devens and helped in the library alongside Pete. She had the day off but was pleased to help us. With the same long dark hair, same general build, and only slightly shorter than Amy, dressed identically, she differed from Amy in that she wore a wedding band.

Eileen ordered the same coffee and pastry that I had ordered for Amy and went to the restroom while the young man behind the counter prepared her order. I stood and requested a repeat for Amy's and my table. Amy also took a minute to freshen up. Eileen's single order left with Amy. She drove away in Eileen's car, Eileen and I sat and finished off my second order.

Pick and roll, just in case anyone was watching, *basketball metaphor courtesy of Steve Chauklin*. Eileen and I were to arrive at the Fort Devens entrance at the same time as Amy walked from Eileen's car to the employee entrance at the prison. Our part was to show ourselves conspicuously.

§

"Lance, Petros Belluno here. It's one o'clock."

"Pete, really, I just walked into my office. Now you're just showing off. You know where I am, and you discovered my private number." Lance knew his victory would be shallow. "My guys tell me that my Amy is late, so close and yet so far away, sitting in the visitor parking lot."

"I'm not showing off, Grimaldi. And, the State Police will arrest your guys with the sniper rifle on that grassy berm overlooking the parking lot here, in less than thirty seconds. My daughter is right here. I'll put her on for you and cover my ears. I don't want to hear the verbal lashing she is going to give you."

"Grimaldi, *tu odioso, scusa patetica per un uomo, tira fuori le...* " (Grimaldi, you hideous, pathetic excuse for a man, grow some...)

§§

CHAPTER 62

Francisco's on Durango's Main Street, iconic for its Mexican fare, was packed. It was a typical Saturday night for June. My first weekend back, I had no mixed feelings as I thought I might, definitely at peace.

"Evening, Cal. Is anyone joining you tonight?" The doorman, friendly, as were all the staff.

"No. No one but me. Thanks, Miguel. Looks busy for you guys, so if you don't have any tables, I'll sit at the bar, though I'm more interested in eating than drinking. Any specials?"

"Chef has put a Serrano rubbed sirloin on the menu tonight, with roasted vegetables and Spanish rice. Sound good?"

"*Si, si tu recomendarlo. Gracias.*" (If you're recommending it. Thanks.)

"*De nada. Ve y siéntate.* (It's nothing. Go and sit.) I'll get Marquita to order it up."

Francisco's decor is the epitome of a Mexican restaurant, with arches, booths, stucco, cacti, inlaid wood tables, terra-cotta tiled floor, and dimly lit. Flickering candles illuminated the tables, and mariachi music played at low volume.

The wooden bar toward the back was polished. The slight lip produced by its attractive molding made it awkward to rest my forearm. Stainless steel dishes, well stocked with limes, lemons, and cherries, decorated the no-skid mat in the garnish rail.

Matt, the bartender, produced a Modelo Negra that I poured straight down the leaning away side of a frosted mug. I attended to the froth with a slurp off the top.

Focus on work had not been a problem, having just gotten back at it today. ProtoBobby was proceeding well in Telluride, with minimal input required from Bobby and me.

My restless thoughts were concerned with Amy at home in Lenox. She needed to be by her dad, understandably.

I had set in motion impressive, productive legal work in the background that put me once again in familiar territory. I couldn't tell Amy any of it.

At a table closer to the restaurant's front was seated a tall tree. It was Steve Chauklin with Chelsea, and Jill and Jack Walsh. What a great circle was nearly complete since I had last spoken to them at Deep Hole in Acworth six years ago.

"Hey, Matt," I spoke to the bartender, "hold my seat; Marquita should bring my out dinner out any minute. I'll be right back."

The rock and mineral shop across the street was open for the residual evening tourist trade. They might still have the heliodor crystal I'd seen there. Forty bucks later, I was back.

"Miguel, could you arrange a distraction? I want to drop off a present, unnoticed, at that table with the tall guy."

"What's up? You know the tall one plays basketball for the Phoenix Suns?"

"It'll be good; you won't want to miss this. Jill, Steve's sister, is Jack, the shorter guy's wife. She'll flip out when she figures out what this is." I held up the crystal. "I plan to do a 'Phoenix' of my own. My magician image needs a spiffing. I'll explain after."

"I'll ask how they are enjoying their meal, check on their service." Miguel grinned, ready to collaborate in whatever mischief I had up my sleeve.

Miguel beguiled, even offered a round of beverages on the house to make up for having only one of two candles on the table lit. All their eyes were on him. He lifted the darkened tea light high and applied his lighter. I had no difficulty in placing the crystal next to Jill's plate before the four of them returned their attention to their conversations, beverages, and enchilada's.

I made my way back to the bar to observe.

The rock's irregular surface irritated Jill's wrist. Quizzically, she inspected the amber crystal that had suddenly appeared. She held it up to the candle to examine it, then displayed it for Jack, Steve, and Chelsea.

"Do you know what this is or where it came from?" Jill racked her memory. This crystal was significant somehow.

None at the table knew.

A golden dawn spread over Jill's countenance.

"I do! *I do!* Do you guys remember, it was way back when; we met after school at that swimming hole in Acworth? Chelsea and I were still in high school. You, Steve, and Jack had a party at your apartment on Green Street. Michael Barton was there swimming, he told me about this. This is a golden beryl crystal; heliodor, he called it." Her revelation cascaded beyond the impossible. "He's here. Cal is here."

"Jill, Cal's dead. Six years ago." Jack weighed in reluctantly.

"Jack, I love you only. But Michael is here!" Jill looked around desperately and caught the eye of Miguel. "Sir? Sir?"

Miguel was not quick enough to avoid the glance and frantic beckoning.

"Yes, ma'am?" Miguel approached the doubting table. "What can I do for you?"

"Is there a man named Cal here?" Jill offered up the heliodor for Miguel's inspection. "Did you help him put this here?"

Miguel turned his head toward the bar and nodded in my direction.

The look of shock and disbelief was one to behold.

I went to their table and knelt, resting my elbows on a free surface.

"Hi, guys."

"Michael Barton, as I live and breathe!" It was Chelsea.

"Close, Chelsea. My name has been Calvin James these last six years, but still Cal. I've been in the Witness Protection Program. Everyone at the Petros Belluno trial was concerned for my safety, in light of my family being murdered, so they whisked me away to Colorado."

Steve's six foot seven frame, quickly stepped around. He raised me up for a handshake and pulled me in for a bear hug. Jack followed suit, Chelsea and Jill each had their turn. Miguel pulled a vacant chair from another table with an approving nod from Steve. Marquita brought my bar fare to the table.

"Thank you, Marquita. Miguel, Marquita meet Steve and Chelsea Chauklin and Jill and Jack Walsh; they're good friends."

After sitting quietly for a long minute. Steve began, "Gosh, where do we start?"

"Nutshell, Steve, I've been dead twice, once as a cover for Michael Barton. What day is today? Just five days ago, I was flat on my back, not breathing, heart stopped, about fifteen miles from here. Yet, here I sit with my longtime friends." An edge in my laugh let them know how close I had come. "Let me talk a little. We've got all night."

"We are all thrilled to see you... and shocked. It will be a while before we absorb it all." Jill spoke for all.

"You guys have been a tremendous support for me. I've seen you here and there at the UA and Suns games. But I had to be invisible. Where to start, indeed. I saw you at my folks' funeral. I was on the backhoe that no one wanted to look at. Thanks for being there. It meant a lot to me.

"Let's see what else. Okay. Before Christmas, the year that I disappeared, I asked Don Warthington to go to a Keene State basketball game the next time he was in Boston. He asked me who to look for. I said, 'He's the guy who elevates everyone else's play.'

"When we talked next, he said he'd not talked to you but spoke to a Plymouth State player that you had fouled. Don noticed that when you'd helped him up, you spoke to him. So he asked the guy what you said. He said that you told him to keep his foot planted when he did a shoulder drop fake. It would open him up for a step-back jumper or a scoop layup. That and the way you played was all he needed."

"You know the Phoenix coach?" Steve exclaimed, "I remember that game. I let a Plymouth player park his elbow in my eye. It was hideous, the eye that is."

"Don sends me Italian dubbed movies," I confirmed.

"He's the one that connected me with a scholarship to UA." Steve quickly came to the natural conclusion. "It was you! You sponsored us all at the University."

"You don't know that for sure. But, I couldn't have you decline a solo offer out of a sense of loyalty to Chelsea, Jill, and Jack. I knew you would. Besides, it would have made your honeymoon trips to Durango and Ouray way more expensive."

"Oh! We didn't know who sent those gift certificates. And there wasn't any time that we could go anywhere exotic; they were so perfect." Chelsea was effusive. "We couldn't send a thank you note. Thank you, Cal."

"I've read the thank you card that you sent Nations Pennsylvania. Very touching."

"But Don Warthington, how do you know him?" Steve still wanted the connection.

"My business partner and I own a construction company. We built Don's house after it got off to a disastrous start. It was our first project. You've seen it and been there. Beams for the basketball court came from that timber frame shop I worked for in Alstead. They never knew I was the one who requested their materials. They couldn't. It stinks not having a real past to share."

§

Miguel reluctantly reminded us of closing time. None of my friends seemed to tire of my story. They had countless questions; I had plenty for them, too. I hadn't broached the subject of Amy. I'd learned of their lives, plans for kids, and Steve's great mentor in the Sun's excellent point guard. Jack, an actuary, was already promoted to department manager. Jill was now a speech pathologist. Chelsea was teaching English as a second language. Jill and Steve's parents were older and were eyeing Sun City for retirement.

"Cal, we should be driving to the Wiesbaden in Ouray tonight, though it's fantastic talking with you. Ouray's a couple of hours away." Chelsea spoke, with nods from all. "So, we ought to go or find a place here."

"Don't drive tonight. Meet me at Don's house. My company is Don's caretaker. I'll get the key from my office. We can all stay there tonight."

§

"So, Cal, witness protection is supposed to stay secret; why are you so open?" Jack sat on Don's sofa next to Jill. We made ourselves comfortable, helping ourselves to Don's Italian vineyard's red.

"Let me answer with a question for Steve and Chelsea. Do you remember the Nuggets game in Denver last December and the girl after? She saw Steve on the floor after the game. When she saw Chelsea and you kiss, she thought it okay to talk with you. You guys were very gracious and entertained, waiting to talk to her boyfriend, who was a great fan. She was embarrassed when he didn't show. I got in deep trouble for that. Her name is Amy Farina. She's the reason I can talk openly now."

"I do remember. There was a Cal Barton vibe about her. Chelsea remarked on it later. Remember, Chel?"

"Dark hair over the shoulder, very Italian gestures, lovely, just right for you, Cal. I do. I asked you, Steve, who does she remind me of? It wasn't until you came out of the locker room. You and Coach were discussing free throws. You were saying that height, angle of release, and velocity were key to lock in before repetition or something that sounded physics-oriented. Then I said, Michael Barton, she reminded me of Michael Barton. It was the way she looked at us and talked with such familiarity."

"I opted out of WITSEC because I wanted to be truly and completely honest with her. You'll be seeing some news soon on the Petros Belluno trial that has to do with my witness protection, too. Do you want to hear more? It's two o'clock."

"Cal," Jack squeezed Jill's hand, she, in turn, patted him on the leg, "when Jill and I talked this morning about what would make us happiest at the end of the day, to be honest, running into Michael Barton didn't come up. But we've learned over the years that there are wonderful exceptions."

"The resurrection of Michael Barton and a love story to boot. Come on, Cal. Who cares if the sun rises and you're still talking." Chelsea received nods from everyone.

§§

If it wasn't clear to anyone else, it was clear to Amy. Janis, Camilla, even her dad encouraged her to make the best of her own life, chase her dreams. She shouldn't let guilt, they all advised, direct her decisions. Guilt was the essence of her decision to live close enough to be an emotional support to her dad. Guilt from not having had a relationship with him, guilt that would follow should she abandon him. Guilt that it was Cal, her special friend, who relegated him to prison.

She now felt guilty about having to tell Cal that her dad in prison was an irreconcilable issue between them. It was the path of least guilt. Aversion to that conversation inspired her to walk from her former Boulder residence to Cal's home. He'd made it a point to be in Boulder when she'd told him that she was coming, that they needed to talk. He would volunteer to relocate to New England. She would let him know that there were issues that his change of residence couldn't resolve. That would be it. She would be gone. Cal would stay.

The walk would do her good; it would calm her spirits and help her hone her arguments. She knew that there was no good choice. Both options were untenable.

She was glad that Cam insisted that she join her for an early dinner of Cobb salad with grilled chicken. Grateful for the companionship, it was a pleasant discussion when it remained not about Cal. Throughout their conversation, Amy thought Cam looked wistful as if she possessed knowledge or held a secret hope that Amy's mind would change.

The evening mountain downdraft, fresh and crisp, should have been invigorating but didn't affect her. The Boulder County Corrections building was a supportive sight, reminding her of her dad's incarceration. A residential neighborhood countered with the splash of child sounds and the occasional whiff of barbecue, a glimpse of what one possible future might have held for her and Cal.

She had done okay without him, hadn't she? Except for his telephone calls and anticipated letters, his support when her mother died, his support after, his rescuing her from Grimaldi, and conversing how nearly perfect Cal was with her dad. Even though, when she went out to dinner with Ted North from Lenox, all she could think about was that Ted wasn't Cal and never could be. She had survived without him, hadn't she? Her dreams were of so much more. But more would never come to fruition.

Mercifully distracted by rock and roll music, she followed the sound emanating from a school gymnasium's open doors. This led her to imagine what the occasion might be, a school dance, a practice arena for some first-rate local talent, or a school play rehearsal with accompaniment.

She made her way to the open doors.

"Good evening, young lady." A man, perhaps in his mid-fifties, complete with cowboy hat and boots, black vest, bolo tie, and a firm handshake, all in good taste, greeted Amy with such enthusiasm that she felt compelled to enter the gym, "there are empty seats over on the far side. If you don't have a Bible, you'll find one under the chairs."

The musicians were skillful. The assembly sang along with them, reading lyrics projected on a screen. The last song ended on an up note, unresolved.

It wasn't altogether foreign to her. Her dad had encouraged her to attend a lecture at L'Abri in Southborough, presenting biblical Christianity reasonably concerning culture and art. The demographic here seemed about the same except for the kids.

Tempted to continue her journey to Cal's house; instead, she sat when when the lead musician made the invitation. Interlocking stack chairs, comfortably padded, were set out in curved rows, the easier to casually glance at other people.

The acoustic guitar player stepped up to the center microphone, having parked his instrument. Papers shuffled along with the man's Bible. At the same time he made small talk with individuals he knew in the gathering about the upcoming baseball expansion team slated for Denver, and in some context, about the Caribou Ranch. That recalled for her, her and Cal's day horseback trip near the Caribou Ranch, complete with the picnic lunch that Cal had prepared.

She noted that personal relationship was highly regarded and not hard to come by here.

"I know, I know," the pastor, Amy had heard him referred to that way, feigned defense, "we're supposed to start First Corinthians chapter 15 in verse 12, but verses 1 through 11, are so essential, we're going to review them.

"Open up your Bibles. If you can't find this evening's text, take the Bible from the person sitting next to you." A handful of laughs dispersed throughout the assembly.

An empty chair separated Amy from a young man who could have been entering high school. He took notice of Amy's unfamiliarity with the proceedings, opened a Bible from under his seat to the passage for the study, and handed it to her with a sheepish smile.

"Lord, open our ears, hearts, and minds to what you would have for us tonight," was the pastor's brief prayer.

Amy found herself reading along, reasoning through.

"Paul, in chapter 15, breaks off his order of worship presentation. He then reminds the Corinthians of the gospel he preached. That they received it, stood in it, and were saved. This is the gospel that Paul preached; we are all sinners, but Jesus was the sinless, perfect, and only begotten Son of God, fully God and fully man. He bore our sins, took our guilt, and was crucified. He died, rose again, and now sits at the right hand of the Father to make intercession for us, so that we might become the righteousness of God in Him.

"It is only by grace through faith in Him that we come to salvation.

"People try to make it complicated, creating a body of doctrine where none exists. 'Well you reject the commandment of God that you may keep your tradition.' These are the words of Jesus from Mark 7:9. The New American Standard Version refers to these traditionalists as experts at rejecting the commandment of God. *Experts!* That's why the priesthood of all believers is so important.

"Paul praised the Bereans when they confirmed Paul's words, not relying on what Paul said, but searching the scriptures, for themselves... Just like you shouldn't take my word, check it out for yourselves.

"The beauty is, one, we don't have to convince anyone. It's not our job; that's for the Holy Spirit. We humbly witness the truth of Jesus. Two, no one is obliged to believe it. As in anything, the choices we make have consequences.

"... remember reading, in the gospels, the temple veil was torn from its top to its bottom... giving access to all.

"... works, what you do, how you live, how you talk, what you do or don't look at, how much and to whom you give charitably, these things only evidence your relationship with Christ. No works by themselves earn salvation."

Here the pastor paused from his hour-long exposition.

"I had a smooth segue for next week, getting into verses 27 and 28. Someone here tonight needs to hear these two verses. Here it is; call it a spoiler. 'For "He, has put all things under His feet." But when He says, "all things are put under Him," it is evident that He who put all things under Him is excepted.' Think about that this coming week."

Amy didn't need a week. She recognized the logic. Two contemporary mathematicians, Zermelo and Fraenkel, were anticipated nineteen centuries earlier by the words in the Bible she held. "... He who put all things under Him is excepted." Astounding. This Biblical inclusion of formal logic was a connection she had never had with the Bible before.

§

It was about nine-thirty when Amy knocked first then came in, although she knew from our earlier telephone conversation that Marv and Tex would only be returning in the early morning hours from a summer fishing expedition in Banff.

"Cal?" She sounded weak. I jumped up and sprinted around the short U-turn from my office to the door.

"Amy, come, sit. Are you okay? I imagined you would have been here earlier." I steered her to the sofa that backed to the picture window. I sat on the stuffed chair opposite her.

"I would have, but was sidetracked. I walked and came by a school over by the foothills. I heard music, so I checked out what was happening. It turned out to be similar to your Easter experience.

"I ran a bit on the way here."

"Glass of water, wine, or soda? I could put on water for tea; I have Earl Grey."

"I'd take some ginger ale, please, Cal."

I jumped to make the quick trip to the refrigerator, smiling at her knowledge of its offerings. I returned with the beverage. Amy took the glass from my hand and held it under her nose, enjoying the aroma of ginger and light sprinkling from the carbonation.

§§

Chapter 64

Through the living room window, behind Amy, I saw a Yellow Cab In-Service light. The vehicle came to a stop as if to disembark a passenger, but no passenger emerged. It was already three in the morning. Neither Amy nor I were ready to set aside our wandering conversation.

"I'll be right back. You're not expecting a cab?" I stepped to the door, a shake of Amy's head confirmed that I'd have to delve into the taxi mystery.

"*Stai attento,* Cal." (Be careful, Cal.)

I poked my head through the cab's opened front passenger window. Over my shoulder, I could see Amy peer out after me. Given our experiences, I thoroughly understood.

"The driver had this address, Denver Cab no less." I offered when I returned. Amy wasn't interested in probing details.

"Did I ever tell you that my Colorado driver's license overstates my age by two years? I'm only a year older than you." For reasons far beyond male comprehension, this produced, from Amy, a smile and a tear.

We returned to the topic of my high school days, Melanie Howe, Steve Chauklin, and the early admission offer I'd received from MIT. In turn, Amy talked about her years in Lenox, her struggles to fit in, and missing her dad during that time. She spoke about understanding Cecelia's stresses better.

At four in the morning, we stepped outside. We both needed fresh air and to stretch our legs. I grabbed a couple of fleece jackets for Amy and myself to ward off the early morning chill. We walked under the streetlights on Hawthorn and traced the familiar bicycle path to the Rec Center. The thinnest sliver of a moon offered only slightly better illumination than the planet Mars. Ambient city light kept us on the concrete. Along the way, we startled several rabbits tempted by the eleven-acre Community Garden's bountiful produce. Amy folded her arms, pulling the jacket closer around her.

"And there's Lepus the Hare at Orion's feet," Amy noted the celestial irony, "how can he be such a great hunter with a rabbit so close and obviously in his sight?"

Our conversation rambled everywhere, but not smoothly the way our banter usually flowed. I could tell more was on her mind that she had not yet shared. We drifted, walking along the greenway toward campus. We only stopped when we reached our rock, not much before daybreak.

"I stopped at a bakery on my way out of Boston, after seeing your dad that awful night. It was in Hampton Beach, John and Marsha's Bakery. It was closed, but the couple who owns it let me in when I asked for a cup of coffee. John advised that I write down the details of what I saw so that if I were to testify, I would be clear. I'd never had coffee that good before."

Amy was tired and agitated from lack of sleep, stress, and not knowing how to transition subtly. Tears were on the verge. She tugged at my arm so that I faced her. With her feet close together, she refolded her arms, clutching again at the fleece.

"Cal, you put my dad in jail." Out gushed her pent-up frustration. "You know, you have your preferences about how long a relationship should be before marriage, when you kiss, why you won't sleep together before you know a girl well. Cal, I can't get mad at you, but I am passionate about family loyalty. I'm going back to Lenox to live. I want you to stay here. Unless you want to wait around for the next fourteen years for my dad to get out of prison..., Cal, until he's out..., I'm not..., I can't see you anymore."

§§

CHAPTER 65

Lance Grimaldi swung his feet around, letting his knees hook over the edge of his cot, careful not to knock his head on the bunk overhead. He contemplated the feel of white cotton socks before he applied them to his feet. His orange slip-on deck shoes were very different from Prada.

§

Sam Wilson never expected to step foot in his parents' Gloucester home again. Ironically, he hadn't. His father, a former school principal, had guided his wheelchair up the ramp, built in anticipation of his arrival. The convalescence period for Sam's knee surgeries would be short; physical therapy, prolonged and painful. He lay in bed, waiting for the Massachusetts State Police's warrant.

§

In typical rural New England fashion, Dave and Betty Harris had been relieved, cooperatively, from their essential chores by their farming neighbors to take a three-day visit to Colorado. Betty beamed excitedly. Dave took stock of his street clothes and puffed on his Meerschaum between the hotel and the taxi stand while waiting for their ride.

§

Steve and Chelsea Chauklin, Jill and Jack Walsh, deplaned from a red-eye Frontier Airline flight from Phoenix. They were surprised to see Don Warthington and his wife waiting for them to share a limousine.

§

Janis Thomas, not used to traveling alone, had adopted Amy's self-confidence aid of dressing up when flying. The United morning flight from Logan was on time at Stapleton. It wasn't hard to spot the basketball players in the luggage claim area. Intimidated, she shyly introduced herself to the group. Alan ran to Janis and the group, having arrived from Bradley minutes before.

§

Dave Cravath, with his wife Meredith, and his recently restored project car, a 1964 Aston Martin DB5, had gathered admiring stares their entire cross-state drive. Pedestrians walking along the University of Colorado campus pointed and chatted excitedly as they drove by.

§

Juan, Angelo, and Jorge, in Juan's Previa, trailed the Aston Martin along Broadway, attracting much less attention. The three discussed between themselves how they would fare in their confidential informant discussion with Peter Nori.

§

Dick Mason fired up his Cessna Skylane, not his favorite aircraft, but a four-seater. For the flight to Boulder Municipal Airport, it was his best choice. At least it had a Lycoming power plant. Dick looked at his wife Cheryl, then to Bobby and Rosa in the rear seats. His attention then shifted to the instructions spoken through his headset.

§

ProtoBobby and his girl, Jill, ducked and stepped aboard a commuter jet at the Telluride Airport.

§

John and Martha's Hampton Beach bakery opened at 6:00 AM. Ready again for another day of business. John and Martha took a rare moment to read an article in the *Boston Herald* together. They had a letter that tipped them off, with a 303 area code number to call later.

§

Thomas and Judy stopped by the bicycle shop, hung their *Gone for a Ride, Be Back Tomorrow* sign in the door, and left.

§

Melanie Howe-Cole had another in her series of anonymous tips; the date, time, and place, where she could find and personally interview the previously undisclosed Boulder, Colorado, police officer for her investigative journalistic series on Lance Grimaldi. She and her husband John boarded the morning flight out of Logan.

§

Annette Smith, wearing last year's Josh Billings t-shirt, slipped into the driver's seat of her rental Camry, with her fiancé beside her. They reviewed the *Rand McNally Road Atlas* for directions to Boulder before departing their rented condominium in Breckenridge, Colorado.

§

Marcia Nori was happy to leave her night shift in the ER, a trade she had made for the day off. It was always the sign of a good day when she could ditch her scrubs and lab coat at the hospital and depart in street clothes.

§

Jim Shipley's wife, June, picked him up at the Nations Pennsylvania Bank to make the hour and twenty-minute drive to Philadelphia International Airport.

§

Jeff Teller sent a telegram, with congratulations, saying he would rain check their Colorado visit. He and his wife were out of the country on a Partners with Haiti trip, visiting a school near Port-au-Prince.

§

Paul Rivers woke with a start. A street musician, whom Paul had known years earlier when Paul recited poetry and soliloquies for tips, stood knocking at his studio apartment door. Accompanied by a Dayton Police officer, Ted Commons spoke first. "Good news, brother. Get dressed and come with me. This officer has a good thing to tell you, too."

§

Tex followed Marv down the stairs. Their girlfriends were at the front door. Both pairs hoped that they would be following in Cal's and Amy's footsteps.

§

Cam, Sue, and Kik let themselves, early, into the café and out again, loaded with thermos bottles of coffee and pastries, compliments of the management.

§§

CHAPTER 66

"Amy, *tesoro mio*, you are dear to me. Everyone is entitled to their internal directives." Amy hadn't anticipated this response. She expected, she wanted, resistance and argument; it would be easier to break off our relationship that way.

I lifted my arms from my side, hands open toward her. The tension was tangible, a barrier between us.

"You know that I respect your passion for family loyalty," I pressed on, "for that matter, I respect all your passions. Your opinions are so important to me. But what if, *mio amore*, I'm not only the one who put your dad in prison, but also the one to get him out?"

Amy threw her clenched fists toward the ground and stamped her feet.

"Even you have your limits, Cal. No matter what you do, my dad has at least fourteen more years to serve. You know that." Amy bawled, crying, and emotionally torn.

"That cab that drove up to my house earlier," I aimed to be calming, "it brought us the *Boston Herald* early edition, flown counter to counter to Stapleton for you and me. I had a clue that we would want a copy, page three, above the fold, byline Melanie Howe-Cole. I haven't been able to glance at it. Would you read it for us?"

Amy grabbed the front section, roiled, and hastily moved to a street lamp, the best illumination available. Noisily ruffling the pages, she found the page three headline, "Former Alleged Crime Family Head Released."

Amy's whole body heaved, gasping at its magnitude. Too astounded to continue her tears, Amy began reading the article aloud.

A cooperative effort, covered exclusively by this Boston Herald reporter, forged between the Boulder, Colorado, Police Department, Boston Police, the Massachusetts Department of Revenue, and the Massachusetts State Police, resulted in a warranted raid Thursday last, at the home of Lance Grimaldi on Revere Street in Boston. Mr. Grimaldi's arrest immediately followed, on numerous counts of extortion, blackmail, bribery, withholding evidence, racketeering, conspiracy to commit murder, and murder.

Mr. Grimaldi refused to comment to this reporter at his arrest, referring all questions to his lawyer.

Amy shook the paper to smooth out a wrinkle. She shivered and shifted her stance. Standing side-by-side, I leaned in so I could see where she was reading.

Massachusetts State Police entered crates of articles, confiscated from a sizable concealed repository within the Grimaldi residence, into the chain of custody. Multiple police armored vehicles transported evidence to the State Police crime lab for immediate analysis, with more to follow. The Federal Bureau of Investigation has also expressed extreme interest in the findings.

Of particular interest to the FBI, Massachusetts, and Boston police, amongst the evidence gathered and impounded at Grimaldi's brownstone address, were a boxed pair of .38 caliber Charter Arms Police Undercover revolvers. A direct result of fingerprint and laboratory analysis and an accompanying document was the clearing of alleged former organized crime boss Petros Belluno of the sensational death of alleged Irish Mafia rival Tom Boyle six years previous. Mr. Belluno had been sentenced to life in prison for the crime, with parole eligibility in twenty years. Judge Taylor, the original presiding judge in the Belluno trial, immediately overturned his conviction...,

Amy let out a delighted squeal.

"Read on," I urged.

"overturned his conviction, in conjunction with former prosecuting attorney Stanton Royce. Judge Taylor ordered Mr. Belluno's immediate release. Pending further investigation, District Attorney Royce has stated his intention to file new charges. He would not comment further.

"Cal, what does this mean? *What happened?*" Amy drew in a deep breath and brought the paper down to her side, gripping it tightly. We squared up, once more face to face, she studying me intently.

"Everything that I saw that night happened exactly the way I testified in court. Your dad had used blanks as he testified. That's what the State Police analysis of the two guns confirmed, fingerprints and fiber. The second gun had Lance's prints with two shots fired from it. Lance had fired real bullets from a gun in his pocket only minutely delayed from Pete's firing blanks. I interpreted that delay to be an echo from the apartment building across the street. The distance and delay didn't match. Besides, the fog should have dampened any echo had there been one."

"I didn't read that in the article. How long have you known about this?" Amy placed her hands on her hips, a stance that she used to show feigned displeasure. It wasn't displeasure right now; neither was it teasing, just intensity.

It was clear that in her eyes, I had abrogated my responsibility for her dad's incarceration.

"Let me clear that up for you. Do you remember Grimaldi saying he would put his stiletto in his trophy room when he was done gutting me with it? You know, the first time we were here? All this discovered evidence is from Grimaldi's trophy room. Your dad knew, intuitively, that it existed; he knows a lot of things that way. He told me, '*Riguardati dai pollastri.*' (Know your chickens.)

"I confirmed Pete's intuition. I broke into, that is, I visited Grimaldi's house in Boston while you and his gang were being chauffeured to Durango in June.

"I called Peter Nori in Chicago from Logan and suggested a "random" tax audit for the companies that remodeled Grimaldi's house. I happened to have the names of his contractors. I didn't offer how I got them, and Peter was wise enough not to ask but forwarded the suggestion and the information to his friend in the Massachusetts State Police.

"The decorator and contractor tax audits showed a significant, nonpermitted, structural modification to Lance's row house. Grimaldi wouldn't have allowed any governmental agency to conduct an inspection of any remodel. A quick review of filings with the State Board of Building Regulations and Standards verified that there was no permit issued.

"The building department obtained a warrant to examine the work. They called in the State Police because of the evidence they found in the process. Unraveling the details of Lance's remodel created a beautiful, documented path of evidence for multiple collaborating law enforcement agencies. FBI, IRS, ATF, Massachusetts State Police, and Department of Revenue, were only a few to benefit. It ended with cascading, court-ordered, warranted discoveries.

"Grimaldi documented everything, which made it easier for law enforcement. Stupid Grimaldi, he identified the gun that killed Tom Boyle as his own. His was the gun with live bullets; he left a signed confession, so freaking arrogant, so assured of his invincibility.

"I wanted to clue you in, but I couldn't in case this plan somehow failed.

"What else does Ms. Howe-Cole have to say?"

Satisfied for the moment, Amy didn't take any pause before she continued with her reading. Side-by-side again, she leaned into me, found her place, and read more.

Police acquired substantial incriminating information regarding the gangland slaying of Phillip Barton Sr., Stephanie Barton, and Phillip Barton Jr., the father, mother, and brother of Michael Barton (now deceased), a key witness in the Petros Belluno trial.

"Grimaldi ordered those hits on my family to further incriminate Pete. It appears as though I was included on that list."

Amy wiped her eyes with the side of her index finger and continued.

Revelations in additional high profile cases, including the lurid and mysterious death of former CEO of Auric Enterprises, Tyler Simmons, will be made public concurrent with arrest warrants and suspects taken into custody.

Other evidence encompassing uncounted photographs, tape recordings, and numerous stolen property items have instantly cleared many other faulty convictions throughout the state, from Lenox to Chatham and from Taunton to Amesbury. Law enforcement agencies are reopening dozens of cold cases.

"Lenox?" Amy quizzed.

"Your friend, Paul Rivers, was cleared." I nodded and blinked.

She continued reading and leaned closer. I put my arm around her.

State Police spokesperson, Toni Ames, told this reporter, before her public news conference Friday, that the startling discoveries in the Grimaldi cache would keep police busy for months with analysis, dismissing and overturning old convictions, and compiling new charges.

Amy took a step away, rolled up the newspaper, and playfully swatted me with it repeatedly, only stopping when I carelessly looked past her, dropping my guard.

"Peter, I'm being assaulted. Will you arrest this girl?"

"Not on your life. Assist her, maybe." Peter Nori reassured.

"Cal," Amy guessed Peter had an active role in setting up the morning's revelations didn't look toward him, "before I beat you in front of a peace officer, tell me he's not alone."

"He does have a companion with him. I think they stopped by my house and found it empty. I kind of left them a note that we'd be here."

Amy lunged at me, still not turning toward our newly arrived early morning companions. She pounded both of her fists into my chest, hair wild and beautiful. Tears of pure joy released and flooded her cheeks.

"Dad?" She sobbed.

"Yes, Amy, dear. Be careful not to hurt my man."

Pivoting off an additional, two-fisted blow to my chest, she whirled 180 degrees and flew into her dad's arms. After dowsing Petros Belluno's lapel, she released one of his arms for a side hug. She grabbed Peter Nori's arm and dragged him in for a kiss on his cheek.

Amy released Peter and Pete, who, on mutual cue, stepped back.

"Well, Cal, do we add escape artist and magician to master sleuth on your résumé? Is there anything else up your sleeve this morning?" Amy once again struggled to grasp onto a single emotion. We interlocked gazes.

"There is something else I wanted to clear up." I stepped closer, not breaking eye contact, and knelt on one knee. "Amy, I've never said, plainly, that I love you. Let me say it now. I do love you, always will. You are the reason my heart beats literally and figuratively. You can't jump start it and then break it. Since seeing you the first time, the sun hasn't risen without my having dreamed of your smile. The sun has not set without thoughts of you in my mind, love in my heart, and knowing that I want to spend my life with you. You are my love and my best friend, my *Anni Verde*.

"Amy Farina, will you marry me?"

The ability to ask this question was my plummet from six years of identity in suspension.

"Shouldn't you ask my dad first?"

"Pft. Details. I had Pete's approval two months ago."

Her dad nodded, earning him another hug. Amy sidestepped quickly and gave Peter Nori a quick hug and another peck on the cheek.

"Yes! Cal, yes, I'll marry you. I love you, too. I think I knew it when you said, '*Sto andando al negozio di biciclette.*'"

Amused, she smiled down at me. "Can you never cease to amaze me?"

Not seconds elapsed before I had taken a single caret cushioned diamond solitaire out of my shirt pocket and slipped it onto her lovely ring finger.

Standing, I realized I didn't know what to do next. I froze.

Peter Nori inclined a nod toward Amy. Then he repeated the gesture. He saw that I was still dumbfounded at what I had asked and blurted, "Kiss the girl!"

I hadn't let go of her hand yet, making it easy to gather her in. We broke off a divine, passionate kiss sooner than we might have otherwise, in consideration of our company.

I extended my hand to her dad for a shake and over the shoulder hug, warmly received.

"Amy," recovered, I was ready to have a long-postponed bit of levity, "do you remember the time we first spoke?"

"You mean when you swept me off my feet with your carefully crafted romantic pick up line, 'Hey'? How could I forget that?"

"Before that."

She struggled for recollection.

"Huh? We'd never met before that day."

"Sure, you shouted at me, 'Nice form.' I shouted back, 'Thanks. Have fun. Be careful'."

Puzzlement lingered on Amy's face.

"Bennington Hill, late spring, 1987. I was spinning, high cadence, climbing up near the top on a dark blue Trek. You were all Bianchi Blue and dropping to a tuck. My heart knew, in that one moment, I was the luckiest guy in the world. Thank you, by the way." I stole a kiss on her cheek. I turned to look at my companion with a broad smile.

A long pause followed before she registered recognition.

"Yes. Yes, I do. I skipped school that day. That was you? You remembered me?"

"Even then it was, *tutto un fuoco, amore a prima vista*, (ball of fire, love at first sight,) I knew you were the one, unlikely as it was that I would ever see you again. If I did, I would be the most privileged, lucky, most appreciative guy ever. You don't know how that memory of you has haunted me for years."

"When did you figure out that that girl and I are the same?"

"How about two seconds before I said *'Sto andando al negozio di biciclette'*?" I held out my hand to take Amy's once again.

"I should let you all know; there will be a few folks dropping by my house... our house throughout the day today. Peter, will the city of Boulder be abused if you give us all a ride back in your cruiser?"

§§§

Final Notes:

Many places in this fictional story are real. The swimming hole in Acworth, New Hampshire, Deep Hole, is a real place. In the twenty-first century's litigious frame, and because it is privately owned, it is understandably no longer available to the public.

§

"overreaching branches created noontide twilight" is incorrectly but intentionally attributed in Chapter 46 (page 254, in the printed version) as a Hawthorne quote. Instead, it is a statement about Nathaniel Hawthorne in *Old Paths and Legends of the New England Border: Connecticut, Deerfield, Berkshire* by Katherine Abbott. G. P. Putnam's Sons. 1907

"With one accord, we arose from the ground, and made our way through the tangled undergrowth towards one of those pleasant wood-paths that wound among the overarching trees." paraphrased in Chapter 46 (page 257, in the printed version). From *A Blithedale Romance* by Nathaniel Hawthorne, Published 1852, Chapter XIV. Eliot's Pulpit.

Heinrich Hertz quoted in Chapter 1 and Chapter 49 (pages 16 and 273 in the printed version), from *The Identity of Light and Electricity* in *Popular Science Monthly*, Volume 38, December 1890, page 182.

Frederick Law Olmstead quoted in chapter 10 (pages 61 and 62 in the printed version), from *Public Parks and the Enlargement of Towns*, Riverside Press, Cambridge, Massachusetts. 1870, page 22

Made in the USA
Middletown, DE
07 February 2021

33321976R00219